JOANNA SHUPE

"Nothing makes me happier than a new book from Joanna Shupe!"
—Sarah MacLean

THE Devil OF Downtown

⸻ UPTOWN GIRLS ⸻

Don't miss the novels in Joanna Shupe's
UPTOWN GIRLS SERIES . . .

And the novels in her
FOUR HUNDRED SERIES . . .

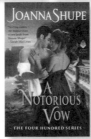

❧

Damn it. He hadn't meant to run the do-gooder off, not until they were finished.

I'll make you regret it.

Was she threatening him? *Him?* Christ, the idea of it had his balls twitching in excitement.

The entire city believed this woman was filled with pure goodness, not an evil bone in her body. Yet, she vexed Jack at every turn. A sharp tongue and blistering reprimands lurked behind those boring dresses and high necklines.

The do-gooder had a mean streak. And he loved it.

Perhaps this was the real Justine, after all. He might have been the only man alive to get a glimpse of the steel beneath the fluff. He wanted more. He wanted to know how deep that steel ran. Did it go all the way to her core? Would she bite his lip if they kissed? In bed, would she dig her nails into his skin, scoring his back with evidence of her pleasure?

He caught up and blocked her advance. "Please, stop. I need to speak to you."

She pressed her lips together and folded her hands. Waited. Those dark brown eyes stared at him as if he were an annoyance. A bother she merely tolerated.

He got right to the point. "I wish to collect on my favor."

By Joanna Shupe

Uptown Girls
THE ROGUE OF FIFTH AVENUE
THE PRINCE OF BROADWAY
THE DEVIL OF DOWNTOWN

The Four Hundred series
A DARING ARRANGEMENT
A SCANDALOUS DEAL
A NOTORIOUS VOW

The Knickerbocker Club series
MAGNATE
BARON
MOGUL
TYCOON

The Devil of Downtown

⚬ UPTOWN GIRLS ⚬

JOANNA SHUPE

AVONBOOKS

An Imprint of HarperCollins*Publishers*

THE DEVIL OF DOWNTOWN. Copyright © 2020 by Joanna Shupe. All rights reserved. Printed in the United States of America. No part of this book may be used or reproduced in any manner whatsoever without written permission except in the case of brief quotations embodied in critical articles and reviews. For information, address HarperCollins Publishers, 195 Broadway, New York, NY 10007.

First Avon Books mass market printing: July 2020

Print Edition ISBN: 978-0-06-290685-4
Digital Edition ISBN: 978-0-06-290686-1

Cover design by Guido Caroti
Cover illustration by Jon Paul Ferrara
Author photograph by Kathryn Huang

Avon, Avon & logo, and Avon Books & logo are registered trademarks of HarperCollins Publishers in the United States of America and other countries.

HarperCollins is a registered trademark of HarperCollins Publishers in the United States of America and other countries.

FIRST EDITION

20 21 22 23 24   cwm   10 9 8 7 6 5 4 3 2 1

For Denise and Cherie,
my very own Mamie and Florence.

Chapter One

Great Jones Street
New York City, 1893

𝒯he hairs on the back of Justine's neck suddenly stood up.

This was one of the roughest neighborhoods in the city and she had come here this afternoon, alone, on an errand. Not unusual, considering her volunteer work, but she'd never had trouble before.

Then it happened. The point of a knife dug into her corseted ribs as hot breath hit her ear, and the blood froze in her veins.

She didn't think about what to do next. Instead, instinct took over. She leaned away from the knife and threw out an arm, knocking the large hand away. Spinning, she made a fist and punched the attacker's throat. Hard. The knife clattered to the walk.

It was over in the blink of an eye.

A young man, probably fifteen or sixteen years of age, began staggering backward, clutching his throat, and she rushed forward to help. "Breathe," she said and guided him toward a barrel under a store awning. His face the color of a ripe tomato, he gasped for air and slumped against the oak top. Justine waited, hopeful she hadn't really injured him.

He was thin, much too thin for his age. Clothes hung on his body and his face was gaunt. Streaks of dirt hugged his exposed skin. Sadly, this was not all that uncommon downtown, and hunger had ways of causing desperation. She'd spent enough time south of Houston Street to learn as much. And desperate people deserved aid, not condemnation— something many in this city had forgotten in a rush of greed and corruption.

Seconds passed as the man recovered. Before he could speak, she beat him to it. "Why did you hold a knife to my ribs?"

His eyes narrowed, lips curling into a sneer. "To rob you. Ain't it obvious? Look at how you're dressed."

Her dress, though faded, was of good quality. It wouldn't fool anyone as to her wealthy roots. Yet she wasn't trying to fool anyone. She was down here to help, as she was more and more often of late. The legal aid society was overwhelmed with tasks and Justine was eager to assist in whatever ways possible.

Reaching into the small purse at her waist, she withdrew a gold dollar piece. "Here you go."

He stared at it before snatching the shiny coin. "Why would you help me?"

"Because everyone deserves kindness, no matter his or her past misdeeds. Sometimes we forget that."

"What are you, some kind of zealot?"

"No. I work with the Lower East Side Legal Aid Society." Her sister, Mamie, ran the aid society with her husband, Frank Tripp. While they focused mostly on legal cases, Justine took on other troubles brought to the society. Hence her visit to Great Jones Street today. "Now, if you'd like a free meal, the church at—"

The young man darted off down the street, the mere mention of religion sending him scurrying like a frightened rabbit. Justine sighed. Most churches had good intentions but not everyone wished to hear a sermon over dinner.

She turned toward her destination. Men were clustered in front of the New Belfast Athletic Club, staring at her, their jaws open as if they were catching flies. Had they witnessed her interaction with the young man? She didn't like attention in general, and she knew the type of men who frequented that particular establishment. She definitely didn't want *their* attention.

Unfortunately, she was headed directly into their domain.

She pushed her shoulders back and started across the street, not stopping until she reached the steps. Two men guarded the door and their expressions quickly went from stupefaction to suspicion.

She cleared her throat. "Good afternoon. I am here to see Mr. Mulligan." A man behind her chuckled, but she ignored him and kept focused on the guards.

"Ma'am—" one of them said, his mouth quirking.

"Miss," she corrected. "Miss Justine Greene."

The mood changed instantly. Both guards sobered. One even removed his hat. "Miss Greene."

Oh, excellent. They'd heard of her. She wasn't famous, like an actress or a singer, but when a Knickerbocker's daughter spent as much time as she did downtown, people remembered.

The recognition also meant she would be safe here. Probably. Only a fool would take on her father, Duncan Greene.

"Miss Greene," the other man said. "Please, come inside. I'll see if Mulligan is available." He opened the door for her.

Swallowing her trepidation, she followed him inside to the club's front room. Once there, he quickly excused himself and disappeared up a set of stairs, leaving her alone. She had no choice but to wait. So, she stuck close to the wall and tried to breathe deeply.

A boxing match was underway in the main room, the noise nearly deafening as men crowded around the ring, cheering and shouting. Thankfully, no one paid her a bit of attention. Her muscles relaxed ever so slightly and she took a long look at the surroundings.

Most saloons she'd visited stank from sweat, smoke and blood. Yet this club was new and obviously cared for. Impeccably clean. The men filling the room surprised her, as well. These were no street toughs covered in grime and dirt. Mulligan's crew was well-dressed, clean-shaven. Hair oiled and styled perfectly. She would even call many of them dapper.

These were criminals?

"Miss?" The guard had returned. "Follow me. I'll take you upstairs."

Nerves bubbled in Justine's stomach as she climbed

the steps. Which was ridiculous. She had no reason to fear Mr. Mulligan. Yes, he was dangerous—he ran the biggest criminal empire in the state, for goodness' sake—but he had a reputation as being fair and not tolerating any violence against women whatsoever.

Indeed then, why were her palms sweating? Why was she so jumpy?

He's just a man. You deal with them every day. Gather your nerve.

Besides, this visit was important. She couldn't lose sight of her purpose. A family was counting on her.

For six weeks she'd tracked her quarry. Former places of employment, known hangouts. Interviewing friends and associates. She'd spent more than forty days trailing a man's metaphorical breadcrumbs, a man who had deserted his wife and five children. Justine was determined to find him, no matter where it led her.

Even a criminal kingpin's headquarters.

They arrived at an ornate wooden door. The guard knocked then threw open the heavy wood. Her eyes went wide at what was revealed on the other side. It was like stepping into an uptown salon. Crystal and gold fixtures abounded, along with patterned wallpaper and thick Eastern rugs. The armchairs were clearly French antiques— Second Empire if she wasn't mistaken—and a large Gainsborough hung on the wall. A marble statue of Diana resided in one corner, a piece so old it might seem more at home in the British Museum.

Crime, it appeared, paid quite well.

A door stood ajar on the far side of the room.

Before she could wander over to peek inside, a man appeared in the doorway.

The afternoon light through the windows hit him just so, highlighting impossibly perfect features, and Justine blinked, taken aback at the sight of such handsomeness. Most men in this neighborhood were rough looking, rugged, with crooked noses and scars here and there. Souvenirs of a hard life earned by many on a daily basis.

He was different. This man had a strong jaw and sculpted cheekbones, sharp blue eyes, and full lips that brought to mind thoughts of the wicked variety. Smooth skin with the hint of an evening beard that somehow only made him more appealing. He was dressed in a navy suit, sans coat, with his shirtsleeves rolled up over muscular forearms.

Goodness. She hadn't expected *this*.

It had to be Mulligan. Rumor held there was no more beautiful criminal in the entire city—and now Justine knew why.

Then she noticed his hands. He held a scrap of cloth and was using it to wipe . . . blood off his knuckles. My God. "Are you *bleeding*?"

The side of his mouth curved. "This isn't my blood. Please, have a seat." He disappeared inside the adjacent room and she heard water running.

Chest tight, she went to the chairs opposite his desk and lowered herself into one. *He has someone else's blood on his hands.* Everything told her this was a mistake, that there had to be another way to help Mrs. Gorcey. But that would take time, one thing the mother of five did not possess.

Mulligan was the most efficient solution available. If he agreed to help, of course.

The water shut off and Mulligan strolled out of the washroom. He smoothed his shirtsleeves in place as he approached his desk, then lifted his topcoat off the chair back and slipped it on.

He looked ready to promenade on Fifth Avenue.

He gave her a once-over as he dropped into his seat. "Well, well. Downtown's notorious do-gooder at my door. I am honored."

She couldn't detect any sarcasm, but she wasn't certain. So she pretended he hadn't spoken and launched into her rehearsed speech. "Mr. Mulligan. Thank you for seeing me. I am here—"

"How is your sister?"

The question may have bothered some women, but not Justine. Both her older sisters were stunning, far more beautiful and interesting than her plain self. "Which one?"

"Forgive me. I was referring to Florence. She spent a bit of time here before she and Madden settled things. I enjoyed getting to know her."

Oh. Florence hadn't mentioned as much, but her sister was known for keeping secrets.

More importantly, what did Mulligan mean? The tone sounded fond, and she wondered if he'd developed a tendre for Justine's sister. Well, he wouldn't be the first in that regard. Florence had collected many a heart over the years, even refusing several marriage proposals. "She is well. The casino's nearly finished. She plans to open at the end of the summer."

"I am happy to hear it. Please give her my best. Now, what may I do for you, Miss Greene?"

Justine cleared her throat and got to the point. "I am here on behalf of a client, Mrs. Gorcey. Her husband, one Mr. Robert Gorcey, deserted her months ago, never to be seen again. She is demanding he fulfill his familial obligation by providing for his family."

"And what does this have to do with me?"

"I understand Mr. Gorcey is in your employ. I ask that you allow me to speak with him. I must press him to do the right thing by his family—or I'll be forced to turn him over to the police."

Mulligan stared at her for a long moment, his blue eyes steady and calm. They had hints of gray, almost as if the irises changed colors depending on the light. She couldn't tell what he was thinking as the seconds stretched and his attention started to unnerve her. Just as she opened her mouth to explain, he said one word.

"No."

Deep down, Justine hadn't expected Mulligan to be eager to help. Most people needed convincing. "Why not?"

"Several reasons. She could divorce him and find another man to help her. There has to be a reason Mr. Gorcey left. Furthermore, I see no cause to step into what is strictly a family matter."

"Mr. Gorcey left behind five children, the care of which now falls directly on Mrs. Gorcey's shoulders. She has taken up sewing to earn a bit of money and the two oldest children have gone to work in factories. Have you seen what toiling in a factory all day does to a ten- or twelve-year-old child?"

"No, but I certainly know hardship, Miss Greene. I've lived on these streets nearly all my life."

"As a man, yes. I ask you to put yourself in the shoes of a woman here, one who is alone and without any support. You cannot divorce your husband, because that would require traveling to Reno, thanks to the arcane divorce laws in New York. You don't have the money or the time for such a journey. So you're stuck because the care of children falls on the shoulders of women in this world. And, if you have no financial assistance for that care, then it is your children who suffer most. Children who wake up every day wondering if there will be enough food. Is our society so cruel that we will not force the men—men who co-created such children—to do the honorable thing and live up to their responsibilities?"

She took a breath and unclenched her hands. Lord knew she could get riled when discussing such matters. But it was common sense. Defending the wives against the cruel and selfish men who had deserted them shouldn't be necessary. And yet, here she was.

Mulligan's expression shifted, a gleam in his gaze that hadn't been there before. "Remarkable," she thought he said under his breath.

"I beg your pardon?"

He shook his head, as if to clear it. "I appreciate your passion for Mrs. Gorcey and her children, but I still must refuse. Was that all, Miss Greene?"

"You are choosing to protect Mr. Gorcey instead?"

"Not entirely, but his personal business is his own. C'est la voie du monde."

That was the way of the world? No. Justine refused to believe society was so cynical.

"If that is your answer, fine. But fair warning, I shall find him myself and turn him over to the authorities."

"Mrs. Gorcey has the funds for legal counsel?"

"Mr. Tripp, my brother-in-law."

Mulligan grimaced, obviously aware of Frank Tripp's reputation, but then waved this off with a flick of his hand. "Tripp's assistance aside, I cannot see a court undertaking these sorts of cases in any serious manner. Not when there are real crimes afoot, like murder and arson."

"I assure you, these are real crimes. I have settled eight such cases already, where husbands were located and forced to live up to their obligations."

"Eight? Why haven't I heard of this?"

She smothered a smile, though it was hard not to feel smug about the accomplishment. Those eight men had thought themselves smarter than their wives. Justine had enjoyed proving them wrong. "Are you aware of everything that happens downtown?"

"Yes." The word held no conceit, just a plain and simple fact.

"Then I must be doing something right. It wouldn't do for my purpose to become common knowledge. The husbands would go to greater lengths to hide."

"And the police are assisting you with this?"

"They are." To an extent. Meaning, they gave Justine leave to find these wayward husbands and bring them in. Only one officer gave her a bit of help, and just when he had the time.

"I don't care for coppers sniffing around my men, Miss Greene."

"Then turn over Gorcey, Mr. Mulligan."

"I don't care for that, either."

"It's one or the other, I'm afraid."

"No. There are always other options."

"Such as?"

His gaze narrowed in a speculative way she didn't care for. "Such as I refuse to let you leave."

She couldn't help it—she laughed. "Meaning you'll kidnap me? That's absurd."

"No one said anything about kidnapping."

"What would you call it, then?"

"I would call it keeping you here."

She chuckled again. For whatever reason, perhaps because he spoke French or had priceless works of art in his office, Justine wasn't afraid of him. Mulligan reminded her of her father, Duncan Greene, a man of more bluster than actual bite.

She also knew men like her father and Mulligan were incredibly stubborn. There was no getting them to change their minds.

This meeting was over. Standing, she started for the door. If this was how Mulligan wanted to play it, fine. Justine had encountered resistance before.

"You think I won't do it?" he called after her, obviously back to the kidnapping nonsense.

Pausing with her hand on the doorknob, she turned. He was on his feet behind his desk, his dark brows bunched together, jaw tight. She tried not to notice how his confusion and irritation only increased his handsomeness.

Focus, Justine. This man had just declared himself the enemy of her cause. That meant she was finished with him. "I know you won't. You're not a mustache-twirling villain, like the men in those penny stories."

His jaw dropped open, but she didn't have time for more banter. Gorcey must be found before Mulligan had a chance to warn him. She let herself out and started down the corridor. Just as she reached the stairs, Mulligan came up behind her. "Miss Greene."

She looked up at him. His broad chest and shoulders nearly blocked all of the soft gaslight overhead. "Yes?"

"I may not have a mustache but I am indeed a villain. You'd be wise to remember it."

Chapter Two

❧

Jack Mulligan couldn't recall the last time he'd been so astounded.

He'd seen it all in his thirty-two years on this earth. Had lived a life most men only dreamed of, with the highest of highs and the lowest of lows. Wealth beyond measure, hundreds of men awaiting his command. He had the power to sway elections, to change the landscape of the city. No one took a piss south of Fourteenth Street without his approval.

And one little do-gooder had just laughed in his face.

It was unthinkable. Untenable. Un-fucking-believable.

She had brass ones, that was for certain. He'd beaten men for less than the insult Justine Greene had handed him. Today, in fact.

Ah, but her face . . .

He'd thought her plain at first. Her sister, Florence, was an absolute stunner. The kind of woman every man lusted after, with big tits and a small waist. Smooth skin and blond hair, not to mention a gorgeous smile. Compared to that, Justine was *less.* No bosom to speak of, brown hair pulled back in a severe style, and eyes that neither danced nor twinkled. No one would look twice at her with Florence in the room.

Until Justine began talking. Then she came alive, some fire or inner determination burning bright inside her. Sitting in his office, she'd fairly glowed.

Now, she swept down the stairs, regal as a queen, dismissing him. Christ, that yellow dress was hideous. With her skin tone she needed deeper, warm colors. Her dressmaker should be fired, immediately.

"Miss Greene," he heard himself call, not even certain what he'd say.

She paused on the last step and glanced over her shoulder. "Yes?"

He waited for her to walk back up but she merely stood there. Solid brass, he thought and descended until he was directly above her. "What's in it for me if I help you?"

"Knowing you did the right thing, I suppose."

"You can't tell me everyone you've approached has cooperated."

"No, but I never said I needed your cooperation. It would make things easier, yes. But I don't *need* it. I'm perfectly capable of finding Gorcey on my own."

"And yet, if he's in my employ—which I'm neither confirming nor denying—he is untouchable."

"That's ridiculous. No one is untouchable."

"I am."

It wasn't a boast. Jack had spent the majority of his adult life ensuring he was beyond the reach of the police department. Beyond the reach of city hall, with their corrupt Tammany machine. Above the rest of the criminal class, who worried about being pinched.

Not Jack. Not any longer.

He'd amassed enough money and power that he didn't need to look over his shoulder anymore. The police may not like it, but he had enough of the dirty officers on his payroll that the department couldn't do shit to Jack's organization without his approval. No one held more sway in this part of town than he did—not the mayor, the police commissioners or the head of Tammany Hall.

This hadn't come easy. He'd toiled, fought, plotted and schemed for his position atop downtown's criminal class. Had been knifed and shot. Endured countless brawls and fights. Suffered broken bones and dislocated joints. His face might not tell the story, but below the neck was a different tale. His body was riddled with the scars and marks of his violent past.

Yet he'd emerged the victor—and he would never fucking apologize for it.

Miss Justine Greene didn't appear impressed with him, however. He didn't quite understand it. Women had never posed a problem for Jack. Even when he was poor his face had ensured he was never lonely. Now that he was rich, women were even easier to come by. Singles, pairs, even groups . . . Getting a fuck was like cleaning his teeth.

Yet this one had laughed at him.

He didn't hate her for the slight, though, which surprised him. No, he *admired* her for it.

"You've never come up against someone like me," she said. "I'll get to Gorcey whether you help me or not."

He almost believed her. Of course, he had ways of hiding people that she'd never dreamed of, with her proper uptown upbringing.

Truthfully, Jack didn't like Gorcey. And if the accusation was true? Jack liked him even less. But Jack didn't care for anyone messing with his men or his organization. He preferred to stay in control.

"Well?"

Justine's impatience broke through his thoughts. "I want to see her."

Brown brows dipped in apparent confusion. "See who?"

"Mrs. Gorcey."

"Absolutely not."

He pursed his lips. "Then we are at an impasse."

"Hardly."

"I can make things very difficult for you, do-gooder."

"By kidnapping me?"

He didn't care for the twitching of her lips as she uttered this, as if the notion were ridiculous. He hadn't kidnapped a woman before . . . but this one sorely tempted him, if only to prove that he could.

Just how much would Duncan Greene pay in ransom to get his youngest daughter back? Now, there was a business opportunity to be considered.

Not a villain, indeed. He nearly snorted. This girl had *no* idea.

Suppressing the urge to twirl an imaginary mustache, he said, "If I meet Mrs. Gorcey and hear her side, then I might be willing to force Robert to do right by her."

Instead of appearing appeased, she frowned. "Hear her side? There are no *sides* to this story. The idea that she has to convince you of her hardships so that her husband will live up to his promises is insulting."

Merde, this woman. Was she always so difficult? "Take it or leave it, Miss Greene. You may have your man before the sun sets, or you may flounder for weeks wondering where he's gone."

"Fine. I'll take you to see her."

"I don't think so."

Streaks of gold sparked in the brown depths of her eyes, tiny bolts of lightning that portended her anger. "I haven't time for games, not when—"

"No game. We shall see her here."

Justine folded her arms. "Mr. Mulligan, she has five children to tend. Do you honestly believe she is able to leave them and come traipsing over, merely because you don't wish to be bothered?"

He hadn't thought of that, but he wouldn't budge on the issue. His help, his rules. Always. "The children aren't my problem. You want Gorcey, then the meeting must be here."

"I'll ask her. That's the best I can do. Perhaps one of her neighbors can watch the children."

He shook his head. "You misunderstand. You aren't leaving. I'll have one of the boys fetch Mrs. Gorcey."

"They will terrify her! You cannot do that. At least let me go along."

She stood nearly nose to nose with him, her voice stern like an irate schoolteacher. Or what he assumed a teacher's voice sounded like, seeing as how he never went to school. Something about that tone and the color on her cheeks got to him. This woman did not give up or back down for any reason. He could feel his body responding despite his better judgment.

God knew she was hardly his usual type. He liked them bold and buxom. Experienced. Not some uptown princess who'd faint in shock if he playfully slapped her arse while screwing her from behind.

"I should leave." She started down the remaining stairs. "This was a mistake."

He darted ahead to block her retreat. He moved two steps below her, putting them almost at the same height. "Giving up already?"

"Adjusting my strategy. I had thought, given your reputation for softness toward the female race, that you'd offer your assistance. I have clearly misjudged you."

"No, but you have misunderstood the way things work around here. I am both the judge and the jury, Miss Greene. If there is a problem with one of my men, then I hear the facts and render a decision. Me and only me. Do you understand?"

She seemed to absorb this, her irritable expression easing ever so slightly. "That implies you are capable of remaining impartial."

"I am nothing if not fair."

"Do you know where Gorcey is at this moment?"

"I have a good idea."

She sighed and stared at the wall. There wasn't much to contemplate, as he had the upper hand, but he appreciated her thoroughness. This was a woman who avoided rash behavior, who was careful. He was much the same way.

"If you won't let me fetch her, then I'd like to send along a note to reassure her."

A smile overtook Jack's face, stretching the sides of his mouth. "Of course. Come along."

Jack Mulligan was full of surprises.

During the hour they waited on Mrs. Gorcey, Justine sat across from him in his office, sipping sherry, while Mulligan made polite conversation. He could speak to any topic, from art and culture to politics and classics. He was well-read, intelligent and charming. She could almost forget they were in a boxing club/saloon/criminal headquarters near the Bowery.

All this was a stark contradiction to Mulligan's dangerous reputation, one he'd earned by consolidating the criminal gangs downtown into one massive empire years back. How he'd done it was the stuff of legend, stories shared in saloons late at night across the city. Justine didn't know the details but she could assume that cunning, bravery and bloodshed had each played a part.

She let him do most of the talking. This was nothing unusual. Her two older sisters were gregarious and outspoken. Justine, on the other hand, preferred to listen and observe. Not that she was a wallflower, but her energies were best spent helping others. Gossip and fashion bored her to tears. Parties and social calls were a waste of time. How could any of those things matter when most of the city's residents struggled to provide for themselves and their families?

"Am I boring you?"

She glanced up at Mulligan's question. "Of course not." What had he been talking about? Right, the art he'd seen on a recent trip to Paris. "I haven't been to Paris since I was a girl."

He cocked a brow, his handsome face turning curious. "I thought all good heiresses went to Paris each year for their wardrobes."

"I'm not that sort of heiress."

"What kind of heiress are you, then?"

"The rebellious kind, I suppose."

"I am noticing that. Here I've been trying to impress you and clearly missing the mark."

"Why would you be trying to impress me?"

"Because I am vain. Not only am I a man in the presence of a beautiful woman, that woman happens to come from one of the best families in the city."

Beautiful? She nearly snorted. He'd clearly mistaken her for one of her sisters. "You don't need to impress me. As soon as Mr. Gorcey agrees to take care of his wife, I'll be out of your way."

He drank from his glass of beer. A lager, he'd said, one produced by Mamie's brother-in-law. "Tell me, what does your father think of your charitable endeavors?"

She shifted on the plush seat of the armchair. "Have you met my father?"

"I haven't had the pleasure but I know him by reputation."

"Then you'll understand why I don't always inform him of my every move."

"But surely he is aware of your trips downtown."

"Of course." She didn't mention that her father

believed she spent her time strictly at the legal aid society with her sister.

He seemed to sense her deception. "Ah, I see." He chuckled, the lines around his eyes deepening. He must laugh often, she realized, to have those lines. The amusement caused him to appear younger and even more appealing, and warmth slid through her, her stomach doing funny things.

Never mind the boxing downstairs. Mulligan's looks and charm were a dangerous one-two combination to a woman's peace of mind.

She hated that he affected her at all. No one, not even her sisters, knew there had been a man in Justine's life for part of last year. A few years older than her, Billy Ferris had been a plumber's apprentice. They met when Justine hired Billy's employer to fix some leaky pipes in a tenement on Mott Street. Billy was sweet and kind, the type of man who never argued or became angry. They'd grown apart after a few months, however, their relationship barely intimate, and she hadn't been brokenhearted when Billy called it quits.

She never considered marrying him. As she'd learned, married women had fewer rights than unmarried women, ceding everything to their husbands. The wrong choice was disastrous, no matter the name and pedigree of one's father.

Justine had seen enough results from unfortunate choices to last a lifetime.

Still, she had cared for Billy. If she were to marry, she'd prefer someone boring and predictable, like him. She didn't care for fireworks and passion. She'd rather have comfort and reliability.

So, why was she noticing Mulligan's looks and *feeling* things?

"Tell me of the legal aid society," Mulligan said, breaking into her thoughts. "Busy, I suppose?"

"Busier than we could have dreamed. It has been exhausting but rewarding."

"I'm not surprised. I have met your brother-in-law and he is a force of nature."

"You know Frank?" That surprised her.

"Of course. It was inevitable we would cross paths now and again. He has the best legal mind in the state."

"And you oversee the biggest criminal empire in the state."

If she'd expected him to prevaricate or deny it, he surprised her by doing neither. "Indeed, I do. Does that bother you?"

"Why would it?"

"I couldn't say, do-gooder. But I get the sense I am making you uncomfortable."

"I am not uncomfortable. It's merely that you're not what I expected." In the least.

He opened his mouth but a knock interrupted whatever he'd been about to say. At Mulligan's command, the door opened to reveal a young man followed by Mrs. Gorcey. Wide-eyed and pale, Mrs. Gorcey rushed toward Justine. "Miss Greene, have you really found Robert?"

"I believe so. Mr. Mulligan has agreed to help us."

"Mrs. Gorcey." Mulligan approached and dipped his chin. "Welcome. I do hope we may arrive at a satisfactory conclusion for you today."

"Thank you, Mr. Mulligan. I apologize for bothering you with my problems." Mrs. Gorcey could hardly meet Mulligan's eyes, her voice trembling.

"No need for apologies. I am always happy to help downtown residents whenever possible."

Justine nearly snorted. Hadn't he just asked her what providing help would gain him? She had a feeling that Jack Mulligan was not acting out of the kindness of his heart, yet he'd made no demands. Perhaps her speeches prompting him to do the right thing had affected him.

The door opened once more and two men entered. Mrs. Gorcey stiffened, giving a short intake of breath, and Justine deduced that one of these men must be Mr. Gorcey.

Sure enough, one man locked eyes with Mrs. Gorcey and stopped in his tracks. His gaze then darted around the room, possibly searching for an escape. As if sensing this, the other man put a hand on Gorcey's shoulder and pushed him farther into the room. Still, Gorcey avoided his wife's eyes, not acknowledging her in any manner.

"Robert." Mulligan pointed to a chair. "Have a seat. Mrs. Gorcey?" He held out an arm as if to escort the older woman to a society event, and Justine rolled her eyes at the ceiling.

When everyone was seated, Mulligan crossed his legs and smoothed his perfectly creased trousers. "Robert, we seem to have an issue with your family."

"I don't have any family," was Gorcey's answer.

"No doubt you're wishin' that were the case," Mrs. Gorcey snapped. Justine put a hand on the other woman's arm in comfort and warning. They must remain calm.

"Well, this woman here claims to be your wife," Mulligan said. "She said you have abandoned her and your five children. Have you anything to say about that?"

"She's a liar."

"How dare you—"

Justine squeezed Mrs. Gorcey's arm. This wasn't the first time a husband had lied when presented with evidence of his misdeeds. She turned to Mr. Gorcey. "You are saying you've never seen her before?"

He shot Justine a look full of venom—one so fierce she nearly flinched. "That's what I'm saying."

"So, if she were to reveal something about your person, like a birthmark or a scar, we wouldn't be able to verify that?"

He gave no response, just clenched his jaw and stared at the wall.

"Mrs. Gorcey?" Mulligan asked. "Is there such an identifying mark?"

She nodded and pointed to her right wrist. "He has a scar here from a fight in a saloon. He also has a mole on the left side of his chest."

Mulligan arched a brow. "Gorcey, I'll strip you down if I must to get to the truth. So, is what she says a fact? Before you answer, remember that I don't care for liars nor do I care for having my time wasted. Do you know this woman or not?"

"Aye." The word was bitten out, filled with resentment.

"She is your wife?"

"Not any longer. I told her I wanted to leave and she told me to go."

"That's not true!" Mrs. Gorcey said.

"It is, too." Gorcey's lip curled as he focused on his wife. "You have no claim on me, woman."

Justine quickly intervened. "Did you marry her, Mr. Gorcey?"

"Yes, but—"

"Are you the father of her children?"

"I don't know," he mumbled. "They coulda been fathered by anyone."

"You son of a—" Mrs. Gorcey started before Justine squeezed her arm again.

"Miss Greene, Mrs. Gorcey," Mulligan said as he rose. "I'd like a moment alone with Robert. Excuse us, won't you?"

Without waiting for Robert's cooperation, Mulligan strode to an adjoining door and walked out. There hadn't been a stated threat of any kind but Gorcey's throat worked, his face going alarmingly pale. Without delay, he quickly stood and followed Mulligan from the room.

"Can you believe the nerve?" Mrs. Gorcey hissed when they were alone. "Saying our children were fathered by another man. How dare he?"

"I wish I could say I am surprised. I've heard just about every excuse from these wife deserters." One man had continued lying even when presented with his eldest son, who was the spitting image of his father. That merely illustrated how easy it was for men to shirk their paternal responsibilities.

"What do you think Mr. Mulligan is saying in there?" Mrs. Gorcey's voice was hardly above a whisper, as if she feared Mulligan overhearing her.

Justine thought back to those bloody knuckles and winced. *This isn't my blood.* Would he beat Gorcey into cooperating?

"I don't know," Justine said. "I hope it's something to help your husband admit the truth."

"All I want is financial support," Mrs. Gorcey said. "I don't want him back."

"No one is saying you must take him back. And if this fails, I'll find a way to bring your husband to the police. So, we aren't out of options yet."

The door reopened and Gorcey appeared first. His blank expression lacked all traces of the animosity from before. Mulligan strolled in next, all smiles. He slapped Gorcey on the back, as if they were the oldest of friends. "Go on, Robert."

"I'll pay her ten dollars a month," Gorcey said. "Until the children are of age."

"Twenty-five," Justine countered. "There are six mouths to feed."

Gorcey's face darkened. "That's absolute robbery!"

Mulligan cleared his throat dramatically.

Gorcey's anger withered instantly. He nodded eagerly. "Of course. Twenty-five."

"Hallelujah!" Mrs. Gorcey said.

Justine pressed her lips together to keep from smiling. They weren't quite done yet. "You are to maintain a respectable distance from Mrs. Gorcey at all times. If I discover that you are harassing or abusing her in any manner, I will set the police on you."

Gorcey's gaze glittered with repressed hatred and burning frustration. These men were the most dangerous, in Justine's opinion. She would not put it past him to try and hurt Mrs. Gorcey or the children to get out of making the payments.

"If I am providing for her like a husband, then I intend to claim my—"

"He won't go near her," Mulligan interrupted. "I'll ensure it. The payments will come directly to me and I'll see them forwarded to Mrs. Gorcey."

"No."

The room paused at Justine's refusal. Even Mrs. Gorcey appeared confused. "I don't understand," the other woman said under her breath.

Justine focused on Mulligan. "The payments will go to the legal aid society. We'll see that Mrs. Gorcey receives the money."

Mulligan rubbed his jaw and stared at Justine. She could tell he didn't like it but she would not budge on this. If Gorcey paid Mulligan, then Mrs. Gorcey might never see the money. Or, she'd see a reduced percentage, less a fee for Mulligan's intervention.

Mulligan waved to the guard at the door. "Robert, I'll follow up with you later. You're excused." Gorcey didn't stick around. He quit the room in a flash. "Rye, see Mrs. Gorcey returned home. I'd like a word with Miss Greene. Alone."

Chapter Three

Jack didn't like ceding the upper hand. Not in his business, not in negotiations. Not even in bed. The minute he gave up control was the minute his empire toppled. Men all across the city were waiting for him to grow weak, to let up for one single second. Jack wouldn't give them the satisfaction.

He meant to die while still on top. It was the only option for a man such as himself.

So, he didn't care for Justine arguing with him when he'd solved her little problem. He'd expected her gratitude. Her appreciation. In his dreams, perhaps a celebratory fuck. What he hadn't expected was for her to contradict that resolution.

"Please, sit." He gestured to a chair. If they were to argue, then it was better to do it in a civilized manner.

"I'd rather stand," she said. "This won't take long."

He shook his head but remained on his feet. "Miss Greene, you seem to misunderstand how things work in my world. My decisions are final. I solved your problem with the Gorceys. Do not spit on my benevolence."

"And while I appreciate your help, I do not like the idea of Mrs. Gorcey beholden to you for her monthly stipend."

"She is not beholden to me. You are."

He almost enjoyed the shock that overcame her face. "*Me?* Why?"

"Because I did you a favor. As I said, favors come with a price around here. Quid pro quo, Miss Greene."

"You never said that," she snapped. "You asked what was in it for you if you helped me."

"Implying that I am owed a debt should I lend assistance."

Her arms lifted and fell at her sides. Then her jaw worked as she clenched it. She was glorious in her anger, with her tightly leashed emotion and flushed skin. He wondered whether that lurking fire and spirit would emerge in the bedroom. He doubted it. She gave off a virgin air. Surprising, considering the way the Greene girls ran amok in New York City. God knew none of them worried about propriety. But this was a complex creature, one he hadn't figured out just yet.

Justine's gaze narrowed, her stare full of loathing. If he weren't so amused by her, his balls might have retracted up into his body in the face of her fierce disapproval. "We never agreed to any debt or repayment. I assumed you believed Mrs. Gorcey's story and acted out of compassion and kindness."

He chuckled. "Wrong. I believe Mrs. Gorcey, but there's no compassion or kindness here. I am pure greed, through and through."

"Well, I cannot pay you."

"It's not money that I'm after."

That statement hung in the air and he could tell she didn't understand. Hell, he barely understood it. But, twisted bastard that he was, he knew one should never turn down the opportunity to have the daughter of a prominent family in his debt. He'd be a goddamn fool otherwise.

"I do not understand."

"It's very simple. You owe me a favor, Miss Greene. The time and method of repayment is at my discretion."

"Absolutely not. That is completely unacceptable. There's no telling what you might ask for."

"That is a risk you'll have to take—unless you'd like me to turn Robert Gorcey out on the street without any agreement of future payments, of course."

"That's blackmail."

She said it as if he was wholly unaware of his terms. "Very good."

"What could you possibly want from me? I have no connections . . ." She drifted off as if an idea had occurred and rendered her speechless. "Surely you cannot mean anything . . . physical."

"You're hardly my type," he said by way of answer. "I think I'd scare you witless the second I undressed."

"Then I cannot begin to see what you will require in exchange."

"No one can predict the future. Perhaps I'll never call in that favor." A lie. Of course he would call in the favor, but she needn't know that.

"Doubtful. You seem the kind of man to keep people under your thumb, turning the screws."

The side of his mouth hitched. "I am fond of screwing."

She huffed out a breath and cocked her head. "Was that *innuendo*?"

"If you cannot tell then I've clearly lost my touch."

"I thought I wasn't your type?"

He lifted a shoulder and shoved his hands in his trouser pockets. "The more you argue with me, the more 'my type' you become."

He nearly laughed at the way her lips pressed together, as if she was holding back her arguments by sheer force of will. Silent, she folded her arms and stared at the wall. He could almost see her brain turning it over, trying to arrive at a solution that wouldn't require interacting with him again.

For some reason, he couldn't let that happen.

The moment dragged on. It was warm in his office and he longed for a cool drink at the bar. Still, he wouldn't rush her. He'd learned to negotiate on the streets of Five Points, where winning meant survival. Those skills had been honed against criminals, policemen, politicians . . . One little Knickerbocker wouldn't rattle him. He'd wait her out all week, if necessary.

"What happens if I refuse the repayment request?"

"You won't."

"I certainly will if it is illegal or makes me uncomfortable in any way."

"Lest you think this is a negotiation, allow me to dissuade you. You have no leverage in this situation. Walking out means Mr. Gorcey disappears for good. Are you so cavalier with Mrs. Gorcey's fate?"

Color tinged her cheeks, the gold in her eyes sparking once more as she faced him. So far, he'd embarrassed and angered her. Yet she was still here, staring him down. The girl had spine. "That sounds like a challenge," she threw out. "How about this for leverage? I'll merely pay Mrs. Gorcey myself."

He blinked. Just once, which wouldn't have been memorable coming from any other person on earth. But for Jack Mulligan, who never flinched or backed down or reacted in any manner that he hadn't carefully planned, he might as well have fainted in a fit of the vapors.

Goddamn it. Would she really do that?

"Yes, I really would," she said, somehow able to read his mind.

"With what money? Your father certainly won't approve."

"I don't need his money. I have money of my own."

Shit. Of course. He'd been an idiot to assume her dependent on her father. Girls like her were rolling in money, dripping in dresses and jewels as soon as they left the cradle.

He accepted defeat. He couldn't counter that—

Oh, wait. Yes, he could.

"And what would your father think about your activities here downtown?"

She visibly bristled, her shoulders tight, brows lowered in anger. "Good God. You are a worm, Mulligan. No, you are lower than a worm. You are the scum floating atop a Mulberry Street puddle."

He chuckled. "I will give you credit for creativity, Miss Greene. I don't think I've ever been called puddle scum before."

"I wish I could revel in the achievement. Unfortunately, I'm too busy cursing you inside my head."

"And what curses would those be? I'm curious how an uptown princess curses out a man like me."

She drew closer, unafraid, her hands clenched into tight fists. "I won't dignify that taunt with a response. Only know they are very creative, entirely lewd and ridiculously offensive."

Whether it was her bold attitude or the word *lewd*, lust began to thicken in his blood, warming him everywhere. Christ, she was brave. Grown men wouldn't face him down like this, insulting him. No woman had certainly ever tried before. He liked it, though, at least from Justine. She was like Joan of Arc or Boudica squaring off in battle, and he contemplated all that passion and determination locked inside her. The man who found a way to enjoy it, whether in or out of the bedroom, would reap a hell of a reward.

As he let his mind ruminate on some of the more interesting reward possibilities, she started for the door. "Fine, Mulligan. You have your promise."

He couldn't help but grin as he watched her move across the floor. "I thought you might say that."

"Enjoy it, then, because that's the last one you'll ever get out of me. I know better than to bargain with the devil twice." She stepped into the corridor, slamming the door shut behind her.

"WHAT IS TROUBLING you, my dear?" Granny asked Justine quietly at dinner. Everyone else was talking around them, leaving a rare moment for private conversation. "You seem distracted tonight."

Was it that obvious? "Merely a long day."

With their parents in Europe, the Greene sisters

had taken to dining with their grandmother most every night. Tonight, though, Justine was not exactly up to making polite conversation, not after her meeting with Mulligan. The idea of owing him an undetermined favor at some point in the future turned her stomach.

Granny nudged Justine with her elbow. "A bold-faced lie if I've ever heard one. Something has upset you."

"Why are men so awful?"

She'd blurted the question without thinking, and Granny's eyes grew round like saucers. Justine couldn't blame Granny for the reaction. The two of them weren't particularly close—Florence was Granny's favorite, after all—and they'd never had a single conversation about relationships or marriage. In fact, Justine couldn't remember ever going to their grandmother for advice. Perhaps she should remedy that. Granny was wise and not as conventional as Mama.

Granny's mouth hitched, her eyes twinkling with mirth. "My dear, you might as well ask why the sky is blue. Men are the way they are because we've allowed them to run roughshod over us for centuries. But your generation is changing that, I believe. It takes time for attitudes to shift." She leaned in and whispered, "And you'll come to learn they are good for some things."

I am fond of screwing.

Justine could feel her skin warming and tingling. Mulligan was potent. A heady presence that overwhelmed any room he occupied. He was also a criminal. She could not under any circumstances forget that, no matter his charm and wit.

"Is there a man in your life?" Granny asked under her breath. "You may tell me. I won't share with anyone."

"No," she said. "Which is fine. I do not need one."

"You might change your mind for the right man. You're more practical and sentimental than your sisters. You'll want a family, of course."

Perhaps once she had. But the last few years had shown her the suffering, the helplessness that children endured in this world. "Marriage doesn't mean children." At least, it shouldn't.

"I suppose. But how will our daughters change the world if there are no more daughters?"

Justine thought about that as she chewed. Mr. Gorcey's face flashed in her mind as he lied about fathering any children. Utterly infuriating. Sadly, he was not unique. Countless men walked away from their promises and responsibilities with little thought, leaving women and children to suffer. It sickened her. "Why are sons not taught to change things? Why must the burdens and problems of this world constantly fall on the shoulders of women?"

The wrinkles in Granny's skin deepened as she pursed her lips. "You know, I've never considered it that way. But you're right."

"Exactly."

"I suppose it's for the best. God knows your father isn't in any hurry to see you paired off, not after what he went through with your two sisters. I think he's hoping you'll live here forever, unwed and pure."

Pure, ha.

Her virginity aside, Justine couldn't imagine leaving her family and this house. She loved this place, the only home she'd ever known. Yet things were changing. Mamie lived with Frank a little farther south on Fifth Avenue. Florence would soon move to her casino downtown. Each of her sisters was finding her path. What was Justine's future? She wanted to help people, but what did that mean? More charity work? "Well, I'm not in any hurry, either."

Dinner broke up and everyone started for the salon. Justine was considering escaping to her bedroom when her oldest sister dragged her into an empty sitting room. "I want to talk to you," Mamie said, her mouth set in a determined line that Justine was well familiar with.

"What about?"

"Today."

"And?"

"You were very late, dragging in here looking like someone kicked your dog."

"That's a terrible comparison."

"Justine, focus. What happened?"

Mamie was the only one in the family who knew about Justine's efforts to locate the wife deserters. "I found Mr. Gorcey, the husband I've been searching for the past six weeks."

"That is good news. Unless it didn't go well?"

"No, it did. He's agreed to pay Mrs. Gorcey a monthly stipend to help her raise the children."

Mamie's brows lowered. "Why so glum, then? I should think you'd be elated."

"I am. It's just . . ." She decided to confide in Mamie. "Do you know a man downtown by the name of Jack Mulligan?"

"I know of him. Why?"

"Gorcey works for Mulligan. I went to the New Belfast Athletic Club and asked Mulligan—"

"You *what*?" Mamie grabbed Justine's arm. "Tell me you did not go alone. You shouldn't be around Mulligan, certainly not without an escort."

"It was the middle of the day. I was perfectly safe. Mostly."

That was the wrong thing to say. Mamie paled and rocked back on her heels. "Did someone hurt you?"

"No. Calm down, Mamie. Nothing happened."

Mamie didn't appear to believe that statement, the irritation not leaving her expression. "So, what is this about Mulligan?"

"I needed his help with Gorcey. In exchange I had to promise a favor."

"What kind of favor?"

"He wouldn't say. Just a future favor of his choosing."

"And you agreed to that?" Mamie gaped then put her hands on her hips. "Have Florence and I taught you nothing? Why in God's name would you say yes?"

Justine bristled. "I'm not a child, Mamie. I needed his help. I erroneously thought Mulligan would force Gorcey to pay based on his reputation as a protector of women. Her situation was supposed to appeal to his sense of right and wrong."

"Well, Frank will go and handle Mulligan, get him to remove the debt."

"That isn't necessary. I will handle it. Also, we agreed Frank wasn't to know about what I am doing." Her brother-in-law could make investigating difficult for Justine, if he chose. Or he could tell her father, which would have been infinitely worse.

"I don't like keeping secrets from him," Mamie said. "It's not fair to either of us. He'll be furious if he finds out."

"Which he won't—because you won't say anything. I will stop informing you of what I'm doing if it's so difficult for you to remain quiet."

"Which would only worry me more. At least I may offer assistance if I know what you're doing."

"So, it's settled. I'll deal with Mulligan and you stay out of it."

"I will look after you if I deem it necessary, Justine. Stop being so stubborn. Now, come along before we're missed."

Justine didn't move. Her head was throbbing with thoughts of manipulative kingpins and meddling older sisters. She just wished to be alone. To rebuild her walls and shore up her defenses. Mamie meant well, but Justine was capable of managing her own life. "I am not feeling well. I think I'll go lie down."

"You're trying to avoid me because you know I am right." Mamie lifted her skirts and headed toward the hall. "Fine. Go rest. Just prepare yourself for when I say, 'I told you so.'"

Justine didn't bother correcting her sister. She'd find a way to gain the upper hand over Mulligan. Somehow.

Chapter Four

❧

Jack sat alone at the club's bar and stared into his glass of beer. Noise surrounded him, from the shouts of the boxing match in the front to the music coming from the saloon, but he didn't really hear it. Not tonight. His mind was on something else.

Specifically, some*one* else.

He'd just received his daily report on Miss Justine Greene. For nearly a week, one of Jack's crew had tailed her then reported the intrepid little do-gooder's activities to Jack. It seemed she always stayed busy, hardly stopping to eat. Out early in the mornings, home by dark. Serving meals at a church. Giving out blankets in the tenements. Taking women to see surgeons and midwives. She didn't pay social calls or attend society events.

Hell, if not for her address and last name, one would never know she was from a wealthy, prominent family.

She hadn't returned to the athletic club and had avoided the blocks near Great Jones Street. Almost as if she were avoiding *him*.

All this while he couldn't get her out of his head.

"My, you are distracted tonight."

Jack glanced up and found Maeve, one of his dancers, at his elbow. Maeve was the unelected leader of the girls, the dancer who'd been here the longest. She was sharp and intelligent, and she looked out for the others. He patted the stool next to him. "I am never distracted. Are you here for a drink?"

She shook her head, the blue curls of her wig bouncing as she sat down. "No, I'm looking for you."

"Is there a problem?" Jack didn't normally handle problems personally. In the saloon, several strong men were tasked with keeping the dancers safe from the rowdy drunken idiots.

"There might be." She leaned in and lowered her voice. "Katie isn't certain but she thinks the same man's been following her home the past few nights."

Jack's muscles tightened. The neighborhood knew Jack's dancers, knew they were off-limits. Knew the retribution that would rain down if any of the girls were harmed.

So, who would dare?

There had only been two rivals in recent years: Clayton Madden and Trevor O'Shaughnessy. Madden had given up his empire for love, which was laughable, and O'Shaughnessy was a newcomer, off the boat from Dublin not even five years ago. Was O'Shaughnessy stupid enough to make a move?

Young and full of piss, O'Shaughnessy hadn't witnessed the bloodshed and violence on the streets before Jack consolidated the Five Points and Bowery gangs into one organization. Trevor thought there was enough money and muscle these days to go around. Why should Jack have it all? To that end, he'd slowly been assembling a crew over at Broome Street Hall, where he started as a bouncer. He wasn't a threat to Jack's empire, but he was someone to watch. So Jack kept an eye on those who sided with O'Shaughnessy and the businesses in Trevor's pocket.

Working in O'Shaughnessy's favor was Jack's refusal to operate brothels. After being raised in one and seeing what that life did to women like his mother, Jack would rather die a pauper than condone such a business. Trevor had no such convictions. He peddled both young women and men in his houses outside of Jack's territory.

This meant Jack would never join forces with O'Shaughnessy. There would be no compromise, only annihilation when the time came.

Qui n'avance pas, recule. Who does not move forward, recedes. It was how Jack lived his life.

Suppressing a sigh, he asked, "She recognize him?"

"She couldn't see his face in the dark and said he pulls the brim of his hat low."

"He didn't approach her?"

"No, but it's got her spooked."

Not a surprise. Jack had seen firsthand the sort of violence men could inflict on women, and any woman in her right mind would wish to avoid it. "I'll have the boys start walking each of you home."

Maeve frowned, her face registering her annoyance. "That's not necessary—"

"Do not argue. We must remain vigilant, lest the city come to believe I've gone soft."

"No one with two eyes and a brain would ever

think that. Up and down Broadway, they are still telling the story of how you mailed that thief's fingers to his wife, one by one."

Jack grunted. Not exactly a true story—but criminals gossiped worse than old ladies at a sewing circle. "Nevertheless, I won't risk it. The five of you are my responsibility. I promised to keep you safe, and I will. No matter what. The other option is for you all to stay here."

"No one wants that. We all have families and lives outside of this club. Not to mention people would make assumptions about our role here if we lived on the premises." That the club was part brothel.

"Then accept the escorts."

She studied his face, her gaze thoughtful. "I can see it is one of those nights."

He took a long swallow of the pilsner and tried to hide from her scrutiny. "And what does that mean?"

"It means you have something weighing on your mind and your patience is thin. Anything you want to discuss?"

He considered it. Maeve was wise beyond her years, the oldest of eight children. The money she made dancing in the saloon went to help feed the siblings still at home. If Jack needed advice on women—which he didn't—Maeve would be the logical choice. But Jack never talked about his personal life with anyone. He fucked plenty of women on the sly, but he kept it private. It was a matter of both safety and practicality.

Besides, Justine Greene was not important. He found her fascinating, yes, but she was from another world. There was no use for a woman like that in his bed.

"No, I don't," he said.

"Fine." She slid off her stool. "Let's agree to escorts for a few days. The girls won't like it but they'll tolerate an escort until we are certain there is no threat."

The girls would tolerate escorts for as long as Jack deemed necessary, but he didn't bother mentioning that. He would assess the situation this evening, see if the man could be identified. Then he would take care of it personally. "How's business in there?"

"You haven't been in?"

"Not yet."

"Packed house. Busier than we've been in a few weeks."

"That's good. Let me know if you need anything else."

She rapped her knuckles on the bar. "I will. Enjoy the rest of your night, Mulligan."

Jack watched her go, his mouth turning into a fierce frown. He didn't wish to alarm her or the other girls, but someone bold enough to disrespect a Mulligan employee was disturbing. If O'Shaughnessy was behind it, this could be the opening salvo to a takeover attempt.

Of course, it might not be Trevor's doing. Business had been good the last two years. When Madden bowed out, Jack's share had steadily increased across the city. More saloons, more policy shops, more poolrooms . . . All of it added up to more money. More power. More influence. But that also made him a bigger target.

He sighed and rubbed the back of his neck.

Some days he wondered if all the aggravation was worth it.

Then he'd count his money and decide, fuck yes. It was more than worth it.

JUSTINE CARRIED HER notes up the steps of 300 Mulberry Street, otherwise known as New York City Police Headquarters. Patrolmen strode about, busy and serious, each looking smart in his navy-blue uniform. Though the department was rumored to be rife with corruption, she envied the officers. They held power, real power, to enact change. Having a badge meant the ability to gain compliance.

Unfortunately, many officers could be bought or blackmailed. Nobility was in short supply amongst the city's police, at least according to the lawyers at the legal aid society.

Inside, she went to the raised counter that served as the entry point. Justine had made enough trips here that she wasn't an unfamiliar face. At first, officer upon officer had stopped her to give directions, assuming she was lost. Now they knew better and ignored her.

After checking in with the desk sergeant, she walked deeper into the building. Men in drab suits stood in small clusters, laughing and talking, enjoying their male-only club. The holding pen for the inebriated was full, the tiny space packed with bodies. She kept her head down and focused on her destination.

Detective Ellison had been Justine's contact at the police department for the past eighteen months. Ellison hadn't wished to help her at first, but she had persisted, trying to convince him that husbands must provide for their families, until he finally relented. When she found that initial wife deserter—and the next—Ellison must have decided to tolerate her because he kept assisting her. While the police couldn't officially allocate resources to finding these deserters, Ellison had said she was welcome to try, if she was so inclined.

Today was not about a deserter, however. This had to do with the other problem she often asked Ellison to help with: child labor.

The door to the office was ajar. She knocked on the doorjamb, not caring to catch any of them unaware by barging in. Once she'd seen an officer urinating into a spittoon in the corner. "Hello?" she called.

Several groans erupted at the sound of her voice. "Come in," someone barked.

Four detectives sat at desks crammed into the small room. All heads turned her way. Three pairs of eyes were openly hostile while one set held a curious patience. The latter belonged to Ellison.

"Look who's here with another one of her cases," a detective said. "Shall we ring for tea, Ellison?"

She ignored them. "Good morning, Detective. Might I have a moment of your time?"

"Someone lose another husband?" another detective said, mockingly. "We better mobilize the entire force."

Ellison sent the others a withering stare as they all chuckled. "Fellows, give us the room, will you?" Still laughing, the other men went out the door, leaving Justine alone with Ellison. Standing, he pointed to the empty chair opposite the desk. "Don't let them bother you. They may be rude but they're good detectives."

"I'm not bothered. They are welcome to laugh at me. What I am doing is unusual but it is also important."

"That's the spirit." He retook his seat and leaned back in his chair, the wood creaking underneath him. "What may I do for you, Miss Greene?"

She sat and placed her notes in her lap. "I learned of a shirtwaist factory on Rivington Street and went to see it for myself yesterday. There were women and children there, young boys and girls not more than seven or eight, all working past dark on the fifth floor. The owners had locked the doors from the outside to prevent the workers from leaving."

He shook his head, his lips turned down in disapproval. She'd seen the look many times in their interactions. He was married with small children, and he hated the abuse and violence that many of the city's children faced. "Absolutely abhorrent. Anything to make a quick buck. Unfortunately, I can't help right now. I'm working a big murder case. Son of a politician, which means I have Tammany breathing down my neck."

"You cannot spare an hour to come and talk to them?" Ellison had done it in the past. He'd taken corrupt business owners aside and intimidated them with his badge and rank. He'd even threatened to go to the unions and help workers mobilize if the owners did not treat workers more fairly. All in all, it proved a more effective method than Justine acting on her own.

"I can't. Captain will fire me for certain if I do. Sorry, miss. You know I always like to help but until this case is solved I'm in a pickle."

"But . . ." She didn't know what to say. He had

never refused her before. "Is there someone else who can help, perhaps a detective not on this case?"

He gave a bitter laugh. "The entire precinct is on this case. And even if they weren't, the factory owners aren't doing anything illegal. I doubt I could convince another officer to help you."

In other words, her only choice was Ellison and he was too busy at the moment. Even as she understood this, she struggled to accept it. Something had to be done. "I must try and help them. Do you have any suggestions at all?"

"You could try the new Department of Buildings. Thomas Brady is the superintendent. He might have an issue with the locked doors and whether there's enough egress in case of a fire."

"But the ages of the children and the hours they are forced to work?"

"As reprehensible as we find those practices, Miss Greene, I'm afraid not all agree. They're more fixated on profits than quality of life. Come back in a few weeks and I'll see what I can do, all right?"

Irritation swept across her skin, but she nodded and rose. "Fine. Good luck on your case."

"I really am sorry." He followed her to the door. "Some days I wish they'd just admit women into the department and give you a badge. Then you wouldn't need me to intimidate these factory owners. You could intimidate them all on your own."

She snorted. "As if they would listen to a woman, police officer or not."

"Sadly, you're probably right. Have a care, Miss Greene. It's a rough city out there."

It was what he said to her each time she saw him,

Ellison's special brand of goodbye. "You too, Detective. Thank you."

In the corridor, she ignored the group of men gathered in the corner, whispering as they watched her depart. Ellison once mentioned the detectives teased him about his association with her. It made her so angry, their childishness. The atmosphere here was no better than upper Fifth Avenue, where one had to cater to the "right" people. Outsiders were looked down upon, no matter their net worth. Here, she was viewed as silly and frivolous because of her gender.

Sigh.

Humid air, sticky and heavy, greeted her outside. The responsibility she felt toward these families, these children, working in unsafe, cruel conditions weighted down her shoulders. God help them if there was ever an accident or a fire. Hundreds of lives could be lost.

It was then she heard a familiar deep voice, a cultured tone wholly out of place in this spot. Glancing over, she found him.

He was here. Jack Mulligan. At police headquarters.

She stared, unable to believe the sight. Mulligan was leaning against a sleek black brougham, his booted feet crossed at the ankles. Blue uniforms surrounded him, everyone smiling as they listened intently to whatever Mulligan was saying. He spoke animatedly, his hands gesturing, the life of the party. A perfectly tailored light brown suit hugged his frame, the hue complementing his dark hair and blue eyes. He could have been any industrialist or banker going about his daily business instead of a legendary kingpin.

The entire group broke out into loud laughter, some of the officers wiping tears of mirth from their eyes. She must have made some sound, a disbelieving squeak, because Mulligan's eyes met hers. His mouth twisted into a half smile before he addressed his audience. "Boys, it has been nice catching up but I see a pretty lady that needs my attention." He shook hands and slapped backs, but Justine didn't wait around. Spinning on her heel, she started up the walk and headed north.

He wasn't here for her, was he? Dread pooled in her stomach. If he was here to collect on that stupid agreement, then she'd have to think quickly. By reputation, Mulligan wasn't the type to negotiate or be put off. However, there was a limit to what Justine would agree to as repayment.

If Mulligan thought to bully or intimidate her, he was in for the shock of a lifetime.

"Whoa, wait up." He came alongside, easily matching her stride with his long legs. "What's the hurry, Miss Greene?"

"I have things to do, Mulligan." She dodged a fruit cart and the line of children surrounding it. "Was there something you needed?"

"Where are you headed?"

"Why all the questions?"

"Because I am curious about you. How does one small woman accomplish so much in one day? Serving meals in the Bowery, delivering clothing in the Lower East Side. It seems you never stop."

How . . . ? She halted in her tracks to blink up at him. "Are you having me *followed*?"

"That makes it sound nefarious. It's pure curiosity, I promise."

"Curiosity about what?" She couldn't fathom how she had sparked such interest in their short meeting. "My charity work?"

"That, among other things. Come. Allow me to drive you wherever you need to go."

The street was bare of conveyances, save a police wagon. "With what? The police wagon?"

Mulligan's eyes twinkled in the sunlight, the edge of his mouth kicking up. Lord, he was a handsome man. She ignored the fluttering in her stomach as he put two fingers in his mouth. A whistle pierced the air and she instinctively covered her ears. Seconds later, the sleek black brougham she'd seen outside headquarters rolled to a stop at their side.

Mulligan bowed. "Your chariot, my lady."

THE SILENCE STRETCHED and Jack began to feel like an idiot, bent over like an uptown swell, all in a ridiculous attempt to impress a girl. Something he hadn't bothered with in a long time—at least out of bed, anyway. He straightened and waited, the sun beating down on his back.

Justine looked anything but impressed. She stared at the brougham suspiciously, as if a snake waited inside, ready to strike. "I should have known."

"Known what?"

"You have a reputation for being resourceful."

Damn straight. Being two steps ahead of everyone else was the only way he had survived this long.

He tried for charm once more, offering his arm. "A lady as beautiful as yourself should never walk in this heat."

With a roll of her eyes, she ignored him and went the other way, heading south. Jack watched her, frozen, his arm suspended in the air. Was she *refusing* him? Disappointment sank into his bones as she kept going.

A choking noise that sounded suspiciously like a chuckle caught his attention, and he glared at his second-in-command and frequent driver. "Fuck off, Rye."

Rye quickly sobered. "Sorry, Mulligan." The two had known each other a long time and Jack liked Rye better than most. Not enough, however, to tolerate any disrespect.

He watched Justine get farther away. There was no choice, really. He'd have to chase her.

She hadn't traveled far, just across Houston Street, by the time he caught up with her. Jack matched her stride and nodded politely at people along the way. Private conversation during the walk would prove near impossible. He was well-known here. These streets were in his blood, the blocks where he'd spent nearly his entire life.

He'd brought order here. A measure of safety. Residents could breathe easier knowing Jack Mulligan watched out for them, that he kept other criminal elements and Tammany Hall at bay. No more riots, no more gang fights. He hired as many men as he could for his crew, the number now over fifteen hundred. They weren't choirboys, but they brought money home to their families. Patronized local businesses. Elevated the entire area.

It was why he insisted his men look clean and sharp at all times. They were better than the old gangs, who had worn rags and knifed each other in the streets. No, this was a different way of life and his men had to show as much for the rest of the city to believe it.

"Does that ever grow annoying?"

He tipped his derby at a woman calling out to him from her downstairs window. "The adulation, you mean?"

"Ha. Hardly adulation. More like pandering."

"I cannot help if my people revere me."

"They don't revere you. They *fear* you."

He frowned at her. "I would never hurt the people of these streets." This was his territory. From Broadway to Bowery, East Fourth Street to Five Points, his crew oversaw it all. He even had a foothold in New Jersey, Long Island and Staten Island. Soon, he'd have a lot more than that.

"As long as they do what you want," she said under her breath.

She didn't understand the ways of Lower Manhattan. Really, as an uptown princess, how could she? He moved on to a different topic. "Are you planning on walking all the way down to the legal aid society?" On a hot day like today, the journey would be pure misery. Not to mention the walk would take her directly through Five Points. What was she trying to prove?

"Yes. I need to think."

"About?"

"Mulligan, I do not have time for this. Just tell me what you want and get gone."

That stung. He didn't know why, exactly, but her easy dismissal rankled. "When was the last time you ate?"

She stopped and glared up at him. "Why do you ask?"

"Because it's past lunchtime and I am sensing you hardly slow down long enough to take care of yourself. Am I wrong?"

"I hardly see how that concerns you."

"You are in my debt, Miss Greene. Until I collect on that debt, your well-being is my concern." A completely inane argument, but he wouldn't back down. Not if it got her to dine with him. "Come."

Without waiting on her response, he took her elbow and led her to a German saloon he liked. She didn't fight him, just grumbled under her breath as she took the five steps down to the ground-floor entrance.

The interior was dim, even during the day. A long bar occupied one half of the room and wooden tables took up the rest of the space. He held up a hand in greeting to the man behind the bar, the owner, Mr. Hoffman.

An older woman approached them, an apron tied around her waist. She clapped her hands when she saw his face. "Willkommen, Herr Mulligan!"

He shook her hand. "Hallo, Frau Hoffman. Wie geht es Ihnen?"

"Es geht mir gut. Would you like to sit?"

"Bitte."

Mrs. Hoffman led them to a table in the back, one that would allow Jack a view of the entire first floor. Just as he preferred. "Danke," he told the older woman as he held out a chair for Justine. "Ich hätte gerne zwei pils, bitte."

"And lunch?"

"Yes. The special will suffice." Mrs. Hoffman made all the food herself and it was terrific. Best wiener schnitzel in the city.

A delicate clearing of a throat caught his attention. "Mrs. Hoffman," Justine said. "I would prefer water. And if you could tell me the special before I decide to order it, I'd be most grateful."

She asked nicely enough but Jack got the impression that Justine was annoyed. What had he done wrong?

Mrs. Hoffman explained the dish, sauerbraten, which was roasted meat served with dumplings and cabbage. Justine proclaimed that would be fine and Mrs. Hoffman departed. Jack tapped his fingers on the table. "Don't trust me?"

"I do not care to have my choices taken away from me, no matter how small."

Brass ones. She was no wilting uptown flower. He liked that about her. "I was merely trying to help. Relax, everything here is delicious."

"I am only here because you gave me no choice in the matter."

"Life is short, Miss Greene. We must enjoy what pleasures we can before it's too late."

Her gaze flicked to his mouth on the word *pleasures* and even the dark interior could not hide the color now staining her cheeks. Interesting. He hadn't meant the comment as innuendo but it seemed the little do-gooder was not so innocent.

Very interesting.

Rye entered, tipped his chin at Jack, and headed to the long bar up front where he'd keep watch and chat with Mr. Hoffman. Mrs. Hoffman returned with water for Justine and a pilsner for him. The Hoffmans, along with many of the saloon owners downtown, bought their beer from Jack's brewer, Patrick Murphy. Jack tasted the beer and confirmed the freshness. Patrick would be pleased to hear it.

"Why were you at police headquarters?" he asked when they were alone again.

Justine lifted a shoulder. "There's a detective who often helps me, but he's consumed with a murder case. He said he'll be fired if he works on anything else."

"Big Tom's son, I assume." Tom Wagner's boy had been murdered in a brothel on Mott Street. Wagner was a Tammany Hall man who'd worked his way up at city hall. The deceased son had left debts all over town, including some to Jack. He'd be collecting on those from the father in the very near future.

"Yes, I suppose. I asked my detective friend for a favor but he refused. Now I'll need to figure something else out."

The opening was there and no one had ever accused Jack of squandering an opportunity when it was presented. He took a long sip of his pilsner to hide his smile. "I am also in the habit of granting favors. Why not ask me instead?"

Chapter Five

The way he said it, low and rough, sent tingles through Justine's belly. Somehow "granting favors" sounded lascivious coming out of Mulligan's sinful mouth. Lord, why did he affect her this way? She should be immune to charm and handsomeness. Mulligan was Satan wrapped in a silk brocade vest. Yet knowing that did not prevent her body from warming, her pulse from quickening.

The reaction to him made her angry with herself. Angry with him. He'd made it perfectly clear she wasn't his type—not that she cared. The less they had to do with one another, the better.

"I am already in your debt," she said tartly. "It would be unwise of me to sink any lower."

"What's one more favor to repay?"

"I have no idea, seeing as how you refuse to tell me what the repayment entails."

"It bothers you, doesn't it? Are you reassured to learn there are hundreds of men walking these streets who owe me favors, debts I might call in at any time?"

"No, I am not." First, she wasn't a man. Second,

she didn't like the idea that Mulligan could demand something from her out of the blue. "I am not one of your lackeys."

The charm vanished and his gaze turned assessing, sharp. Keen intelligence blazed from his blue irises, a hint of the man who had forged an empire through cunning and violence. "Yes, I am aware," he said. "Let's make conversation, then. No favors or debts. Tell me about this problem you encountered."

Their food arrived then, the sauerbraten exactly as Mrs. Hoffman had described, and she dug in. It was delicious, hearty and filling, and Justine realized days had passed since she'd sat down to a proper meal. She now avoided dinners with her sisters, knowing Mamie would merely badger her about Mulligan, about her *foolishness*. Mamie and Florence often treated Justine as a child, as if she needed protecting.

Ludicrous. Justine had probably seen more violence and horror in her twenty years on this earth than the two of her sisters combined.

Relaxed by the warm food in her stomach, she began talking. She told Mulligan of the shirtwaist factory on Rivington, the women and children locked inside. How the workers were not allowed to take breaks from the sewing, even to tend to personal needs. The hopelessness and misery she'd found, and how the owner had thrown her out when she'd tried to complain.

"Was that why you sought Ellison out? Hoping he could scare the owners into compassion?"

"Yes. It has worked in the past."

"That's astounding, considering most factory

owners are the greediest bastards alive. They'd sell their own mothers for more profits."

"True, but Ellison's badge and the threat of unionization have been effective thus far."

"I'd suspect it's due to something more than that," Mulligan said, a small mysterious smile on his face. She didn't know what that smile meant but it caused her breath to catch.

Calm down, Justine. Don't fall under his spell.

Silence descended as they both ate. He ordered another pilsner and when it arrived he leaned back and took a long drink. "The legal aid society is busy, no doubt in part to your successful efforts. You're well regarded as a savior in Lower Manhattan."

"That is a gross exaggeration. I've hardly done enough to reduce the suffering and poverty."

"One person cannot solve the city's problems."

"You did."

"Not exactly. I had help. And it was mostly convincing the other fellows that we'd do better together. Stronger in numbers, et cetera."

No doubt he underplayed his importance. He had built a kingdom for himself with men who were not known for compromise. "Why did you do it?"

"Couldn't stand the thought of working for anyone else—and that included the police and Tammany Hall. I knew I'd eventually come under someone's thumb unless the organization was large enough, powerful enough, to eclipse everyone else."

Hard to argue with that. She suddenly had a desire to learn more about him. What had made a man like Mulligan? "Did you grow up downtown?"

"I did. Right in the Bowery."

"And the languages? It's said you speak three in addition to English."

"Four, actually. I learned Italian and German from people in the neighborhood when I was a boy. French and Spanish later from books. I also know a good deal of Yiddish and Russian, but I'm hardly fluent."

"That is impressive. I only learned French."

He lifted a shoulder. "It has come in handy over the years, especially when I need to speak without others understanding what I am saying. Did you study French in finishing school, as all good society girls do?"

"No. Florence was kicked out of finishing school so my mother hired tutors for our education." This had allowed Justine to pursue volunteer work with the city's charities, rather than suffering in a stuffy classroom with girls who only cared about the latest fashions and using the proper fork.

"Why am I not surprised?" Mulligan muttered. "You know, you are different than your sister. More self-possessed. Sure of yourself."

The compliment caught her off guard, so she immediately dismissed it. "Oh, you're wrong. Florence is the bravest of us all. She never cares what anyone thinks."

"There's a difference between knowing who you are and putting on a show to the rest of the world."

"You think Florence is putting on a show?"

"I'm positive of it. I never understood why, though." He took a long sip of his beer. "You, on the other hand, are exactly as one sees. There is no pretense or artifice with you."

He was right. She'd never seen the point in

pretending to be someone other than herself. "I merely want to help people. Anything else is a waste of time."

"And Billy Ferris? Was he a waste of time?"

She sucked in a sharp breath. How on earth had Mulligan learned of Billy? She'd last seen her former beau eight months ago. Was Mulligan looking into her background? She put her fork and knife down on the plate with a snap. "That is none of your business—and stop having me investigated."

"There's no need for concern. I mean you no harm."

"That's hardly the point. You are invading my privacy. My debt to you does not give you the right to spy on me."

"I like information, Miss Greene. I like to know the people with whom I deal."

"We are not in business together. Our association will end the second I repay your favor."

"Yes, but there's no telling how long before that happens."

Incensed, she ground her teeth together. The man talked in circles, justifying his actions through whatever means necessary. "I believe you are enjoying this."

"You would be right. I daresay I haven't enjoyed anything as much in a long time."

"Bully for you. Wipe my debt clean, Mulligan. I won't tolerate being followed and harangued."

"Buying you lunch is hardly haranguing you. And the streets are not safe for a lady. Perhaps I am merely ensuring your safety."

The arrogance was astounding. She'd been working in the city's seedier neighborhoods for almost five years now, where she handled her own problems and had never suffered any serious harm. "I need no keeper. I'm perfectly capable of taking care of myself."

"Indeed, I do not doubt it. The boys at the club cannot stop retelling how you thwarted that robbery attempt when you first came to see me. The story has only added to your legend."

She remembered the boy who'd appeared out of the shadows on Great Jones Street. "Do you know him?"

"We found him later that day. He won't attack another woman, not in my neighborhood."

She frowned, contemplating the meaning behind those words. "What did you do to him? I swear, if you hurt him—"

"Calm down, chérie. He's new and needed to be taught the rules of my territory. But he lived to tell the tale to others."

To spread the word: no violence toward women. Mulligan wouldn't tolerate it. She wanted to ask him why. She had this insane desire to ask him countless questions about his background and life. She wanted to *know* him.

And that terrified her.

She shouldn't wish to spend time with him, to learn intimate details about his life. The more she discovered, the more she liked . . . and that was dangerous.

She had clearly lost her mind. A bit of rest and sauerbraten had gone to her head. This had to end.

Reaching inside the small purse clipped to her belt, she withdrew some bills and slapped them on the table. She met his curious blue gaze. "I'll buy my own lunch, thank you. And you've learned enough about my life. Stop having me followed. If you don't, I'll make you regret it."

Without waiting for his response, Justine stood and dashed from the restaurant. Lunchtime was over.

IGNORING RYE'S SHOCKED expression, Jack tossed money on the table and rushed out of the Hoffmans' saloon, hurrying after Justine. "Wait!" he called to her back. She didn't pause, merely continued walking downtown.

Damn it. He hadn't meant to run the do-gooder off, not until they were finished.

I'll make you regret it.

Was she threatening him? *Him?* Christ, the idea of it had his balls twitching in excitement.

The entire city believed this woman was filled with pure goodness, not an evil bone in her body. Yet, she vexed Jack at every turn. A sharp tongue and blistering reprimands lurked behind those boring dresses and high necklines.

The do-gooder had a mean streak. And he loved it.

Perhaps this was the real Justine, after all. He might have been the only man alive to get a glimpse of the steel beneath the fluff. He wanted more. He wanted to know how deep that steel ran. Did it go all the way to her core? Would she bite his lip if they kissed? In bed, would she dig her nails into his skin, scoring his back with evidence of her pleasure?

He caught up and blocked her advance. "Please, stop. I need to speak to you."

She pressed her lips together and folded her

hands. Waited. Those dark brown eyes stared at him as if he were an annoyance. A bother she merely tolerated.

He got right to the point. "I wish to collect on my favor."

That gained her attention. Her face slackened, her mouth opening slightly. "*Now* you bring this up? Why did you not tell me this at police headquarters or over our interminable lunch?"

Because she would've heard him out and disappeared. Instead, he'd wanted to drag out their encounter. Never mind the reasons why. "That is immaterial. Would you care to hear what I require of you?"

"Yes, with the caveat that I may refuse."

Not a chance. No one reneged on Jack Mulligan.

"Then get in." He gestured to the brougham at the curb, with Rye in the driver's seat.

"No. Tell me here."

So stubborn. He almost admired her for it. "No. This is too public for my tastes. I prefer to have my conversations away from those who might be listening."

She glanced at the brougham, examining it for a long moment. Jack couldn't fathom what she hoped to see.

"No tricks," he said. "I merely wish for a private conversation while I give you a ride downtown. I'll keep my hands to myself."

Her head swiveled sharply, her face taut. "I am hardly worried about *that*. You've made it abundantly clear I am not your type."

"And you believe I am puddle scum, as I recall. So, I think we are both safe for the short journey."

"Fine, but you still owe me the ride even if I refuse your request."

Hardly a request, but he didn't bother to point that out. He could allow her to believe she had the upper hand. For now.

They ascended into the carriage, which provided a bit of shade to cut the city heat. Rye wasted no time in flicking the reins and getting them moving along the street. A slight breeze filtered through the conveyance. Justine located a fan on her person and began using it to cool herself. "Well?"

Removing his derby, Jack withdrew a silk handkerchief from his pocket and dotted the sweat on his brow. "I understand the legal aid society is hosting a large fundraiser at the Metropolitan Opera House."

Her hand stilled, the fan hanging in the air, useless, as she shifted to face him. "And?"

"I'd like to escort you."

"I . . . *What?*"

"Me, your escort. At the event."

"You wish to attend the fundraiser?"

"Yes."

She blinked a few times, her lovely face registering a myriad of emotions. "I don't understand. This is a society event. You're not the usual guest."

"I understand. However, I need to be there. I'm even prepared to make a large donation to the legal aid society, as well." He knew their legal aid society lived and died by donations. Money kept an organization like that afloat and it took a lot of dough. From what he'd heard, funding was always tight.

"How large?"

He smothered a smile. Of course the do-gooder would ask such a question. "I was thinking five thousand."

"Fifty."

Air hissed through his teeth. "That's extortion. You owe me, remember?"

"My repayment is allowing you to escort me. That alone will cause nothing short of a riot. In fact, my family will likely disown me. Therefore, if you want me to go along with it, then you need to give the legal aid society fifty thousand dollars."

He could tell by the smug expression on her face that she thought this stipulation would shut down the conversation. That the amount was far too high for him and would prevent his attendance that night.

She underestimated him. Underestimated his reasons for wishing to attend. There was a deal to be made at that particular event, one he couldn't possibly undertake elsewhere. A deal that would transform him into one of the richest men in the entire country.

More money, more power . . . Wasn't that the American way?

The idea had come to him a few days ago, when he'd learned of the fundraiser. His interests and her social standing were colliding, and he meant to use the opportunity to the fullest.

And so, he decided to call her bluff.

"Fine. Fifty thousand to your legal aid society."

She dropped her fan. It clattered to the floor of the brougham but neither of them bothered to retrieve it. "Are you serious?"

"As a pastor on Sunday morning."

"What if I refuse?"

He'd expected nothing less than a fight from her. She was no idiot. His presence would prove scandalous in her world. She'd likely never be received anywhere decent ever again. The Greenes were powerful, but not so powerful as to bring a criminal into decent society. Hell, those uptown folks snubbed someone for wearing the same dress twice. Jack's offenses ran a bit deeper than clothing.

Agreeing would, in short, ruin her standing.

That wasn't his problem. She owed him a debt and he meant to collect.

It was time to turn the screws. "If you refuse, the legal aid society gets nothing. Would you really deprive them of much-needed funding just to save yourself from embarrassment?"

He could almost hear her gnashing her teeth. "It's hardly embarrassment. What you are asking me to do is rock the very foundation on which society is built."

"And that bothers you?"

She sighed, her fingers tapping on her knee. "Not necessarily. Society is not for me. I've known that for years. However, tradition means quite a bit to my parents."

Jack didn't bother pointing out that her eldest sister had married a lawyer who'd assumed a false name, and her other sister, now a casino owner, was playing house with a former casino owner. Tradition was on shaky ground in the Greene household in Jack's opinion.

"Perhaps I'll go unrecognized." A slim possibility, but he thought it was worth mentioning.

"You're new. That alone would have people talking."

He stayed quiet. The wheels continued to roll, the familiar buildings and businesses passing outside the window. These were his streets. He knew the locations of the secret opium dens, cockfights and boxing matches. The sex clubs that offered privacy and safety. The policy shops, poolrooms and card games.

And while he loved every bit of it, nothing lasted forever. A king only remained a king if he learned how to adapt.

To do that, he needed Justine.

"Tell me why."

"Why?"

"Do not play dense. You're far too keen for that. Tell me why you need to attend this particular fundraiser."

She was considering it, and Jack could taste victory. He decided to give her a hint of his goal. "I am a man who deals in favors—"

"I am aware, Mulligan. Skip ahead to the fundraiser."

Arousal slid through him, an unexpected tightening in his groin at her sharp words. He didn't want to find her sour disposition attractive and yet he liked it. A lot. Most people he encountered were respectful. Courteous. They understood this was Jack's game and therefore Jack's rules. And not playing by Jack's rules meant consequences.

Nearly everyone avoided those consequences.

Everyone except this woman, it seemed.

And fuck, if that didn't make him hard.

She snapped her gloved fingers in front of his face. "Jack, pay attention. Where did you go?"

"As I said, I deal in favors. Nearly every man, at some point, comes into contact with one of my businesses. I can find ways to reach them and get what I want. A few men, however, remain beyond my reach for one reason or another. Unfortunately, one of these men is necessary for a business proposition I'd like to undertake."

"Let me get this straight." She cocked her head and studied him. "There is a man you need to speak to and this fundraiser is the only place you can do it."

"Precisely."

"You cannot go to this man's home and see him there?"

Jack fingered the brim of his derby. "He won't receive me."

"Ah." She stared out the window, grabbing for the strap as they turned a corner. "And you're hoping to ambush him at the fundraiser. How do you know he'll be in attendance?"

"*Ambush* is a strong word—and I know he'll be there."

"Then it must be someone important, someone involved with the legal aid society. Hmm."

He could almost hear her thinking, trying to reason it through. "I won't tell you his name, so don't bother trying to figure it out."

"Or perhaps he is close to my father? Or Frank Tripp?"

Damn it. She was circling the correct answer and he couldn't allow that. "Do you agree or not?"

"Could I arrange for a meeting with this man outside of the fundraiser?"

The particular man Jack needed would never agree. "You could, but the legal aid society won't get my donation in such a case."

She huffed in response, a sign of annoyance, he supposed. But that didn't bother him. Whether she liked this or not wasn't his concern. He just needed her cooperation.

"Let me out here." She rapped on the roof. The carriage slowed and began making its way to the curb.

They were still several blocks north of the legal aid society. "We haven't arrived yet."

"I would rather walk."

Stubborn girl. He reached down and retrieved her fan. "You might need this, then."

She took the fan. "The fundraiser is Saturday," she informed him, as if he wasn't perfectly aware.

"Yes, I know."

"Evening dress. I'll meet you outside at eight o'clock."

He couldn't help but grin. "I'll be there."

She reached over him to throw open the door. Without waiting for anyone to hand her down, she climbed out of the brougham and jumped to the street. "Good. After that you may consider my debt wiped clean. You'll never see me again, Mulligan."

The door slammed shut and she disappeared into the crowds of people on the walk. Jack tried to find her in the chaos of carts, shoppers, bootblacks and hawkers. But she was gone.

"Want me to follow her?" Rye called from the front.

"No."

"Never seen one so eager to get away from you. Usually you're scrapin' the ladies off, not the other way around."

Jack drummed his fingers on the side of the carriage. Justine was hell on a man's confidence. If he were a weaker man, he might take offense.

A slow smile spread over his face. Good thing he wasn't weak. Not in the least.

Chapter Six

When she arrived at the legal aid society, Justine went straight to Frank's office. "Hello?"

"Come in," her brother-in-law called.

When Justine entered the office, her stomach sank. Mamie was there, as well. Justine had hoped to tell Frank of the donation and avoid questions from her older sister today. Sadly, that was not to be. *Best get this over with.* "Do you have a moment?"

"Barely." Frank waved her closer. "Come and settle this dispute for us. Then I have something for you."

"Dispute?"

Mamie gestured toward her husband. "He's being difficult. We are discussing the fundraiser."

"Oh, good. I must speak with you about the fundraiser, as well."

"Fine, but first my question. As for the reception, I want to serve Moët, but Frank says to go with something less expensive. What do you think?"

"Moët. Nearly everyone there that night will know if you serve low-quality champagne." Probably not Jack Mulligan, of course. She'd only seen him drink beer. Did he care for champagne? *You'll soon find out.*

"Exactly!" Mamie pointed at Frank. "I told you. If you want proper donations, then this must be a proper fundraiser."

"Fine, but every penny you spend is a penny we cannot use for the legal aid society."

Mamie patted his hand. "I'll raise enough to cover the cost of Moët, my hardworking and handsome lawyer." She glanced at Justine. "Now, what did you need to say about the fundraiser? I hope it's not in relation to the hors d'oeuvres because I've already set that menu."

"No, it's not about the food. I wanted to let you know that I'll be bringing an escort."

"Oh." Mamie paused and studied Justine. Understandable, as the family had never seen Justine with a man before at any event. Or ever. "Do I know him?"

She pretended not to hear the question. "And he has agreed to make a substantial donation to the legal aid society."

"That's what I like to hear," Frank said, rubbing his palms together. "How much is substantial?"

Justine cleared her throat. "Fifty thousand dollars."

Papers fluttered from Mamie's hands onto the floor and Frank's jaw fell open. "Fifty *thousand*?" Frank repeated. "Are you serious?"

"Very. He has agreed and I don't believe he'd go back on his word."

"Who?" Mamie squeaked as she retrieved her papers. "Who is this?"

"A friend. You'll meet him at the event."

"I'd rather have a name now," her sister said.

"You won't get it." Justine could be stubborn, too.

"That means you do not wish for me to know. You think I won't approve."

Heat washed over her, yet she did not break her sister's stare. "I do not need your approval. He's just an acquaintance, Mamie." An acquaintance that made her heart race.

Mamie said nothing and the two of them watched each other for a long minute. Justine thought for certain her sister would guess the identity of the escort, blurt it out in front of Frank, but Mamie finally looked away. "I need to visit with Louis Sherry to finalize these details," she told Frank. "I'll see you later."

He came over and kissed her cheek. "Indeed, you shall."

Mamie walked past Justine on her way toward the door. "This discussion is not finished," Mamie said softly. Then her sister disappeared into the corridor.

Ready to move on to another topic, she turned to her brother-in-law. "How may I assist you?"

"Come with me to see Mr. Solomon. He thinks he has another wife deserter for you, if you feel up to it."

Justine sighed inwardly. She wished these sorts of cases were rare, but they were not. She'd barely solved Mrs. Gorcey's problem when now she had another missing husband on her hands. "Of course. What do you know?"

They went down the hallway and turned left where the other offices were located. "Husband is missing," he said. "He could have deserted the family or been kidnapped to work on a ship headed out of port. We aren't sure which, but legally there's nothing we can do. Maybe you'll have luck in finding this husband, as you did with the others."

He knocked on a door. "Come in," a deep voice called.

They went in and found a woman sitting across from Mr. Solomon. She was young, perhaps twenty or so, and wearing a faded gray cotton dress. She cradled a baby on her lap and a small child fidgeted in the chair next to her. She began to rise, but Mr. Solomon said something in German and the woman relaxed.

"Miss Greene, Mr. Tripp, this is Mrs. von Briesen." He made the introductions in German for his client. Frank excused himself, off to other duties, and Justine came to stand near Mrs. von Briesen.

"Guten tag, Frau von Briesen."

The other woman smiled slightly and returned the greeting. Mr. Solomon then spoke to his client in German. When he finished, she nodded and he explained to Justine, "I let her know that I would repeat the conversation for you in English."

"Very good."

Mr. Solomon began speaking to Mrs. von Briesen, pausing every two or three sentences to speak in English. "We know her husband visited the World Poolroom in the Bowery on the nineteenth of June. We believe he encountered a group of peter players who drugged and robbed him, then put him on the street."

Justine winced. Peter players used chloral hydrate in drinks to knock out unsuspecting saloon patrons, leaving the mark completely vulnerable. It was an awful, horrible thing to do.

Mr. Solomon went back to speaking with his client in German. Justine picked up some words here and there, but she mainly watched Mrs. von Briesen for clues. There weren't any, unfortunately. The other woman showed no reaction, her expression stoic throughout the report. The older child was quiet as well, listening and observing, while the baby slept peacefully on his or her mother's lap.

"We do know," Mr. Solomon said in English, "that some of his things turned up at one of the nearby pawnshops. From there we lost track of Mr. von Briesen. He may have been thrown onto a ship leaving the harbor, or he could be living under an assumed name in another part of the city."

Mrs. von Briesen spoke and Mr. Solomon began a lengthy exchange in German with the other woman. Justine waited patiently, her mind spinning with how to locate Mr. von Briesen. The poolroom was likely her best bet, to see if anyone recalled what happened after von Briesen was put out on the street. Otto Rosen, the society's head investigator, was thorough, but Justine often had luck in speaking with the girls in the area, the streetwalkers and serving girls. She had a knack for finding men who didn't wish to be found.

With an apology, Solomon turned to Justine. "She asked why the authorities could not be contacted to find him." He lifted his shoulders. "I wish I could answer that myself."

Justine knew why. It was because men ran the world. Devoting police time and resources to locating husbands who had decided to desert their wives was considered a waste. Many officers had even told Justine, *There was probably a good reason why he wanted to leave her in the first place.* They always added a shrug for good measure.

What kind of world prevented women from divorcing terrible husbands, but shrugged whenever husbands up and left whenever they felt like it?

"What happens next?"

"I'm afraid that's all we are able to do at this point."

When Mr. Solomon repeated this for Mrs. von Briesen, she began to tremble, her eyes filling with tears. Justine held out her hand, giving the other woman the opportunity to take comfort if she needed, and Mrs. von Briesen clasped it tightly. Justine squeezed, trying to offer a bit of strength. This had to be nothing short of a nightmare.

"Please tell her that I would like to help her and her family," Justine said, and Solomon relayed the message. Mrs. von Briesen nodded in understanding. Justine looked back to Mr. Solomon. "I will try to find her husband."

Solomon appeared relieved. "I know you've had some success in the past, Miss Greene, and I do hope you are able to find him. Breaks my heart to turn anyone away when they come to us for assistance."

"Me, as well. Please, tell her."

The lawyer informed Mrs. von Briesen of Justine's pledge and the other woman turned to Justine, her gaze solemn and grateful. "Thank you," she said in accented English.

"You are welcome," Justine replied. Then she held out her free hand toward Solomon. "Her file, please. I'll take it from here."

JACK PUSHED OPEN the door of the Little Water Street Brewery. Rye and Cooper, Jack's usual shadows for neighborhood errands, trailed him inside. This would certainly prove a more pleasant stop than some of the others they'd made today. The brewery was a passion of Jack's, a partnership started with Patrick Murphy, the brewer.

They met seven years ago, when Jack tasted Patrick's homemade lager. Patrick had been brewing and selling it out of the back of a drugstore on Pearl Street. Jack knew quality beer when he found it, having been raised on the drink like mother's milk. Patrick had a gift for flavors. Within months, the two of them had gone into business together, eventually opening this brewery. The beer was now sold all over Lower Manhattan and Brooklyn, thanks to Jack's distribution genius.

Jack saw big things ahead for this brewery. And for him.

The pungent smell of hops and grain sank into his lungs. Heat hung in the air surrounding the huge copper kettles, where yeast had been added to the wort and would ferment until it was properly aged. Assistants were carrying ledgers, recording temperatures and checking levels.

"Mulligan!"

Jack turned to the sound and found Patrick hurrying toward him. "Afternoon, Patrick. I see you are hard at work, as usual."

The two shook hands. "I had to add two more kettles this week just to handle the new orders. I don't know how you managed to get us sold in Madison Square Garden, but I am grateful."

"I happened to meet one of the Garden's investors and I made the pitch." It turned out the investor had a hop habit, and Jack had promised not to reveal such details to the investor's wife in exchange for the deal. But, there was no use sullying Patrick's mind with the dirty details. "Do you have a moment to spare for me?"

"Indeed, I do. Would you like to try a sample of something I'm working on?"

"That's like asking if I'd like to watch Rembrandt paint."

Color washed over Patrick's neck. "A ridiculous comparison but I'll take the compliment. Let's sit at the bar."

Jack followed Patrick to the corner, where a high table and chairs served as the room's bar. The two of them often sat here to discuss the business or taste ingredients. Jack much preferred to see the main brewing room than be sequestered back in Patrick's office.

Patrick shouted to one of the workers. "Jimmy, bring us a bottle of that Saaz lager, will you?"

They settled in the chairs. "How are things in general?" Jack asked. "Need more staff?"

"No, not after the last round of hires. It's a good group." Patrick rolled his sleeves up. "Why? Do you have someone in mind?"

Jack thought of Justine and the shirtwaist factory. "Just wanted to ensure the hours and wages are fair. That we keep workers happy and reduce accidents."

"I have them in six-hour shifts, and they make more here than any factory in the neighborhood. Besides, they get free beer each week. Hell, some of them would work for that perk alone, if I'd let them."

"Good, I'm glad to hear it. How is your brother?"

They were interrupted as Jimmy arrived with a large brown bottle and two glasses, which he placed on the table between Patrick and Jack. Patrick quickly opened the bottle and held it out. "Smell."

Jack put his nose close to the opening. "Sweet. A little grassy."

"Very good." Patrick poured the lager into two glasses, ensuring he poured into the center of the glass and not along the sides. An impressive head formed atop each glass. "Now swirl."

As he'd done plenty of times, Jack picked up his glass and gently swirled the contents, agitating the beer. He'd learned from Patrick this unlocked the flavor and enhanced the aroma. He smelled it again. "Nice. It's clean, not overpowering."

"Wait until you taste it." Patrick's eyes shone with excitement, as they always did when discussing beer. He dipped his chin toward Jack's glass. "It should be ready."

Jack took a slow sip and held it, allowing the liquid to flow over every part of his tongue. It was delicious. Smooth, with lots of flavor. Was that caramel? The swallow was clean. Crisp. Well-balanced. Unlike anything he'd ever had.

He stared at the glass. There was nothing like this on the market. Not anywhere around here, at least. "What the hell is in here?"

"Do you like it?"

"Like it? It's perfection. Sweet and dry, but flavorful. It'll appeal to anyone, whether they like beer or not. How did you manage it?"

"A few things. Water from the Catskills along

with two-row barley. Then we've imported the hops from Bohemia."

Jack took a long draught. Christ, it just kept getting better. So much innovation in one small glass. "It is impressive, Patrick. If we hadn't just missed the competition at the World's Fair, I would have entered it."

Patrick made a sound, always humble about his gift. "Well, let's not get ahead of ourselves."

"This is better than Pabst's supposed blue ribbon winner, that's for damn certain. Start bottling it."

"Soon." Patrick grinned and drank from his own glass. "I'm glad you like it. Now, you asked about my brother. Is that why you're here?"

Patrick's brother was Frank Tripp, brother-in-law to Justine Greene. Frank was one of the rarified individuals who could straddle both ends of Manhattan, having served as a lawyer to both the city's uptown elite and downtown criminal class. "Partly. I was wondering if Frank had invited you to his fundraiser."

"For the legal aid society?" At Jack's nod, Patrick said, "Yes, though I have no desire to attend. Those types of events are more to my brother's tastes than mine."

"I would like you to go. I plan on attending."

Patrick's gaze widened, though he quickly recovered. "You realize it's being held at the Metropolitan Opera House. If I know my sister-in-law, every blue-blooded snob in the city will be there."

"I am counting on it, in fact. There is one snob who won't receive me in his home. I hope to corner him at the event, however, and it would be helpful if you were there, as well."

"Ah." Patrick relaxed as he began to unravel what was left unsaid. "This is about Julius Hatcher, isn't it?"

Jack hid his smile by taking another sip of the outstanding beer. A reclusive financial genius, Hatcher had fingers in almost every pie—including the brewery in which Jack now sat. Hatcher had invested a few years back, with Jack's permission, and urged Patrick to take the beer national. They hadn't been ready at the time, but Jack had been doing some math. The time was now ripe to brew, pasteurize and ship a national product. They just needed Hatcher's buy-in.

They would get it, of course, but Hatcher would want to control the entire venture. Jack had no intention of allowing that to happen. If this went forward, it was under his leadership.

"He is your brother's closest friend," Jack said by way of answer.

"Do you really think we can pull it off? What about refrigeration?"

"Refrigerated train cars. Then we buy a railroad."

Patrick whistled. "That sounds like a huge investment."

"That is where Hatcher comes in." Jack finished his glass and stood. "You just keep working. My job is to find ways to share your genius with the world. Together, we're going to make a load of fucking money."

"I like the sound of that. Incidentally, did my brother get you into the fundraiser?"

"No. I'm escorting his sister-in-law."

"*Florence?*" Patrick nearly screeched the word. "Madden will skin you alive then set you on fire."

"Not Florence. Justine, the youngest Greene daughter."

The look on Patrick's face would've made Jack laugh, if he hadn't been expecting it. No one would ever believe a man like Jack would associate with the angelic do-gooder. If she were even so angelic. Jack had his doubts.

Though he looked forward to discovering the answer.

"You're joking," Patrick managed.

"Absolutely not. We are quite friendly, actually."

"You . . . and Justine Greene. Friendly?" He scratched his jaw. "What am I missing?"

"There's nothing to it. She needs my help from time to time with her little projects in my part of town."

"Oh, I see." Patrick's confusion cleared up, his lips stretching into a smooth smile. "The business of favors. A Mulligan specialty."

"They do come in handy. You just be at that fundraiser."

"You with Justine Greene at the Metropolitan Opera House in front of all New York high society? I wouldn't miss that spectacle for the world."

Jack clapped Patrick on the back. "Then dust off your evening jacket. We'll show those Knickerbockers a thing or two."

JUSTINE COULDN'T RECALL ever being this nervous.

Draped in one of Mamie's old evening gowns, she hovered near the entrance of the Metropolitan Opera House. It was crowded, with nearly everyone of consequence here this evening. To bear witness to her and Mulligan. Together.

Thank goodness that her mother and father were

in Europe at the moment. It would be weeks before they learned of Mulligan's involvement at the fund-raiser. By that time, Justine would have rid herself of Mulligan altogether. They would have no reason to interact any longer, and her bizarre fascination with him would subside.

Fascination? More like fantasies.

Fine, yes. She'd had her share of fantasies lately about Mulligan. Lewd and exciting fantasies where he kissed and touched her everywhere, his bright blue eyes burning with desire. His hands eager, his body hard. Dark words of appreciation and en-couragement. She had pleasured herself in the bath tonight just thinking about it.

But fantasy and reality were two entirely differ-ent worlds.

He stood for everything she worked against, like violence and crime. She helped people but never stepped outside the law. Mulligan created his own set of rules, anything that furthered his interests.

Therefore, she had to suppress her body's bizarre reaction to him, the craving that hummed along her skin in his presence.

The line of conveyances moved and a slick black brougham inched to the curb. Nothing on the out-side hinted that it was any different than the other fancy carriages on the street, but something, some strange feeling, made the hairs on the back of Jus-tine's neck stand up.

The door flung open and a leg clad in perfectly creased black wool shot out. The leather shoe was so shiny she thought she saw her reflection on the surface. Then a large frame twisted and slowly emerged, each movement deliberate, almost flamboyant. The yellow lamplight illuminated the sharp angles of his jaw, the perfectly chiseled features. He wore an arrogant smile, his bearing proud and straight, as he placed a silk top hat on his head.

Elegant. Impossibly handsome.

Mulligan had arrived.

He made no effort to advance toward the entrance. Instead, he pulled on his cuffs. Brushed his sleeves and smoothed his vest, seemingly preening for the crowd. Mouth gone dry, Justine swallowed as she watched from the shadows. He was Adonis, all lean male beauty and strength. A man the gods would fight over. His black-and-white evening clothes, worn here by every man like a uniform, only caused him to stand out from the crowd. It was as if the cloth had been woven just for him, sewn to highlight his broad shoulders and trim frame.

Everyone around them stopped to stare. The woman next to Justine actually gasped.

Justine didn't move, her back glued to the brick. In general, she didn't care for attention. *Too late now. You agreed to let him escort you.* All eyes would be on them tonight.

One evening. One fundraiser. Then you're through with Mulligan.

Unless she decided to ask for help with finding Mrs. von Briesen's husband.

No, you can do it on your own. No more debts to Mulligan. No more favors, no more contact. They were even after tonight.

"Miss Greene!"

Oh, Lord. He'd spotted her. Heads turned her way, and she had no choice but to step forward. "Good evening."

He strode toward her, his long legs eating up the pavement that separated them. Then he took her hand and brought it to his mouth, his full lips brushing the thin cloth of her glove. "Miss Greene," he said, his voice deep and intimate. A ripple went down her spine. "How lovely you are this evening."

She could feel her skin heating, like she'd been in the sun too long. Eyes were everywhere, silent and judging, but she forced herself to ignore them. *One night. You can do it.* She clutched his arm and began leading him inside. "That was quite an entrance," she murmured.

"They were going to stare no matter what I did. Besides, cowering by the side of a building isn't really my style."

"I was not cowering." Not really, anyway. More like enjoying her last few minutes of solitude.

"If you say so."

She ignored him and focused on the impending crush. The inside of the opera house bustled with activity. Patrons hurried to their seats while ushers assisted. Keeping her face down, Justine tugged him up the stairs and toward the bottom tier of boxes.

"May we slow down?" he asked. "I wasn't aware this was a race."

"They'll cease staring once we are in the box." *Maybe.*

"I had no idea you were so eager for us to reach your family."

She stopped suddenly, nearly causing the couple behind them to collide into her back. Oh, heavens. Her *family*. In moments, she would walk in with Mulligan. How strong was her grandmother's heart?

Offering a smooth apology to the other patrons,

Mulligan neatly moved her out of the fray and into a small alcove. He leaned in, the hint of cigar and mint clinging to him, and brushed a lock of hair behind her ear. She froze, tingles shooting down her legs all the way to her toes. The unexpected touch had been gentle, so different from her fantasies. But she liked it. A lot.

"Breathe, Justine. The part about being eager was a joke."

"Are you certain you must attend tonight?"

The side of his mouth hitched. "I am, chérie. But I promise, you'll emerge unscathed. I swear my life on it."

Ha. He had no idea how vicious society could be, how this would affect her family. Justine would end up very much scathed. "Let's get this over with."

He stared down at her, his blue eyes startling even in the dim light. "Do you trust me?"

"Absolutely not."

That caused him to throw his head back and laugh. "Smart girl. Considering the thoughts running through my head at the moment, you'd be wise not to."

"What do you mean?"

His head tilted as he perused her from head to toe. Something about the slow examination made her feel both hot and cold at the same time. "Impure thoughts," he rasped. "About you."

Oh, heavens. *He's having impure thoughts about me.* The idea was dizzying.

Yet, this was not the time or the place for her fantasies to come to life.

Exhaling, she struggled not to reveal how much he affected her. "After tonight, you will never see me again."

"Do you honestly believe that?"

"Of course I do."

"We shall see, I suppose. Come on. Let's face the dragons together." He presented his arm and, after she sucked in a deep breath for courage, she accepted it. They departed the alcove and moved along the corridor to the Greene box.

"Prepare yourself," she warned as they drew near. "We may be asked to leave."

"Not a chance in hell. This is a fundraiser. No one wishes to lose my generous donation."

She almost groaned. How could she have forgotten? "I suppose that guarantees *you* won't be asked to leave."

"Mon ange, if anyone hurts or disrespects you, I shall grow very angry. Then they will have to deal with them." He bent closer. "I will protect you."

"Do not call me that." She was no angel, nor did she belong to him.

Looking up, she noted they'd arrived. *Oh, sweet mercy.* He had distracted her with his flirting and nicknames, and now they stood in front of the Greene box. *More like Pandora's box, considering all the trouble they were about to unleash.*

"Go on," the devil urged over her shoulder. "If I know one thing it's that you are no quitter, Miss Greene."

A little burst of confidence filled her. He was right. She was no quitter. Resigned, she pushed through the velvet curtains at the back of the box.

Mamie and Granny were in the salon sipping cocktails when Justine stepped in. "There you are," her grandmother said. "We were wondering—"

The words disappeared and silence descended as her escort entered behind her. She cleared her throat. "May I present Mr. Mulligan? Mr. Mulligan, this is my sister, Mrs. Tripp. My grandmother, Mrs. Greene."

He strode deeper into the room and performed a bow worthy of a prince. "Good evening, ladies. Mrs. Tripp, it is my honor to attend for such a worthy cause."

"I wasn't aware Justine was bringing an escort tonight," Granny said. "A Mulligan, you say? Are you one of the Boston Mulligans?"

"Indeed, I am not," Jack said. "New York through and through. In fact I was born and raised in the Sixth—"

"On Sixth Avenue," Justine blurted. "Near Washington Square Park."

"Oh, that is a fine area," Granny said. "Our family had a home on the park for years. Perhaps we knew some of your people—"

"Granny, let's not get into boring social pedigrees before we've even taken a seat." Justine turned to her sister. "How is the crowd tonight? Will you raise a lot of money?"

Mamie's eyes flashed fire, a knowing gleam that proved her sister was aware of Mulligan's identity. No doubt she'd latch on to the first opportunity to get Justine alone. "The crowd is unexpected, to say the least."

Justine had no response to that, so she gestured

toward the sideboard. "Shall we stay and have a drink?"

"Go," Granny said, shooing them toward the box. "No need to sit in here with us. Go and find a seat. Tripp will bring out drinks soon enough."

Her grandmother's angle was glaringly apparent. Justine had been considered unmarriageable for so long that her family wished for all of society to finally see her with a handsome escort. If only Granny knew. Then she'd insist Justine stay sequestered tonight.

"Oh, there's no rush," Mamie said. "Sit here and have a drink—"

"I agree with Mrs. Greene," Jack said smoothly. "After all, the purpose of these events is to be seen, isn't it? And you look so beautiful this evening, Miss Greene. It would be a shame if the entire city were not to bear witness."

Justine could have sworn her grandmother sighed at the flattery. Before she could refuse, Jack lifted her hand and placed it on his arm. Then he led her into the box.

The bright glow of the theater's electric lights greeted her. This was the "Diamond Horseshoe," the most desirable tier in the entire opera house. Everyone would be able to see them from this spot. At the moment, however, she couldn't take in the crowd surrounding them. She was stuck, rooted to the spot.

Frank Tripp, and Frank's brother, Patrick, stood in the box. When Frank's eyes landed on Mulligan's face, his jaw fell open. "What in the ever-loving hell . . . ?"

Chapter Seven

Jack didn't make it two steps before Frank Tripp grabbed his arm. "Excuse us," the lawyer said before towing Jack like a side of beef toward the exit.

"You are wrinkling my coat," Jack muttered. "Not to mention annoying me."

Frank released him but didn't stop. He jerked the curtain aside and gestured. "Keep going. I want to talk to you. Alone."

Fine. Jack supposed he couldn't avoid this. Strolling through the salon, he winked at the two women. "Ladies."

Once in the corridor, Tripp pointed to a room on the opposite side. Two men were smoking cigars in the small salon. "Gentlemen, I need the room," Tripp announced. Like sheep, the two swells nodded, stamped out their cigars and departed.

"What's your next trick?" Jack drawled as he perched on the arm of a sofa. "Getting them to quack like ducks?"

"What the fuck are you doing here? With *Justine Greene*, of all people?"

"What does that mean, of all people? What

are you insinuating, Murphy?" It was low, using Frank's birth name to remind him they were on more even footing than Tripp might admit. But Jack would not be judged, not by this man.

"It means that she is my sister-in-law and a good person. How do the two of you even know one another?"

"I know just about everyone who works and lives in the Sixth. That shouldn't surprise you."

"And yet, it does. How on earth did you get her to agree to bring you tonight? And more importantly, why?"

Jack needed Frank's help tonight, so he decided to be honest. "I did her a favor. This was my repayment. I need to see Julius Hatcher."

Frank's brows climbed up his forehead. "This is about meeting Julius? Why didn't you ask me to simply arrange it?"

"Because Hatcher would never agree. He's refused my attempts at every turn."

"So you're here to ambush him?" At Jack's curt nod, Frank blew out a long breath. "Jesus Christ. If I had known you were planning to sabotage the evening, I would have kidnapped Hatcher and brought him to you myself. My wife will never recover. Her entire fundraiser will be ruined."

"Nonsense. If you get Hatcher to meet me, I'll get you more donations than your legal aid society could possibly handle."

"How?"

"Never mind that. Just get Hatcher to see me at the first intermission."

"No sense in waiting that long. We'll visit him as soon as the performance starts."

"Excellent. See how easy that was?"

"So easy you didn't need to drag my sister-in-law into it." Frank studied Jack's face for a long moment. "You haven't . . ."

The implication was clear. Jack hadn't defiled the uptown princess, had he? "No. She's made her feelings on that subject painfully clear. 'Puddle scum,' I believe she called me."

That hadn't stopped Jack from contemplating said defiling more and more often lately. He hadn't been kidding when he'd told her she inspired impure thoughts. Currently, his preferred fantasy was her bent over his desk while he took her from behind. When she came, he imagined his little do-gooder screaming his name loud enough to shake the rafters of the club.

Oblivious to Jack's inner thoughts, Frank appeared relieved by this news. "Good. See that it remains that way. I'd hate to have to shoot you."

As if he could. "I should return. I promised she'd remain unscathed."

"There's very little chance of that. Her reputation will be in tatters. Not to mention what will happen when her father returns from Europe and finds out."

"I'm hardly scared of Duncan Greene." There was nothing he could do about Justine's reputation, though he suspected it wouldn't suffer as much as she feared. Jack knew one thing about this city: New York loved a spectacle.

And he was prepared to give them one.

"Jesus, Mulligan." Frank pinched the bridge of his nose. "Next time leave Justine out of it and come see me."

Who did Tripp think he was talking to? This patronizing speech was starting to offend Jack. "I'm not one of your clients. When I need saving, I'll let you know."

"I realize that but . . . the Greenes are good people. They do not deserve to be embarrassed."

"Stop wringing your hands, Tripp." Jack stood and crossed to the exit. He was finished with this conversation. "It's going to be fine."

Once in the corridor, the two of them returned to the Greene box. Frank pulled back the curtain. "I hope you know what you're doing," he murmured.

"I always know what I'm doing." A requirement in Jack's life—or else he'd end up dead.

The salon was now empty, the family having gathered in the box for the impending performance. Jack could hear the orchestra warming up. It sounded a hell of a lot better than what he was used to at the saloons and dance halls below Fourteenth Street. He wondered if they served beer here.

Frank went into the box first, Jack directly behind. Heads turned but Jack had eyes for only Justine, who looked alarmingly pale. He was instantly at her side, concern burning behind his ribs. Had someone said something to her? Damn Tripp for taking Jack away and leaving her vulnerable.

"Miss Greene." He leaned in closer to speak in her ear. "Tell me. What is wrong?"

A throat cleared behind him.

He moved beside Justine and turned, partially blocking her. Mrs. Tripp stood there, her expression fierce and angry. "She's just been snubbed, that's what. Our neighbors, friends of our family,

have both cut Justine for bringing you here tonight." She gestured to the box on the right, where
Justine's grandmother was currently speaking to
an older couple.

"Mamie," Justine started, but her sister would
not back down, apparently.

"No, Justine. He must know. Whatever his reason
for attending, he must be made aware of the consequences."

Jack slipped his hands in his trouser pockets, un-
moved. "If you expect me to lose sleep over those
with small minds and hateful hearts, you'll be
sorely disappointed."

"Exactly," Justine said. "No one cares, Mamie.
Society doesn't matter in the real world."

"Perhaps not to you," Mamie snapped. "However,
it matters to Granny and our parents. It matters to
me, if only for tonight's fundraiser."

"You'll have your donations," Jack said. "I promise."

"I hope you are right," Frank put in. "Because we
need the money."

Jack nodded once. "I'm never wrong, not when it
comes to money. Now, shall we all sit?"

"Are you really the man who runs downtown's
criminal syndicate?"

Jack turned toward the sound of the voice, Justine's grandmother. She had finished with the
neighbors, who obviously gave her an earful, and
returned to the Greene family.

He saw no reason to lie. "Yes, I am."

Instead of revulsion, she looked at him with fascination. "Is that so? I bet you have all kinds of
stories . . ."

"Granny," Mamie hissed, "we should be discouraging this."

"Oh, I've smoothed things over with the Stewarts. They believe he's here as one of Frank's clients, a man in the grips of redemption."

Jack snorted. Redemption wouldn't keep him alive, considering his vast number of enemies. The instant he loosened his grip on his territory was the beginning of the end. Still, he was grateful for the lie if it saved Justine's reputation.

He didn't know when he'd started caring about her reputation. Likely when he'd seen the pallor of her skin a few moments ago, the embarrassment lurking in her gaze. He hadn't expected to feel anything tonight, certainly not remorse. Jack looked ahead, always. Never behind.

"That was kind of you, Granny," Justine said, "but not necessary. I am prepared to deal with the ramifications of the evening."

"You will have to," Mamie said. "Granny cannot spread that tale to everyone in the theater."

"Now is not the time," Frank said in a low voice. "Not with ears everywhere. Let's sit and enjoy the performance."

The eldest Greene sister gave him a dark look before she left the box, while everyone else settled into seats. Frank kept glancing over his shoulder, as if Jack might pounce on Justine at any moment and steal her innocence.

Thoughts of innocence left him wondering . . . had Justine slept with Billy Ferris last year? If so, something told Jack that Ferris had done a lousy job of it. The two hadn't lasted even three months together. That didn't exactly scream "passionate affair."

Now, if Jack had bedded Justine . . . he'd keep her naked, in bed, for days on end, worshipping her. She deserved to be studied and mapped, drawn and painted. The woman was layers upon layers of contradiction. Virginal and feisty. Pure and fierce. Selfless and dedicated. What did all that dedication feel like when it was directed toward a man's pleasure? Fuck, he could grow hard just contemplating it.

And why couldn't he stop thinking about her?

She thinks you are puddle scum.

Yes, there was that.

"You look very dashing tonight," she whispered.

A compliment? If he were a schoolgirl he might have blushed. "Thank you."

Hmm, perhaps she was reconsidering her opinion of him. He didn't know whether to be grateful or terrified of the idea. If she were attracted to him, then he might consider exploring it, seeing where this battle of wills between them would lead.

Even though something told him he wouldn't come out on top.

MINUTES LATER, THE footlights at the base of the stage were illuminated. From the wings came Mrs. Tripp, a graceful queen, to the center of the stage. The audience grew quiet, but Jack watched with only partial interest. He was more curious about the woman next to him.

He snuck a glance at Justine and the proud smile she wore as she watched her sister. A tiny spark of jealousy lit his chest. Jack had no family nearby. After his brother's acquittal—an event that began Jack's association with Frank Tripp—Jack had shipped him off to Cleveland. They hadn't seen one another in four years.

As far as parents went, Jack's mother died when he was eleven. The identity of his father had never been shared with him, a secret his mother took to her grave. Most of his memories of her were from the days in the Green Dragon Saloon, a Bowery mainstay that had seen the worst of the Dead Rabbits and Bowery B'hoy fights in the late '50s.

Inside those shabby walls, he grew up hearing stories about the gangs and their destruction, the bludgeons and brickbats, how the men would fight each other instead of everyone else. It hadn't escaped his notice how the women in the brothel took care of one another, banding together against an unruly client or speaking out when the owner enacted a policy they didn't like.

He learned one important lesson in his childhood. Alone, you were vulnerable. Together meant you were infinitely stronger. Those ideals, camaraderie and brotherhood, had earned Jack an empire.

"Ladies and gentlemen," Mamie said. "Thank you for attending this evening. I am Mrs. Frank Tripp. My husband runs the Lower East Side Legal Aid Society. As many of you know, we serve the needy and underrepresented in New York by offering them free legal assistance, helping to find lost family members, filing papers, and so much more. Why, last year alone we . . ."

She continued on but Jack ignored the speech. He admired what the Tripps were doing downtown, but the elites in this audience didn't live there. Each night, they settled in their fancy uptown mansions, with servants and cooks and French furniture.

They didn't know what it was like to struggle, to wonder where your next meal was coming from.

Donating to these causes eased some of the guilt these Knickerbockers experienced over their privilege . . . but it didn't absolve them. Because this crowd wouldn't dare socialize with the Irish or Italians. Sneered at the Jewish businessmen. They forced the free African Americans and the former enslaved from their homes, using their land for parks and fancy houses. They voted for politicians who'd signed the Chinese Exclusion Act into law.

The hypocrisy made Jack nauseous.

He'd grown rich over the years, yes, but he did his best to take care of his people, his neighborhood, no matter their skin color or background. Gang violence had almost ceased. Unions were on the rise. He meted out punishments and kept things organized—in his favor, of course. It was not a democracy, per se, but he was hardly a dictator. A benevolent king, perhaps.

And weren't kings supposed to be blessed by angels?

That brought his attention back to his little dogooder. She was grinning, her expression full of satisfaction and happiness, and he felt something loosen in his chest. Indeed, she was different than the people in this crowd. She didn't merely write a banknote and go about her merry way. Justine worked incredibly hard, day after day, with the downtown residents, giving of her time and energy until she was exhausted. His men had complained, quite vociferously, about how difficult it had been to keep up with her.

She was remarkable.

The crowd broke into applause at the conclusion of Mrs. Tripp's speech, and Frank stood from his seat near the front of the box. He started up the aisle toward Jack. "Come," he snapped without breaking stride.

Had Tripp arranged a meeting with Hatcher so quickly? It would have been a miracle, considering Jack hadn't seen Tripp leave his seat or send a note via an attendant.

"Excuse me," Jack whispered to Justine before motioning to Patrick. The brewer left his seat as well and they trailed Tripp out of the box.

The performance started as they entered the corridor. Theater employees were rushing from various salons and rooms, hurrying to ensure the wealthy patrons lacked for nothing. Tripp led Jack and Patrick to the center of the tier, where he pushed aside the velvet curtains and entered a salon.

Julius Hatcher reclined on a sofa, paperwork on his lap. He glanced up sharply. "Ah, Frank. Are you here to—" Hatcher's mouth closed abruptly when he saw Jack and Patrick. "Well, it seems you come bearing gifts."

Frank walked deeper into the room and lowered himself into one of the armchairs. "Sorry to barge in unannounced, but I believe you all know one another."

"Indeed we do. Patrick, good to see you again." Hatcher paused. "Mulligan."

The less-than-enthusiastic greeting was not lost on Jack. "Would anyone care for a drink?" He hooked his thumb toward the well-stocked sideboard. "Brandy? Bourbon?"

"Help yourself," Hatcher said. "Patrick? Frank?"

"Bourbon," Frank answered. "I fear I'll need it for once we're done here."

"How on earth did you sneak Mulligan in?" Hatcher asked as Jack busied himself at the sideboard.

"He is Justine's escort."

"*Justine?* Your sister-in-law?" Hatcher whistled. "Bet Duncan will have a thing or two to say about that. What's this to do with me?"

Jack took this as his cue. He handed out the crystal tumblers of bourbon then sat in an empty chair. "I'm here tonight to see you. I fear I had no other choice."

"I haven't agreed to see you because there's nothing we need to discuss, Mulligan."

"I respectfully disagree. I have an idea, one I think you'll like."

"Doubtful. And my wife is in our box, watching the performance. I'd rather she didn't come back here and see us together."

"So I'll be brief."

"No, you'll be leaving." Hatcher started to rise, but Frank held up his hand.

"Please, hear him out. I can't have Mulligan continuing an association with Justine."

"That's not my problem," Hatcher said sharply. "And you shouldn't have brought him in here without asking me first."

"I know, and you may yell at me later. But I need Mulligan out of the building before my wife's fundraiser is ruined."

Hatcher glared at Tripp. "You are lucky I like your wife better than I like you."

"Everyone does. Now get on with it, Mulligan, so that we may get out of here."

Jack cleared his throat. "I wish to take the brewery national and I need your help to do it."

Hatcher's expression grew even darker. "As I recall, I had that idea several years ago and you turned it down."

"I had my reasons. The time wasn't right. So, we took you on as an investor and I believe that investment has made you a lot of money."

"As do all of my investments. But, I have no desire to play catch-up. You missed your chance while other local breweries like Pabst and Anheuser have thrived and started to expand regionally."

"You've already tasted Patrick's creations. You know anything he has far outshines what they are brewing in the Midwest."

"He is gifted, without a doubt. So are others. No offense, Patrick."

"None taken," Patrick said and sipped his bourbon. "I realize I'm not the only brewmaster in the country."

Jack knew they wouldn't be so flippant about Patrick's genius if they had tasted the brewer's recent Saaz lager. That revelation would come once Jack had Hatcher's buy-in. "Such may be the case but we now have the perfect opportunity."

Hatcher looked bored as he arched a brow. "Is that so?"

"The key to shipping beer across the nation is about maximizing profit and maintaining freshness. I've solved both problems. First, profit. For that, we need to buy a railroad. A number of them are in trouble."

"That's putting it mildly," Hatcher said. "Railroads and banks are failing across the country. President Cleveland is going to send this country into a depression. He's completely inept to handle the financial crisis—despite my best advice on how to proceed." Hatcher was a Wall Street wizard who could sink or save businesses with a well-placed word.

"Nevertheless," Jack said, "we should capitalize on the current downturn. If we bought a centrally located railroad, we could ship anywhere in the country in just a few days."

"And the freshness? How would you keep the beer cold?"

This was the best part. Jack sat back and held his palms out like he was making an offering. "Refrigerated train cars. I've seen drawings for them and talked to fruit growers in Georgia who use them for peaches. It would work for beer."

"Hmm." Hatcher scratched his jaw and stared at his bourbon. "If I'm being honest, I don't relish going into business with you. The silent investor role is a hard one for me. And you're talking a lot of capital for this venture."

Jack could feel the other man's interest like an electric current in the room. "I realize that and wouldn't expect you to remain silent."

"You are willing to share control?"

"Yes, to a degree. You and Patrick would both have a say."

After a pause, Hatcher said, "The Northern Transportation Railway might work."

Jack smothered a grin. If Hatcher was picking apart the idea and making suggestions, that meant he was on board. "I like the Great Lakes Northern better."

"Yes, I'd forgotten about them. Regardless, I need to think about it."

Jack nodded. He'd brokered enough deals to know when it was prudent to back off and let the information stew awhile. "You know how to find me."

"Yes, I do. In the meantime, have the plans for the refrigerated railcars sent to me. I'd like to look them over."

"Of course."

"It seems you've thought this through, Mulligan." Hatcher placed his empty crystal tumbler on the side table. "So, tell me. If Patrick is in charge of the beer and I'm in charge of the money, what exactly do I need you for?"

"It's my deal. And you need me for my distribution contacts."

"Don't you have enough on your plate at the moment?"

Yes, but more money and power were always worth the trouble. Qui n'avance pas, recule.

He spread his hands helpfully. "I am happy to buy out your share in the brewery."

Hatcher took the hint and dropped the issue. He stood and everyone else followed suit. "We'll speak later, Mulligan, after I've reviewed the plans."

"Patrick, are you all right with this?" Frank asked his brother.

"It's worth a try." Patrick shrugged. "Someone else will do it if we don't. Thank you for considering the idea, Mr. Hatcher." Patrick held out his hand.

"I like you, Patrick," Hatcher said as he shook

the brewer's hand. "You're a genius with hops and barley. It's your partner that I am not sold on quite yet."

Jack merely smiled. Hatcher would come around eventually to see things Jack's way.

They always did.

Chapter Eight

Justine glanced over her shoulder for what felt like the hundredth time. Infuriatingly, the curtains of the Greene box remained closed. Where in Hades was Mulligan? He'd left with Frank and his brother more than twenty minutes ago.

What were those three up to?

The waiting was killing her. Every time their neighbors looked at her, Justine had to feign indifference and concentrate on the performance. Finally, the curtain opened and Justine held her breath. She exhaled. It was merely her oldest sister returning to the box.

Mamie slid into the empty seat next to Justine instead of taking a seat down front. Justine braced herself. While she loved Mamie dearly, she did not quite feel up to a heart-to-heart at the moment.

"So, Mulligan," Mamie whispered behind her fan. "I cannot believe you brought him here."

"I had no choice."

"There is always a choice. Which meant part of you relished thumbing your nose at everyone tonight. Not to mention ruining my fundraiser."

Had she? Justine hadn't ever been brash and willfully disobedient like her two older sisters. No, she quietly volunteered and worked, instead of going to saloons and dance halls. If she were the type to thumb her nose at society, wouldn't she have flaunted Billy around town when she had the chance? After all, even considering the drama of her sisters' love matches, a Greene heiress with a plumber's apprentice would have created quite a stir along upper Fifth Avenue.

No, that was not it. She'd brought Mulligan because she'd given her word about repaying his favor. Now they were even.

"You know I don't care for attention," she said. "This is the repayment for his favor. Nothing more. And it will not ruin your fundraiser."

"Are you sweet on him?"

"Mamie, be serious."

"I am serious. And your lack of surprise at the question makes me wonder."

"A waste of time on your part, then. There's nothing between us."

Her sister made a noise in her throat. "Tina," she said, using her childhood nickname for Justine. "There's unsuitable, like Clayton Madden. And then there's catastrophic, like Mulligan. Do not confuse the two. Daddy and Mama might come to terms with unsuitable. However, you'll be shipped off to a convent in Europe before they allow catastrophic."

Justine bristled, her shoulders pinching. She hated being treated like a child, especially from older sisters who had certainly caused their share of scandal. The truth spilled out of her mouth.

"You do not need to worry about that. He flat out declared I am not his type."

Mamie's eyes rounded. "I don't believe it. I saw how he looked at you. How he treated you. He's interested. Mark my words."

Ludicrous. Justine would never appeal to a man like Mulligan. Her sister Florence, a vivacious and beautiful vixen, was more his type. Justine wasn't a woman to command a room; she was happiest in the background, helping people.

The first act ended and the audience broke out into polite applause. Mamie came to her feet. "There are a few boxes I must visit. I'll return at the start of the second act." She flung the velvet curtains apart and disappeared.

Justine didn't bother getting up. She would rather poke herself in the thigh with a sharp stick than mingle in the ladies' retiring room.

Her grandmother came up the aisle. "Would you care for a drink?"

"No, thank you. I'll remain here."

Granny sat and began fanning herself. "I am curious how you are acquainted with this dangerous man."

"Through my work at the legal aid society."

"He visits the legal aid society?"

"No, but I like to be in the neighborhoods, calling on the clients and helping out."

"I do hope you are being safe. Does your father know you are unescorted on the streets?"

"No. I wouldn't want him to worry." *Or lock me in my room.*

"Indeed, I worry about what you are doing. It was bad enough your sisters went higgledy-piggledy in their day. What can you hope to accomplish through this recklessness?"

"I am helping families. Women and young children in this city. People who are starving, who are struggling. The legal aid society offers assistance, but only in the short term. Which makes sense, given their resources. Frank cannot serve meals at the soup kitchen. Mamie cannot tend to five children for a mother who must spend all day looking for work. That's the kind of thing I do. I assist them with seeing a physician, filing paperwork with the city. Locating a place to live. Mr. Mulligan helped me track down a wife deserter some weeks back. In exchange for his assistance I promised a favor in return. Tonight is that favor."

"I admire your dedication but you could be hurt on any of those errands. At the very least, why not take a maid or one of the grooms? Someone else to serve as a chaperone."

"The only people who care about chaperones live above Thirty-Fourth Street. I am perfectly fine downtown during the day."

The crowd suddenly quieted and Justine glanced at the stage. She sucked in a harsh breath. Mulligan was walking across the stage.

Mulligan was *onstage*. Striding across the wood and rays of light like he owned the place.

What on earth was he doing?

She covered her mouth with her hand, too shocked to move. Her grandmother leaned in. "Is that Mulligan? What in heaven's name . . . ?"

When he reached the center of the stage, he gave the crowd a dazzling smile. "Bonsoir, mesdames et messieurs. Good evening. My name is Mr. Jack

Mulligan." Someone in the audience gasped loudly. Jack merely chuckled. "It appears some of you may have heard of me." He looked around dramatically. "Is this not the Bowery Theatre?"

Guffaws erupted throughout the audience, everywhere except the Greene box.

Then he gestured toward Justine and her grandmother. "Thank you to the Greene family for allowing me to come tonight so that I may speak about the legal aid society and their importance to the citizens of downtown Manhattan. You see, newspapermen like to focus on the fantastic stories that sell papers. They would have you believe that below Fourteenth Street lies nothing but sin and immorality, dirt and violence. They won't tell you about the young girls who are forced to work in factories. Or, the mother who sews by candlelight to make ends meet for her family. The boys who work around the clock shining shoes and selling papers. The husbands breaking their backs on the docks and in the slaughterhouses."

He paused and looked around the audience. "But I will. I see these people every day. I know their names. These are good people, decent people. Many have come here from faraway places, hoping for a better life. They live in one- or two-room flats, often with three and four to a bed. They work hard, but they may not know our language or customs as well as we do."

Justine could see where he was going with this. It was a stroke of brilliance. Brazen, too. Who would have ever thought he'd do such a thing?

"That is why the legal aid society is so important. Mr. Tripp and his team of lawyers are able to help our city's residents with tasks that would otherwise elude them. This is not just about funding a criminal defense in case of arrest. This is about helping those with unfair landlords and cheating employers. Completing job applications and citizenship papers. And"—his gaze locked with Justine's—"even locating husbands who have deserted their wives and families. It is about sticking up for those who have been wronged yet lack the means to procure justice on their own. So tonight, we ask for your assistance. The legal aid society must remain free of politics and the heavy hand of the city's government. This means they rely exclusively on private donations to operate."

Every person in the audience was rapt, watching Mulligan with unwavering concentration. Intermissions were normally loud and chaotic. This one was quiet, with Mulligan commanding the room. A crusader for the underprivileged. Justine knew he was magnetic and had a powerful presence, yet it was glorious to see it on such broad display. *And for such a good cause.*

Warmth slid through her, a slow spread of heat that stretched and filled every part of her. Her breathing picked up, her chest rising and falling, and her breasts pushed against the cage of her corset. She could feel her heartbeat between her legs, and hear the blood rushing in her ears. The fan in her hand did nothing to stem the blaze inside her.

She might not be his type, but right now, at this moment, Mulligan was very much *her* type.

"And so I ask you, the very brightest jewels of New York society, won't you open your hearts and your billfolds? I myself have donated fifty thousand dollars. I wonder if any here could match that donation. Mr. Cavendish?" He pointed to a box on the second tier. "Mr. Bryce? Mr. Irvin? Mr. Randolph? I look forward to hearing of your generosity, and the generosity of everyone else tonight. Thank you for listening, and now on with the performance."

With a carefree grin, Mulligan strode to the wings. Polite applause ripped throughout the cavernous space.

"Clever man," Justine's grandmother muttered.

"Yes. That was quite a speech," Justine said.

"It was more than that. He practically blackmailed those four gentlemen to match his donation or else."

Justine frowned. Blackmail? Granny was being dramatic. Mulligan had issued a challenge to those men, but that was no blackmail threat. "No, that was not what he meant."

"My dear, I have lived long enough to read between what is said and not said. A man like Mulligan must have damning information on nearly everyone of consequence in this city. If it suited his purposes, he wouldn't hesitate to use it any way he saw fit."

"I do not doubt it. But, why on earth would he care? Why threaten anyone here at the fundraiser tonight? What would he possibly hope to gain?"

"Clearly he hopes to gain the one thing he'll never have: *you.*"

More fluttering in her chest. "That's absurd. We are acquaintances, nothing more."

"After tonight, it had better not even be that. I do not want to see you hurt. And your father will never approve."

"I hadn't planned on seeing Mulligan again. You do not need to worry about me. I'm hardly Mamie or Florence."

"That is precisely what worries me. For all their wild ways, your sisters are able to handle themselves in any situation. You are more thoughtful, more reserved. More trusting. I wouldn't like anyone taking advantage of you."

"Trusting and reserved do not equate with weak, Granny."

"True, but you must admit that Mulligan is beyond the bounds of what your father or mother will tolerate. There are limits, Justine—and he is one of them."

"I have no interest in him that way." Her tongue felt awkward, the words sounding flat. Still, she soldiered on. "You are worrying for nothing."

Granny patted Justine's knee. "Good. See that it stays that way."

JACK PROWLED THE length of his office, restless despite the late hour.

He'd left the opera house directly after his speech. The reasons for the speech were complicated. He had no desire to dig deeper as to why he'd felt it necessary, especially when no one had asked such a thing of him. No, like an imbecile he'd volunteered.

But he'd hated the way they treated Justine for bringing him there. Recalling the look on her face after being snubbed made Jack want to punch the wall. God, he hadn't felt this violent in years. Thought he'd buried it under his bespoke suits and fine manners.

In that moment, he'd wanted nothing more than to protect her. Soothe her. To hold her close with one hand while he ripped the offenders apart with the other. He hadn't experienced the feeling since his mother died. Hadn't even thought himself capable of it again until now.

Until *her*.

How could anyone ever find fault with her? Jack might have seen the lioness underneath the silk and pearls, but as far as everyone else knew, Justine was good, obedient and pure. Selfless and caring. An altruistic angel. Certainly better than her father, who'd inherited most of his fortune then earned the rest through means both fair and foul.

Oh, but when the criminals lived above Forty-Second Street, they were called *tycoons*.

Jack had seen them in the crowd tonight, the men he knew from years of doing business in this city. They might not recall their misdeeds—but Jack did. He remembered the ones who'd come to him for help, or the ones who'd begged forgiveness. Cheaters and thieves, murderers and swindlers. They might dine with Mrs. Astor, but they were no better than the men locked up in the Tombs. These Knickerbockers just had the funds for better lawyers.

He blew out a long breath and tried to collect himself.

Anger was a dangerous emotion, one he worked hard to suppress. Anger clouded a man's head. Took away his ability to reason. Jack prided himself on remaining cool no matter the situation. It had kept him alive more times than he could count.

He rolled his shoulders. This was ridiculous. He'd have a beer and get to work. Soon, he'd relax and forget all about earlier tonight.

Striding to his office door, he found Cooper standing guard at the top of the stairs. "Have some beer brought up, will you?"

"Sure thing, Mulligan."

Five minutes later, Cooper returned with a bucket containing ice and several bottles of Jack's preferred lager. He set the whole thing down on the sideboard. "Want a glass?"

"What am I, an animal? Yes, a glass."

Cooper placed a bottle and a glass on Jack's desk. As Jack poured, Cooper said, "Brady is downstairs, waiting to talk to you."

Brady was the man assigned to walking Maeve and Katie home each night. Walters, another one of Jack's men, escorted the other dancers. Jack had ordered that Brady provide regular updates on any trouble or anything out of the ordinary. "Have him come up."

By the time Brady walked in, Jack had downed half the beer in his glass. "Sit," he told the other man. "Report."

"Haven't had any trouble until last night." Brady lowered himself into a chair. "Katie always gets dropped off first. Then Maeve and I wind along to East First Street. Last night I noticed a man about half a block behind us, keeping pace. Head down, hat pulled low. He followed us across Bowery toward Second Avenue. I didn't want him to see where she lived, so we doubled back on Houston. He kept after us."

Goddamn it. "Did you try and grab him?"

Brady nodded. "Put Maeve in Big Stevie's place," he said, referring to one of Jack's poolrooms. "Then I ran after him. He was fast, though, and dodged me somewhere around McGurk's Saloon."

"You'd never find him in that hellhole, if he did go inside. Shit!" He smacked his palm on the desk. "First he follows Katie, now Maeve. And he's not scared off by you? How stupid is this bastard?"

"I couldn't say, but this rules out that it's an old beau of Katie's. This guy is either working up his nerve or trying to scare them."

"I don't like either of those possibilities." Jack drummed his fingers on the desk. "Take more men. I want him caught if he shows his face again. If Maeve gives you any trouble, then tell her the girls can all sleep here instead."

"Will do. Do you think he's one of O'Shaughnessy's men?"

"Hard to say. Catch him next time, though, and I fucking guarantee we'll find out."

The door opened and Cooper stuck his head in the room. "A visitor."

Christ almighty. He was not in the mood for this tonight. Couldn't he work in peace? "Who?"

Cooper's lips twitched like he was fighting a smile. "The do-gooder."

Jack straightened in his chair. Justine was here. Downtown. At this hour? "Send her up."

Cooper left, and Brady came to his feet. "I'll let you know if we see anything else."

"No matter how small, Brady. Even if it seems insignificant. I won't have my people intimidated. We need to catch him."

After a nod, Brady departed. Jack downed the

rest of his beer and opened another bottle. He hadn't changed out of his evening clothes, though he'd removed his coat. The ends of his bowtie hung loose around his neck, his collar unpinned. A gentleman would redress in the presence of a lady.

Jack was no goddamn gentleman.

Anticipation swirled in his gut, an unsettled feeling. Edgy. He couldn't imagine what she wanted, seeing as how their association had ended several hours ago.

You look very dashing tonight.

The compliment, given almost reluctantly, shyly, had been no false praise or flattery. Justine didn't have a dishonest bone in her body. There had been something in her eyes when she'd first watched him approach on the walk, an appreciation. Feminine interest. Just the hint of a flame waiting for the right match.

And God help him, because he was a terrible man, the *worst* man, he'd love nothing more than to watch her burn.

The door swung inward and his muscles tightened in readiness. Justine appeared, wrapped in a long black cloak. She stepped in and he could see she still wore her evening gown from the fundraiser. He hadn't been lying when he said she was lovely. The silver gown gave her a regal air, like an ethereal princess. Delicate—though he knew she was the complete opposite.

No, this girl was stronger than the bedrock holding up the island of Manhattan.

He was walking across the room before he even realized it. Kept going until the tips of his shoes brushed the hem of her skirts and the scent of her, flowery and clean, filled his lungs. It was the best thing he'd ever smelled.

He could see the light smattering of freckles on her nose, the sweep of her dark lashes. The gentle bow of her upper lip. Had he once thought her eyes boring? Now they blazed up at him, gold flecks dancing in the gaslight.

To keep from touching her, he thrust his hands in his trouser pockets. He had no intention of making it easy for her. Merely stood and waited. They both knew she had no good reason to be here at this hour, and he wanted her to own it.

The tip of her tongue emerged and she dragged it across her lips. Jack felt that caress in his cock. *Does she have any idea of the dirty, depraved things I wish to do to her?*

"I apologize for interrupting," she said. "You left abruptly and I did not have a chance to thank you."

That diverted his attention away from her mouth. "Thank me?"

"Yes, for your speech." Another sweep of her pink tongue. "Mamie said they had a record number of donations. The highest amount they've ever received at a fundraiser."

Good. His not-so-subtle nudging of a few particular gentlemen must've paid off. Those bastards could well afford it. "And?"

"And no one shunned me. In fact, I was quite the hero for bringing you to speak."

"I meant what did you think of the speech?"

"It was tremendous." The compliment came out in a breathy rush. "I hadn't guessed you'd do anything like that, so it caught me off guard. But you were . . . quite impressive."

Dashing *and* impressive?

He was starting to think she wanted him just as much as he wanted her.

Impossible.

Pitching his voice low, he asked, "Why are you really here this evening?"

Her eyes went wide. The question had startled her. *Good.* "I told you. I had to thank you."

"That is what letters and telegrams are for. Tell me honestly. Why did you come all the way downtown to my club?"

She blinked a few times but didn't drop her gaze. "You want me to say it was to see you once more in person. Is that it?"

"I hardly think it's a lie."

"Then you have grossly misinterpreted the situation."

"Have I?" Without touching her, he leaned in and brought his mouth right to her ear. Near enough that she would feel his warm breath on her skin. "I think I've interpreted the situation correctly. You want to be here. With me."

Her breath caught, goose bumps breaking out on her exposed skin. He was inches away, so close he could see the pulse pounding in her throat. The proof of her excitement only heightened his, and he longed to sink his teeth into the soft skin where her neck met her shoulder. It had been weeks since he'd fucked a woman and Justine would be just as good as anyone else.

Liar.

She would be better. She was so fierce and pure, so *decent.* A bold angel he didn't deserve. He wanted to charm and seduce her. To pleasure her beyond reason. To absolutely *wreck* her.

He didn't move and she didn't pull away. The overhead gasolier hissed and faint noises drifted up from the club below them. Her shoulders rose and fell with the force of her rapid breaths and his cock thickened, lengthened in his trousers. He was half-hard and hadn't even kissed her yet.

"You said I wasn't your type." Her voice was barely above a whisper.

"I lied. Shall I prove it to you?"

Chapter Nine

Justine swallowed. Hard. Mulligan was potent, heat rolling off his large body like waves from a furnace. He wore no coat, his collar unfastened to reveal the strong column of his throat. She couldn't seem to move. Frozen by whatever was happening in this room.

Why was she here? There was no good answer for that question. She'd gone home with Mamie after the fundraiser and then snuck out of the house with one destination in mind. To see Jack.

A hum had started under her skin the second he'd descended from his carriage at the curb. It had only worsened when he walked off the opera house stage. She'd been possessed by an undeniable impulse to talk to him, to see him. But it couldn't mean anything more. Could it?

She licked her dry lips again and Jack's eyes flashed as he watched her mouth. It was as if an electric current ran between the two of them, a dark need she could almost taste. She'd never experienced it before, this urgent craving, as if her body belonged to someone else. Something else. An animal in heat, one incapable of higher reasoning. A creature of flesh and blood and *wanting*.

And he'd taunted her. *Shall I prove it to you?*

Oh, yes. She'd like nothing more right now. To attack and be attacked. To finally feel what the poets and storytellers meant when they talked about passion. To feel *alive*.

Her life had been about others for so long that she forgot what it felt like to live just for herself. To take instead of giving, giving, giving all the time. The idea of being wicked and selfish was a thrill just waiting there, beckoning in the sizzle of his gaze as he stared down at her.

Danger. You're in danger, Justine.

He wouldn't hurt her, not in the physical sense. However, no one would ever believe that Mulligan could be good for her. He was worldly and charming. Cunning. A man who dressed like a duke but traded in violence and crime. An elegant sword dipped in poison.

So why had she come here tonight?

"Stay," he whispered and inched closer, and she held her breath. "Stay and I'll make all your darkest dreams come true."

Lust tore through her, a pulse of fire and need that centered between her legs. A battle waged inside her like two sides of a coin. Heads was sin and debauchery, the wicked man in front of her. Tails was life beyond these walls, the real world in which she lived with responsibilities and conventions. In this moment she wasn't sure which side she favored.

Hot breath hit her skin an instant before she felt the rough, wet tip of his tongue press to the sensitive spot behind her ear. She gasped and stumbled backward, shocked.

Sweet Lord. He'd *licked* her. Her gaze locked with his, and she expected to see a smug arrogance reflected there.

Instead, she found raw, naked desire.

Fumbling behind her, she clutched the knob and turned. Then she hurried into the hall, nearly running to the stairs. A man stood at the landing but she didn't acknowledge him. She merely lifted her skirts and flew down the steps. Toward the street. Toward safety. She didn't care if anyone followed. Her only thought was to escape.

But you liked it. Go back so he may continue.

No, she told her inner voice. That was impossible. Justine didn't belong with Mulligan. It was like Little Red Riding Hood choosing the wolf over her grandmother. It made no sense. *They* made no sense.

A boxing match was in full swing as she darted through the club's main room. Thankfully, no one paid her any attention. Once out the front door, she tried to dodge the two young men on the stoop.

"Ho!" One of them caught her arm.

"Let me go."

He instantly released her but the other guard stepped in front of her, blocking her path. "Beg your pardon, Miss Greene, but you can't be runnin' the streets of the neighborhood at this hour."

"I will hire a hack. I'll be fine."

The first boy jerked his thumb at the brougham parked up the street. "We'll have Rye take you wherever you need to go."

"That's not necessary—"

"Miss, if we let you tear out of here, alone, Mulligan'll string us up by our toenails. Please, take the carriage."

They both looked young and sincere, and Justine didn't wish to cause them trouble with their employer. "Fine."

Satisfied, one of the guards ran inside, presumably to find Mr. Rye. Justine tried not to fidget as they waited. She watched the boxing match through the glass panes at the front of the club. The flurry of fists and feet was dizzying, a battle so primitive it was beautiful. The fighters' bare chests, one light and one dark, dripped with sweat, their attention focused solely on each other. Spectators surrounded the ring, cheering and shouting, some even shoving one another. This was Mulligan's world, where men battled for dominance with their fists.

What was she doing here? And why in God's name was she so fascinated by it?

"Hello, miss." Rye came up alongside her. "Just give me your address and we'll get you home all nice, safe and sound."

Safe and sound. In another word, boring.

Was that how everyone saw her? Was that how *he* saw her?

She blinked up at the brightly lit windows on the second floor. Mulligan stood there, expressionless, leaning against the window, a glass of beer in his hand as he watched her below. He made no effort to look away.

How long had he been standing there?

He hadn't seemed surprised when she'd fled the club. Hadn't come after her, either. Perhaps the touch of his tongue had been meant to scare her. To prove she wasn't strong enough to handle what was between them.

If so, he underestimated her.

Justine was much stronger than she appeared. He'd caught her off guard, was all.

And while he may be a wolf in fancy clothing, she was no innocent lamb looking to get slaughtered. She could take care of herself. That meant staying away from Great Jones Street and Mulligan.

She gave him a jaunty salute then started for the brougham. *Good luck, wolf. Find another lamb to play with.*

BROOME STREET HALL was a classic Bowery dive. It had a plain storefront with two big windows on either side of a double door. A large sign proclaimed *Lager Beer* along the front, though many patrons here preferred a punch that contained cocaine sweepings, benzene, camphor, hot rum and whiskey. Jack had seen what it did to patrons; if they were lucky, they might only have a day or two of useless oblivion. The unlucky ones never woke up.

He glanced over at Cooper. "He's here?"

"Yes, confirmed. Up front in the saloon."

Last night, one of Jack's policy shops had been robbed. The particular location happened to border O'Shaughnessy's territory to the east. Though no one had been caught, it did not take a genius to figure out who had been behind the holdup.

Jack meant to send a message. One that would not be misinterpreted.

He had two of his men with him. Thirty men

would've made it seem like Jack was scared of O'Shaughnessy, which was laughable. Ten men would have been smart, merely to ensure nothing happened. Two was an insult, one meant to get under O'Shaughnessy's skin.

Jack wasn't worried. O'Shaughnessy wouldn't dare hurt him. To do so would bring fire and brimstone to the Lower East Side and everything Trevor had worked for destroyed. Just like years ago, when gang warfare used to be the normal state of affairs downtown. When hundreds of innocent lives were lost.

That reminded Jack of his little do-gooder. Perhaps he'd scared her off for good after the fundraiser the other night. She'd run from the club as if rabid hounds were chasing her—or one very aroused male.

Christ, how he'd wanted her.

But he'd purposely pushed, testing her. His words and touch had frightened her, proving he couldn't be what she needed, a gentle man who fucked with the lights off every other Saturday night. That wasn't Jack. Though he wore bespoke suits and oiled his hair, he had been raised in a brothel as well as on the streets. Justine might have a strong will, but so did he—with the blood on his hands to prove it.

He would only horrify her. No, she was better off.

Pushing that away, he focused on the task at hand. "Let's go."

He crossed Broome and started for the doors. Night had fallen hours ago, the gaslights casting yellow gloom on the dirt, piss and animal excrement in the street. Cooper opened the door and

Jack stepped inside—and all conversation ceased. Even the piano player in the corner froze, the notes hanging in midair until they dissipated.

Good.

The place was packed with men, young and old, gathered around small wooden tables on the scuffed tile floor. A table with food had been set up in the corner, flanking the long wooden bar along the far wall.

At the bar stood Trevor O'Shaughnessy.

He wore a black cap pulled low, but Jack could still see the hatred in Trevor's gaze reflected in the mirror behind the bar as he watched Jack's approach.

Removing his derby, Jack went toward the bar. He ignored the patrons gawking at him. Two men at tables closest to the bar shot to their feet, but Cooper and Rye, who flanked Jack like foot soldiers, blocked them.

When he reached the bar, Jack stepped directly between O'Shaughnessy and another man. "A beer," he told the bartender.

The bartender shot a glance toward O'Shaughnessy, who discreetly nodded his head. A few seconds later a beer appeared in front of Jack. He went to dig a coin out of his pocket, but the bartender waved him off. "It's on the house," the man said.

Jack lifted the glass in thanks and took a long sip. It was terrible, nothing but watered-down piss. Cradling the glass in his hand, he turned, put his back against the bar and studied the crowd. Roughnecks and thugs stared at him, a room full of men who had no ambition or drive. Their hands were dirty and their clothing tattered. No thought to distinguish themselves from the butchers and hooligans of the past. A shame, really. Not forward thinkers, this crew.

He made no effort to speak. Just took up space while he drank the beer. Years of experience had taught him that employing silence was often the most threatening thing a man could do.

O'Shaughnessy was short and stocky. He had black hair, a thick neck and misshapen ears from years of boxing. By all accounts, he had a hair-trigger temper.

Sure enough, Jack didn't have to wait long.

"What the fuck do you want, Mulligan?"

So, O'Shaughnessy could speak, after all.

Jack didn't turn. "You should know why I'm here, Trevor."

"I don't. Why don't you spell it out and then leave?"

"Such hospitality," Jack drawled sarcastically. "Careful, or I might think I'm not wanted around here."

Trevor put his glass down with a thump. "Get to the point. I don't have time for you or your games."

Spinning, Jack hurled his beer glass at the mirror behind the bar. The mirror exploded in an unholy crash, shards raining down to the floor along with discarded beer. O'Shaughnessy stiffened and chairs scraped behind them.

Jack leaned in and kept his voice low. "Have time for me fucking *now*?"

A muscle clenched in O'Shaughnessy's jaw but he didn't move.

"Nothing to say?" Jack taunted. "Fine. I'll speak

enough for both of us." He straightened and pulled on his cuffs, smoothed his vest. Style mattered in situations such as this.

"I know you are responsible for what happened to my policy shop last night. Whether it was under orders from you or some of your men gone rogue, I don't care. I expect you to make restitution. I want every dollar, every penny stolen from me returned by the end of the week."

"That's absurd. You have no proof that I or any of my men are responsible."

"I don't need proof. This isn't a court of law. I am the one deciding fates in these parts."

"Maybe word's gettin' out that you're slipping, Mulligan. You cannot blame me for everything that goes wrong."

Slipping? Burying his fury, Jack smirked at the younger man. "I cut my teeth on bastards like you before I had hair on my balls. I took them down and I'll be happy to take you down, too."

"We've stayed to our neighborhood. Haven't bothered your businesses. You have no right to come in here and threaten me."

"Are you calling me a liar? Because there are men trailing my dancers and my policy shops are being robbed. No one other than you would even dare."

"You have a lot of enemies, Mulligan. More than you can imagine."

Did O'Shaughnessy think this was new information? "Comes with being at the top, which you'd be wise to remember." The other man said nothing, merely stared at Jack with burning resentment. Jack slapped a one-hundred-dollar bill on the bar. "For the damage," he told the bartender.

"We don't need your money," O'Shaughnessy snapped.

"Apparently you do, or else you wouldn't be robbing my policy shops. One week, Trevor. Every penny. And stop following my dancers."

"Or what?"

"Or I'll unleash hell on you and anyone loyal to you." It had been a long time since someone had challenged Jack like this. He'd missed it, actually. As if they were old friends, Jack clapped O'Shaughnessy on the shoulder. "Though part of me hopes you won't show. I haven't completely annihilated a man in a while."

"A week or two, at least," Rye put in.

Jack laughed and started for the door. "Sorry to interrupt your night, fellows," he told the crowd. "Next round's on me."

Silence trailed them out of the saloon and onto the street. Jack began whistling as they started for the carriage. "That went well."

"He reacted exactly as you said he would," Cooper noted.

"It's what I would have done in his shoes."

"So what do you think he'll do next?"

"Repay the money and plot my imminent demise." Again, Jack would have done the same in similar circumstances.

Cooper held open the carriage door. "I didn't expect you to part with a hundred dollars."

"Counterfeit." Jack had access to quite a lot of fake money, thanks to a man he'd met a few years back. One who owed him a favor, naturally. "O'Shaughnessy tries to use it and he'll have the Secret Service at his door."

Rye and Cooper both chuckled. "You are devious, Mulligan."

"Goddamn right I am. Only way to succeed in this city."

HURRYING DOWN RIVINGTON Street, Justine dodged a group of children playing ball. The Lower East Side was comprised of many groups, mostly Eastern Europeans from Germany, Poland and Russia. It was a neighborhood always changing, growing and stretching upward to accommodate those who took up residence here. A synagogue was under construction across the street, while a German newspaper was opening down the block. Justine loved watching the transition as the immigrants made this city more vibrant, more diverse.

Moreover, this particular neighborhood wasn't directly associated with Mulligan. Chances of running into him here were slim.

Was she avoiding him? Absolutely.

Three days had passed since she'd foolishly gone to the athletic club to see him. In that time, she'd remained busy, as always, taking care to circumvent the blocks that Mulligan claimed. She could have almost forgotten about him altogether if not for the incessant questions from Mamie and Frank.

Those, and her dreams at night. Mulligan had starred in more than a few, his touch hot and knowing, leaving her sweaty and shaken in the morning. It was mortifying. She was nearly afraid to fall asleep at night.

A familiar figure lingered outside a five-story building at the end of the block. He was tossing a baseball back and forth with a young boy when Justine arrived. "Thank you for meeting me," she said, trying to catch her breath. "Have you been waiting long?"

Detective Ellison patted the boy on the head, gave him the ball and turned to Justine. "Not long. Only a few moments."

"Well, I appreciate you taking the time. Your case, the politician's son, is it over?"

"Yes. We've made an arrest, so I have some free time today."

"Who was responsible?"

"A friend of the deceased. Nothing sordid, just two drunken idiots fighting. One ended up dead. So, this is the shirtwaist factory you were telling me about." He glanced at the structure behind her.

"Yes, on the fifth floor. I'll show you the way."

They went inside, the dark interior serving as a blessed respite from the outdoor heat. She wiped the perspiration from her forehead with a handkerchief. Bustling about the city in the summer was not for the faint of heart. Which probably explained why most of high society left for Newport in June and didn't return until after Labor Day.

Not Justine, though. She stayed in town. The beach was boring and tedious.

"The usual plan of attack?" Ellison asked as they climbed.

"Yes, I think so. I have already seen the conditions. You are welcome to the owner, Mr. Bay." One of the legal aid clients had mentioned this shirtwaist factory, complaining of the cruel conditions and long hours, and Justine had come to see the horrors for herself. It had been easy to gain

access to the floor after telling the secretary she
was there to interview for a position. Mr. Bay had
asked her to leave, of course, but not before she
saw what was happening inside.

Then she'd waited outside after hours and approached a few of the workers. Employees often had a lot to say when their employer wasn't
around, such as the hours and conditions, the
wages and requirements for keeping their positions. Using this information, Justine would bring
Detective Ellison for a visit with the owner. Ellison was quite good at intimidating these men.
Shaming them into doing better by their workers.
A badge helped, of course.

At the top of the fifth flight of stairs, Justine bent
over and put a hand to her stomach. This was her
third climb today above four floors and her legs
were growing tired. "The door is just over there."

Ellison went first, not bothering to knock before
he entered. His detective badge was clipped to his
lapel, visible to all. Justine followed and closed the
door. A secretary looked up from her desk in the
reception area. "May I help you?"

"Yes," Ellison said. "We'd like to see the owner."

She eyed his badge and returned her gaze to his
face. "Mr. Bay isn't available at the moment. Perhaps
you'd care to come back another time?"

"When will he return?" Justine asked.

"I could not say," the woman answered.

"Is there someone else we may speak with? A
manager or supervisor?"

"I'm afraid not."

Frowning, Ellison exchanged a look with Justine. Without another word, he walked around the

desk toward the factory. The secretary popped up and tried to stop him, but he was already over the threshold. Justine trailed him, darting around the girl and into the corridor. The workspace was a long dark room in the back of the building, the windows having been boarded up at some point. Owners often did this, claiming it prevented employee theft. What it really prevented was proper airflow and respiratory health.

When they arrived, however, an entirely different scene greeted her.

Gone were the dark windows and gloomy interior. Today, the windows were open, allowing in a slight breeze, and the overhead bulbs were lit. The terrified silence of her previous visit had also disappeared. Workers were chatting and laughing, sewing while socializing. A few even stood, stretching their arms and shoulders, before walking to the washrooms in the back—washrooms that had been locked the last time she'd been here.

Most shocking? Not a child in sight.

Her jaw dropped. What had happened here? It was definitely the right address, the same shirtwaist factory. She even recognized some of the workers from before.

"Uh, this isn't exactly what I expected," Ellison murmured.

"It was much different. No light, no air. And there were children here, locked in."

"Well, they are not here now."

Confused, Justine walked to the tables where the workers were busy sewing and talking behind their machines. She approached one. "Good afternoon, ma'am."

The woman's gaze darted nervously to Ellison before settling on Justine. "Hello, miss."

"I was here a week or so ago and everything was different. What happened?"

"It's a miracle." She grinned. "A few men came in the other day and took Mr. Bay into the back. We didn't think anything of it until the thumps started."

"Thumps?"

"Loud noises. Like a fight."

A fight? Justine looked over at Ellison, who put his hands on his hips. "Then what happened?" he asked.

"The men left after a bit. Mr. Bay came out and his face was"—she waved her hand in front of her face—"swollen and bleeding. He left and hasn't been back since."

"Who were these men?"

"I couldn't say, miss. One was handsome, well-dressed. Looked like the leader. I overheard talk that he was some important man from over near Five Points, but you know how girls gossip."

Justine blinked several times. An important man from Five Points . . . handsome and well-dressed? It couldn't be.

It *couldn't* be.

Who else, then? What other handsome Five Points man would come here to rough up the owner? There was no one else.

She'd offhandedly mentioned this factory to Mulligan during their lunch, including its location. He must have decided to come intimidate Mr. Bay into treating the workers fairly.

But, why?

Granny's words floated through her mind. *Clearly he hopes to gain the one thing he'll never have: you.*

That made no sense. None of this made sense. She'd run out on him three nights ago. There was no reason for the two of them to ever cross paths again.

So, why had he bothered?

"You know who it was, don't you?" Ellison asked, staring carefully at Justine's face.

"I might," she hedged then thanked the worker. "If there is any further trouble when Mr. Bay returns, please find Detective Ellison at police headquarters."

The woman nodded. "Whoever that man was, he was like our guardian angel."

Justine wasn't so certain about that, but she couldn't deny that Mulligan had done a good deed for these workers. She and Ellison left, the angry secretary glowering at them on the way.

"All right, come clean." Ellison followed her down the steps, his boots slapping on the wood. "How do you know Jack Mulligan?"

Chapter Ten

～

Justine concentrated on taking the steps carefully in the dim stairwell. "We cannot be certain it was Mulligan."

"Important and handsome man from Five Points? There aren't many who fit that description, and only one has the power to scare that factory owner into changing his entire operation. That's Mulligan. So, tell me how you have him doing favors for you, too."

She waited until they were on the walk before she answered. "I never asked him to come here and intervene. I . . . We had lunch one day and I told him about this factory. The day you turned me away."

"You and Mulligan had *lunch*?" Ellison made a choking sound in his throat. "Are you pulling my leg?"

"No. He practically forced me to go because I hadn't eaten." It sounded stupid to say the words aloud.

"And you agreed? Do you know who he is? How he lives his life? He runs most of the illegal activity south of Fourteenth Street."

She hated Ellison's tone, as if she were a daft female, one too naive to be trusted. "I am well aware, Detective. I know of Mulligan's reputation."

"Do you? Do you, really? Because if you did, I don't think you'd get within ten feet of the man, let alone have lunch with him."

"I know he operates some saloons and pool-rooms. That he oversees most of the gambling downtown."

"And the booze and the smuggling. Oh, and let's not forget blackmail. The boxing matches alone could get him thrown in the Tombs. He's swimming in criminal activity." Ellison dragged a hand through his hair. "He's not a nice man. I daresay there's not a gentleman to be found in New Belfast Athletic Club."

"No one has harmed me there—"

"You've been *inside*?" He walked in a tight circle, muttering what she suspected were curse words. "Are you *insane*?"

This was ridiculous. She appreciated Ellison's concern, but he wasn't her father or her husband. He was a police detective who had helped her on occasion. As such, that did not give him the right to make her feel small and helpless. "I will take your words under advisement, Detective. However, I am perfectly capable of handling myself in the Sixth Ward—or anywhere else for that matter."

"Is that so? And the rapes and murders there, you think you could handle yourself? The women kidnapped and forced to work in brothels, that wouldn't happen to you because you're the daughter of Duncan Greene, correct?" He leaned in, his expression hard as his voice rose in volume. "Wise up, Miss Greene. All those things happen in this city and they happen to all kinds of women. Your Fifth Avenue address won't save you. In fact, it makes you a bigger target because they'll know your father will pay a king's ransom to get you back."

She didn't want to fall victim to his hysterics but he was starting to make her nervous. *Relax. You're careful when you're traveling the city alone.* Not to mention that she carried a pistol on the rare occasions when she was out at night. So, she wasn't completely defenseless. "Are you saying Mulligan will kidnap me for ransom? Because he has enough money."

"There's never enough money for a thug like Mulligan. You need to stay as far away from him as possible. I know you like to come downtown and save people, but he is beyond redemption."

Was that why Mulligan appealed to her, because she thought to save him? That hadn't occurred to her before Ellison mentioned it. She'd been drawn to Mulligan, but not for altruistic motives—at least not that she was aware of. He was handsome and charming. Dressed like a swell and spoke like an aristocrat. A woman would need to be dead not to be drawn to that sort of man. "Noted."

Ellison blew out a long breath. This was as agitated as she'd ever seen the calm detective. "I apologize for yelling. It's just . . . The things I've seen in these neighborhoods. I'd hate for them to happen to a woman like you."

What did that mean, a woman like her? An uptown heiress? Justine didn't care for the implication that her status and trust fund made her more valuable. Meaning, women without those things were allowed to be raped, murdered and kidnapped? "Thank you, Detective. I appreciate your concern. For the record I do not plan on furthering my acquaintance with Mr. Mulligan."

If her response was a bit frosty, he didn't notice. He gestured toward the sidewalk. "Good. Now, come on. I'll walk you to the elevated. My wife is cooking a roast and I have a chance of actually making it home in time for a hot meal."

They started toward the train line. She decided to bring up an idea to Ellison, one she'd been considering. "You once said things would be easier if I had my own badge. I am starting to think you're right. With whom should I speak in order to get one?"

Ellison made a noise as he dodged a child sprinting up the walk. "It isn't as easy as that. There are no women on the force who carry a badge and have the power to arrest someone."

"So, I'll be the first."

"You don't understand. This isn't like asking for an invitation to a ball. Female detectives aren't done."

"Chicago has one."

"That's Chicago. They're provincial. It's practically the Wild West out there."

"That seems unfair. They are hosting the World's Fair to worldwide acclaim. Have you ever been?"

He frowned down at her. "No, but I don't need to visit somewhere to know what the place is like."

Um, wasn't that exactly why one visited, to have a true picture of a city? Ellison continued to surprise her today, with his condescension and ignorance. He'd always been so willing to help her that she'd considered him progressive. A supporter of women's rights and the rights of workers. Had she misjudged him?

"Listen, if you just tell me with whom to speak,

I'll try and convince him. I won't even say it was your idea to begin with."

"That's because it wasn't my idea. It was an off-handed comment made when I was overworked."

"Think about it," she continued. "I could handle the types of cases the male detectives can't."

"Like wife deserters and child labor?" He stopped in the street and put his hands on his hips. Just as he opened his mouth to speak, he was bumped from behind.

"Move it, copper."

Ellison glared at the offender's back then looked at Justine. "See that? And if that's what they do to male detectives, imagine what they'd do to female detectives. The idea is preposterous."

"That's not what I asked. Tell me who to speak with. I'll take care of the rest."

"Fine, you have time to waste? Go see Richard Croker."

"The head of Tammany Hall?"

Ellison's lips curled into a mocking smile. "Tammany makes nearly all of the recommendations for appointments and promotions. And the fact you don't know that shows you are not ready to work in the police department."

No, she hadn't known. She assumed the police department worked on merit, which now sounded ridiculous. She really ought to have known better. Corruption ran through New York City faster than water. "Is that how you were appointed?"

"To detective, yes. I had been a roundsman for four years. Helped keep a ward boss safe during an election night altercation in '90. He repaid me by having me promoted."

Her stomach sank a bit—and it must have shown on her face. He said, "That's how the city works, Miss Greene. You are kidding yourself if you believe otherwise."

"I still have to try. Perhaps my father could help."

"Or perhaps you could ask Mulligan."

She frowned at his sarcastic tone. "That was unnecessary, Detective."

"I apologize." His mouth twisted with what seemed like honest regret, like he'd take the words back if he could. "I admit, I am a little bothered by your association with him. Here I thought I was helping you because you had no other option. Only, it turns out you're cozy with one of the city's biggest criminals."

"It almost sounds like you're jealous."

"Maybe I am."

Sweet Lord. She'd been joking but his response was utterly serious. Her jaw fell open and she took a step back, putting distance between them. Contrition washed over his features and he held up his hands. "No, not like that. Not in a romantic sense. But, in a professional sense. I thought you needed me."

Confused, she tried to make sense of what he was saying. He wanted her to be dependent on him and only him? He wouldn't assist her in getting a position in the department and he told her to stay away from Mulligan. Was this what men considered as professional "advancement" for women? She thought her gender had been gaining ground, with new jobs and new possibilities. Soon, women would get the vote. And yet.

Would there always be a man holding them back?

The idea was depressing.

"I'll speak to Croker. Thank you for the advice. You know, I've changed my mind about the elevated. I feel like walking a bit. Take care, Detective." She darted in front of an omnibus to cross the street and then kept heading west. On her own.

Without anyone telling her what to do.

THE NEXT AFTERNOON, Justine was back downtown, staring at the front of the building. She'd loitered on the walk for a good twenty minutes now, waiting. Keeping a sharp eye on her surroundings.

It was the middle of the day, yet no matter the hour, the World Poolroom was one of the most dangerous places in the Bowery. Thieves, confidence men, smugglers . . . any manner of rough character might be found drinking and gambling in there. She decided to wait on the walk instead of risking life and limb by going inside. Someone would eventually leave and she could ask him or her about Mr. von Briesen out here.

Minutes later, she was rewarded when a red-haired woman stumbled out of the poolroom door and onto the walk. The woman squinted into the sun, wincing as if in pain. Her clothes were wrinkled and stained, her gait unsteady. Was she inebriated, or recovering from being inebriated earlier? Justine couldn't tell.

"Excuse me," she called. "Might I speak to you for a moment?"

The woman rocked on her feet then put her arms out to catch her balance. "Who wants to know?"

"My name is Justine. I would like to ask you a question or two."

"I don't have time for questions. Barkeep's fixin' to fight me about my tab." She started off down the street, her steps wobbly but fast.

Just then, the door flew open again and a man emerged. He had a white apron tied around his waist, his mouth carved into a fierce scowl framed by bushy brown muttonchops. When he spotted the retreating redhead, he darted after her, catching up easily and forcibly dragging her back toward the poolroom. "You're gonna work off that money, Bess. Upstairs, in one of the rooms."

"Fuck off," the redhead spat as she tried to squirm out of his grip. "I ain't no whore."

Justine couldn't prevent herself from intervening. "Wait, how much does she owe you?"

The barkeep narrowed his eyes on Justine. "Thirty-five dollars."

Thirty-five dollars! That was outrageous. "For a morning bar tab?"

"Try four days' worth of tab. I'm tired of carrying her. She's gonna pay up one way or another."

"How?"

"I hardly see how that's your concern, miss." The barkeep opened the door and started to tow Bess inside.

"Wait! I'll give you the money for her tab if you'll let her go."

"Why?"

It was a fair question. She was a stranger on the street, offering to square up this woman's expensive bar tab.

Yet, she couldn't watch someone be forced into an illicit act against her will, merely because she was short of funds. Plus, if Bess had a four-day bar tab here, perhaps she was well versed in the goings-on at the World Poolroom. She might be a font of information, anything that might lead to Mr. von Briesen.

"Yeah, why?" Bess parroted. "You can keep whatever religious pamphlets you're peddlin', honey. I don't want 'em."

"No, I'm not here to save your soul. I have some questions, is all."

The barkeep lifted a shoulder. "Suit yourself. If you have thirty-five dollars to spare, I'll take it and you can get this loudmouth harridan out of my bar."

Justine dug in her small purse for the bills to settle Bess's tab. Counting it carefully, she handed the money to the barkeep. "There you go. Now release her."

He shoved Bess roughly, causing the redhead to stumble, before disappearing inside. Justine put a hand out to steady the other woman and helped her to the shade near the side of the building. They sat on the stoop of the rooming house next door.

"Go on, ask your questions." Bess practically sneered at Justine, but Justine ignored it. They weren't here to become friends, and she didn't expect gratitude for paying the bar tab. She'd given the money because it had been the right thing to do.

Reaching in her small purse, Justine took out the sketch of Mr. von Briesen. A sketch artist hired by the legal aid society had assisted with the portrait based on his wife's description. "Do you recognize this man?"

"No. Should I?"

"He disappeared. The nineteenth of June, to be

exact. The last place anyone saw him was here at
the World Poolroom."

Bess took another peek at the portrait. "Never
seen him before."

"I understand there are peter players here, that
this man may have been a victim. Is there anyone
who might know what happened once they put
him on the street?"

"Take your pick." Bess waved her hand around
them to indicate the Bowery. "Anyone might have
seen."

"Are there girls working inside the poolroom?
Serving girls or . . . others?"

"Prostitutes, you mean? They're on the upper
floors."

"I'd like to talk to some of them. Do you think
you'd be able to help me—?"

Bess pushed off the stone step and got to her feet.
"You want to see 'em, pay for an hour just like ev-
erybody else. I'm done talking. I'm going back inside."

"You're going back in? After you were chased
out?"

"Sure. I got some nice lady to pay my tab for me.
Now I can run it up again." Bess sauntered to the
poolroom door and disappeared inside. Because
of the bright sunlight, Justine couldn't see through
the glass to make sure the woman was all right. She
supposed the barkeep would either serve Bess or
toss her out again.

Justine sighed, disappointed but not discouraged.
It took more than one surly drunk to cause her to
give up. These investigations were all about talking
to people and gaining their trust. She hadn't really

expected to solve Mr. von Briesen's disappearance on the first try.

The trick would be getting to the second floor to speak with the girls there. If Mr. von Briesen had hired a companion for the night, perhaps one or two of the women might remember him.

Shielding her gaze from the bright light, she craned her neck to look at the upper floors of the building. Was there another way up there, other than through the poolroom?

Noise at the curb caught her attention. A black brougham skidded to a halt in front of the poolroom, the driver jerking hard on the reins. The driver was familiar, and a shiver ran down Justine's spine despite the heat.

Mulligan.

Before she could blink, he was out of the brougham and on his way to her. The look on his face was far from pleasant. In fact, he looked downright irritated. His mouth, the mouth that had nearly kissed her the other night, was flat and unwelcoming.

He licked me.

She could almost still feel that brief, warm wet slide on her skin. Tasting her. What would that tongue be able to do elsewhere, on other parts of her body? Swallowing, she pushed all those thoughts aside for later. As in, never.

So, what was he doing here?

"What are you doing here?"

She shielded her eyes from the sun with her hand. "I was just wondering the same about you. Have you come to bet on the horse races?" She could think of no other reason why Mulligan was here, glowering at her outside the World Poolroom. Then a horrible thought struck her. "Is this one of yours?"

"No, my poolrooms are just poolrooms. We don't drug and rob patrons as a regular practice. Seeing as we've cleared that up, tell me why you are visiting this particular establishment."

"I am looking for someone. He was last seen here on June 19th."

"Who?"

"A German man, von Briesen. We think a group of peter players robbed him and put him on the street. His family is quite concerned."

"Do your brother-in-law and Otto Rosen know you are investigating here, at this particular place?"

"I don't know. Why?"

"Because they will both answer to me if the answer is yes. You have no business being in this particular stretch of the Bowery. It's dangerous."

"Is this why you are here? Because of me?"

"When they told me you were here, I came as fast as I could."

Part of her was flattered that he worried over her safety, but the bigger part of her was annoyed he thought she was in danger. "That was unnecessary. I am perfectly safe."

"No one is perfectly safe here, least of all an unaccompanied woman."

"It's the middle of the day and I have no intention of going in. My plan is to question patrons out here, which I have already started doing." He appeared confused so she elaborated. "A woman came out from the poolroom and she was fairly inebriated. The barkeep chased her down because she owed him money, so I helped out. In return, she answered my questions."

"Helped out?"

"Paid her bar tab in exchange for answers. I showed her the sketch of von Briesen. Unfortunately, she hadn't ever seen him before and went back inside."

He shook his head and muttered a string of French curse words. "Let's go get your money back."

"What? Where?"

"Inside. Come on."

He started toward the poolroom door so Justine grabbed his arm, stopping him. "Wait. I don't need my money returned. I offered up my assistance free and clear. He was going to make her do terrible things to work off her debt."

Jack's expression softened, his gaze turning warm, almost affectionate. Her chest fluttered at that look, one that probably caused women to swoon at his feet. The foot traffic streamed on both sides of them, but this man commanded every bit of her attention with his bright blue eyes and chiseled face. He lifted a hand and dragged the backs of his knuckles gently across her cheek. Her knees trembled, her body caught under his spell. Had she melted into a puddle on the sidewalk yet?

"You have a good heart, and I admire you for it," he said. "But you've been swindled, chérie, and I mean to make it right."

Chapter Eleven

Jack could tell by her face that she didn't believe him. God save him from uptown do-gooder heiresses.

She blinked at him and he dropped his hand, already missing the feel of her soft skin. "No, Mulligan. You're wrong. She was inebriated, and cursed and spat at him. He said she owed four days' worth of bar tab."

"Justine, this is more my area of expertise than yours. You were swindled. They probably saw you standing out here on the walk and decided to con you."

Stubborn until the end, she shook her head. "No."

"Shall we place a wager on it?"

Ah, there was the seed of doubt. She bit her lip and chewed it, indecision pinching her lovely brows. He waited, the fear at her roaming this neighborhood alone slowly ebbing. He had vowed to forget her after she left his club in fear. Then the second he'd learned of her errand at the World, he'd raced to her side. Had he ever traveled south so quickly? The news had terrified him.

She's here. She's safe.

And Tripp and Rosen would be answering for this.

But that was for another day. Right now, he had to prove himself right and perhaps gain another favor from Miss Greene. The possibility made him dizzy.

This favor would not be so innocent as allowing him to escort her to a fundraiser.

Perhaps she read his intent on his face because she asked, "What would the wager entail?"

"If I'm right, you owe me a favor. And I offer the same in reverse should I be proven wrong."

"So if I'm right then you owe me a favor."

"Yes."

"I can't think of anything I want from you," she said with a wrinkle of her nose.

"You can't?" he murmured. "What a pity."

There were many, many things he'd like from Justine, not all of them suitable for polite conversation. Most of them centered on the topic of her pussy and his tongue.

Then she grinned. A sly, secretive grin that caused Jack's knees to damn near weaken and goose bumps to break out on his skin. Jesus God, that look. As if a wicked thought had crossed her mind. No, more like a dirty, illicit thought. And he very well might die if he didn't discover it.

Though he doubted hers had been as dirty as his own.

"I have something," she said, eyes shining. "A favor I need with Tammany Hall."

Disappointment punched through his stomach. Indeed, what had he expected? She wasn't corrupt and wicked, like him. Never would be.

He started for the World's main entrance and waved her along behind him. "Well, certainly don't spoil the surprise by telling me. Come along."

He flung open the heavy door. The stench of sweat, blood and whiskey filled his nostrils, the scent as familiar as breathing. The interior was bright enough for him to quickly take stock of the room, the number and positions of everyone inside. The place was as safe as he could reasonably expect, so he headed toward the long wooden bar. Several patrons were standing at the bar, their backs to him.

He leaned against the edge, right next to a redhead he'd know anywhere. "Bess! How have you been, love?"

Bess turned, her face registering surprise then genuine pleasure. "Damn, Mulligan. It's been a long time."

"It has. You are looking well, though. Paul, good to see you," he said to the barkeep. "I like the new look." He pointed to the man's expertly groomed muttonchops.

Paul cast a wary glance at Justine before coming back to Jack. "Hello, Mulligan. We don't see you often in these parts. Did you come down for a drink or to place a bet?"

"No, I have my own places for that. I'm actually here with my friend." He hooked a thumb to where Justine stood. "I understand you took her for thirty-five dollars. I'll be wanting that back."

Paul and Bess exchanged a look. "Now, Mulligan. We don't want any trouble," Paul said.

"Which is why you'll return my friend's money and give her an apology."

"Aw, damn," Bess said. "You can't blame a girl for trying. Do you see the way she's dressed? She can afford it."

"That's hardly the point and you know it." Jack rapped his knuckles on the bar. "Thirty-five. Right now."

Bess reached inside her bodice while Paul dug into his apron. Within seconds Jack held thirty-five dollars. "Now, the apology."

Both mumbled apologies to Justine, who'd drawn closer during the exchange. "No harm done," she said without a hint of ill will and took the money. "You're forgiven."

"Good. That's settled. You know a man named von Briesen?"

"Of German descent," Justine put in. "Last seen here on June 19th."

Bess and Paul both denied knowing the man. "Check with Mac. He does the books in the back. He might remember."

Jack led Justine to the poolroom, which was packed with bodies. Men of every color and background were clustered around small wooden tables where they stared at the race results on the wall. A screen in the corner hid a telegraph machine that steadily transmitted results from the track. Everyone along the line made a fortune off the city's poolrooms, even Western Union.

Payouts were handled much like a bank, with a counter surrounded by bars. There were guards, as well. If anyone thought to rob the place, they'd never make it ten feet before they were gutted.

Jack walked up to the counter and leaned an elbow on the wood. "Good day. You must be Mac."

"I am, sir."

"My name is Mulligan. I need some information."

The banker's eyes went huge. "Mulligan, as in . . ."

There were a hundred ways to finish that sentence. Instead of bothering, Jack gave the man an easy smile. "Listen, you know a man named von Briesen? German fellow." Justine slipped the paper sketch through the bars.

"No." Mac passed the paper back. "Sorry."

"We'll go upstairs to ask the women next, if that's all right."

"Sure." Mac pointed. "Polly's the woman in charge. Through that door there."

Jack started toward the door Mac had indicated— only to realize Justine wasn't with him. Instead, she was glued to the action in the betting room. Boys carried slips of paper back and forth from the screen in the corner to the wall. These were the race results, which were then written on the board. Minimum bets here were cheap, not like Jack's rooms, which made the World more affordable for the average Bowery resident.

"Do you own many poolrooms?" she asked.

He actually ran a syndicate of eighteen poolrooms throughout downtown and up to Twenty-Third Street. It was a lucrative business. "I do, yes."

"Are they like this?"

"Mine are a bit fancier." A Mulligan poolroom was carpeted, with free drinks and a buffet dinner. That attracted a higher, wealthier clientele, one that tended to stay a good long while. And that meant more money. "Have you ever bet on the races before?"

"I haven't. That's more Florence's tastes than mine."

"How do you know if you've never tried it?"

She lifted a delicate shoulder. "I fail to see the appeal. So, a horse comes in first, second or third. What is the fuss?"

Jack lifted a hand and beckoned one of the young boys. He withdrew five dollars. "The lady wishes to place a bet in the next race." Addressing Justine, he pointed to the board. Bets were being taken for the fifth race at Sheepshead Bay. "Pick a horse."

"Do we really have time for this?"

"There's as much time as you need. Choose a horse."

"Number three. It's my favorite number."

The boy wrote on a small slip of paper then handed the betting receipt to Justine. "Race is being called in a few minutes."

She continued to watch the crowd, so Jack cast a surreptitious glance over his shoulder and caught the eye of the bouncer behind the counter. He dropped a twenty-dollar bill on the wood then held up three fingers behind Justine's back, his brows raised meaningfully. The bouncer accepted the money and stepped out from behind the counter, hurrying toward the screen in the corner.

"Did you meet with the owner of the shirtwaist factory on Rivington?"

Jack's mouth hitched. *Meet* was certainly an interesting term for his interaction with Mr. Bay. "So, you went back."

"I did. Detective Ellison and I were surprised by the fresh air and unlocked doors. The women were laughing and smiling. Quite a difference."

Good. As long as Mr. Bay stuck to the agreement then Jack wouldn't need to return. "I am pleased to hear it."

"I don't understand. It usually takes Ellison two or three visits, showing his badge and making threats, to get a result. And yet you managed it in one."

"Haven't you learned by now who really has all the power in this city?"

"What does that mean?"

"It means that I am the man who gets things done in New York." Not a boast. Just a fact. He'd worked damn hard for it, too.

"Did you hit him?"

"No." It was true. Jack hadn't hit Bay. Generally, he didn't like to get blood on his suit if it could be avoided.

"Did someone *else* hit him, then?"

"Mon ange, don't ask how the soup is made if you like the way it tastes. Just enjoy it."

She let out a huff of breath. "That is a ridiculous answer. There would be no recipe books if that were true."

"It's an analogy. Relax, do not worry about Mr. Bay. Think of the happy workers who won't perish should a fire start on that floor."

"That is a grim thought."

"Life is grim. You should know that by now, considering all you've witnessed."

"Betting for the fifth is closed!" the man at the board shouted. This meant the race was about to start.

"About upstairs," he started. "Would you rather I went up alone and asked—?"

"Do not insult me." Her head whipped toward him, her brows pulled low. "I am not afraid to meet with these women. It won't be the first time—or the last."

There was the backbone. So angelic and fierce at the same time. He cleared his throat and tried not to drool. "Again, does your brother-in-law know what you're up to?"

She waved her hand. "We are wasting time. Let's go speak to this Polly."

"Wouldn't you like to see if you've won?"

"I suppose. Will it take long?"

He smothered a smile. She was adorable. "Mere seconds."

"And number three is the winner!" the man at the board announced a few seconds later. "Followed by numbers one and eight. See the window for your winnings."

She clutched Jack's arm. "I cannot believe it. I won. I've never won anything before."

"See?" He grinned, the happiness in her expression causing his belly to twist and turn. "Go, collect your winnings." He jerked his head toward Mac and the window.

She presented her receipt to Mac. "It appears I've won."

"Indeed you have, miss. Here you are." He slid forward a fifty-dollar bill.

"Oh, no. That can't be right." She turned to Jack. "Fifty dollars?"

"Guess number three had some long odds." Reaching out, he palmed the bill and presented it to her. "Congratulations. Thanks, fellows," he said to the men behind the counter and led her toward a side door.

It was time to go upstairs.

FIFTY DOLLARS. IT was unbelievable. "What am I supposed to do with this money?" The soup kitchen at the Bowery Mission could certainly use the help. Or Justine could donate it to one of the nearby schools. The legal aid society. One of the new settlement houses—

"No doubt there's a pretty dress or hat you've had your eye on," Mulligan said over his shoulder as they weaved through the crowded room.

She frowned at his back, though he couldn't see it. Didn't he know her at all? Her mother might care about new dresses and accessories, but Justine didn't. "That is not what I would spend my money on."

Stopping beside the door, he cocked his head as he examined her. "What if I ordered you to spend that money on yourself, for something selfish? Not for anyone else. What would you buy?"

Her mind blanked. Just yawning emptiness and fragments of thoughts. There wasn't a thing she wanted. Moreover, she came from privilege. If she desired clothing or jewelry, her family could afford it. "I don't know."

"Not one thing? A meal or a trip? A pair of earrings? New corset or stockings?" His gaze darted to her bosom and sparks tingled under her skin. Was he thinking about her breasts?

"I could never waste the money on me when I know others need it more." Her voice sounded strange, low and raspy. Had he noticed?

The way he stared at her—with a heat and intensity she felt everywhere, even the tips of her toes—said he absolutely had.

They stayed there, suspended in time, watching the other, as the moment stretched. He stood mere inches away, far closer than any decent man would dare in public. The thick fringe of his lashes, the slashing brows, full lips . . . all of it close enough to touch. To kiss. Her heart felt like it was trying to force its way out of her chest. She wished she knew what was going on in his head.

Stay and I'll make all your darkest dreams come true.

Was he remembering, too? She could hardly stop thinking about that promise and all the wicked possibilities it might entail.

"So pure," he murmured. "All that decentness is the worst kind of temptation to a man like me."

"Why?" she croaked.

Bending at the waist, he put his lips near her ear. "Because I want to sink inside and bathe myself in it, then destroy it."

She sucked in a ragged breath. Raw and erotic, his words raced through her like an electric current. Her nipples tightened to hard points in her clothing, her breasts heavy and full. Sakes alive, how could he say things like that aloud, in broad daylight?

Even so, she wouldn't run from him. She was stronger than he credited her for. "Perhaps it would have the opposite effect. Perhaps it could save you."

He straightened, his mouth twisting with a hint of what seemed like regret. "I am past the point of saving, *cara*." Before she could argue that no one was past the point of saving, he threw open the door to the second floor. "Up you go."

Exhaling, she started up the stairs. She'd never been so affected by a man before. Mulligan had a way of sliding under her skin and twisting her inside out. He also was proving to be efficient at solving her problems. She wasn't certain how to feel about that.

Haven't you learned by now who really has all the power in this city?

Nevertheless, she couldn't rely on him. He was not helping her out of the goodness of his heart.

Which reminded her. She now owed him another favor. God help her.

A woman appeared at the top of the stairs, her mouth turned into an unhappy frown at the sight of Justine. "Stop," she called. "You do not have permission to be up here—" Her lips curved when she spotted Mulligan. "Well, hello there, sir. Welcome to Polly's."

The woman sidled up to Mulligan on the landing and ran a hand down his lapel. "You look familiar. Have we met?"

"Doubtful," he said, unusually subdued. Normally, he oozed charm. "I am Jack Mulligan."

"Mr. Mulligan! Goodness, it is our lucky day. I am Polly, the purveyor of the fine entertainment on this floor. Now, my love. Tell me, what are you in the mood for? I've got girls of every type and background. Young and old, experienced and not. You can have two or even three, if you wish. I've heard the rumors."

Rumors? Justine's brain tripped on that word as she tried to make sense of it. Mulligan bedded multiple women . . . at a time? How did that even work?

"Tempting," he said with what sounded like

polite disinterest. "However, we are here to ask you and your girls about someone. A man. He has been missing for several weeks."

Polly's gaze narrowed on Justine. "What are you, a Pinkerton?"

"No, ma'am. I work for the Lower East Side Legal Aid Society. We're trying to find a Mr. von Briesen. Does that name sound familiar?"

"We don't get a lot of real names around here." She returned her attention to Mulligan. "My girls are very busy. This ain't the sort of thing we have time for."

"We have money," Justine blurted, needing to draw this woman's focus back to her. For some reason, she couldn't let Polly fawn all over Mulligan any longer. Best not to examine why.

"Well, I would certainly hope so. How much?"

"Fifty dollars."

Mulligan made a strangled noise in his throat. "Chérie, have I taught you nothing?"

Actually, no. He hadn't taught her anything. She took the newly acquired fifty-dollar bill out of her handbag and held it up. Polly went to grab it, but Justine jerked the paper out of reach. "After we speak with your girls."

Polly dropped the flirtatious manner like a hot iron. Instantly, she was brisk and all business. "Follow me."

She was going to be the death of him.

They would find him buried under the mounds of her blind trust and faith in humanity. It wasn't exactly naivete; no, she'd witnessed too much for that. But, she took people at their word. She believed the best of everyone.

Including him.

Not once had she asked why he was helping her. Hadn't questioned his motivation in aiding her little cause today. Because she believed he was good. Like her.

She'd find out his true motives soon enough. Because "good" didn't factor into it. Not by a long shot.

Polly led them to the back, probably to the salon. This was a room where potential clients gathered, looked the girls over before making a selection. *Run along, Jack. Mama's going to entertain her friend for a while.* How many times had he heard that as a boy? The men never even spared Jack a second look.

The sounds inside the house had been the worst, the grunts and slapping of bodies. The rattle of bed frames. After, the men would leave and the women would soak their bits in tubs or clean their cunts with syringes full of vinegar. Every now and then, they'd see the doctor for a cure or remedy. They had no choice but to take it, to endure. Coppers didn't care, either. In fact, many came by for freebies or bribes.

To his ten-year-old mind, it was like the entire world wanted to make money off what lay between a woman's legs . . . then punish them for it.

His mother told him he was wrong, that her life was better than most. Many women walked the streets with no protection or medical care whatsoever. Or, she could have been in a miserable marriage with a cruel man, an escape from which was nigh impossible. She was saving money so the two of them could move to Omaha. His mother had cousins there, and she talked for hours about this clean city with opportunities for work. Where they would live with fresh flowers and white picket fences.

Then she'd died from what they'd said was cancer. Before he was twelve, he'd been turned out on the street. Into the arms of the gangs he'd one day control, now with a brother to care for.

He shook off those morose memories as their little group reached the main salon.

"Are you all right?" Justine said out of the side of her mouth.

"Fine."

She paused and lingered on his face, watching him. "Would you prefer to wait downstairs?"

"And leave you here alone? Absolutely not."

Now in the room, she put a hand up to block her mouth and dropped her voice. "It's a room full of women, Mulligan. I think I'll be safe."

He'd heard numerous stories over the years that might point to the contrary, but he didn't mention as much. Instead, he marveled at her concern. For him. When was the last time someone had worried about him? His throat tightened and he cleared it, shoving away any pesky tenderness. "Stop coddling me and get to your questioning."

"You know, if you weren't smiling right now, I might take offense to being ordered around."

"Ladies," Polly was saying. "This is Mr. Mulligan and his friend. They wish to ask you all a few questions."

Jack looked carefully around the room. The women were young but appeared well cared for. No bruises that he could see. They were smiling and clear-eyed, their dresses old but clean. The tension between his shoulder blades eased somewhat. He still didn't like it, but he wouldn't need to intervene.

Justine presented her sketch to the girls on the left side of the room. "Ladies, I am searching for a Mr. von Briesen. Here's a sketch of what he looks like. Please pass it along, if you will. He is German. Has a wife and two small children. They are quite concerned about him since his disappearance."

Each girl studied the picture, shook her head and passed it on. It wasn't until the next to the last girl before they had a reaction.

"Oh, I know him," she said with a nod. "He's the shoemaker. Every Thursday like clockwork."

"When did he stop coming to see you?" Jack asked.

"He hasn't. Was just here last week."

"We were told he was robbed by some peter players downstairs and put out on the street."

"Not that I heard." The girl exchanged a look with Polly. "That is to say, we don't have peter players here."

Jack nearly snorted at the bald lie. "Can you tell us anything about him? Where he lives, for example?"

"I know he likes his bum hole tickled while he's getting sucked off." All the girls laughed and clapped, and Justine turned a bright shade of scarlet. Jack hid a smile.

"Anything that might help us locate him?" Justine asked. "A neighborhood or family member he talks about?"

The girl shrugged. "None that I am able to recall."

Jack could see the direction this was headed. It was already Tuesday. "What time does he usually arrive on Thursdays?"

"Nine o'clock," the girl answered. "Might be a few minutes early but he's never late."

"I'll be here to have a chat with him. Do not say anything to alert him or give him cause to disappear until I arrive. Is that clear?" He glared at both Polly and the girl so there would be no misunderstanding.

"I'll come, as well," Justine said. Jack didn't contradict her, but under no circumstances would he allow her to return here during the evening. Jack would deal with von Briesen himself.

"You'll need to pay for the time," Polly said.

Jack nodded once. "I'm good for it."

"I bet you are, sweetheart," one of the women drawled.

Everyone laughed, including Justine, and Jack had a sudden urge to get her alone. He wanted to kiss her smiles and swallow her laughter. He wanted her all to himself. He tipped his chin toward the exit. "We should go."

"Thank you, ladies," Justine said, withdrawing the fifty-dollar bill from her purse. "You've helped us immensely."

Before she could hand the bill to Polly, Jack snatched it. "See that it's evenly distributed," he said to the proprietress. "Fairly and equally."

Though she paled, Polly gave a brisk nod. Jack pressed the money into her palm. "Ladies, that money is for all of you. I'll check on Thursday to make certain you all received an equal share." He paused for effect. "And if you haven't, if even one of you has been cheated, there will be consequences." The last bit was directed at Polly.

Convinced he'd made his point, he led Justine out of the room and toward the stairs. It was time to collect on his good deed.

Chapter Twelve

Justine could sense Mulligan's dark mood. Something had changed in him the instant they'd entered the second floor. He was no longer his charming, congenial self. Instead, his eyes had gone flat, his shoulders bunched. An air of anger and resentment had clung to him like an overcoat.

When they reached the street, he gestured toward his brougham lingering at the curb. "Come along," he said. "We'll drop you wherever you're headed."

She didn't argue. A ride to the train would be faster than walking. Also, she was curious as to what had caused the shift in his personality. Perhaps she could drag it out of him on the ride.

"Afternoon, miss." Rye tipped his hat as they approached. "Where are you headed?"

"I suppose I'm done for the day. The elevated station will do."

"That's ridiculous," Mulligan said as he handed her up. "We'll take her uptown, Rye."

"I couldn't ask that." She settled into the seat and watched as he smoothly folded his lanky frame into the tiny interior. "You must have other more pressing things to do than to take me all the way home."

"Of course, but that is the best part of being me. I may do whatever I wish, whenever I wish."

She chuckled. There was a bit of his old spark. He removed his derby and rapped on the side. The wheels began to turn, leading them away from the World Poolroom.

He was quiet, which only confirmed her suspicions that something was off. But she was distracted, as well. His large thigh pressed against her leg, their shoulders locked tight. Everywhere they touched now prickled, like ants were crawling over her skin. Why was there no air in this dashed carriage?

She dug for her fan and tried to cool herself. "Tell me why you were so uncomfortable up there."

"What do you mean?"

"At first I thought you were worried about my safety or reputation. But the longer we stayed I realized it was something else."

"You're imagining things."

"Hardly. I know you well enough by now to see a difference in your moods."

He shifted, his body crowding hers in the most delicious way. "I hadn't realized we were so intimate, mon ange."

"And you're attempting to deflect my question with flirtation." Her heart thumped in her chest, the strings on her corset growing tighter by the second. She tried to breathe deeply, keep the blood flowing to her brain.

"Is it working?"

"No," she lied and pushed at his chest with her palms. "Stay to your side, Mulligan."

He sighed dramatically but allowed her to put distance between them. "It's decidedly less fun on my side, though. Are you certain I cannot crawl onto yours?"

Goodness, he was alluring, always knowing just what to say to draw a smile out of her. But she would not be distracted. "Tell me. Please."

"Haven't I done enough for you today? Now I must bare my soul, as well? We haven't even discussed my repayment."

Oh, that. She'd nearly forgotten about their wager. They had been a formidable team this afternoon, investigating side by side to find Mr. von Briesen. It had been nice. For a brief moment, she'd almost believed he acted out of a sense of responsibility toward her. Perhaps even a touch of affection.

I am a man who deals in favors.

Idiot. How could she have believed his actions were anything other than a way to gain control over her? That was Mulligan's modus operandi. He did nothing out of the kindness of his heart.

And that made her realize something else. "I didn't really win that fifty dollars, did I?"

Surprise flashed across his features before he masked it. "Your horse came in first, didn't it?"

His reaction confirmed it. Somehow Mulligan had rigged that race. "Was the scene outside the poolroom also your doing?" He'd arrived quite quickly, after all.

"Why would I do such a thing?"

"To gain another favor from me. You were so eager to suggest the wager."

"Because it was impossible I'd lose. And I like having you in my debt."

"Why?"

His expression turned positively predatory, like he was ready to devour her. She shivered under his hot blue stare, unable to look away. "Isn't it obvious?" he said. "You're a beautiful and charismatic woman. What man wouldn't angle to have you at his mercy?"

The memory of his tongue on her skin caused goose bumps to travel all over her body. She felt off balance, like she'd been thrown into the deep part of the lake without learning how to swim first. There was no pamphlet or guidebook for what was happening. No map or report. Merely these huge, impossible feelings inside her, ones much too big for her flesh to contain.

She wasn't ready. Whatever this was, it was happening too fast.

In an attempt to regain control of the situation, she said, "Tell me about what happened on the second floor. Then we'll discuss your favor."

"You are very tenacious when you want something, cara. I almost pity those wife deserters. They do not stand a chance."

"Fine." She turned to the window, done with this maddening conversation. If he didn't trust her enough to be honest with her, then there was no reason to pester him. He could keep his glower and his secrets. See if she cared.

The brougham crossed Houston Street. Would she really have to ride in silence all the way to upper Fifth Avenue?

Mulligan heaved a sigh. "Christ, you are maddening." He pounded on the glass behind Rye's back. "Bond Street instead."

Rye darted a glance over his shoulder and Justine could see the surprise in his expression. "Are you sure?" he asked. "Because I'm thinkin'—"

"Do as I say," Jack said calmly. "And watch the street."

She frowned, unsure about this new direction. "What is on Bond Street? Are we shopping?"

"Do you know how to bowl?"

She opened her mouth to answer—then promptly closed it. Bowling? Was he serious? "Uh, yes. I do. I mean, I've been once. With my sisters. When we were young."

His lips curled into a satisfied smirk. "Good. I've decided on my favor."

"Oh. We're to bowl one of these days?"

"No. We're to bowl now."

"Now?"

"I earned this favor fair and square, Justine. And I've decided that bowling it shall be. Right now."

"On Bond Street?"

"Yes."

Was there a bowling alley on Bond Street? She wasn't certain. The area was in the heart of Mulligan's kingdom. Returning there at night wasn't exactly wise, even if she had him by her side. Though he was just as dangerous, but for different reasons.

Stay and I'll make all your darkest dreams come true.

Sakes alive, she'd nearly collapsed at his feet, overcome with lust.

With a mental shake of her head, she relaxed in the plush seat. She was overreacting. It was merely bowling. With other people doing the same on the adjoining lanes. Mulligan couldn't possibly seduce her in such a scenario.

A pang went through her and she ducked her head, mortified. Goodness, had that been disappointment?

They turned along Bond Street and she peered out the window. "Is the bowling alley on this block?"

"No."

The brougham began to slow. That made no sense. "Are we stopping?"

He watched out the window, his hand on the latch. "Do you always ask so many questions?"

"Only when others are purposely evasive."

The vehicle jerked to a stop. Mulligan threw open the door and hopped down to the walk. He held out a hand for her.

This block was residential. There were no businesses here, and certainly no bowling alley. "I don't understand."

"Come along, do-gooder."

With a huff, she accepted his help in getting down. He led her up the steps to one of the largest houses on the block. A beautiful limestone structure with large windows and elegant cornices. Definitely not a bowling alley. When he produced a key from his pocket, she frowned. "Wait, who lives here?"

The lock clicked and he turned the brass knob. "I do."

JACK HADN'T EVER brought a woman here. Hell, he never brought *anyone* here.

No one knew of his home, except Rye and Cooper. Everyone else believed he lived on the top floor of the athletic club because it was off-limits to just about everyone but Jack. And there was a bed on that floor, one he used often but not for sleeping.

Instead, he resided a block over, here on Bond Street, in the former mansion of a wealthy merchant who'd moved uptown more than a decade ago. Jack bought the place because he'd discovered a tunnel that ran under his club leading to this property a block away. The tunnel had been reinforced and this passage allowed him to travel back and forth at will. Such tunnels existed all over Five Points and Lower Manhattan, but he never told a soul about his.

So, hard to say why he'd brought Justine here tonight. Except he wished to spend more time with her, away from prying eyes. Somewhere they could be absolutely alone.

And his world, his rules. Whatever he wanted, he got.

"Wait a moment." Justine stepped inside his home, her head swiveling. "You live here. You, Mulligan, the bogeyman of downtown, live *here*?"

"Yes, though I'm not certain *bogeyman* is the right word to describe me."

"What word would you prefer, then?"

"King."

She laughed, her face full of joy, so heart-stoppingly beautiful, that his mouth dried out. "America doesn't have kings."

"Just wait." The entire country would know him when he took the brewery nationwide. The only two things Americans cared about were alcohol and money. He would soon have a lot of both.

Then Justine sobered, as she looked around at

the cavernous entry and the darkened rooms. "Do you have servants?"

"No. Maids come in once a week but that's it. Are you scared to be alone with me?"

"Should I be?"

"Ma belle, I would never hurt you or ask you to do anything that frightens you. Rye will come in after seeing to the horses. However, if you want to leave, he will drive you home."

"But I won't get to see your house."

"That's true. You also won't get to bowl with me."

"You have a bowling alley here?" He nodded, and she continued, "You actually bowl?"

"Indeed—and if you tell anyone I'll deny it until my dying breath."

That caused her to giggle and he'd never seen her look happier. Heart pounding, he was utterly charmed. Dazzled. Unable to take his eyes off her. The young boy he'd never been wished to pick posies for her or dip her hair in ink.

The man he was now longed to drop to his knees and suck on her clitoris until her eyes rolled back in her head.

Fuck, he had to stop. He needed to remain distant, keep his urges under control. Not scare her or intimidate her. This was no widow or barmaid. Justine was an uptown princess with an altruistic streak. He couldn't forget that.

"So, what's it going to be?" he asked.

"I don't know." She bit her bottom lip in that adorable way she had of doing. "I should return home. It's getting late."

"Not so late. Besides, I thought your parents were away."

"Yes, they are in Europe. But my sister . . ." He shot her a disbelieving look and she smiled. "You're right. No doubt Florence is out, too, and Granny had other plans."

"Then there's no reason to leave." She still didn't appear convinced, so he turned the screws. "When was the last time you did something hedonistic? Something just for yourself?"

Stay here.

Join me.

Let me show you how much fun we can have together.

"Fine. One game, then I'll go."

A dark thrill shot through his veins, the sweet taste of victory like a drug in his system. "One game and then you'll go. Follow me."

The house was dark but he knew the corridors well. He threw switches to illuminate their way as they twisted and turned toward the stairs that led to the basement. Once downstairs, he flipped on the lights surrounding the two bowling lanes.

They were beauties, with glossy oak floors and white wooden pins at the opposite end. A groove flanked each lane. A high bench allowed a place for a pin boy to cool his heels between throws. Jack used the lanes every few weeks, bowling by himself to relax.

"This is stunning," she said. "What fun."

"I thought you might like it. Do you remember how to play?"

"Roll the ball and knock pins over, correct?"

"Basically, yes. Let's get started." He shrugged out of his topcoat and tossed it onto the back of a chair. She examined him through her lashes, as if she didn't wish to stare but couldn't look away.

Interesting. He took full advantage—how could he resist?—by removing his cufflinks, slipping them in his pocket and slowly rolling his shirtsleeves up his arms. *Look your fill, little do-gooder.*

She suddenly presented him with her back, then unpinned and removed her small hat. Now it was his turn to gawk. Light glinted off the strands, and he noted a fascinating mix of colors, from honey to wheat, chestnut to auburn. Was it a trick of the lighting, or was her hair as complicated as the woman herself?

More importantly, what would all that glory look like swirling about her creamy shoulders?

She smoothed her skirts and avoided his gaze. "What's first?"

"Choose your ball." There were eight to decide between, all in varying degrees of heaviness. "One you can lift easily."

She took her time. He dropped into the chair behind the scoring table and enjoyed watching her, here in his home. Another person in his space should have made him nervous. Hundreds of people in this city would pay good money to learn where Jack slept. Yet, he wasn't worried about his secret in Justine's capable hands. The woman always did the right thing. Nobler than a nun. If he asked her not to inform anyone of his address, he was absolutely certain she wouldn't spill.

Her bustle twitched as she moved, her waist begging for a man to span it with his hands. She bent over . . . and he nearly groaned. *Sweet Jesus.* That brought forth recent fantasies starring her arse and his palms.

He needed to move this along before an erection

prevented any bowling whatsoever. "Try the dark brown one," he said, his voice low and rough.

"Stop rushing me."

The sass did little to ease the lust simmering beneath his skin. She might have the nobility of a nun, but she had the fire of a three-star general. Damn, if that contradiction didn't arouse him.

"Ready."

She held the dark brown ball, but he made no comment as to selecting his suggestion. With the flick of a switch he powered up the lanes. Light ran above the alleys and pins, making everything easier to see.

Rye entered at that point, and Jack suspected his second-in-command had been lurking in the basement until this precise moment. Jack tipped his chin. "We're ready for you back there."

"Right-io," Rye said with a small salute. He walked down the lane, around the pins, and jumped up on the bench to wait.

Jack swept his hand out. "After you."

Chapter Thirteen

Good heavens. He'd merely removed his coat and Justine was suddenly sweating. Had the temperature in the room climbed by forty degrees?

Mulligan had a bowling alley. In his *fancy house.* Never would she have imagined it. He was so much more than he appeared. Dangerous, yes, but he was also intelligent and cultured. Kind, as evidenced by his speech at the fundraiser. And something about him set her stomach afire every time he walked into a room.

Taking a deep breath, she decided to focus on this one game. Then she could return home and . . . What? Face an empty house? Perhaps Mulligan was right. Perhaps she would benefit from a little hedonism.

Honestly, though, bowling wasn't what came to mind when she considered a walk down Hedonism Lane. She'd pictured sweaty limbs and passionate kisses. A big bed and hooded blue eyes. Bowling felt more like a turn along Spinster Alley.

Stop complaining. Do you wish for him to ravish you right on the lanes?

She sort of did, actually.

Oh, she was perfectly aware that she wasn't the kind of woman to inspire passion in a man, but it would be nice just *once* to drown in desire. Billy had kissed her a few times, but they had been tepid, almost polite kisses. Perfunctory. Boring. She hadn't craved his touch or kiss like women were supposed to. Florence and Mamie discussed these things all the time when they thought Justine wasn't listening, so she knew women lusted every bit as fiercely as men.

But, the most desire she'd ever felt was the other night when Mulligan had licked that spot behind her ear. One quick press of his tongue—and she'd nearly combusted. Then she'd run away.

He must have thought her a complete fool.

Exhaling, she pushed all those worries aside. She couldn't change the past, anyway.

So, bowling. Her one attempt had been ages ago. But, really, how hard could it be? Roll ball, hit pins. She started to step onto the lane.

"Oh no, you don't."

Mulligan's deep voice startled her. "Have I done something wrong?"

He crooked a finger at her, his expression slightly devious. "You cannot step on my lanes in those boots."

Her black low-heeled boots? They were practical, everyday shoes. Not fancy in the least. "Why not?"

"They'll ruin the wood, cara. Come here."

Confused, she closed the distance between them. Was she going to sit this game out? What was happening?

He patted the seat next to him. "Sit down."

Oh. Disappointment pressed on her chest, just like all the times her sisters had excluded her from fun in the past. They thought Justine hadn't noticed or cared, but she had.

She dropped into the seat and presented the ball to him. "Here you go. I'll watch you."

"No, that isn't what I mean." He took the ball from her and set it on the ground. Then strong fingers wrapped around her ankle. She squeaked and tried to jerk away. "Stop," he said. "All I am doing is removing your boot."

"You cannot remove my boot. It's . . . improper."

Straightening, he lifted her foot and placed it on his knee. She stared at her boot . . . resting on Mulligan's leg. Her heart galloped in her chest, a wild rhythm keeping time in this unchartered territory. When she met his gaze, she was surprised to find him watching her intently, the lines of his face stark. His expression gave nothing away, yet she shivered all the same.

His big hands held her foot steady. "I won't do anything against your wishes, but you cannot bowl in these shoes. If you don't turn an ankle, you'll damage the wood."

She swallowed, unsure. Casting a glance at Rye over her shoulder, she was relieved to see the driver was reading a book, not paying attention to her and Mulligan in the least. What was the harm in removing her footwear? Did she really wish to refuse and cut the evening short?

No.

"You're right." Removing her own shoes while

still dressed was near impossible, but she had to try. She stretched forward as far as her corset allowed, sucking in to reach her laces.

"Wait." He waved her away. "Will you allow me?"

She dropped her arms. This was silly. He was asking to remove her shoes, not her drawers. She tried to relax. "Yes, please."

He shifted her skirts to completely reveal the boot, while the rest of her leg remained covered. Graceful fingers plucked at the knot at the top, undoing it. Then he began to unlace the strings. The muscles of his forearm shifted as he worked, and she couldn't take her eyes away from that patch of skin. Veins and tendons moved under skin that was lightly covered in dark hair. For a man steeped in the city's underworld, he certainly had long, capable fingers that were surprisingly gentle.

He slid the string out of the eyelets, left then right, left then right, loosening her shoe. His free hand held her foot steady. It was so . . . intimate. Warmth slid through her, building behind her sternum and sliding into her stomach. Then lower, between her legs. Every inch of her felt restless and on edge, excitement coiling in her limbs. The more laces that were undone, the more *she* was undone.

Her eyes drifted to the sight of his strong thigh encased in dark blue wool. The fabric molded to his leg and she could see he wasn't rangy or thin. No, he was solid. Powerful. Impressive.

Sweet mercy, why was that so arousing?

When the laces came loose, he dragged her boot off gradually, as if he didn't wish to rush the process. Was he enjoying this, too? Her stocking-covered ankle came into view, then the top of her foot. Finally her toes. They both held perfectly still, silent, as the boot hit the ground.

Neither of them moved. It shouldn't have felt so extraordinary—it was merely her foot, for heaven's sake—and yet it did. The sheer silk stockings hid nothing and she could *feel* the heat pouring off him under her leg. She had the insane desire to slide her silk-covered toes all along the slope of his inner thigh. Then even higher . . .

Oh, Lord.

That shouldn't sound so delicious.

She closed her eyes in an effort to collect herself. Without warning, the backs of his knuckles brushed her instep. She sucked in a breath, her lids flying open, as tingles trailed in his wake.

He froze, his hand in midair. "Have I hurt you?"

"No." She tried to sound casual but most likely failed.

"I apologize." He lifted her foot and placed it on the ground. "I got carried away. I shouldn't have touched you."

Some wild urge prompted her to blurt, "I didn't mind."

Don't stop.

Touch me.

Lick me again.

The thoughts came lightning fast as a flood of wanting crashed through her.

He picked up her other foot and brought it to his knee. "You shouldn't encourage a man like me."

"What do you mean, a man like you?"

"A man who can be ruthless when he sees something he wants."

She couldn't think of anything to say. Was he

hinting that he wanted her? Or that he *might* want her? It was maddening.

What man wouldn't angle to have you at his mercy?

He made quick work of her second boot, then put her foot down and straightened. She wiggled her toes against the wooden floor and watched him through her lashes. After toeing off his shoes, he strode to select his own bowling ball from the rack. He wore blue silk socks that matched the color of his trousers, his feet long and narrow. How . . . fascinating.

When he turned, he put the two bowling balls on the wooden track at their lane. Then he swept his arm out. "Ladies first."

EIGHT PINS TUMBLED to the back of the lane. Rye hustled to gather them while Justine jumped and clapped. Spinning, she pointed at Jack. "Take that, Mulligan!"

Jack couldn't help but grin back at her. He couldn't remember the last time he'd had this much fun.

Whatever she lacked in bowling experience she made up for in total dedication. She asked for tips and concentrated on implementing them. Then laughed at herself easily when she failed, cheered loudly when she succeeded. He was absolutely mesmerized.

Best of all, he hadn't thought about the club or the books or Trevor O'Shaughnessy in hours. The noise in his head, the worries that dogged him daily, was quiet tonight. It was easy to be with her. Relaxing. She was funny and charming, completely at ease with him.

Even after he'd made such a fool of himself when removing her boot. *What a disaster.*

He'd removed plenty of women's clothing over the years. Hell, he could undress and dress a woman in the dark with gloves on, if necessary. But there was something about Justine's delicate foot—so tempting in her fancy silk stocking—that had nearly driven him over the edge.

Which was ludicrous. It was a foot, no different than any other woman's foot. And yet, it had been different. Because the foot belonged to Justine. Somehow that sight had caused arousal to spike in his groin.

He was beginning to fear his reaction to her. He seemed to lose his mind every time he was in her presence. No matter how often he told himself she wasn't for him, his body had other ideas. God help him if this woman ever decided she'd like a night in his bed. He'd probably come in his trousers.

She dropped into the chair next to him, her skin glowing from exertion. How in hell had he ever thought her plain?

"Nicely done. You are improving."

"I won't beat you, of course, but at least I've stopped throwing them in the gutter." Her first five balls had gone directly to the side.

"Progress, chérie. Progress."

Rising, he lifted his ball, aimed, then stepped and threw it. All ten pins crashed into the back of the lane, causing Rye to flinch.

"Easy, Mulligan!" Rye called. "I don't fancy a trip to the bonesetter!"

Justine clapped for Jack, as well. "Outstanding,"

she said when he returned to their seats. "How did you ever learn to do that?"

He lifted a shoulder. "I asked."

"Who? The best bowler in the city?"

"Yes," he said, completely serious. "He owed me a favor and I asked for instruction in exchange."

"Don't tell me. I don't wish to hear any more of your deals."

"I got his wife a job at city hall. Not all my *deals* are of a criminal nature."

"Just most of them."

He chuckled, even though she was poking fun at him. When was the last time someone had dared? Justine kept him on his toes, certainly.

She approached the lane then glanced over her shoulder. "Will you teach me?"

"To bowl?"

"Yes. Show me all of your tricks, Mulligan."

Oh, cara. If only. He'd keep her in bed for *weeks*.

He rose slowly. "We have only one more frame. Are you certain you don't wish to finish this game?" *And then leave?* He didn't voice the latter, but she hadn't exactly been thrilled to stay tonight. There was no sense in pushing and scaring her. He'd much rather use patience and cunning to win her over.

And he would win her over. It was only a matter of time before he got her in bed. He'd decided as much about two frames ago.

"All the more reason to finish strong in the last frame. Come on."

Now at the mouth of the lane, he shoved his hands in his trouser pockets. "First, you're trying to roll the ball directly down the middle. Bowling is about angles, speed and rotation. The best way to get all the pins is to hit them slightly off-center."

Her brows lowered as she thought about this. "That is why your ball swings out to the right at first and then curves back in."

"Correct. To do that, you have to turn your hand as you release the ball. Flick your wrist over your thumb."

"That doesn't make any sense." She examined her ball.

"Here, let me show you." He took her ball and put his two fingers in the holes. It was a tight fit, but he showed her what he meant, how you had to create the proper rotation for the ball to curve. "When you release it, move like this."

"Let me try." With the ball in her hand, she rotated her hand to the side. "Like this?"

As if it were the most natural thing in the world, he moved behind her and started to reach for her hands. Then he paused. "May I show you?"

"Please."

He cupped his hands over hers on the ball, his arms surrounding her. "You're almost there. Do this." He showed her the best motion to get both spin and rotation. "Feel that?"

She didn't respond, just nodded. With her back pressed against his chest, her body was caged between his arms. He stood, rooted to the spot. He didn't want to let her go. She smelled clean and bright, like flowers and freshness. Like someone unsullied by everything dark and cold in this city. He longed to breathe her in, just inhale until his lungs were full of her scent, so he'd never forget it.

Then he remembered her mad dash out of the club when he'd pressed his tongue to her skin.

He couldn't rush her. Or coerce her. Whatever happened between them had to be consensual, with her full participation. Better yet, he preferred if she initiated it.

Easing his grip, he started to step back. "Now you—"

"Wait." She clutched his arm with her free hand. "Show me one more time."

Satisfaction shot through him. He pulled his arms tighter, closer, and put his mouth to her ear. "Like this," he whispered.

Before he could blink, she relinquished the ball to his palms and spun around. Her hands landed on his shoulders, her mouth inches from his. Fire licked through his groin, swift and hot, and he'd never wanted anyone more. This virginal uptown princess—an angel, a perpetual do-gooder—had turned him inside out. He couldn't tell if he hoped a little of her goodness would rub off on him . . . or if he prayed his wickedness rubbed off on her.

Perhaps both.

He studied her flushed face and the pulse pounding in her neck. "You're missing the lesson."

"I'd rather have a different lesson right now."

"What kind of lesson, cara?"

"The one where you stop talking."

She didn't wait. Rising on her toes, she crushed her mouth to his. It was clumsy, but the effect was like being punched in the chest by a fistful of brass knuckles. She robbed him of breath.

Jesus God, she'd kissed him. Was *still* kissing him. And it was better than he'd imagined. She was lush and sweet and responsive, her lips soft and determined as they moved over his, learning him. Had he assumed her inexperienced? He'd been a fool, then. Because the way she was kissing right now had him hard and aching in seconds.

He dropped the ball on the ground with a thud. Wood was likely damaged, but who fucking cared? Holding her jaw in his palms, he dipped his head and dove at her like a dying man. He kissed her deep then changed the angle, only to continue kissing her some more. Everything in him focused on this one place, on *her*. He didn't ever want to stop.

Somehow their mouths opened and his tongue found hers. Or maybe hers found his. He didn't know but he was damn grateful. His tongue wound around hers, stroking and rubbing, while her fingernails dug into his shoulders. His chest heaved, lungs screaming for air, but he couldn't stop. He'd been waiting for this for so long—years, it seemed—and he meant to keep going as long as possible. Because he was a greedy bastard, he wanted everything she had to give.

Perhaps more.

Then she broke away, putting space between them, and his stomach sank. This was when she'd retreat. Run away again, leaving him to contemplate what might have been.

Silent, he merely tried to catch his breath. She glanced behind him. "Is there . . . ? Could we sit somewhere? My legs are feeling a bit weak."

She wasn't trying to leave? Blinking, he put the pieces together. She was asking to sit so that she might stay longer. "Of course," he rushed out.

"I forgot about Rye." She craned her neck toward the end of the lanes. "Is he still there?"

Rye had been wise enough to depart when Jack had started kissing Justine. "No. He left quite some time ago." Taking her hand, he led her to an armchair against the back wall. He dropped into the seat and, before she could complain, pulled her onto his lap. "Is this better?"

"Much. Does this mean you're interested in continuing?"

Chapter Fourteen

Justine held her breath while awaiting his answer. The moment felt huge and important, the beginning of something momentous. All she knew was she desperately needed more of Mulligan's kisses. Though if he refused, she could hardly complain. She had attacked the man, after all.

With his free hand, he swept his thumb over her lips, up over the slope of her cheekbone, then down to the curve of her jaw. It was as if he were mapping her face with his fingertips. "You are so lovely," he said, his voice deep and gruff. Not his usual cultured tone at all.

He was being kind, and she was grateful for it. "Thank you. I know I'm not—"

"Stop. If you are about to disparage yourself, I do not want to hear it. Not now, not ever, mon ange."

Her heart tripped over itself in her chest as it expanded and solidified. She wouldn't be surprised if he could see her heart beating through the layers of clothing. "Mulligan," she breathed, unable to say more than that one word. She hoped he understood what he was doing to her.

"Jack."

"What?"

Leaning in, he dragged his nose along her neck, and she heard him inhale. Was he smelling her? "Say my first name when you sigh like that."

She bit her lip, trying not to smile, and met his eyes through her lashes. "Jack."

"Perfect." He gave her a swift kiss. "Christ, you are utterly perfect."

He took her mouth again, using his lips and teeth and tongue to scramble her brains. She no longer feared herself incapable of passion. Jack had her panting, straining, *dying* for more. Her breasts were heavy, aching behind her corset, her body straining toward his. Desire pooled between her legs, and she could feel her pulse like an insistent drumbeat in that one spot, calling for attention. Demanding satisfaction.

His hand dropped to her hip, and she nearly vibrated with the need for him to touch her somewhere. Anywhere.

Everywhere.

Since the moment he removed her boot, she'd been thinking about when he might kiss her. For a brief, horrifying minute it had seemed like the night might end with bowling. Thank God it hadn't. Any embarrassment over throwing herself at him was worth it for *this*.

Because Jack Mulligan knew how to kiss exceedingly well. The right amount of pressure, not wet or sloppy. Enticing but not overwhelming. A girl might walk through fire for a few moments of recklessness with this man. No matter what happened between them after tonight, she would never regret this.

His mouth drifted to her jaw then along the sensitive skin of her neck. Teeth scraped between hot openmouthed kisses. His hand moved from her hip to cover her ribs. He dropped his forehead onto her shoulder, his breath every bit as labored as hers. "What do you want tonight?"

There was quite a long list, actually. "Must I say it out loud?"

"Yes, you must. I cannot read your mind and I'd rather not guess. I may intimidate others into doing what I wish, but I'd never intimidate you."

"What do *you* want tonight?" She sank her teeth into his earlobe and felt a tremor go through him. Nice to know she could affect him, as well.

He kissed her shoulder. "I wouldn't like to scare you. It's better if you tell me instead."

"You cannot scare me. Haven't you learned that by now?"

"Chérie, I touched my tongue to your skin and you ran from the club like it was on fire."

"I was merely caught off guard, not scared. Not to mention, you've done a lot more with your tongue tonight and I haven't run screaming."

"Yet."

"Jack, come on." She nudged his shoulder. "I am braver than I appear."

"Really?"

His voice was laced with sarcasm and she couldn't tell if he was teasing her. "Indeed."

"I know you are brave—I knew it within seconds of meeting you—but there is *brave* and then there is *daring*. The latter requires fearlessness with a sense of adventure."

"You think I lack a sense of adventure?"

"I think you are a woman who gives much of

herself to others without considering what she wants most."

He was annoyingly correct. However, considering her wants and desires almost seemed selfish. No one, other than Jack, had ever encouraged her to try. "What I want right now is for you to tell me what you'd like to do, regardless of whether it scares me or not."

"Do not say I didn't warn you." He pressed his tongue in the same spot as the other night, perhaps to test her. She didn't run this time, merely leaned in to get closer. He growled, his chest rumbling, fingers digging into her sides, and he put his mouth near her ear. "I'd start by leading you to my bedroom. I've never had a woman there and I'm keen to see you spread out on my bed. I'd undress you, of course, until you were in just your stockings. Then I want to feel your silk-covered feet digging into my back as I'm tonguing your pussy."

She inhaled sharply, her lids sweeping closed on a wave of lust so strong that she nearly moaned. She'd never heard anyone speak such words. She should probably feel appalled or embarrassed. Marginally horrified. Yet, she *loved* it.

The devil kept going. "I want to suck on your clit until you come on my tongue. I want to lap up your juices and smell your sweetness until I'm drowning in it."

God in heaven, she could almost imagine it. She'd seen the cards under Florence's bed, so she knew adults fornicated in many different positions. Never had she considered the possibility of him putting his mouth between her legs. Was this something all couples performed?

While she may not have known about it a few

minutes ago, her body now longed for it. She and Billy hadn't done more than some kissing and casual groping. Orgasms had taken place in her bed at night, alone. What would it feel like if someone else pleasured you? Was it better?

Something told her Jack would be very, very good at it.

She shuddered and sighed, her body melting into his. "I want that, too."

He straightened, nearly sending her off his lap and onto the floor. "You . . . what?"

"Oh, is it selfish of me to ask for it? Should I offer to—?"

"No! Jesus fuck, allowing me to pleasure you would be the greatest gift I've ever received." Slipping his free hand under her knees, he stood in one fluid motion and began carrying her toward the stairs. "Asking for what you want is not selfish. None of this is about who wins or loses. We don't keep score. If any man ever tries to tell you otherwise, he deserves to be beaten."

"Are you really taking me to your bedroom?" She wrapped her arms around his neck. "Am I about to see where the legendary Jack Mulligan sleeps?"

He started up the main staircase. "Other than the maids and me, you will be the only other person to see it."

"And they say you aren't romantic."

His laugh echoed off the intricate plaster ceilings. "Cara, I am about to show you more romance than your little body can possibly handle."

"MORE ROMANCE THAN I can handle? Goodness, someone is full of hyperbole tonight."

Jack grinned as he managed the rest of the steps. Christ, his little do-gooder had spirit. He'd show her. Never once had he made an idle threat. If it killed him tonight, she'd regret taunting him. *No mercy.*

At the landing, he hurried to the large master suite in the back of the house. His bedroom was dark, full of the shadows he preferred. Tonight, however, he needed to see, to catch every moment of her pleasure. He didn't want to miss a single second of it.

So he placed Justine on the bed and went to the windows, throwing open the drapes. Moonlight filtered in, brightening the room just enough for his memories and her comfort.

Once on the bed, he reached for her, pulled her close to him and kissed her. Gently at first, until she softened, her lips growing hot and eager, and then he slipped his tongue in her mouth, desperate to taste her. The kiss dragged on, their bodies flush, and he had to keep from grinding his erection into her thigh. He couldn't remember the last time he'd been this worked up.

She was actually here. In his bedroom. Where he'd brought himself off many times merely thinking about her. It was too fantastic to believe.

She rubbed her toes against his shins in the most delicious way. He couldn't wait to feel those silk stockings on his back and shoulders in a few minutes. He paused, panting above her mouth. "May I undress you?" When she hesitated, he said, "It's fine to change your mind, you know."

"I haven't changed my mind. I've been thinking about this for a while."

Oh, these were thoughts he needed to hear. In great detail. "You have? And what exactly have you been thinking about?"

"You told me you'd make all my darkest dreams come true." She scraped her teeth over his bottom lip. "I spent a lot of time imagining what that might entail."

He cupped her breast through her clothing, pleased when she arched into his touch. "Did your imaginings involve touching yourself?"

"Of course."

Closing his eyes, he struggled to keep his wits about him. The idea of Justine using her fingers to pleasure herself was an image he'd relive later when he was alone. With his cock in his fist.

"So, you haven't changed your mind," he confirmed. When she shook her head, he asked, "Would you rather leave your clothes on?"

"But I thought you needed . . ."

"I don't actually need them off. That was merely my fantasy."

"I want you to enjoy this, so if that is your fantasy, then yes."

"Cara, I will enjoy this no matter what. You should be comfortable so that *you* may enjoy it." He tilted his head and kissed her, trying to tell her without words how much she affected him. How much he wanted her. How it was what *she* wanted that mattered.

Perhaps it was better to show her.

Sliding down the bed, he rearranged her skirts and positioned himself between her legs. She observed quietly, her gaze rounded and her skin flushed with excitement. "Here we are," he said. "Ready?"

She nodded once, and he watched her carefully as he moved her skirts out of the way. If at any point she appeared uncomfortable, he would abandon this. They could always try again another night.

Yet, she didn't stop him or cringe. Her breathing picked up as her lower half was revealed, but not from panic. Her hooded dark eyes told another story, and he dared not look away. By the time her clothing reached her waist she was panting. He waited patiently, frozen, watching her for signs of discomfort.

"You're coddling me."

"I am being careful with you."

She blinked a few times then shook her head, her hair spilling out of its pins. "You don't need to be careful. I won't change my mind."

"Then spread your legs and hold your drawers open for me."

Her throat worked but he'd backed her into a corner. He needed her full participation. Slowly, she widened her legs and made room for his shoulders. He could smell the sharp spice of her arousal, and he nearly humped the mattress. Christ, he wanted to sink inside her so desperately. Then her hands began creeping south, toward her middle, through mounds of cotton and silk, until she reached her drawers. Her fingers found the part and pulled, spreading the fabric wide.

He got his first look at her then, all pink, glistening skin. It made his mouth water. Her clitoris was already swollen, begging for his tongue. "Stop me at any time. Though I sincerely hope you don't."

Shifting forward, he dragged the flat of his tongue through her folds, her flavor exploding in his mouth and causing him to groan. She was dripping. Thick arousal coated her skin and pooled at her entrance. It was like all the birthday and Christmas gifts he'd never received rolled up into one. "Fuck," he breathed. "I could stay here for hours."

He worked slowly, tracing the length of her folds with the tip of his tongue, then sucking the plump lips gently, merely trying to learn her. What did she like? Some women liked a tongue thrust inside; others liked a scrape of teeth on their clit. Fingers, or no fingers? He had to discover exactly what this particular woman preferred—because he planned to do this as many times as he could possibly manage in the coming months.

Her hands found their way into his hair, holding him closer. Subconsciously signaling she was ready for more. Shifting, he found her clit and began with light pressure, easing off after a few seconds and then returning again. Teasing her. A few minutes later her hips began rocking, seeking. She made the most adorable low sounds in her throat, her teeth clamped into her bottom lip.

He wanted to make this last, so he licked her entrance, then pushed his tongue inside. She gasped and he did it a few more times before returning to her clit, which was even more swollen now. Excellent. He kissed it ever so gently.

"Please," she whispered. "I'm dying."

He took pity and wrapped his lips around the taut bud, sucking on it. Her thighs began to shake around his shoulders, her moans echoing inside the room. He slipped a finger in her pussy, filling her, and her back bowed off the bed. "Oh, my God." She sounded mystified, bewildered by the strength of what was happening. Another finger and she shouted, her inner walls clamping down, contracting, as her limbs trembled. The orgasm went on and on, her hips bucking and her grip tightening in his hair. He loved the strength of her reaction. It made him feel like the most powerful man in the world.

When she began to relax, he softened his touch. He loved this part, when a woman was limp and soaking wet. With any other partner, he might rise up and slide his cock inside her. With Justine, however, he had another plan in mind.

He pumped his fingers, stretching her. She panted, her hips rocking to pull him in deeper, and he smiled. He kept his kisses light and gentle, biding his time. She was tight around his fingers but so hot and slick. Her channel would have felt like absolute heaven wrapped around his cock, if tonight had been about fucking her.

Soon, but not now. When he finally took her, he wanted her begging for it. Absolutely certain, with no chance for regret.

This time was about showing her how good it was between them and earning her trust. Making her feel adored and cherished. Pleasuring her until she couldn't stand.

"That was amazing," she said. Her eyes were closed and she had a satisfied smile on her face.

"I am glad you thought so, chérie. However, if you're still capable of complete sentences, then that means I'm not quite done yet."

And he started the entire process all over again.

Chapter Fifteen

As shaky as a newborn foal, Justine crept into the Greene kitchen, careful of her every move. Though it was the middle of the night—and her parents were still away—she didn't wish to wake any of the servants. It wasn't easy. Her coordination and agility had been left on Mulligan's bed about an hour ago.

She'd come three times before he finally poured her into Rye's carriage and saw her off. The goodbye barely registered, she'd been so dazed. She remembered him kissing her sweetly, his mouth and tongue tasting of her, and saying he hoped she'd enjoyed herself.

Hoped she'd enjoyed herself? Any more enjoyment and she'd have died.

By the end, she had begged to touch him. He merely laughed and told her not tonight, but soon. When, soon? Tomorrow night? She needed to see him equally undone, pleasured by her hand. Or mouth. Or . . . elsewhere.

Her sore lady bits gave a squeeze in anticipation. She took the stairs slowly. Her legs felt like leaden

weights. Her drawers were soaked, too, likely ruined. A small price to pay for a night she'd never,
ever forget.

Though she was tired, a bath sounded like absolute heaven at the moment.

The house was dark and quiet, but she knew these
halls well. She made not a sound as she crept past
Florence's room on the way to her own—though it
was likely a wasted effort. With their parents gone,
Florence had been spending every free moment
with Clayton Madden. Justine couldn't blame Florence, even if she did miss her sister's presence in
the big house.

Turning the knob on her door, she slipped
inside—and nearly tripped when the light suddenly switched on.

Her two sisters were sitting on Justine's bed,
waiting. Arms folded, both wore flat and unhappy
expressions.

Worry slid along Justine's spine. "What is
wrong?" Had something happened to their parents? Granny? "Has someone died?"

"Where have you been?" Florence asked.

Where had she . . . ? *Oh.* "Wait, why are you both
here?"

"We have been waiting for you since ten o'clock,"
Mamie said. "It's now"—she glanced at the mantel
clock—"half past three."

"Waiting for me? Why?"

Florence's hazel gaze narrowed. "You didn't
show up for dinner and we waited to show you the
telegram from Daddy that arrived tonight."

Dinner? That reminded her, she was starving.
"What did it say?"

"You have not answered my question. Where were you, Justine?"

Justine looked from one sister to the other. "Are you both upset with me for sneaking out? Because that would be incredibly hypocritical of you."

"No, not necessarily," Mamie said. "We're more concerned as to whom you are sneaking out to see."

"I don't see how that is any business of yours." She met Florence's eyes. "Or yours."

"If you are doing something dangerous, then it is our business."

Justine barked a laugh. "I don't recall making it my business when you two were running amok a few years ago. Casinos, dance halls, poolrooms . . . neither of you worried about safety or propriety."

"This is different," Mamie said.

"How?"

"Because we know you've been with Mulligan." Florence gestured to Justine's hair. "Intimately."

Justine put her hands up to her disheveled hair and began pulling pins loose. "And?"

Mamie's jaw fell open. "And how do you not see the problem? Mulligan is the worst criminal in the city. He's dangerous, Justine. You cannot have a relationship with him."

"We do not have a relationship. We're . . ." She thought of the fundraiser and the shirtwaist factory. Mrs. Gorcey. His help with Mrs. von Briesen. No one laughed or teased her at his club, which was more than she could say for the police station. "We're friends."

"No, absolutely not," Mamie snapped. "You cannot be friends with Mulligan."

Florence held a palm up to silence Mamie. "Justine,

I met Mulligan and spent some time with him in his club. He's charming and intelligent, I know. He's a gorgeous bundle of charisma dressed like an English duke. I understand an attraction to him. But this won't lead anywhere beneficial for you. He'll ruin you."

"The way Clay ruined you?" Then she pointed at Mamie. "Or the way Frank ruined you?"

"You cannot . . ." Mamie exchanged a glance with Florence before coming back to Justine. "You cannot be thinking of marrying him."

"No one is discussing marriage!" Justine crossed the room and dropped onto the bench at her dressing table. "I meant physical activities. Taking my virginity."

"Has he?" Florence asked on a gasp.

"No—not that I'd tell either of you if he had." Any tiredness she felt evaporated like smoke. She pushed off the bench and began pacing the room. "You both have quite a lot of nerve lecturing me. Neither of you saved yourself for marriage. Neither of you followed the rules or conventions of high society. You did whatever you pleased, and neither one of you checked with me first to see what I thought!"

"Justine, you are the youngest," Mamie said, using her big-sister tone. "It is our job to look out for you. To help you."

"Even when I don't require it?"

Florence gave a dry laugh. "You think you can handle Mulligan? Don't you think you are a little out of your depth, Justine?"

The words squeezed her chest, shrinking her airways. Making her feel small. No matter how much she accomplished, the wife deserters she'd located, the people she helped, she would always be inexperienced, naive Justine to these two.

You're too young to come downtown with us, Justine.

We're talking about things you wouldn't understand, Justine.

Stay behind and tell Mama I'm not feeling well, Justine.

Her sisters had no idea of the woman she'd become. Or the things she'd done and the things she hoped to do. Her sisters gambled, drank and kissed their way across the city . . . but they wouldn't dare let her do the same.

And she was tired of it.

She threw her shoulders back, refusing to let them intimidate her. "Whether I am out of my depth or not, that's for me to figure out. Not you. Do you know when I first started making trips downtown?" Both women stared at her, so she answered. "When I was thirteen. Neither of you had any idea, but I'd go to the Madison Square mission and pass out bread on Saturdays. I paid our governess to take me and not tell anyone. So, please do not lecture me on what I can and cannot handle."

"Justine," Mamie said calmly, as if her younger sister were hysterical, "passing out bread in a church hardly equates to keeping pace with Mulligan. We wouldn't wish to see you hurt."

"Mulligan won't hurt me."

Florence rolled her eyes heavenward. "You have no way of knowing that. He's not a gentleman. Not even close."

Frustrated beyond measure, Justine reached for her brush and began dragging it through her hair. "Let's not forget that Chauncey, who is a gentleman, attacked Mamie in our gazebo. So please, do not extol the virtues of gentlemen to me."

"She's not listening to us," Florence said to Mamie. "We're wasting our breath."

"Yes, you are," Justine agreed. "So leave."

"Justine, please believe us. I know you are stubborn and independent, but this goes too far. If you keep seeing him, I'll have to tell Mama and Daddy."

The brush fell from Justine's hand onto the floor. "What?"

Mamie lifted her chin. "You heard me. Do not force me to tell them. Cease seeing Mulligan."

"Get out."

Florence frowned. "We are trying to help—"

"No, you aren't," Justine snapped. "You are acting like hypocrites. You assume you know what's best for me, but you do not. So, get out. I need to sleep."

Florence shook her head while Mamie sighed. "Fine," she said. "We'll leave. But I will tell Mama and Daddy if I think you're in danger. You're awfully important to us, Justine."

The sentiment came too late. Justine was too angry to appreciate it, her resentment bubbling over to clog her throat. She merely pointed at the door.

Her sisters left, both looking worried, and Justine headed to the bath. Now that she was wide-awake she might as well soak for a while. Then it occurred to her: she hadn't asked them about the contents of Daddy's telegram.

She considered following them to inquire but decided against it. At the moment, the less she saw of her sisters, the better.

WHISTLING, JACK SIGNALED to Cooper, who lifted his chin in acknowledgment and started across the main room of the club. Once Cooper arrived at his side, Jack explained, "You and Rye are with me. We're going to see a man at the brothel inside the World."

Cooper's brows lifted but he said nothing, merely nodded. They left the club and found Rye waiting at the curb with the carriage. The ride was a short one with the streets mostly clear, now that dark had fallen. Jack hopped out and waited for Rye to secure the horses. Cooper descended as well and stared at the World Poolroom, the inside of which was already rowdy. "Anything I should know?" Cooper asked.

"There's a fellow upstairs. Sees one of the girls here on the regular. He's run out on his wife. We're going to convince him to return to her."

"Got it."

Rye joined them and Jack took a step toward the World—then froze in his tracks.

Justine stood a few feet away, her face and hair obscured by a thick black cloak. "You weren't going in without me, were you?"

"What are you doing here?" he growled. His gaze swept the street, looking for trouble. "Have you lost your mind?"

"I told you I was coming." She walked toward them and smiled at the man on Jack's left. "Hello, Rye."

Rye grinned and tipped his derby. "Miss." The older man had taken a shine to Justine after the bowling. Annoyingly, he'd been singing her praises for almost two full days.

"I'm Cooper," the younger man said, and Jack had to suppress the urge to smack both of his men.

"Hello, Mr. Cooper. I am Justine."

"Excuse us, fellows." Jack grabbed Justine's hand and pulled her out of earshot. "Chérie, this is a dangerous spot after dark. I don't like the idea of you waiting here by yourself."

"I wasn't by myself. I stayed in a carriage across the street until I saw you arrive."

He sighed. She wasn't getting it. "You need to let Rye take you home. Or to my home. Anywhere but here."

"Jack," she said in a low, soft voice, one that spoke of intimacy and affection, and the sound was like a caress to his balls. "I've had enough of lectures this week. I'm perfectly safe with you. So let's go take care of Mr. von Briesen. Then perhaps we might find some privacy and take care of other, more delicate things."

Christ almighty. His mouth went dry. He didn't even care if she was managing him. *Find some privacy.* Fuck, he liked the sound of that. Blood began pulsing in his groin and he would've done just about anything she asked at that point.

Stepping closer, he bent and put his lips near her ear. "We'll finish this as quickly as I can manage. Then you'd best be wet and ready to take care of those delicate things because they are *aching* for you."

He heard her tiny gasp and smiled. He so enjoyed corrupting his little do-gooder.

Sweeping out his arm, he said, "Stay close. I'll kill any man who even looks at you funny."

"No, you won't. Besides, no one will hurt me when I am at your side."

True, but this crowd was unpredictable. "Do not drink anything while we're inside. And do not turn your back or wander off."

"I won't. I promise." She bit her lip, her eyes gleaming with what he supposed was triumph.

Resigned, he brought her to where Rye and Cooper waited, his twin shadows not even bothering to look away or pretend they weren't watching closely. "Do not let her out of your sight," he told his men. "Not for a single second."

Their group started for the door. Rye sidled up to Jack and muttered, "See she's got you dancin' to her tune. Now I like her even more."

"Fuck off." He shoved Rye out of the way and hurried to open the door. "I'll go through first," he told Justine. "Stay together."

She clasped her hands together and waited, the picture of obedience. Jack knew better. She was about as obedient as a wild fox.

Inside was a crush of lowlifes and degenerates. The saloon reeked of tobacco, piss and sweat. Jesus, had none of these men ever had a bath? Justine remained close, and the three men formed a protective triangle around her as they moved through the crowd.

The poolroom was still busy, though the race-tracks had closed for the day. Now patrons were racing rats on the pool tables, with logs set up like rails. Men were throwing money around, eager to bet on anything, even vermin.

Jack kept going, directing their group to the brothel's main door. Soon they were all climbing the stairs, and Jack took his first full deep breath since finding Justine on the front walk.

Polly appeared at the landing. Her expression was less than welcoming. "I was hoping you'd forgotten."

Jack slipped her a wad of cash, which disappeared into the madam's bodice. "We won't be long. Just show us which room."

"Third door on the left." She pointed down the hall. "He's been here about fifteen minutes."

Excellent. That meant things should be well underway. Sliding a glance at Justine, he told her, "Wait in the salon."

Her brows knitted. "Why?"

The truth, that he wished to speak to von Briesen alone, would only cause her to dig in her heels. Instead, he went with a partial truth. "Because he'll likely be undressed. And busy. Let us get him decent, and then you may come in and talk to him."

Justine started to speak until Rye put in, "He's right, miss. You don't need to be seein' his dangly bits. Let us get him sorted and then we'll call you in."

"Fine." She didn't appear happy about it, but at least she refrained from arguing.

"Remember what I said," Jack warned. He didn't trust Polly any more than the men downstairs.

"Just hurry."

With Rye and Cooper behind him, Jack went to the room where von Briesen was currently "relaxing." He didn't bother to knock. Throwing open the door, the three of them stepped inside. Von Briesen was on the bed in just an undergarment, a woman's head bobbing between his legs. His eyes widened at the intrusion and the woman quickly pulled off, leaving von Briesen to cover himself. "What are you doing here?" His voice had a thick German accent. "This is a private room."

Rye shut them in and Jack handed the woman a stack of cash. "Give us a few minutes, will you?" After she left, he thrust his hands in his pockets. "Are you Mr. von Briesen?"

The man's head swiveled between Rye, Cooper and Jack. "Y-yes. Why?"

"You recently left your wife."

Von Briesen swallowed. "I don't see why that is any concern of yours."

Jack approached and sat on the side of the bed, his posture relaxed. He took a moment to smooth out his trousers. "My name is Mulligan. I have a little club not far from here called the New Belfast Athletic Club. Perhaps you've heard of me?"

The other man said nothing but his face paled. His hands began trembling on the bedclothes.

"I see you have. Good, that saves us time. We're going to have a quick little chat, the four of us, about your family. Then I'm going to call in a friend of mine and you're going to tell her how you plan to return to that family."

"But . . ." He glanced at the two other men before returning his gaze to Jack. "I do not plan on returning."

"You will. Trust me."

"No, my wife, she's always after me about money and helping with the children. I do not want to go back."

"Well, we'll have to see what we can do to convince you."

Chapter Sixteen

So, he didn't argue at all?"

They were now in the carriage, and Justine was having a hard time wrapping her head around how easy the night had been. Von Briesen had eagerly agreed to return to his wife, his eyes even tearing up with remorse. Jack, Cooper and Rye had promised to check up on von Briesen's wife to ensure the man kept his promise. After that, they'd all departed the World Poolroom.

It had been so effortless.

Almost *too* effortless.

Cooper had taken another way home so Justine and Jack were alone, with Rye in the driver's seat. Jack leaned close and traced the shell of her ear with his finger. "He might have argued a little."

"So you intimidated him." Then she remembered the shirtwaist factory owner. "You didn't . . . beat him, did you?"

"No beating. We were a bit more creative than that. But he quickly came around to see our way of thinking."

"Jack," she said on a sigh. "I didn't want you to hurt him."

"He leaves unharmed, cara."

"Is that the truth?"

He took her gloved hand and laced their fingers together. Then he kissed her knuckles. "I will never lie to you. I might not give you every tiny detail but I will never lie."

"Well, thank you. His wife will be relieved to have him home, though I daresay she might be better off without him. I hadn't realized as much when I agreed to find him."

"Such is the risk when one tracks down these wife deserters."

True. "I believe she loves him, though. She was quite distraught at his absence."

"If nothing else, the financial support will come as a relief to her." He kissed her knuckles again and sparks raced along her skin. "Nevertheless, you have done your best in resolving the issue."

"Because you helped me."

"You would have resolved it without my help, if necessary."

"But it would have taken me weeks, perhaps months, to do what you accomplished in three days." It would be easier if she had a badge and the power to arrest, of course. Her hands were tied because of her gender. Being a woman meant she could not join the New York City police force. At least not yet. She still liked the idea of being the first.

"As I told you," he said, "power in this city rests in the hands of those who are strong and those who are rich. I happen to be both."

Which made him considerably powerful. At least he was using his influence for good. The shirtwaist factory, the fundraiser. Now von Briesen. Perhaps she was rubbing off on him.

And really, if the end results were the same, why was she questioning the methods? Mrs. von Briesen would get her husband back sooner and Justine could move on to another case or issue. She could assist someone else in need. Everyone came out ahead.

"People certainly are more accommodating when you are involved," she said.

"True. That is why you should allow me to assist you on all your errands."

"Even the boring ones?"

"I suspect nothing is ever boring with you, chérie." He turned her hand over and unbuttoned her glove. Then he began removing the cloth from her fingers, one by one. "Now, let's discuss these delicate matters that require our attention."

She angled to see him better in the dim light. His normally bright eyes were dark, his stare almost hypnotic as he watched her. He was so beautiful that her stomach flipped over. "You have something in mind, I suspect."

"Of course. I am a first-class deviant, after all." He tossed her glove onto the seat and started on the other hand. "But you also have a say. What were you thinking?"

The comment had been made lightly, a way to tease him outside the poolroom. She hadn't really expected him to push her for answers. Especially when her experience in no way matched his.

Though she couldn't deny she had been thinking about it. A lot. In the past two days she had contemplated all the things she and Jack might do together, even the things she'd never attempted before.

Especially the things she'd never attempted before.

Skin aflame, she mumbled, "Something akin to the other night. Except reciprocated."

"I'm sorry, I could not hear you. You'll have to say it again and speak up."

She nearly rolled her eyes. The scoundrel had heard every word. "You are being difficult and trying to embarrass me."

"You are the smartest and bravest woman I've ever met. When you want something, you go after it. So, what do you want?"

The praise melted her insides, and she burned the words into memory for the next time one of her sisters called her naive or sheltered. It also gave her the courage to voice her desires, something she couldn't have done a few days ago. "I want to explore you. Pleasure you as you pleasured me the other night."

He crowded her against the carriage seat, his clean familiar scent wrapping around her. Bringing his face to her neck, he slid his nose along her jaw, his humid breath gusting over her skin. "You wish to take my cock in your mouth. Is that it?"

She knew the gist of how it worked thanks to Florence's erotic cards. Justine licked her lips. "Yes. I wish to suck your . . . cock."

Groaning, he threw his head back. "Fuck, that gets me so hard. Hearing you say the word *cock* is like all my darkest fantasies come to life."

Indeed? She had no idea she could affect him like

this. She, Justine Greene. The boring sister. The one passed over by all the gentlemen at the balls and soirees.

Surprised and intrigued by her power over him, she sidled closer, crowding him this time. She slipped her hand onto his thigh and moved it higher, slowly, until she reached the bulge in his trousers. Jack froze, his gaze locked on her fingers, as she tentatively touched him through his clothing.

"Mon ange," he wheezed. "You are killing me."

"Not quite, if you are still able to manage complete sentences."

"Throwing my words back at me, I see. Very well, if you want to play, I am more than happy to oblige you." He turned to glance through the window. "We have several blocks still."

She wanted him writhing in ecstasy, as she had been. And the carriage was dark. Intimate. She wasn't certain she could be so bold in his bedroom. "What if I want to do more than play?"

"Meaning?"

She scraped her fingernails over his erection and his expression slackened in surprise as a moan escaped his mouth. He blinked and his lips twisted. "Oh, I see. So, that's how it is. Angling to make me come, do-gooder?"

His tone, rough and authoritative and altogether new, had her sex throbbing from a rush of pure lust. The charmer was long gone; this was the man underneath the slick suits and fancy French. She imagined it was the voice he used when ordering his legion of followers to do his bidding. The tone should have irritated her . . . but it had the complete opposite effect. Every cell strained to get closer to him. "I do."

"Then take it out."

"I . . . What?"

Silent, he watched her carefully, and she suspected he was testing her. Pushing her to see if she'd follow. *You are the smartest and bravest woman I've ever met.* Indeed, she was, dash it.

And she wanted this. Desperately.

She reached for his trouser fastening but he put a hand on hers, stopping her. "Look at me, Justine." She met his gaze, unsure what he was about. "I might tease you and push you," he said. "But you do not have to do this. You may stop at any time."

His consideration was thoughtful. Unnecessary, but thoughtful. She decided to tease him. "Are you saying you don't want it?"

"Oh, I want it all right." He moved his hands out of the way. "More than you can possibly imagine."

JACK HELD HIS breath, anticipation crawling through him like a million tiny insects. Was she really going to suck his cock in this carriage? The idea of it was dizzying. Unbelievable. And highly fucking erotic.

Though she was clearly not a deft hand with men's clothing, she got his trousers open and undergarment unbuttoned in minutes. He held his breath, nearly coming out of his skin with wanting. Then she wrapped her fingers around his length, her grip strong and sure. She bent and placed a chaste kiss on the tip, the touch featherlight. "How is it so hard and yet so soft at the same time?"

"One of its many tricks. Keep sucking and licking and you'll soon see another of its tricks."

She smiled seductively at him through her lashes. "I cannot wait."

With the flat of her tongue she gave him a long lick. Sparks raced through his groin and he sucked in air. The sight of her mouth on him was almost enough to send him over the edge. "More."

With a sweep of her tongue over the crown, she worked around the sensitive ridge then down the shaft itself. Wetting her lips, she slipped him inside her mouth. Tight heat enveloped him, and the back of his head smacked against the wood of the carriage. "Christ, you have no idea how amazing that feels."

She hummed, the vibration sinking into his skin and down to his balls. Groaning, he gripped the edge of the carriage seat and resisted the urge to thrust into her mouth. Then she began to move, her head bobbing as she sucked him. God, he wished he could see her face, watch her lips stretch around his shaft. As it was, he could only see the top of her head and *feel* her mouth on him. She kept up a steady pace, using her tongue to hit that sweet spot on the underside. Fuck, he liked that.

Turned out his uptown do-gooder was damn proficient at sucking cock.

It shouldn't surprise him. Whatever the task, Justine dedicated herself to it. Selflessly gave and gave with every piece of her soul. And he was bastard enough to take it.

"I like the way you taste," she whispered, almost shyly. His blood sizzled at that confession, his balls tightening. He'd give anything to draw this out, to drive around the city for hours while Justine's mouth kept working on him. But it was too good and he had bigger plans for the night. As it was, they had only a few blocks before they arrived at Bond Street.

He remembered the way her gaze had darkened when he'd talked to her. She seemed to like it.

He liked it, too.

"Wrap your hand around the base," he told her. "Squeeze me." One of her hands moved from his thigh to grip the base of his shaft. "Harder, cara."

She tightened her fingers and his eyes nearly rolled back in his head. "God, that's perfect. Now work the head. Use your tongue on that—" He bit off the words as she read his mind perfectly. The tip of her tongue teased that sensitive spot and he could feel his orgasm building, gathering steam in his toes. "I'm going to come if you keep doing that."

Pulling off briefly, she said, "That is generally the point, is it not?" Then she went back to her task, with the perfect amount of enthusiasm and pressure.

It was too much.

Curses tumbled from his mouth, his fingers digging into the velvet seat. His chest heaved as his lids fell closed. The pleasure coiled, sharpened inside him, then radiated outward. His heartbeat echoed in his cock, pulsing, driving the need to thrust. A second later, his muscles tensed. It was too much, too powerful, and he couldn't stop it if he tried. "Now. I'm coming now," he growled, warning her.

Instead of pulling off, she held on tighter—and his body began contracting, wave after wave of bliss slamming into him as he poured into her mouth. His mind went blank, limbs trembling. He might have shouted.

It was over quickly, but he couldn't move. She pulled off and pressed a final kiss to the hyper-sensitive crown, which would've caused him to shiver if he were capable of it. He heard her laugh. "Should I worry that you'll fall asleep?"

"No, but I need a minute before I'm able to think again."

She sat up and settled into the seat beside him. "That was fun."

"Hmm. Fun, indeed." He might never recover. "I haven't spent that fast since I was a lad."

"Really?"

He nodded. "You are quite unexpected."

"In a good way, I hope."

Opening his eyes, he leaned over and pressed a kiss to her soft and swollen lips. "The very best way." Lights outside the carriage caught his eye. He recognized the spires of Grace Church. "What in the hell . . . ?"

As quickly as he could, he tucked his cock away, buttoned up his trousers and then pounded on the side of the carriage. "Where are you going? Why are we on Broadway?" he shouted to Rye.

"Don't be cross with him," Justine said. "I told him to take me back uptown. I have to return home."

"Home? Why?"

"My sisters are watching me more carefully than I'd thought, it turns out. I'd rather not have to an-swer questions when I return late."

"Damn it. I had plans for you tonight."

"You'll have to save them for an afternoon instead."

He considered fucking her in his bed with sunlight streaming through the windows, a light breeze blowing through the room . . . and his disappointment ebbed slightly. "Tell me what they said."

"It's not worth discussing."

Reaching over, he pulled her onto his lap. She fit perfectly against him. He liked holding her, probably more than he should. "It is worth discussing if it upset you."

She rested her head on his shoulder. "They think I am out of my depth with you. That you'll hurt me."

Mrs. Tripp might possibly believe as much, but Florence should know him better than to say that. "I would never hurt you, cara. I'd rather saw off my own arm with a rusty blade."

"I told them I was perfectly safe, but they do not believe it. Mamie said she would tell our parents if I don't quit seeing you."

Jack's jaw clenched, but he forced an easy tone. "Bit hypocritical of her, isn't it? Frank Tripp wasn't exactly squeaky clean when they met."

"Precisely what I said. And Clay was no angel, either. It is ridiculous."

Understatement. Clayton Madden was like Jack, only without the charisma, charm and good looks. Though Clay had given up his enterprise for Florence Greene. "I'm not afraid of your father, if that's your concern."

"Nor am I. The worst is they might ship me off to a convent in Europe." She shrugged. "That wouldn't be so bad."

"It wouldn't?" It sounded like hell on earth to him.

"They perform a lot of charity endeavors. Not to

mention that convents are peaceful and pretty. I've considered it."

"You considered joining a convent? Taking of the vows, the celibacy?"

"Why are you so surprised? It wasn't until recently that I even knew what I'd be missing."

He didn't begrudge any woman for answering a higher calling, but Manhattan without this clever do-gooder trying to save it? Unthinkable. He began gathering her skirts in one hand, exposing her legs.

"What are you doing?" She tried to push the cloth down and he stopped to explain.

"I plan on making you come at least once during this journey. In the interest of showing you more of what you'd be missing, of course."

"Oh." She moved her hand. "Show away, then."

Jack spent the rest of the ride with his hand between her legs, the joy of her non-celibacy ringing in his ears.

Chapter Seventeen

Justine knocked on the door of salon number twenty-five inside the Hoffman House Hotel. Male voices could be heard arguing inside. After a few seconds, she knocked again, louder. The door opened and a man appeared, frowning at her. "Who are you?"

"We wish to speak with Mr. Keller."

"Again, who are you?"

"Miss Greene and Mrs. Frank Tripp."

The man scrutinized Justine then Mamie. "Hold on." He closed the door with a snap.

"You owe me ten favors in exchange for this errand," Mamie whispered.

"Fine," Justine answered with a roll of her eyes. "Just be quiet. I shall do all the talking."

The Hoffman House Hotel was one of the very best in the city, where famous actors and English dukes came to stay. It was also where Tammany men gathered to plot and scheme their stranglehold on New York City politics and business.

Through one of the attorneys at the legal aid society, Justine learned that Mr. Keller, second-in-command at Tammany Hall, handled the appointments for the police department. It also happened that Keller convened every afternoon inside a Hoffman House salon for a long business-related lunch.

Justine hadn't bothered trying to get an appointment. Keller certainly would not have agreed to meet and catching him unaware, before he had time to form a counterargument, seemed a wiser plan.

"I don't like how secretive you are being," Mamie hissed.

Justine hadn't told Mamie anything about today's errand. First, Mamie would have tried to talk her out of it. Second, Mamie would have told Florence, who would have tried to talk Justine out of it.

Still, she hadn't wished to come alone. Keller might've made assumptions about an unmarried woman alone that were completely wrong. She might ignore propriety to suit her purposes downtown, but there were times when acting the part mattered.

Today was about presenting Miss Justine Greene, daughter of Mr. Duncan Greene, as a serious candidate for the New York City Metropolitan Police Department.

She had considered asking Jack to come with her, but immediately rejected the idea. She could do this on her own. For years, she had been looking after herself. Merely because he kissed her from time to time didn't mean she could trouble him with every little problem. He likely had a thousand problems every day. She refused to burden him with more of hers.

They hadn't yet discussed where things stood between them. She liked him—quite a bit, actually—but he was just a friend. Not that he'd asked for more, but she wasn't ready for something serious.

Perhaps in a few years. Their encounters were fun and satisfying . . . and that's all she let herself dwell on at the moment. Worries were for another day.

She cut her eyes toward her sister. "Relax, it is nothing dangerous."

"Is this related to some case at the legal aid society?"

"Not directly."

"Remind me to strangle you when we leave. I swear, I'm never doing another errand with you unless I know—"

The door opened once more and the same man appeared. "Come in."

Justine stepped inside the salon, where a group of six men were gathered. Cigars were being extinguished, whiskey tumblers set aside. All of them stood, but only one man walked forward. He was short in stature, a beard setting off his dark eyes.

"Miss Greene, Mrs. Tripp. I am Mr. Keller."

"Mr. Keller." Justine strode forward with her hand extended, which Keller shook. "Thank you for seeing us."

"It's not often that women such as yourselves seek out an audience. Please have a seat."

The rest of the men in the room disappeared, save Keller and the man who'd opened the door. Justine and Mamie sat, as did Keller. He asked, "How may I help you ladies?"

"I work with my sister Mrs. Tripp and my brother-in-law at the Lower East Side Legal Aid Society," Justine said.

"I am aware," Keller said. "You have made quite a name for yourselves in that endeavor. I have known Mr. Tripp a long time."

Mamie did not seem the least bit surprised to hear it. Everyone knew Frank Tripp.

"Even before that work," Justine continued, "I spent quite a lot of time downtown helping people through various charities and organizations. Though I've had some success, it has often been difficult to get lasting results without authority behind me."

"That's not my impression. They speak of you as if you're some sort of miracle worker."

"A generous implication at best. I could accomplish much more if I were given a certain level of status with the city."

"Such as?"

"I wish to join the police force. Not as a matron. I'd like to carry a badge and investigate cases. With full arrest capabilities."

Mamie went perfectly still but said nothing, thankfully. Keller just stroked his beard and studied Justine. "I don't understand. I heard you've been working with Mulligan."

Justine's mouth opened and closed. How had Keller come by such information? "I am not . . . That is, we are not working together. Mr. Mulligan and I are friendly and have collaborated recently on a few projects. However, those have been resolved."

"Ah. Does Mulligan know that?"

She frowned, uncertain why that should matter. "I believe so. And it is a totally separate issue from what I am requesting."

"Not exactly separate, but we'll leave that for now. You are aware there are no female officers in the department."

"I am aware. However, there are many cases that women could handle exclusively—"

"What you are suggesting would take jobs away from men, men who must provide for families at home. Whom exactly are you providing for?"

"That's not the point."

Keller shook his head, as if she were a child incapable of understanding the adults in the room. "That is precisely the point. You wish to take the spot of a man, one without your family's resources and privilege, and leave him out of a job."

"But there are cases not being investigated because the department does not have the resources or the ability to follow up on them."

"Such as?"

"Husbands who desert their wives. Labor issues involving women and children."

Keller's lips twisted. "Are you presuming to know more about labor issues than I do, Miss Greene? We oversee the unions in this city. Are we not doing a sufficient enough job for you?"

This was deteriorating quickly. Keller wasn't understanding her, clearly. "What about the husbands who desert their wives?"

"A family issue, one the police shouldn't interfere with."

Justine could feel her skin heating, frustration building in her veins. Remaining calm was normally not an issue for her, but Keller made her want to jump up and scream.

Mamie must've sensed Justine's mood because she spoke up. "Mr. Keller, my sister is not suggesting that she replace a man on the department staff. She is asking to be added, to be allowed to join them, not displace them."

"Mrs. Tripp, all due respect to you and your husband, but these are not the kind of men who wish to work side by side with a woman. Their jobs are often dangerous. How are we to ensure everyone's safety if they're worried about a hysterical woman in their midst?"

"Perhaps Justine is capable of looking after herself. I have seen her in many situations, in all sorts of neighborhoods, and never once has she been close to hysterical."

"Serving soup and handing out pamphlets hardly qualifies as the kinds of work she'd be involved in as a police officer."

Mamie's eyes narrowed at his condescending tone. "Yes, taking bribes and looking the other way from crime requires a special skill."

The temperature in the room plummeted. Keller's expression hardened, his eyes cold. "I'm certain our fine officers wouldn't appreciate such characterization of their work."

Justine rushed to smooth things over by trying another tack. "Mr. Keller, women make up almost half the city. We should have some sort of representation on the police force."

"You do. There are matrons, not to mention that most of the officers have wives."

"Wives? How does that help, exactly?"

Keller waved a hand. "You know, as Mrs. Tripp assists her husband at the legal aid society. A sounding board when he requires it, a comforting ear at home."

"A sounding board?" Mamie's voice rose about eight octaves. "I am more than my husband's sounding board."

"I mean no offense, Mrs. Tripp. But surely, Miss

Greene, you can now see that the highly emotional state of a woman has no place on the police force. They rely on science and logic, which men are more naturally inclined toward." He rose and thrust his hands in his pockets. "In time, you'll come to see it's for the best."

Justine rose, her shoulders weighted down with defeat. Mamie appeared one hair's breadth away from ripping Keller's beard off his face. Justine gave her sister a warning glance before facing Keller once more. "I implore you to speak with Detective Ellison at police headquarters. He and I have collaborated on a number of cases and he can speak to my relevant experience."

Keller's expression remained unchanged. "That won't be necessary. I cannot recommend you for the department. There's nothing in it for me or Tammany except bearing the unhappiness of every other officer on the force."

"This was a waste of time," Mamie told Justine. "Let's go."

Justine exhaled and stared at the floor, her mind spinning. How was she supposed to fight such antiquated ideas about women and the workplace? Was her gender to be forever circumscribed to secretarial work and department stores? "You are wrong, Mr. Keller. Women and children are suffering in this city, being left behind because no one watches out for them. Someday—and I hope it is soon—we will get the vote and men will then be answerable to us."

"No offense, but I hope Hades freezes over first." He bowed. "Mrs. Tripp, give your husband my best. And Miss Greene, please pass on my regards to Mulligan."

Justine headed for the door, not intending to do anything of the kind. She planned to see Jack imminently . . . and Keller would not enjoy the results.

JACK SQUINTED UP at O'Shaughnessy's man. "You don't mind if I count it, do you?"

Whip, as the errand boy was called, said nothing, his eyes filled with resentment. Jack nearly sighed. *The lack of respect in these young men today . . .*

He peeled apart the handles of the satchel Whip had presented. Large stacks of money rested inside. Was it enough? If O'Shaughnessy thought Jack would accept one cent less than what had been stolen, he was sorely mistaken.

"Have a seat, Whip. Cooper will fix you a drink. I should have this sorted in no time." No one could count money faster than Jack.

Cooper didn't offer options, merely poured a glass of whiskey and set it on Jack's desk. Jack busied himself with the cash, Rye propped against the wall behind him. No one spoke. Other than Jack, no one moved. Tension hovered, the room bracing itself for disaster to strike at any moment. Jack tried not to think about that as he counted.

Really, he didn't want to war with O'Shaughnessy. He would, if provoked or pushed, but he wouldn't enjoy it. Not like the Jack of a few years ago— hell, a few months ago—who would've relished the challenge. But warring with O'Shaughnessy would put everything he'd built in danger, not to mention everyone in his life. That included one beautiful, captivating do-gooder.

O'Shaughnessy wouldn't hesitate to use Justine

to hurt Jack, and God only knew what she would be subjected to in the wrong hands. Jack would never be able to live with himself if something happened to her. Even the idea of it filled him with terror.

So, he had to keep her safe. No matter what. If things with O'Shaughnessy turned serious, he'd send her out of town for a bit. She wouldn't like it but he wouldn't give her a choice. Perhaps a short stay at a quiet convent, where the ugliness of his life wouldn't touch her. How could she object to that?

If O'Shaughnessy was anything like Jack, the plotting to take over had probably already started. Jack would need to put the entire crew on alert, plus see if his informants could find anything out. With Justine running about downtown he couldn't risk her safety by waiting to see what Trevor would do. He needed to cut the threat off before it gained legs.

Why do all your decisions revolve around Justine these days?

He ignored that voice. There was no debating his need to keep her safe. It was vital to his peace of mind. Like his secret Bond Street home and the bank accounts no one knew about. Those things allowed him to sleep at night.

He finished up with the last stack. "That's all of it." He came to his feet. "This concludes our visit, Whip. I hope you've enjoyed it as much as I have."

Without speaking, the young man stood and started for the door. Jack held up a hand and Cooper instantly blocked Whip's path. Jack strolled forward, drew closer, until he was in Whip's space. He clasped him on the shoulder and lowered his voice. "Tell O'Shaughnessy this had better never happen again."

Whip tensed but didn't respond. Just as Jack

released him, the door flew open and bounced into Cooper's back. A feminine voice said, "Oh, goodness. I apologize. I didn't realize anyone was standing there."

Justine.

What was she doing here? More importantly, how had she arrived at his office unannounced?

Cooper stepped aside and Justine entered. She took in the room. "Good afternoon," she said politely to Whip. Instead of answering, Whip darted through the cracked door and disappeared into the corridor. After a quick look from Jack, Cooper followed O'Shaughnessy's man. They didn't need the enemy lingering, especially with Justine on the premises.

"Find out who is on the front door," Jack said to Rye with a meaningful glance.

"Is that because of me?" Justine's eyes darted between them. "If so, I came in through the kitchens."

Jack frowned. That was worse. "I'll see to it," Rye said, noting Jack's expression and hurrying out.

Now alone, Jack gave his full concentration to her. The brown skirt and white shirtwaist were boring and serviceable, but she still appeared delectable to his eyes. "Not that I am unhappy to see you, but why the kitchens? Did you think you'd be refused at the door?"

"I didn't wish for the entire world to know I was here." She stared at the floor, not meeting his eyes. The skin of her neck had turned a delightful pink.

What was happening?

If he didn't know better, he'd say she was embarrassed. And, why did she wish to keep her presence at the club a secret?

The Devil of Downtown   231

Then it hit him. Was she here for the afternoon pleasure they'd discussed? Lust rolled through him to settle in his groin. He hadn't expected this so soon but he was absolutely ready and willing.

Coming closer, he slid a hand onto her hip and pulled her into him. She fit perfectly, all sweet softness and feminine curves. Everything inside him quieted, settled. His mind calmed, no longer going full speed with worries and dollars and things to do. He focused solely on her, from the pulse jumping wildly in her neck to the silky strands of hair falling to frame her lovely face. Bringing his mouth to hover above hers, he whispered, "Shall we go to Bond Street, cara? Where I may spread you out on my bed and feast on your pussy until sundown."

"Yes," she breathed, then seemed to shake herself. "I mean no."

"No?"

"No, that isn't why I'm here." She pushed away from him. "I mean, perhaps it could be why I'm here—but later. After we've talked."

"What is it we need to discuss?"

"Should we sit, or . . . ?"

This was a new tentative side of her. He was missing something, clearly. "Of course. Would you care for a drink?"

"Whatever you're having." She lowered herself into an armchair and fussed with her skirts.

Also unusual. She was normally confident, telling him exactly what he'd be doing and when. He poured them two lagers and set the cold glasses on his desk. "There you are." He dropped into the armchair beside her. "Try it. This is one of the beers I hope to sell across the country."

Justine brought the glass to her mouth. Foam coated the sweet bow of her upper lip after she drank, which she licked with the tip of her tongue. *Oh, that tongue. How I've missed it.* "It's good," she said. "Normally I do not care for beer."

Grinning, Jack took a sip from his own glass. Her reaction was precisely how he knew this beer would make them all very rich. "Now tell me. To what do I owe the pleasure of your company this afternoon?"

She set her glass down. Clasped her hands in her lap. "I need a favor."

Sweet Jesus, those words. The extraordinary amount of delight he experienced at hearing them come out of her mouth should have embarrassed him. Before, he'd cajoled and bartered with her. Now she was here making a simple request for his help. They'd turned a corner—and the victory was fucking satisfying.

He struggled to keep his face completely impassive. "And what is that, *mon ange?*"

"I wish to become the first female detective on the New York City police force."

"No, you don't." He started to rise. "Now, we can take the tunnel to my house or—"

She put a hand on his arm, stopping him. "Yes, I do."

He returned to his seat and took a sip of beer, thinking on how best to put this. "I realize how this sounds coming from me, but they are criminals— and bad ones at that. You do not want to join their morally corrupt ranks."

"Not all of them are criminals. And even if that were the case, I would not be a criminal. I could do a lot of good for the women and children of this city."

"You *are* doing a lot of good for the women and children of this city. In fact, you hardly ever stop doing good."

"Don't you see? If I had a badge and real authority, then I wouldn't need—"

Her jaw slammed shut and he finally understood. Disappointment burned in his chest, a hot poker of realization. He forced himself to say it. "You wouldn't need me."

"That's not what I meant. I wouldn't need anyone. Not Detective Ellison or my father. Not even my brother-in-law. I could make real change in this city."

He didn't believe her, but he let it go. Furthermore, hadn't she spent enough time with him to see how things really worked in New York? "I keep telling you, the coppers aren't who make change in this city."

"It will not always be that way, though. Would the force not benefit from women investigating the types of crime the men refuse to touch?"

"The sorts of cases you're already investigating?" He thought of the factory owner, Mr. Bay. Von Briesen and Gorcey. "Is that what you mean?"

"Yes."

"If you think a badge commands respect and will make things easier for you, I hate to disappoint you with the truth."

"I don't believe that. I have seen the way people respond to Ellison, how he's able to back up his threats with jail time."

"You are not Ellison, however."

"I know, but it would be better than what I have now. Which is nothing."

No, he wanted to say. *You have me.*

But he couldn't offer her that. She certainly didn't want it, not after just declaring her eagerness to be rid of him. Besides, he had O'Shaughnessy likely planning his demise at this very minute. It was in her best interest to leave here and never return.

Not that he would let her go. Not yet, anyway. They weren't quite finished with whatever this was between them.

He shot to his feet and moved toward the desk, his hands deep in his pockets. Everything in him told him to refuse. To keep her tethered tightly to him. Yet, how could he not give her everything she wanted, even if it took her away from him?

Her eyes were full of hope, looking at him as if he could do anything. Could solve any problem. It made him feel like the most powerful man in the world, a god among men. He'd give his entire fortune to avoid disappointing her.

Smothering a sigh, he nodded once. "I will speak with a man named Mr. Keller. He handles these things."

"I just came from meeting him."

He tried not to appear as surprised as he felt. "You met with Keller?"

Her throat worked as she swallowed. "He told me no. That I'd be taking a job away from a man who needed to support his family. He was . . ."

"He was, what?"

Fury tightened the angles of her face, her mouth hard and angry. "Condescending and awful. And so very smug."

Keller was most definitely all those things.

She added, "He said to pass on his regards to you."

Interesting. That meant his association with Justine hadn't gone unnoticed by the Tammany boys. Though why they cared Jack couldn't say. One thing he did know was that Keller would answer for upsetting this glorious creature. His do-gooder. "Is this what you really want?"

"Yes."

"Then consider it done."

Her mouth worked but no sound emerged. Finally, she said, "J-just like that? Don't you need to speak to Keller first?"

"Do you honestly think he'll refuse me?"

"No." Her lips twisted as she gave him a playful smirk. "Is this where you tell me I should have come to you first?"

Reaching over, he helped her out of the chair. Though they were close, he didn't move away. Instead, he ran the pad of his thumb over the smooth skin of her throat. "I won't deny that I like when you need my help, but I hate dwelling in the past. You did what you thought was right in the moment." He pressed his lips to her cheek, the slope of her brow, the edge of her mouth . . . tiny kisses to reacquaint himself with the taste and feel of her skin. "And there are better things to discuss, such as how I'd like to take you to my bedroom, whereby I will make you come many times."

She clutched at him, her fingertips pressing into his chest. "I'm in favor of such a discussion."

"Then follow me."

Chapter Eighteen

Warm afternoon light streamed through his bedroom windows as he undressed her. He went slowly, drawing it out, clearly trying to drive her mad. It seemed each naked inch of her was new terrain that must be explored by his hands, mouth and lips. Her body burned, the yearning so deep and fierce that she could barely stay on her feet. By the time he removed her corset, she was panting, her heartbeat thrumming in her ears.

He remained annoyingly clothed. She itched to touch him, to investigate all the muscles and ridges under that fancy suit. Not to mention that she wanted to drive him wild, as well. Make him as mindless as he'd been in the carriage, when he had spent in her mouth. Just the thought of it had her pressing her thighs together to ease the ache in her core.

Her shift ended up on the floor, quickly followed by her drawers. Before she could worry about her nakedness, he laid her out on the bed and stretched out beside her. One large thigh slid between her legs, pressing into her bare flesh, the wool of his trousers rubbing in all the best places. His bright blue gaze raked over her. "You are so lovely," he murmured, cupping one of her breasts. "I think I've died and gone to heaven."

Rising up slightly, she sealed her mouth to his. He froze for a half second before he kissed her back, his hand angling her head to where he wanted before his tongue delved past her lips. She couldn't get close enough to him as their tongues swirled and tangled, their shared exhalations rough in the quiet room. The connection felt necessary, important to her very survival. There was no rationalization or serious thought, other than *more* and *yes.*

The pulse between her legs turned demanding, and she rolled her hips, seeking. Fabric dragged against the nub at the apex of her folds, his leg weighting her down like an anchor to hold her in place. *Oh, God.* Sparkles danced behind her eyelids and pleasure rippled throughout her core. She did it again and gasped, breaking off from his mouth to suck in air.

"Keep going," he whispered into her throat. "Use my leg to make yourself come."

His hand went to her hip, encouraging, and then he bent to lick and suck the tip of her breast, with each draw on her nipple echoing deep inside her. She didn't think, just began moving, churning her hips as the pleasure built. Rocking her body against his to satisfy the raw need coursing through her.

When her rhythm faltered, he began moving, sliding his thigh back and forth, until she shattered, her limbs shaking. She moaned as her womb contracted, the orgasm going on and on. After she floated down, she marveled at how fast that had all happened. He'd barely touched her.

"That was the single most arousing thing I've ever witnessed." He kissed her like he couldn't get enough. Like she was the air he needed to breathe. "I cannot wait to see you do that again."

His reaction eased any embarrassment she might have felt. "Another time. Right now, I want to explore you." She tried to roll him over so that she could undress him.

"Not yet." He dragged his teeth over her earlobe, along the side of her throat. "I want to taste you first. Make you come on my tongue."

Goodness, she wanted that. A lot. Jack was incredibly talented with his mouth. But today was about something else, something bigger.

Something she'd been thinking about for a while now.

"Jack, get undressed. Please. I want . . . Let me feel you inside me."

Unblinking hypnotic eyes focused on her. "Are you certain? There are many other ways to pleasure one another. We don't have to—"

"I want to. Desperately. Unless you don't want to?" She hadn't considered that possibility, but of course he might not want to. "Is there someone else?"

"Justine, no. Definitely not that—and I absolutely want to fuck you. I just need you to be certain."

He never wrapped the words in pretty euphemisms. For a charmer, he had a dirty, dirty mouth. And she liked it. He was real and raw, a man half the city feared. To her, however, he was her knight in tarnished yet impenetrable armor.

She trusted him. To keep her safe, to watch out for her. To slay her dragons. No matter what happened between them in the future, she wouldn't regret sharing his bed.

Placing her palm on his cheek, she didn't try to hide her emotions from him. "Have you ever known me to be uncertain about anything?"

He chuckled, looking so handsome and carefree that her heart stuttered. "True. You are a woman who knows her own mind." His smile fell. "This isn't some sort of repayment for speaking to Keller, is it?"

The idea hadn't even occurred to her. "No, absolutely not. I would never . . ." *Sleep with you as a way to trade favors*. She couldn't even say the repulsive concept aloud.

"I didn't think so, but some have tried. I apologize." The side of his mouth hitched. "I forgot for a brief second that the most noble and trustworthy woman in the city was here in my bed. Spread your legs for me, chérie."

She did as he asked, trying not to think about the other women in his past. Then his fingers swept along her folds, through the moisture at her entrance, and her worries disappeared. He slipped a digit inside her, the thickness dragging against her inner walls. She threw her head back, the sensitive tissue magnifying the pleasure rippling through her. "What about your clothes?" she asked when her ability to speak returned.

"Soon." He drew on her nipple while his finger slid in and out, stretching her. "We need to ready you first."

The sensations created by his mouth and hands were amazing. Better than amazing, actually. "I'm ready," she breathed and clutched at him.

She felt him smile against her skin. "Not quite. I wouldn't like to hurt you."

Hurry, hurry, hurry, she wanted to tell him. Instead, her hands started on his vest buttons, pushing them through the holes. When she couldn't reach any more, he finished then shrugged out of the garment. Next came necktie, studs, shirt collar . . . He was able to focus on several things at once, getting undressed while still touching and licking her. If she weren't so desperate she would've been impressed.

He removed his fingers for an instant as he whipped his shirt over his head, and then returned to pleasuring her. More pressure as he added a second finger. "You are so hot and wet. So tight. I cannot remember ever wanting something more."

"Now." She was wheezing, barely able to draw in air fast enough. "Please, Jack."

He ignored her. Teeth gently scraped her nipple before his tongue soothed her. She moaned, helpless.

A third finger had her rolling her hips once more, chasing the bliss that lay just out of reach. His thumb swept over her clitoris and her back bowed. Her lids slammed shut and every muscle tightened. "Oh, God."

Close. She was so close.

The fingers disappeared as he shifted. He unfastened his trousers, hands working quickly and efficiently to get them off. Then he moved between her legs, his big thighs pushing her wider as he worked on the tiny buttons of his undergarment. The cloth was tight, clinging to every part of him, making her mouth water. She couldn't wait to taste and touch all that rough skin.

He took his erection into his fist. His eyes were wild as they focused on her sex. Pressing forward, he notched the crown at her entrance. Then he caught her gaze and held it. "You may change your mind, you know."

"I won't. I'm not. Please, Jack."

His throat worked as he swallowed, then he pushed inside. There was no pain, only a heavy fullness. He didn't look away from where they were joined, while she watched him. Skin flushed, muscles bulging . . . he was the most beautiful man.

She wanted to see all of him.

Her hands reached for the tiny buttons on his remaining garment, intent in divesting him of the cloth. Glancing up, he stopped her with a large palm. "Not now."

Why would he rather keep clothed? "I want to touch you."

"I'd much rather watch you touch yourself."

"What? Where?"

Dark mischief lit his eyes just before he captured her hand. "Right here." He brought her fingers to her clitoris. "Stroke yourself for me."

Her skin went up in flames. Touch herself there . . . while he *watched*?

"There is no right or wrong, not with me. Only what makes you feel good. It will also help keep you wet for your first time." He jerked his chin to where he was barely inside her.

"Oh."

If this would help, how could she refuse? She slid the pad of her finger over the taut nub, her hips jerking slightly. That brought him deeper inside her channel. "Fuck," he gritted out, his lids closing as his hands dug into the outsides of her thighs. "I'm trying to go slow."

She didn't need slow or careful. She wasn't breakable.

Her sisters viewed her as naive and weak, but she wasn't. She was brave and strong, a woman who knew her own mind.

Soon to be the first female police detective.

She lifted her hips once more, and Jack slid deeper. Once more and their hips met. His chest heaved, the lines of his face etched in painful ecstasy. "Oh, Christ. You're killing me."

There. It was done. He was inside her . . . and it was better than she'd even imaged. She closed her eyes, letting the feeling wash over her. Jack was a part of her. There was no pain, only a delicious fullness that radiated from her core.

"All right?" he asked. "Because I need to either pull out or start moving."

She nodded, incapable of anything else. He braced himself on his arms and began thrusting inside her, slowly at first then picking up pace. "Move with me," he told her, "while you rub yourself."

Reaching between them, she circled the nub with her fingers as he pumped his hips. They worked together, two bodies straining and climbing. His hooded blue gaze remained on her face, gauging her reactions. When she gasped, he growled, almost as if her pleasure fed his own. It felt like they were joined more than just physically, that he was deep in her brain. Wrapped around her heart. A part of her in a way she'd never shared with another person.

She was falling in love with this man.

Her toes curled and she threw her head back, the heat and light dragging her to another place where thought and worry didn't exist. She trembled and clutched at him, everything else disappearing but this strong and caring man.

"That's it." His thrusts turned rough and hard, drawing out her climax. "Good girl. Yes, keep coming. God, you are fucking beautiful. I don't want this to end." He finished on a shout as he withdrew suddenly, sitting back on his haunches. Thick ropes of milky liquid landed on her stomach, his hand flying over his shaft. His big shoulders shuddered, his face slack with his release while she tried to recover.

Seconds later it was over and the only sounds in the room were their harsh breathing. Just when she was about to fill the silence, he looked up. "I don't believe I've ever come that hard in my life."

She bit her lip, the compliment settling inside her chest like a heavy blanket. "When may we do it again?"

JACK COULD NOT believe this woman.

Only minutes ago he came so hard that he nearly passed out . . . and she wanted him to do it again? He hadn't expected that.

Then again, when had he ever predicted anything Justine said or did?

Grinning, he tucked his cock back into his union suit and rolled off the bed. She was sprawled on his bedclothes, dark hair every which way, with his spend coating her lovely skin. Indeed, he could get used to this vision. A better man might have felt remorse or guilt over taking this woman's innocence.

Jack did not. Virginity wasn't a prize or badge of honor for a man to earn. He was damn grateful to have her in his bed, no matter her level of experience. "Perhaps I should clean you up first. Then we may discuss a second round."

He strode to the washroom. "Don't move, you glorious creature." Shutting the door, he turned on the tap and grabbed a cloth. The water was ice-cold, so he quickly unbuttoned his undergarment and used the freezing water to wash his cock. It took all of a few seconds, then he re-dressed. With the water now warm, he wet a cloth and brought it out to Justine.

She hadn't moved and her gaze tracked him as he crossed the room. He put a knee on the bed and used the cloth to clean his semen from her stomach.

"Thank you."

He lifted his head. "For what?"

"Thinking of pulling out. We hadn't discussed that, preventing a baby, but I'm grateful you were aware enough to withdraw."

Finished with the cloth, he tossed it in the direction of the washroom. Then he stretched out next to her. "I would never burden you or any other woman with an unplanned baby." The words just tumbled out. "I was raised in a brothel and I've seen those consequences firsthand."

She searched his face, but he read no pity there. Just understanding. "That is why you don't run any brothels yourself."

"Correct." He traced the line of her jaw with his thumb. "My mother was a whore."

Her brows pinched ever so slightly. "Your mother earned her living the best way she knew how. It was her job, not who she was."

He thought of his mother reading to him at night. Though he couldn't have been more than five or six, he remembered the sound of her voice so clearly. During the day, she took him to the harbor to watch the boats or to the fish market. To visit the neighbors, so he could learn to speak German and Italian. Any activity she could think of to "stimulate his mind." She'd been smart and kind, but without options when it had come to making a living.

"You're right," he told Justine. "She was a great mother."

"I do not doubt it. Look at how you turned out. Besides, women should not be shamed for selling sexual favors. Many enjoy it. Many even prefer it. I can introduce you to some of those ladies, if you don't believe me."

"Oh, I believe you. My mother said as much when I asked her why she worked in a brothel."

"She sounds like an intelligent woman." Justine shifted closer, facing him, and he drew her into his side. He hadn't ever cuddled with a woman in bed before, but he wasn't ready for this to be over. She threw one leg over his and rested her head on his shoulder. "What happened?"

"She died. There was no one to look after us so my brother and I left. I wasn't yet twelve."

"Oh, I am sorry, Jack. That must have been hard to lose her at such a young age. Where did you go?"

"Here and there. Nowhere, really. Just kept moving and fighting. Young boys on the street must sleep with one eye open. I lived in constant fear of being killed, shanghaied or raped."

"What happened then?"

"I fell in with the Five Points Gang."

"And the rest is New York City history."

He huffed a laugh. "Not quite. It took me years to work my way up. I had to gain enough trust to convince several downtown enterprises to work together."

"You say that as if it were easy."

"It was not. People were resistant at first. There were fights and takeover attempts along the way." But he'd survived. Barely.

"Do you ever worry about what will happen in a few years?"

All the time. "No. Why would I?"

"Because what you do is dangerous."

Astute woman. "I have plans in place for the future." *Qui n'avance pas, recule.*

"You're being vague."

Kissing her forehead, he smiled. "Yes, I am. This is not the time or place to discuss my future. We should be discussing our present. For example, how late are you able to stay?"

"Another hour, at least." She swept her hand over his stomach and up his chest, her fingers toying with the tiny buttons of his undergarment. When she started to undress him, he stayed her hand and rolled on top of her.

"Let me focus on you instead." He bent to kiss her, but she put a palm on his shoulder and pressed him back.

"Why don't you wish to undress with me?"

He paused. Had he been so obvious? "That is rid—"

"Don't you dare say it is ridiculous. You told me you would not lie to me, Jack."

He tried for an affable grin. "It's your first time and I don't want to scare you."

"What would scare me?"

"Have you ever seen a completely naked man before?"

"I have." He blinked at her, the answer unexpected. She bit her lip. "Not in person, but I've seen statues and Florence has these playing cards . . . Anyway, you won't scare me."

Indeed, I would.

Sliding his hand below her waist, he petted the soft mound of hair between her legs. Her expression slackened, eyes going dreamy. Christ, he loved the way she looked right now. Lips swollen from his kisses, skin glowing from exertion. Muscles lax with pleasure. He wanted to keep her here for eons.

"You're trying to distract me."

Her observation startled him enough that she was able to get him on his back. Leaning over him, she stared at him as if trying to unlock all of his secrets. "Tell me."

Heat crawled up his neck. Shame. He hadn't allowed himself to experience it in years. "There are scars, cara. I only look perfect from the neck up."

She didn't appreciate his attempt at levity, apparently, because she gave him a fierce scowl. "I neither asked for nor expected perfection. What I want is *you*."

He swallowed. The life he'd lived—dangerous and precarious—showed on his naked skin. He avoided looking at it whenever possible. "You have me."

Her gaze flickered between his eyes. "No, I really don't." Leaning in, she brought her hand to his cheek, their foreheads touching. They paused, trading breath back and forth. "Trust me enough to understand, Jack."

Indecision warred while he closed his eyes. He hadn't trusted anyone, not like this, in a long time. Justine wasn't just anyone, however. She was kindness and generosity, selflessness and light. She hadn't judged him for the way he lived his life. He'd shown her parts of himself that he hadn't revealed to anyone else. What was one more secret uncovered?

And what if he horrified her?

Then whatever this is between them ends sooner rather than later.

Above all, he couldn't stand to disappoint her. Whatever he had in his power to grant her, he would. Full stop.

Shifting, he slid out from under her and sat up. "Be careful what you wish for," he said as he started unbuttoning his union suit.

She said nothing and he could feel her watching. He kept going, trying not to think about what she was about to see. The knife wounds that became jagged scars. The bullet wounds. Razor slashes. They started at his knees and kept going to his collarbones.

He stood and stripped off the thin fabric. Now naked in front of her, he kept his gaze on the wall just above her head.

He heard her move. Clenching his muscles, he prepared himself. Now she'd try to tell him the marks weren't so horrible and then make excuses to leave. *It's for the best.*

A featherlight touch swept over the worst of the scars, the one on his chest. He sucked in a breath and held perfectly still. Then he felt another gentle caress over his stomach. His hip. All the way up to his shoulder. Bold fingers explored, not shying away from the ugliness on his skin.

Pressure built in his chest, an emotion stronger than anything he'd experienced before. It was overwhelming and confusing. How was she not horrified?

Her lips followed the path of her hands and Jack's knees wobbled. His heart hammered as she pressed soft kisses all over him, as if she were soothing those old injuries. "You are a warrior," she whispered. "A survivor. Never be ashamed of that, Jack."

His lungs refused to pull in air past the knot in his throat. She made him feel normal, that he hadn't lived a life of cruelty and violence. That he didn't deserve every one of these scars to atone for his sins. The tenderness he felt in that moment was larger than him or this room; the feeling threatened to consume him. His cock was already hard, her touch and proximity all that was required for it to swell between his legs, but this was about more than easing his lust. He wanted to devour her. To crawl inside her and never leave.

Grabbing her hair, he tilted her head back and captured her mouth with his. The kiss was hard and frantic, his lips moving over hers desperately. She met him eagerly, matching his frenzied pace. And thank God for that. He needed her. Now.

He cupped her breast and gently squeezed a nipple. "Are you sore?"

"No." Panting, she arched her back to give him better access. "Please, Jack."

Placing her down on the bed, he stood on the floor between her splayed thighs. She watched through hooded lids as he pushed inside her, the moisture at her entrance easing the way. Tight heat surrounded him as he sank deeper, the pleasure heightened because it was *her*. Justine. His little do-gooder with the pure heart. A woman he didn't deserve but would fight to the death to keep.

"Oh, my sweet heaven," she whispered, her fists curling into the bedclothes.

"Am I hurting you?"

"Goodness, no. It's so much better, and I thought that impossible."

He angled over her, desperate to feel her skin against his. "Wrap your legs around me." She did as he asked and then he covered her, his hands flat on the bed. "It's about to get better still."

And he said nothing more, but proceeded to show her exactly what he meant.

Chapter Nineteen

Justine entered the legal aid society around ten o'clock. She'd meant to get up earlier, but the energetic hours with Jack were catching up with her. For the past week she'd spent afternoons with him, returning home around suppertime. Her sisters hadn't said anything more about Jack and Justine hadn't offered up any information. It was none of their concern.

They wouldn't approve, anyway. They thought she was naive and foolish and unable to handle a man like Jack. Absolutely ridiculous. Jack had complained yesterday that he was barely able to keep up with *her*, not the other way around.

She smiled to herself as she crossed the waiting area. The two of them were evenly matched, and she'd never felt closer to another person. She loved the hours they spent in his Bond Street home, completely secluded from the rest of the world. He was attentive and sweet, a force of nature when he wanted something—usually her.

How could she complain?

"Miss Greene!"

She spun at the voice and studied the faces in the anteroom. A woman she recognized approached her. "Mrs. Gorcey, good morning." Her smile quickly faded when she caught the expression on the other woman's face. "What is wrong?"

"It is my husband," she started.

Justine took her hand. "Come with me. Let's find a private space to talk." Nodding at Mrs. Rand, the secretary, Justine took Mrs. Gorcey inside. Just as she was about to go into an empty office, her brother-in-law turned the corner.

Frank's brows lowered as he studied both women. "Mrs. Gorcey. I thought things were settled."

"No." She clasped her hands together. "My husband has stopped paying me. The lady at the front said there is no money for me."

Frank swept his arm out toward the empty office. "Please, sit down."

The three of them sat. "Tell me what happened," Justine said to Mrs. Gorcey.

"Well, like you and Mr. Mulligan arranged, the money from my husband was supposed to come here each week. At first, I had money waiting. Last week, nothing. Again this week, nothing." Moisture pooled on her lids. "I do not know what to do, Miss Greene. I need that money to buy food. To pay my rent."

"Why didn't you tell me last week?"

"I didn't wish to trouble you. You and Mr. Mulligan have done so much for me already."

Frank's fingers drummed on the table, a heavy silence on his side of the room. Justine ignored him, reaching across to clasp Mrs. Gorcey's hand. "I will have answers this afternoon. I know where to find him. You will have your money soon, I promise."

"Oh, thank you, Miss Greene. I hated to bother you but I didn't know where else to turn. And I didn't think I should visit Mr. Mulligan alone."

"No, definitely not. You did the right thing. I'll stop by with your money today."

Mrs. Gorcey appeared relieved at that news. "I appreciate your help. Bless you, Miss Greene."

Frank stood and pulled Mrs. Gorcey's chair out for her. "Thank you for coming, Mrs. Gorcey. I am pleased that the Lower East Side Legal Aid Society could help you."

Mrs. Gorcey nodded and then bid them goodbye. Justine started for the door, prepared to finish her errand here and then go see Jack. How dare Gorcey just not pay his wife—?

"A moment, please."

She turned to her brother-in-law. "I need to see Mr. Rosen." She had questions about the police department.

"That will need to wait. Sit down."

"Why?"

Instead of answering, Frank went to the doorway and spoke to someone in the corridor. "Send in my wife, will you?"

Unease slid down Justine's spine. "Why do you need Mamie in here?"

He said nothing, merely crossed his arms and frowned at her.

Skirts rustled in the hall. "Frank, I'm busy. What do you want?" Mamie stormed into the room, as regal and unafraid as ever. Then she saw Justine and stopped. "Oh, hello, Tina." She looked between them and cocked her head. "What's this about?"

"I have no idea. He won't let me leave." Justine dropped into a chair.

"Shut the door," Frank told Mamie.

Mamie did as he asked but didn't sit. "What's wrong?"

"Did you know?" Frank asked.

"Did I know what?"

"That she's been working with Mulligan on our cases?"

Mamie's lips pressed together and she apologized to Justine with her gaze. "Yes."

Frank made an angry sound in the back of his throat, something between a huff and a growl. "Goddamn it, Mamie. Why would you not tell me?"

"Well, you saw him at the fundraiser with her. This cannot be a surprise to you."

"He said he did a favor for her. I had no idea that was in relation to our cases. She took Mrs. Gorcey to see him, for God's sake."

"Because Gorcey works for Jack."

Frank sent Justine a withering glance. "Oh, it's Jack now?"

"Stop it," Mamie snapped at him. "Be angry with me, but do not take it out on Justine. She's done nothing wrong."

"Are you serious?" He dragged his hands through his hair. "How many cases has he helped you with, Justine?"

She cleared her throat and debated on how to answer. "Do you mean my own efforts, or cases brought to the legal aid society?"

Frank pinched the bridge of his nose between his thumb and two fingers. "Jesus Christ," he muttered.

Mamie smacked his shoulder. "Language, please. And that's all in the past. She's not seeing him anymore. Are you, Justine?"

"Jack and I are friends," she said, not giving a direct answer. "Furthermore, it's none of anyone's business."

"It is my business." Frank motioned to the room. "Literally, this is my business. And if you are involving Jack Mulligan in it, then I damn well should have a say about it."

"I am not involving him in legal aid business."

"Then what was that?" He pointed to the door Mrs. Gorcey had just gone through. "Because that felt like involving him. You are planning to go see him, aren't you? To find out why Gorcey hasn't been paying."

"Yes. I owe her answers and Jack can get them for me."

"Do you hear yourself?" Frank put his hands on his hips. "Jack Mulligan is like a spider, Justine. You've fallen into his web and the more you let him, the deeper he'll pull you in."

"That's absurd."

"I have to agree with Frank," Mamie said. "Mulligan trades in favors and bribes. The more help you ask him for, the more he'll demand from you in return."

But I've already given him everything.

She didn't tell her sister that, though. If Mamie found out the true depth of Justine's feelings for

Jack, her sister would go straight to their parents and tell them. That would bring about a series of uncomfortable conversations Justine would rather not have right now. Not when things were so perfect with Jack.

"You're wrong. Jack doesn't mind helping me."

"Of course he doesn't," Frank said. "He's trying to corrupt you. To get you and your family in his debt."

"That's not why he helps me."

Frank exchanged a glance with Mamie, and Justine could tell exactly what they were thinking. That Jack was taking advantage of her, likely physically. And that she sounded like a naive fool for falling for it.

She was very tired of being underestimated and dismissed.

Coming to her feet, she stared them both down. "If I am able to help people, including the clients here, then what is the difference how I go about it? You never questioned my methods before."

Mamie shook her head. "This is different, Justine. And you know it."

"No, it's not. What I do know is that neither of you think I am able to handle myself. That I'm following Mulligan down a path of rack and ruin."

"We are right to be worried," Frank said, a little more gently this time. "I've known Mulligan a long time, the kinds of things in which he's involved. You're not cut from the same cloth."

She strode to the door. This conversation was going nowhere and only serving to upset her. "Maybe, but I hardly see how that matters. People change."

As she went into the corridor, she thought she heard Frank say, "Yes, they certainly do."

JACK WAS IN his office, getting his weekly manicure, when the door burst open. Frank Tripp appeared, his expression as dark as a thundercloud. Only, the lawyer wasn't alone. Behind him was Clayton Madden, the former casino owner and Jack's biggest rival until Florence Greene came along.

Oh, Christ. What was all this? He was glad to see Cooper trail the other two men inside. Mrs. Jenkins didn't look up from her seat at the side of Jack's desk, her concentration remaining on Jack's hands.

"Afternoon, Mulligan," Frank said, removing his derby. "Hope you don't mind the intrusion."

He did, actually. Once his nails were finished, he had a stack of reports and tallies to get through before he could meet Justine over at Bond Street in an hour. "Not at all," he lied as Mrs. Jenkins began filing his nails. "Always happy to see you both. Some more than others, of course."

Clayton said, "Being rude won't get rid of me."

Pity. "You are looking well, Madden. How is the lovely Florence?"

Clayton's eyes flashed with violent intent. She was a sore spot between the two of them. He clearly hadn't forgotten how Florence came running to Jack when Clayton had been stupid enough to kick her out. "She is exceedingly well, thank you."

"I am relieved to hear so. Please send her my regards. And if I may help her casino in any way—"

"She doesn't need your help," Clayton snapped.

"Perhaps, but my door is always open for her."

"If you're not too busy with your primping, that is." He tilted his chin toward Jack's hands.

"Hold up, you two," Frank said. "That's not why we are here. We're here to talk about my other sister-in-law."

Justine? Jack ground his back teeth together, fighting an outward reaction. He hated being caught off guard. However, he needed to keep his wits about him at all times. Stupid equaled sloppy equaled dead in Jack's world.

Jack said quietly to the manicurist, "Mrs. Jenkins, would you mind excusing us for just a few moments?"

The woman nodded and put down her file. Cooper showed her into the hallway and shut the door behind her. Jack faced his two guests. "And what about Miss Greene?"

Clayton strolled over to the sideboard and poured drinks for them. "You and Miss Justine Greene," he drawled and handed out glasses of bourbon. "I wouldn't think luring uptown debutantes to their ruin was your raison d'être, but here we are."

Jack set the glass aside. "Making money is my raison d'être, a quality we both share. And, I hardly see how this involves you. Isn't there a gloomy hallway missing your glower right about now?"

"Stop sniping at each other," Frank said. "Mulligan, my wife is concerned about your association with her sister."

"Miss Greene is a grown woman and makes her own choices. I am not forcing her to do anything against her will."

"That's a load of shit," Clayton put in as he leaned

against the wall, drink in hand. "You're seducing her into trusting you."

"You make me sound positively Machiavellian."

"Because it's not far from the truth," Frank said. "I am begging you to leave her alone. This can only end badly and I won't be able to help you. Her father will come after you."

"Please." That was beyond insulting. Jack shook his head. "Considering all I've faced in my thirty-two years, do you honestly believe I am scared of Duncan Greene?"

Frank's mouth flattened and Jack imagined the lawyer was fighting the urge to talk this problem to death. "I want you to stop involving yourself in my clients' cases."

"I'm hardly involved. Your sister-in-law asks for my assistance from time to time and I see no reason to refuse her."

"I am asking you to refuse. I do not want you mixed up in my business."

"Except for my donations."

Frank grimaced. "I realize how that sounds, but yes. I prefer to help clients legally, not through bribes and intimidation. And the legal aid society remains open only through generous donations."

At least he was honest. "May I ask where this is coming from?"

"Mrs. Gorcey returned this morning saying her husband has missed the last two payments. Apparently, you and Justine settled on some arrangement with the Gorceys."

Goddamn Gorcey, the idiot. Jack caught Cooper's eye. "Find him." Cooper nodded once and disappeared out the door.

"I'll learn what happened," he told Frank. "Gorcey is one of my men."

"He should have been arrested and brought before a judge. If this were handled in the courts, then Mrs. Gorcey would have legal recompense."

"And I prefer to handle it myself, seeing as how Gorcey is under my command."

"Which makes Mrs. Gorcey dependent on you."

"I suppose, though she has no reason to doubt my word that it will be handled."

"You cannot possibly think to foresee every possibility. What if something happens to you? What if Gorcey jumps a train out west? She has no legal hold over receiving money from him."

"Then you're in a bind because I don't turn my men over to the coppers. I prefer to deal with my own problems."

Frank's frown revealed his frustration but Jack wouldn't back down. The lawyer said, "What about the other cases? Do those involve your men, as well?"

"I hardly see how that matters." He held up his palms. "If she asks for my help, I will give it. Gladly."

"I don't get it. Do you have feelings for this girl?" Frank asked, seemingly exasperated. "Or are you poking a hornet's nest merely for amusement's sake?"

This was starting to grow tedious. "Miss Greene is perfectly capable of taking care of herself. You are concerned over nothing."

"Wrong. She is kind and gentle, a caring soul. Your complete opposite in every way. You must know an association with you will tarnish her."

Yes, he was aware. And, if he were a good man, he would heed Tripp's words. But he was not that man. Instead, he'd crawled out of the gutter to oversee the city's biggest criminal enterprise, one he ruled with relish. To astonishing success. That man would do what he pleased, when he pleased.

And he wouldn't stand here and be taken to task like a goddamn errant schoolboy.

"Tripp, it is my appreciation of what you did for my brother all those years ago that prevents me from throwing you out on your arse at the moment. However, make no mistake, I do not take advice from anyone other than myself. If Duncan Greene—or anyone else—doesn't like that, you may tell him I said to not-so-very-politely fuck off."

"I told you he wouldn't listen," Clayton said, his mouth curving into an annoying smirk.

Jack pierced him with a harsh stare, one that had cowed many a man over the years. "Do not forget who assisted you in your hour of need, when you came begging to get back in Florence's good graces."

Clayton had no rejoinder for that, so Jack returned his attention to Frank. "Are we finished?"

"Yes, we're finished. For now."

"Then by all means, don't let me prevent you from leaving."

Clayton finished his drink, set the glass down and left. Frank didn't immediately follow. Instead, he narrowed his eyes on Jack's face, his expression solemn. "We all have an hour of need, Jack. You'd best hope you still have some friends left when yours arrives."

Jack was still mulling those words over a few

minutes later when Cooper returned. "How is it everyone walks around here unannounced? Tripp and Madden just stormed my office like I'm a French aristocrat."

Cooper scratched his jaw, seemingly confused. "Tripp said you were expecting him."

That lying bastard. "Forget it. I want the door guarded at all times. O'Shaughnessy will retaliate at some point and I'd rather have a fighting chance when it happens."

"Got it."

"Any luck in locating Gorcey?"

"No. Hasn't been around in over a week, apparently."

Jack sighed, his leg bouncing with irritation. "Fucking find him. Search the city. In the meantime, send the missing payments to his wife with my apologies."

"I'll handle it. By the way, Rye wants to know if you're going to the fights tonight or if you're headed over to Bond Street this afternoon."

"Bond Street." Cooper's mouth twitched like this answer amused him. Jack snapped, "Something to say before you fetch Mrs. Jenkins for me?"

"I think it's sweet, is all. Rye and I both like her."

Before Jack could reply, Cooper slipped out the door and into the hall, leaving Jack alone with his thoughts. *Yes, I like her, too.*

More than he'd ever believed possible . . . and he wasn't quite certain what to do about that.

Chapter Twenty

Rising, Justine put down the telegram and rang for her maid. She hated to cancel on Jack this afternoon but her presence was needed elsewhere. He'd understand. After all, they'd seen each other nearly every day for the last week.

Mrs. Grant, her friend at the Mulberry Mission, just cabled to ask for help with the soup kitchen. Justine was always happy to lend a hand when necessary, and today was no exception. Even if she craved Jack's touch.

She dashed off her own telegram.

CANNOT MEET YOU. AM NEEDED AT THE MISSION FOR DINNER. TRY NOT TO MISS ME.

She then sent the cable with her maid, who could be counted on as discreet. Thirty minutes later, as Justine readied to leave the house, a messenger boy from Western Union arrived on a bicycle. He handed her a paper then waited in case there was a response. The message read:

IMPOSSIBLE. I ALWAYS MISS YOU WHEN
YOU ARE NOT HERE. WHICH MISSION?

She bit her lip. The charmer. "Do you have a pencil?" she asked the messenger. "I'd like to send a response."

The boy handed her a stack of papers and a pencil. She quickly wrote out her response.

MULBERRY. WILL BE THINKING OF YOU.

She handed him the papers, pencil and a coin. "Thank you." He tipped his cap and sped off, legs pumping as he disappeared into the city's traffic. Justine hailed a hansom and set off downtown.

The mission was already crowded when she arrived, with men, women and children lined up outside the brick building to wait for supper. She smiled and offered a polite hello as she passed. There were so many that needed help in this city. How could anyone turn a blind eye to all of the suffering here?

She went through the heavy double wooden doors and hurried toward the kitchens. Mrs. Grant found her right away. "Thank goodness," the older woman explained as she hugged Justine. "We've had four workers laid out with illness this week. I'm at my wit's end."

"Tell me what to do."

That was the last conversation Justine remembered. From that point on, she was too busy to think straight. She and the workers struggled to prepare and cook the meal, ready the utensils and plates and put chairs and tables out for the guests.

It was almost a relief when the doors opened because then she could merely focus on putting food onto plates.

With fewer staff on hand, it took longer to fill each plate. Justine did her best, moving as quickly as she was able. Sweat rolled down her back but she kept going.

Out of the corner of her eye, she saw someone step in on her right. "Move over."

Her head snapped up at the familiar voice, certain she'd misheard. Certain she'd missed him enough to conjure his voice at every turn.

No, he was here. Jack was here. At the mission.

He wore his usual fancy suit, his hair slicked to perfection. His eyes dancing and lips twisted with satisfaction, he was clearly enjoying her surprise. She blurted, "What are you doing?"

"Helping, if you'll let me." He flicked his fingers to indicate that she should slide over. "Hand me that ladle."

She gave him the soup ladle and moved to the potatoes. "I do not understand."

"There's nothing to understand. I wanted to see you and this is where you are."

Heat flooded her skin as she scooped roasted potatoes onto a plate. The woman holding the plate gave Justine a wink. "You've got a keeper in that one, dearie."

Yes, she rather thought she did.

"Don't you have better things to do?" she asked out of the side of her mouth.

"Surprisingly, no. And the more help on hand, the sooner you'll be finished."

That was when she saw Cooper and Rye in the

crowd, helping to clear dishes and chatting with the guests. *Oh, dear Lord.* Her insides melted, her heart squeezing tight like a fist. "Thank you."

"You're welcome. I'll let you properly thank me later."

She was certain someone overheard that comment, but it seemed no one did. She couldn't stop grinning.

Jack was a natural at making people feel at ease. It shouldn't have surprised her, yet it did. He spoke to many of the guests in their native language, from German and Italian, to bits of Polish and Russian. He made them laugh, charming the women and joking with the men. Some recognized him, expressing their astonishment that Jack Mulligan would be here, at a soup kitchen, serving meals. He assured them of his love for the neighborhood and its people, whether they worked for him or not.

When the food had been served, he walked through the tables, sitting and visiting with people. He had soup stains on his cuffs, but he didn't seem to notice. As she helped to clean up, she stole glances at him. Her heart felt as if it might burst.

"And who is your friend?" Mrs. Grant asked quietly. "He's certainly a handsome one."

"That is Mr. Mulligan."

"Well, it appears many of our guests already know him. Is he a politician? Or a fancy railroad magnate?"

"He's . . ." She hesitated. "A businessman." It felt wrong to dissemble but the description wasn't exactly a lie.

"That ain't no businessman," one of their guests

said as he passed by. "That's Jack Mulligan. South of Fourteenth Street they call him the very devil."

Mrs. Grant's face changed, wariness creeping into her expression. "Oh, I hadn't realized it was *that* Mr. Mulligan."

"He's not as bad as that," Justine said. "He's quite generous."

"But he's also dangerous." Mrs. Grant watched Jack as he shook hands with a table of men. "I've heard stories. Should you be associating with a man like that, Miss Greene?"

Her back straightened, the urge to defend him tightening her muscles. She wished the world knew him as she did: a sweet, funny and kind man. Who else would have rushed here to help tonight, merely because he wished to spend time with her? Who else would have made a speech at the Metropolitan Opera House as a way of saving her reputation? What about teaching her bowling and promising to help get her into the police department? He'd done all that and more since she met him. "He's merely a friend."

"If you say so. Please tell him we are grateful for his help tonight." Mrs. Grant picked up a serving dish and took it into the kitchen to be washed.

It was clear the older woman wasn't convinced. Someday, though. Someday the entire city would see him as Justine did.

The main dining room was empty by the time Justine left. She hadn't seen Jack depart but why would he remain? There must have been a hundred other things requiring his attention. She'd find a hansom uptown and meet her family at home for dinner.

Pushing open the heavy wooden doors, she emerged outside. Cool night air washed over her just as she spotted a slick black carriage waiting at the curb. Her heart stuttered. A good-looking man leaned against the side, his hands in his trouser pockets. He looked delectable—like an ice cream cone, an ear of roasted corn and a chocolate bonbon all rolled into one.

His mouth hitched when she started toward him. Warmth shone in his startling blue eyes. "A ride, miss?"

"I am looking for the bighearted, good-looking man who was inside a few moments ago. Have you seen him?"

"Perhaps. Was there some sort of reward being offered?"

She stepped closer, mere inches from him. "Most definitely. A large reward just for him."

Jack's throat worked as he swallowed. "Then come aboard. We'll see about locating him for you."

He handed her up and she settled against the velvet seats. She was kissing him before the wheels even started rolling. Warm heat spread through her as their lips brushed, a sense of rightness that had been missing all day until this second. She was nearly in his lap when they paused to breathe. "You were very impressive tonight, Mr. Mulligan."

"Was I?" He sucked on her bottom lip, pulling it through his teeth and making her gasp. "I hadn't realized charity work affected you this way."

"I hadn't realized it, either. But seeing you helping people, talking with them, turns me ravenous, apparently."

His hands bracketed her waist and slid along her

rib cage until they rested under her breasts. "How long do I have you for tonight?"

"Probably no more than an hour."

"Then I had best make the most of that hour."

JACK SAT INSIDE the brewery, a glass of lager sweating on the table in front of him. He drummed his fingers, his eyes never leaving the front door. Workers moved about the copper kettles, the beer production here unrelenting thanks to the demand for Patrick's creations. They'd added two big new orders this week. Soon, they'd have to expand to larger facilities. Perhaps Jack should start scouting buildings in New Jersey or Pennsylvania.

"He's only a few minutes late," Patrick said. "You're too jumpy."

"I won't believe he's coming until he walks through the door."

Julius Hatcher had called this meeting today, and Jack prayed that the financier was prepared to go all in on the brewery project. Taking Little Water Street national was so close Jack could practically taste it.

This gathering was the only thing keeping him away from Bond Street and seeing Justine. He'd postponed their afternoon rendezvous in lieu of hearing Hatcher's answer on the brewery. Perhaps he'd cable her when they finished. He'd come to look forward to their time together. She was enthusiastic and adventurous in bed, sweet and gentle out of it. They talked about everything, from his childhood and her charity efforts, to their families and aspirations. Nothing was off-limits. He'd never felt closer to another person in his life, not even his mother.

He liked her so much that he'd spent time at a soup kitchen just to be near her.

Not that he was against charity. Quite the contrary. He donated to several around the city, but anonymously. It wouldn't do for his reputation if people knew. A man like Jack had to be hard and impenetrable to enemies. Not a softhearted do-gooder.

Which brought to mind his softhearted do-gooder and how much he missed her. Where the fuck was Hatcher?

"Drink that lager," Patrick ordered. "I hate seeing good beer go to waste."

Though Jack took orders from no one—not even a genius brewmaster—he shoved aside his impatience and sipped the beer. "Damn, that's excellent."

"I know."

The door swung open and Jack's body tensed. Sure enough, Hatcher walked in. He came alone, without lawyers or associates. Jack hoped that didn't signal bad news.

Hatcher's gaze searched the interior until it landed on Patrick and Jack in the rear of the large room. They rose to shake Hatcher's hand. "Glad you could come down," Jack said.

"Hello, Mulligan. Patrick."

Once they were all settled, Jack motioned for Cooper to bring over another beer. The glass was placed in front of Hatcher. "That's not necessary," the financier said. "I'm not staying long."

Jack tried to tamp down his mounting disappointment. "Then I suppose we best get right to it. Have you made a decision?"

"I have." Hatcher eyed the copper kettles, the workers moving around to taste and take measurements. "You're busy. Busier than the last time I visited."

"We've expanded," Patrick said. "We're producing nearly one hundred barrels a week."

Hatcher whistled. "Impressive. I hope that doesn't prevent you from doing a hell of a lot more."

Patrick reacted first. "Does that mean . . . ?"

"It means I have decided to sink a lot of money into this idea. Let's take this beer national."

Jack clapped his hands once, elation soaring in his veins. "Christ, that is good news."

"Indeed, it is." Patrick reached out to pump Hatcher's hand. "Thank you, Mr. Hatcher. You won't regret this."

"I hope not," Hatcher said. "I have my reservations about this little trio, but you aren't the problem, Patrick."

"You're welcome to sell me your shares," Jack said. "And I'll find another investor who isn't so squeamish."

Hatcher stared at Jack, his expression unreadable. "I want my own accountants on this, Mulligan, at every step of the way. I want this completely separate from everything else you're involved in. Nothing crosses over. Do we understand each other?"

"Of course. This isn't something my crew will be involved with. Only us."

"It had better stay that way." Hatcher stood from the table. "I've looked into the Great Lakes Northern. It's ripe for a takeover. I can get it tomorrow, if we wish."

"Soon," Jack said, also rising. "Did you like the train car design?"

"I do. I couldn't find any flaws, and neither could the four engineers I consulted. We should get the cars into production."

"I'm ready. Just say the word."

"Send the contract out to two or three steel companies and have them send me proposals. I'll get it underway."

"Excellent." Patrick rubbed his hands together. "So this is really happening? Little Water Street Brewery all over the country?"

Hatcher slapped Patrick on the back. "This is really happening. Prepare yourself. If this goes well, there may be big changes coming for you and your family."

"Indeed," Jack agreed. "Soon, maybe your brother won't be the only famous one in the family."

"Walk me to the door, will you, Mulligan?" Hatcher said.

Jack nodded and matched Hatcher's pace toward the glass windows at the front of the brewery. "This is where you remind me you meant what you said earlier."

Hatcher paused and thrust his hands in his trouser pockets. "It is. I do not want anyone losing money because you run this like a gambling syndicate and not a legit business."

"Everything will be aboveboard. You have my word."

"I don't come from a world where a man's word is law. This isn't going to be a handshake deal. No, you're going to sign legal papers that clearly state the penalties if you don't abide by our agreement. And fair warning, they will be stiff."

"I'll sign anything you want, Hatcher. I'm prepared to do this right."

"I am relieved to hear it. Patrick may trust you but I do not. And I've seen too many businesses fail because of misplaced trust. I won't allow this to be one of those casualties."

If Jack didn't want this deal so damn bad, he'd tell Hatcher to fuck off. This lecture, treating Jack as a rube or an outright thief, was beginning to grate on his nerves. "I am just as invested in this as you are, perhaps more so. And I'll work my fingers to the bone to see it succeed—"

Glass erupted, a sudden crash splitting the air. Something hit his side, what felt like a pebble or a rock. On instinct, Jack grabbed Hatcher and pulled them both to the wooden floor. Pain exploded in Jack's right side, but he wasn't certain of the cause just yet. He fought through a wave of dizziness as Cooper tore out of the front door to investigate. Rye crawled to Jack's side. "Are you all right?"

"What was that?" Hatcher barked, shifting from his position on the floor to better see the window.

"Don't move, you idiot," Jack said, grimacing as he grabbed at Hatcher. His entire body was on fire, a searing pain in each cell.

"Let me see if you're hurt," Rye said to Jack. "You're sweating."

Jack didn't want to answer just yet. He knew what the hot burning sensation all throughout his body meant. "Hatcher, you hurt?"

"Merely sore from where you slammed me into the ground. Was that a damn gunshot?"

Jack met Rye's worried gaze. "See that everyone gets to safety."

"What about you?" Rye looked away, down toward Jack's legs. "Jesus, is that blood?"

And that was when everything turned black.

Chapter Twenty-One

Justine raced up the steps of the Bond Street house, her mind whirling. She was not a worst-case scenario person, but panic had overruled her ability to calmly rationalize.

Shot.

Jack had been *shot*.

Rye hadn't said much when he found her, only that Jack had been shot and she should come right away. The older man looked as if he'd aged a decade since she saw him last, which showed how worried he was for Jack. He'd driven her here quickly, during which time she'd nearly gnawed off four fingernails. The not knowing was an awful black pit inside her chest. Jack could be maimed or dead, for all she knew.

Please, let him live.

He wasn't a terrible man. Underneath that fancy suit beat the heart of a caring and gentle soul. A man who loved and lived fiercely.

A man with whom she had fallen in love.

It was the only way to explain her sheer terror at the thought of losing him. In a very short time he'd come to mean everything to her. His sly smiles, the rough tone he used when he forgot himself. The way he saw her as no one else ever had.

I think you are a woman who gives much of herself to others without considering what she wants most.

You are the smartest and bravest woman I've ever met.

I'll kill any man who even looks at you funny.

I'm going to come if you keep doing that.

Quick snippets of their time together, every dirty and sweet thing he'd ever said to her, played through her head. She did not want to lose him, not when she'd just found him.

She didn't pause on the landing. Instead, she ran to Jack's bedroom, intent on seeing him. Cooper stood outside the closed door, blood on his shirt-front. Justine tried not to stare at the stain or think about what that blood meant. He shifted to block her from entering. "Miss, the surgeon's in there now. You cannot go in."

A surgeon who could be using leeches or dirty hands on Jack. "I must go in. I've seen enough blood not to be frightened of it, and I need to ensure everything's clean and sterilized. Please."

Cooper shook his head. "That's Dr. Moore in there. He's the house surgeon at Bellevue."

Justine's jaw nearly fell open. This was no random sawbones working on Jack. Moore had recently been lauded for removing the appendix of the mayor's wife—a dangerous operation the woman had easily survived. How on earth had Jack managed to get Dr. Moore here at a moment's notice? She pushed that aside to contemplate later. "What happened? Is Jack all right?"

"He was shot at the brewery. Bullet clipped him

on his right side. He lost a lot of blood. We don't know yet how he's doing. He fainted before we got him here."

He lost a lot of blood. The words took up all the space in her brain, preventing her from thinking about anything else. She could hear the sound of her heartbeat, an eerie echo of sheer terror that she'd never experienced before. He *fainted*. That invincible charmer had *fainted*.

"Here, now. Why don't you take a moment, miss?" Rye arrived at her side with an armchair, gesturing for her to sit down.

She shook herself. What was she doing, wringing her hands like a hysterical fictional character? This was real life and, while she wasn't a medical professional, she'd witnessed several procedures and nursed many patients back to health. There were things to ready, supplies to be gathered. The surgeon was merely the first step.

"How long has the surgeon been working on him?"

"Almost two hours," Rye answered. "As soon as he got here, I came to find you."

"Thank you, Rye. Might I make a list of items we'll need in the coming days? Perhaps you and Cooper could see about procuring them for me."

Rye's face lightened, a weary smile breaking free. "I knew bringing you here was exactly what he needed."

Goodness, she hoped so. She would definitely fight tooth and nail to keep him alive. "He might not agree once he's awake."

"He needs you," Rye said. "Don't ever let him convince you otherwise."

The door opened, preventing her from responding. They all turned to see a bearded man with spectacles emerge from Jack's bedroom. *Dr. Moore.* He did not appear surprised to find a small group gathered in the hall. He placed a black bag on the ground and began unrolling his cuffs. She could see dark marks and scars on the inside of his arm.

"I'm finished," Moore said without much enthusiasm. "The bullet nicked him, so I've sewn that up and removed the glass. He has some sutures that'll need to come out in a week or so. Laudanum for the pain as needed. Have him stay abed as long as possible, if you can manage it."

"So, he's going to live?" Justine held her breath, too hopeful to exhale.

"Indeed he shall, miss. Do not worry about Mulligan. He'll live to swindle and blackmail for a good long time."

"Thank Christ," Rye muttered, and even Cooper smiled.

Relief poured through her, until she remembered how many patients died after surgery. "What about infection?"

Moore's gaze turned hard as he examined her. "I washed my hands and all my equipment has been sterilized in antiseptic. This is not my first surgery, miss. Perhaps you'd like to check my sutures?"

She would be doing exactly that, but didn't bother to say so. "I apologize, Dr. Moore. Not every doctor goes to such lengths, however."

Moore ignored her and focused on Rye. "Tell him this makes us even. If the wound starts to ooze or he runs a high fever, come and get me. Otherwise, we better never see each other ever again."

"Appreciate it, Doctor. Do you want me to take you—?"

"God, no. I'll find my own way home." Pushing through them, Moore disappeared down the corridor.

Justine didn't wait. She hurried inside Jack's room. He was pale, flat on his back, and there were drops of blood on the floor. However, he was breathing, his chest slowly moving up and down. That would have to do for now.

Moore had tossed strips of bloody cloth and Jack's ruined clothing to the corner of the room. "Get rid of those," she told Cooper. "Burn it all. Then wash your hands with soap."

To Rye, she said, "We need to get him on clean sheets. Do you know where to find those?"

"Aye. I'll be back."

A big basin of red water was on top of the dresser, clearly where Moore had washed up. Blood had never bothered her before, but this was Jack's blood. Seeing it had her gut cramping, sweat breaking out on the back of her neck. Someone had *shot* at him.

She went to his side and placed her hand on his head. The warmth of his skin sank into her fingers, reassuring her, and she closed her eyes to let the rest of her worry recede. While her sisters believed her naive, Justine was not. She was well aware of the danger surrounding Jack and his position in this city. Yet, she hadn't expected him to suffer a gunshot in broad daylight.

Rye returned with clean sheets, which they quickly got under Jack. She then cleaned the room with the help of Rye and Cooper, scrubbing the floors and the bloody basin. After, she made a list of things for Cooper to purchase for Jack's recovery. She also sent word to Florence that she was nursing a sick friend tonight. It wasn't unheard of, so the statement shouldn't bring about too much suspicion.

Then, she sat at his bedside. There was nothing to do but wait.

IT TOOK HIM three days before he was able to get out of bed. His body ached, sore everywhere, but he pushed through the pain. He'd refused laudanum, even when he couldn't sleep. Jack could not appear weak. Strength and cunning were everything in his line of work.

He'd sent Justine home to rest yesterday, though she'd argued against it. For two days she had hovered by his bedside, tending to him like the angel he often called her. She didn't want to admit it, but she was tired. Jack wasn't a very good patient.

Staying abed was pure misery. There was too much to do, including finding out the identity of the shooter. He had his suspicions, of course. Instinct told him it was Trevor O'Shaughnessy, and Jack had to find a way to confirm it. Quickly.

He also needed to follow up with Julius Hatcher. Rye confirmed Hatcher had walked away from the brewery unscathed, thankfully. And the sooner their plans were put into place, the better.

Cooper was covering for Jack at the club, making it seem as if Jack were on the premises but too busy to see anyone. This would only work for so long. The men would grow restless and suspicious the longer Jack was absent.

So, he forced himself to walk a bit in the house today, even if Rye had to hold him up.

"Steady," Rye said as they turned the corner. "I wouldn't like to explain to Miss Greene how those stitches came undone."

Rye and Justine got along like old friends. Though Jack grumbled loudly in their presence about them ganging up on him, he secretly liked that two of the most important people in his life were fond of one another. "She'll be angry with me, not you. This was my idea, remember?"

"She'll be angry with the both of us, I daresay. She is scared you'll develop an infection."

This was nothing new. Justine had been harping on the notion ever since his eyes opened after the injury. "I won't. I'll be fine."

"She loves you, you know."

Jack frowned, using his arm to steady himself on the door frame. "You're insane."

"You didn't see her face when she learned you'd been plugged."

A large lump settled in his throat. He didn't like the thought of causing her pain or worry. With all she took on at the legal aid society and her various charity efforts, she had enough weighing on her that he couldn't add to it. It was one of the reasons he'd never attached himself to any one woman before. His life was dangerous, complicated. No one deserved to have all that thrust upon them.

And yet . . .

Hope seeped into his chest like water through cracks in a wall. Did she care for him? Love seemed a bit far-fetched, but he'd settle for strong affection.

After all, she was young and of a completely different class. She was everything he wasn't—and he was a selfish bastard for not giving her up.

But he wouldn't, not when he'd just found her. Not when she brought joy and life to a dark and desolate world, her touch both calming and necessary to his well-being. Not when he wasn't certain how he'd manage to survive without her.

Indeed, a selfish bastard.

Rye chuckled. "You should have seen her standing up to Dr. Moore. Wanting to make sure he'd cleaned and sterilized everything."

With Moore's raging cocaine addiction, one could never be too certain. "Good. But I wish you hadn't bothered her. Two days was too long for her to stay here. Her family must be worried."

"No, she told them she was tending to a sick friend. Which I suppose you are, so it ain't a lie."

"Any word from Cooper on the shooter?"

"None. You still thinkin' O'Shaughnessy?"

"Of course. It's what I'd do in his position."

Rye snorted. "You wouldn't have shot through a window in broad daylight. You'd have come at him when he least expected it."

"True, but then O'Shaughnessy doesn't have my flair."

"What are you doing?"

The high-pitched shout startled Jack and he nearly tripped. He slumped against the wall for support. "Jesus, Justine." She must've come in using the key Rye gave her—an item given without asking Jack's permission first, he might add—and had snuck up on them. "How are you so quiet?"

She drew closer, her gaze sweeping his face, assessing. "I thought you might be asleep. How was I to know you were promenading along the corridor?"

"I'm stretching my legs."

"You look about ready to pass out." She pinned Rye with a hard stare. "He needs to be in bed."

Rye raised his palms, all innocence. "I just follow orders, miss. He's not one to listen to me, not like he does to you."

"I knew I should have stayed." She put her shoulder under Jack, taking some of his weight. "Back to bed with you."

"You cannot stay here round the clock," Jack said. "And Rye is perfectly capable of—"

"Letting you run roughshod over him, apparently. Though he did shave you, so I cannot complain too much about him."

They hobbled into Jack's bedroom. "So you like my whisker-free face, do you?"

"You know that I do, you vain man."

Slowly, he lowered himself onto the mattress, Justine holding on to one of his arms. When he was flat on his back, she said, "I want to check your incision."

"No more poking and prodding, cara. I am fine."

"You are not fine and I will be checking. I'm quite happy to have Rye hold you down while I do so, if necessary."

Christ. Had he admired her stubbornness before? "I'll allow it on one condition."

One brown brow shot up and her arms crossed over her chest. "Bargaining, Jack? Really?"

"If you don't wish to check the sutures . . ."

She smirked and shook her head in what he assumed was extreme exasperation. "What is your condition?"

"That you get into bed with me when you're done."

"That is not a good idea. Any sort of vigorous activity could reopen that wound."

"Not for vigorous activity. I merely want to hold you. On my good side, I swear."

Her expression softened into something affectionate and tender. His chest expanded at that look and what it might mean, the feelings it might convey. He held out his hand, desperate to feel her. "I miss touching you."

"All right." She slipped her hand into his and squeezed. "On your good side."

She released him and went to clean her hands in his washroom. When she returned, she peeled open his dressing gown, unbuttoned his union suit and lifted the bandage. He held still, letting her satisfy her curiosity, though he knew she wouldn't see any sign of infection there. While she didn't touch the wound, she brushed his skin as she worked, her cool fingers skimming his stomach as she refastened his clothing. Her flowery clean scent wrapped around him, and he inhaled, dragging this reminder of her into his lungs. Lying here, smelling and feeling her, almost made being injured worth it.

"There. I am finished. See, that wasn't so terrible."

"I never thought it would be. I just wanted you to lie down with me."

She chuckled and collected her skirts in preparation of climbing on the bed. "You are a devious man." Paper crinkled in her skirts. "Oh, I nearly forgot. Cooper asked me to give these to you. I saw him outside."

Cooper had been outside? "What are they?"

"Messages from the club, I believe." She handed over a stack of paper. Jack began flipping through the notes and letters. Most could wait.

A cable near the bottom caught his eye. He tore it open.

DEAL OFF. YOUR ASSOCIATION IN
VENTURE TOO RISKY.

HATCHER

Fuck.

Jack's fist tightened around the paper, crumpling it. The shooting had obviously scared Hatcher. Jack understood this even as he hated it. But no one had been shooting at Hatcher. And they were going into business together, not socializing on a regular basis. As far as Jack was concerned, he and Hatcher never need be in the same room again for the rest of their lives.

"Bad news?"

He blinked up at Justine, who watched his face carefully. "Nothing I cannot fix, I hope."

She plucked all the messages and letters from his hands. "You may look at all these later." Then she settled on the mattress and gingerly nestled into his uninjured side. The warmth of her sank into his bones. He felt a little embarrassed at the pleasure he derived from just being with her.

"Would you like to talk about it?"

An automatic refusal sprang to his lips . . . but he quashed it. Perhaps due to her proximity and how relaxed she made him, but he did want to talk about it with her. He couldn't remember the last time he'd discussed his business with someone other than Rye or Cooper. However, Justine was smart and even-tempered. Logical. She might have insight into some of the problems he faced.

"Remember the man I needed to meet with at the fundraiser?"

"I do."

"His name is Julius Hatcher. He's an investor in the Little Water Street Brewery."

"I've met Mr. Hatcher. His wife is a friend of my oldest sister."

"I am in the process of taking the brewery national. We'll produce and ship beer all over the country. And I need Hatcher's support to do it."

"What a great idea." She caressed his chest. "You are so clever."

"Thank you. I know it's a great idea and I thought I had Hatcher convinced."

"But?"

"But then I was shot. During our meeting at the brewery."

"You were meeting with Hatcher when you were shot?"

"I was."

She exhaled slowly. "And now he's reconsidering the venture?"

He pressed his lips to the top of her head. Smart, this woman. "Correct. He says my association makes the entire thing too risky."

"You can hardly fault him. Poor man's probably still in shock. He's a notorious recluse and seeing you shot in front of his eyes undoubtedly had a lasting impression on him."

"None of it is my fault, either. Not to mention that I'm the one who was shot, not him."

"I would say some of it is your fault. You lead the life of your own choosing—and it's a dangerous one. You've never made any excuses for it, but you have to know the risks."

He did, all too well. The proof was the burning ache in his side at present.

"I am not asking him to share office space with me. We don't even need to see one another in person again. There's no risk to his physical person."

"True, but there is risk to *your* physical person. What happens to this beer business if you're killed? I'm assuming, as it is your idea, that you are doing the hard labor in the distribution and transportation of the beer. Hatcher could hire someone to replace you, but would they have your ambition or contacts? Your charm or business acumen? My guess is that Hatcher knows no one can pull off such a feat but you."

Jack stared at the ceiling and considered this. Was this why the shooting had spooked Hatcher? If so, Jack could arrange for contingencies should something happen to one of the three partners. Doing so might ease Hatcher's concerns enough to change his mind.

He squeezed her tight to his side. "You might be right. Consequently, I really need to kiss you right now. Come up here."

"Absolutely not. You need to rest, not get all worked up."

"I promise not to get worked up. All I want is a kiss."

Carefully, she leaned up on her elbow and met his lips with her own. She tried to keep it chaste, but he dragged his mouth over hers, his arm clamped around her back to prevent an instant retreat. He was starving for her, a bone-deep lust that not even a terrible injury could prevent. Thrusting his tongue past her lips, he tasted her, swirling and stroking, until they were both out of breath.

He pressed his face into the silken strands of her hair. "I would beg to fuck you if I thought you wouldn't worry about my injury."

"No begging would be required if you were healed."

"Then I guess I'd better heal damn quickly."

Chapter Twenty-Two

Though it was the afternoon, the club buzzed with activity. Justine hadn't been here since before Jack's injury nearly a week ago. Jack had insisted on returning to his duties the day after receiving Hatcher's cable, determined to make the national brewery happen. The incision was healing, becoming what would end up as another scar on his battered body.

She hoped to see that body again soon. Perhaps tonight.

Her sisters had dropped the issue of Jack, thankfully. Remaining home each night must have reassured them that nothing was going on between their youngest sister and Jack Mulligan. Florence was in the house more often of late, coming into Justine's room at odd hours to "ask a question." Everyone thought Florence was a terrific liar, but Justine knew what her sister was doing. Merely ensuring that Justine was in the house, not sneaking off to see Jack.

Justine felt slightly guilty about deceiving them. As a rule she didn't care for lying. However, this was different. The matter was none of their business—especially when both sisters had done the exact same thing recently. Justine had never interfered with their romantic lives, never forbidding them to see a man from a different background.

And Jack was a good man. Perhaps a bit rough around the edges, but he was decent and kind.

Surprisingly, he'd asked her to come to the club today instead of Bond Street. She had no idea what this was about. He hadn't mentioned a thing yesterday during their time together.

Climbing the stairs, she passed Cooper. "Hello. Are you well today, Cooper?"

"Fine, thank you, miss. He said to send you right in."

Justine didn't bother knocking on Jack's door. She turned the knob and stepped inside. Jack saw her and rose from behind his desk, and the man seated across from him turned around.

It was Keller, the Tammany Hall man who'd refused her request for the police department.

Her heart began racing, anticipation skipping through her. Was this a meeting about that request?

Keller stood, as well. He didn't look nearly as put together as the last time she'd seen him. This man was sweaty, flushed. His hands clutched a black derby so hard the hatband had crumpled.

"Miss Greene, thank you for coming." Jack's booming voice echoed throughout the room. "Won't you shut the door, please?"

Justine closed the door behind her and approached the desk. "Hello, gentlemen. I trust I am not interrupting."

"Not a bit. We were just discussing you." Jack

came forward and gave her a bow worthy of a viscount. "Come have a seat. You know Mr. Keller, I'm told."

"Good afternoon, Mr. Keller." She took the open seat across from Jack's desk.

Keller dipped his chin politely. "Miss Greene."

Jack relaxed in his large chair and steepled his fingers. "I believe Mr. Keller has some good news for you, Miss Greene."

"Indeed, I do." He cast a quick glance in Jack's direction before meeting Justine's eyes. "We would be honored to appoint you as the first woman to the New York City Police Department."

Jack had promised it, but Justine hadn't believed the appointment would happen until she actually heard the words. She clasped her hands together in her lap to try and control her excitement. If the room were empty she would have danced a jig. Instead, she tried to look calm and mature. "That is excellent news, Mr. Keller. You won't regret this. I shall work very hard."

"We know you will."

"That is kind of you to say. I hope to earn my detective's badge within two or three years."

Keller's brows drew together, and he appeared even more nervous. "You don't understand, Miss Greene. You need not earn a detective's badge. I am having you appointed as a detective, not a roundsman."

Not earn it? "I suppose I don't understand, then. All officers start as roundsmen. Then they are promoted to detective after proving their abilities."

"You've already proven your abilities." Jack gave her a patient and fond smile. "There's no need for you to struggle your way up the ladder. Right, Keller?"

Keller swallowed, his nod a touch too emphatic. "Definitely. Yes. Indeed, no need at all."

"But, you told me I would be taking a job away from a man with a family to support."

"We don't need to worry about that any longer."

Didn't need to worry about that? Unease swept through her and her stomach turned over. Something was not right. She was being given a position she did not deserve. One she wanted, but only after she had earned it.

And she knew why this was happening.

You asked for his help. This is what Jack Mulligan's help looks like.

She thought he would get her in, not have her running the place. The other men would never respect her if she waltzed in as a detective. They would barely respect her after she proved her worth. But at least it would be something. Coming in at a higher rank would merely earn her enemies.

"I would like to start out as everyone else. Then I'll earn my spot as detective."

Keller shot a look at Jack, one that spoke volumes. It said Keller had no idea how to respond and that he was deferring to Jack in this matter.

Do you honestly think he'll refuse me?

"That's unnecessary," Jack said. "You are already a detective. The badge will merely make it official."

Was this what she wanted? To be granted favors based on Jack's power of persuasion? Or worse, because of intimidation or blackmail? How could she ever live with herself if she took the appointment of detective without working for it?

You took his help on everything else. Why stop now?

Perhaps, but it hadn't been so blatant, so obvious.

Liar. You were able to justify it because it was for a good cause.

Her heart sank, shame crawling through her veins. She had justified it at every step. Help with Gorcey and von Briesen. The fundraiser. She told herself the method didn't matter as long as the desired result was achieved.

Jack Mulligan is like a spider, Justine. You've fallen into his web and the more you let him, the deeper he'll pull you in.

And here she was, caught in his web. About to wear a police detective badge she hadn't earned. So many people had tried to tell her and she hadn't listened. Had defended him because she cared about him.

Wrong, you love him.

Yes, she did love him, more than anything. But, she could not become this person. This was not who she was, someone who traded in deals and favors. She believed in honesty and fairness, speaking up for those without a voice. Doing the right thing, no matter what.

And this was not right. Not by a mile.

Silence descended and she could sense Jack's confusion as he stared at her. She ached at the sight of his handsome face, those piercing blue eyes that could steal a woman's soul.

As they'd almost stolen hers.

There was only one thing to do. "I apologize, but I must refuse the position."

Both men gaped at her, but Jack recovered first. "Refuse it? But this is what you wanted."

Under no circumstances did she wish to have this conversation in front of Keller. She stood and held out her hand. "Mr. Keller, thank you for your time. I am sorry it was in vain."

Keller rose slowly, gaze darting over to Jack for a brief second before he shook Justine's hand. "Ah, well. I understand. If you change your mind, please come and see me."

"I won't but I appreciate the offer."

Jack sighed heavily and came to his feet. "Keller, thank you for coming down."

"Anytime, Mulligan." He shoved his derby on his head, touching the brim. "Miss Greene." Without looking back, he disappeared out the door.

Silence descended and Justine forged ahead.

Drawing in a deep breath, she faced Jack. "I cannot see you anymore."

JACK FROZE, CERTAIN he'd misheard. "You cannot see me anymore?"

"Correct."

Was she feeling all right? She'd just turned down an appointment to police detective, the one thing she'd truly wanted, and now she was breaking things off with him. What had he missed? "I don't understand. You're angry with me about meeting with Keller?"

"No. I asked you to meet with him. I am angry with myself for not foreseeing what that request meant."

"And what did that request mean?"

"That you would intimidate or blackmail Keller into giving me what I wanted."

"I did neither, actually." He had merely asked—

because Keller was smart enough to know what happened if he refused.

"Because you are Jack Mulligan. The intimidation and blackmail are assumed."

Annoyance and confusion melded in his brain, yet he struggled for calm. "Which you were perfectly aware of when you asked me to speak to him on your behalf."

"Perhaps, which is why I am truly disappointed in myself."

"So you're disappointed I approached Keller?"

"No, Jack. Don't you see? I am disappointed that I asked you to intervene. That I would trip down this path of favors and bribes with you, remaining convinced it doesn't touch me. Yet it does. Until now, I have managed to justify your help because it benefitted other people."

Shame washed over him but he beat it down. He would not apologize for his life, his empire. He'd been a boy born with nothing, tossed out on the street like garbage before his voice had even changed. From that he'd grown into one of the city's most powerful and richest men. Almost two thousand under his command, nearly everything downtown under his thumb. And he'd built it all his way, the only way he knew how.

If she wished for him to regret it, she would be disappointed.

He crossed his arms over his chest. "This path of favors and bribes as you call it has done a lot of good over the years. Including for you."

"I realize that and I am grateful for what you've done up to this point. However, you once told me not to ask how the soup was made if I liked the way it tasted. I cannot do that any longer—not even if I get what I want."

She's slipping away. Say something. Do something. You are going to lose her.

He came around the desk and drew closer. "Mon ange," he said quietly, "I only want to make things easier for you. I wasn't attempting to corrupt you or take away your choices. But if I went too far, then I'll stop. I won't interfere in your cases any longer."

She started shaking her head before he even ceased speaking, moving away from him as if he were diseased. "I cannot do this anymore. The temptation will always be there. I won't be able to keep from talking about my problems and you won't be able to keep from solving them. I cannot keep eating the soup. At some point it'll change me—if it hasn't already."

Anger built in his chest, a rising tide he had worked hard to control in recent years. He'd been so angry in those early days on the streets. Fighting had been like breathing, a way to survive but also a way to purge the emotions roiling inside him. He hadn't felt so furious, so helpless in eons. Until now.

"You are being ridiculous," he snapped. "I haven't changed or done anything different. All I've done is let you in. You've seen my home, my skin. I trusted you. And this is what you think of me, that I'll poison you with my presence?"

"I do not think you will poison me. It's that I'll come to see the poison as normal. I will accept it, drink it willingly."

"You're saying I will corrupt you."

"Yes. I've already made compromises since meeting you. How far am I willing to go?" She pressed her lips together. "I cannot do it. I cannot turn my back on everything I believe, everything I am, merely because you make things easier for me."

He didn't know what to say. Using words to get what he wanted was his specialty, yet his attempts to convince her were failing. It was like being tossed over the side of a cliff and trying to hang on by one's fingernails. Desperation and panic were beginning to set in. "We are good together. Tell me, are you so eager to throw that away, too?"

Hurt flashed across her face and he almost took the words back. Instead, he fell silent and let her think about what walking out meant.

It meant no more bowling or afternoons on Bond Street.

It meant no more kisses or carriage rides.

It meant no more laughing or fucking or just breathing together.

And if she took all that away, he'd never be the same.

"Jack," she said on a sigh, as if she might reconsider.

Hopeful, he came closer, slowly, determined to press his case one last time. Before she decided, she had to understand how he felt about her. "Justine, I've never met anyone like you. There's never been another woman in my life, not in this way. Not someone I cared for and trusted as I do you. Who knows what would have happened after my injury if you hadn't looked after me? This isn't all one-sided. I feel just as off-balance and unsure of myself around you. But, I don't want to give you up. Please, cara, do not leave me."

She sucked in a ragged breath and he could see the moisture gathering in her eyes.

"I don't wish to make you cry," he whispered and dragged his knuckles over the tender skin covering her jaw. "Je ne peux pas vivre sans toi."

Sniffing, she put a hand to her mouth. "Do not say that."

"It's true. I cannot live without you." A fat tear rolled down her cheek, the effect like a punch to his stomach. "You are killing me. Say you'll stay."

Silence stretched. He couldn't read her expression and his anxiety mounted. Noise from the club below echoed, the familiar sounds of his life usually reassuring. Now they only served to accentuate the quiet in this room, the momentous decision being made outside of his control.

After what seemed like a decade, she shifted to cup his cheek in her palm. "I cannot. This is not my world—it's yours. And I do not like who I am becoming by remaining in it. Thank you for everything you've done, for every minute we have spent together. I'll never forget you."

The words knocked the air from his lungs, the pain so swift, so sharp that his knees nearly buckled. It was like a thousand tiny razor cuts to the inside of his chest. But he would not show weakness. He already begged once. He would not beg further—not today, not ever—and he was done trying to prevent the inevitable.

You should have seen this coming. You should have prepared for this.

Yes, he should have. He was Jack fucking Mulligan. He was never vulnerable. Anger rose within him like a beast, feral and fierce, clawing, ready to lash out.

But he would not let it break free. Not yet.

He took a step back and her arm dropped to her side. Shoving his hands in his pockets, he said, "That's a shame because I'll do everything in my power to forget about *you*."

Her bottom lip quivered as more tears gathered in her eyes, and she spun toward the door. Flinging it open, she lunged into the corridor and he could hear her skirts rustling as she ran away from him.

You made her cry. You hurt her, you monster.

Fuck his conscience. This was his world, as she'd said, and he'd say and do whatever the hell he wished. There were no consequences, none that he cared about any longer. Let her go back uptown to her boring parties and banal suitors.

If she didn't like it here, then he didn't want her.

She was gone. *Gone.* She thought him poison and she'd left for good—even after he'd fucking begged her to stay. Begged her, like a lovesick fool.

And now he was alone.

Rage poured through his veins, scalding him from the inside out. His ears buzzed with it, every part of him aflame, his limbs trembling. He couldn't control it. The feelings built and expanded, doubled and tripled, pain exploding in his skull . . . until he grabbed the edge of his desk, lifted the heavy oak piece off the ground and, with a roar, he tipped it over onto the floor. Papers and glass flew everywhere, the thump shaking the entire building.

Seconds later, Rye appeared. "What in the ever lovin' hell?"

Jack stabbed a finger toward his second-in-command. "She is banned from both Bond Street and the club. No one lets her in—not the boys at the front or the kitchen staff. If she crawls in through a goddamn mousehole, heads are going to roll. Do you understand me?"

"Aye, I'd say that I do. What happened between you two?"

"Never mind that. Just know that as far as I am concerned, Justine Greene never existed."

Chapter Twenty-Three

The door opened but Justine didn't bother looking up from her spot by the window.

"Justine, have you seen that necklace that . . ." Florence's voice trailed off. "Are you still knitting? Do you plan on making sweaters for the entire city?"

Yes, she was still knitting. So far, she had three blankets finished. Sleep had eluded her, and she hadn't done much of anything except knit since leaving Jack's club. It was pathetic, really. But she refused to cry. After all, she was the one who'd left. There was no reason for melancholy. It had been her decision to end things. And, in her heart, she knew it was the right decision. Everything she'd said to him was true.

I'll do everything in my power to forget about you.

Goodness, that hurt—far worse than the time she'd been thrown from a horse. This pain was like she'd been stabbed in the heart. With something dull and thick. Like a knitting needle.

"Justine? Did you hear me?" Florence appeared

in Justine's eyeline. Her sister's gaze went wide. "*Sweet Mary.* What on earth has happened to you?"

"I'm fine." Her voice cracked from disuse. She cleared her throat. "Go away, Florence."

"You're not fine." Florence set her palm on Justine's forehead. "No fever. Are you suffering from chills or dyspepsia?"

"Oh, for goodness' sake." She knocked Florence's hand away. "I am not a child. There's nothing wrong with me."

"When was the last time you ate?"

Why wouldn't her sister leave? All Justine wanted was to be left alone to knit until the awful ache receded. Then she could resume her life as it had been before Jack Mulligan turned everything upside down.

You are killing me. Say you'll stay.

"Come on." Florence bent and got a shoulder under Justine's arm, dragging her to her feet. "I'm putting you in the bath."

"I do not need a bath. I need to knit." For a hundred years. Then she would have forgotten all about Jack and his bright blue eyes and handsome face. And the way his breath hitched when she trailed kisses over his throat. How he'd stared at her as if she were the only person on earth.

She burst into tears.

Florence nearly stumbled as they moved toward the washroom. "You're scaring me. Please, tell me what is wrong."

"I can't." Her sisters had warned her about Jack, and the last thing Justine could tolerate at the moment was any smug righteousness over her misery.

Florence said nothing else, thankfully, and Justine sat, numb, while her sister drew a bath. When Justine sank in the warm water, she was grateful for Florence's bossiness. She hadn't realized just how much she needed to get clean.

The problem with the bath, however, was it allowed her to *think*. Which led to more sadness. She hated this feeling. If there had been any other way, she would have stayed with him. But she was a perpetual do-gooder, as he liked to call her, and he was the criminal kingpin of Manhattan. There was no path forward where one of them didn't compromise their beliefs. Where one of them didn't bend. He certainly wouldn't, and it would destroy her to wake up one day and realize she'd turned against the very principles she'd spent a lifetime affirming. She would hate herself—and eventually hate him.

She missed him, though. More than she'd ever thought possible.

Would he really do his best to forget her?

A knock sounded. "You've been in there over an hour," Florence said from the other side of the door. "If you don't come out in the next five minutes, I'm barging in."

Florence would absolutely do it, too. "I'll get out soon."

"Now, Tina. The water must be ice-cold."

She peeked at her toes and noted a bluish cast to her skin. Sighing, she rose and reached for a towel. "You may stop hovering," she called.

No one answered. Hopefully, Florence had gone away and would remain so. Justine hated lying to either of her sisters. Sooner or later they'd find out what happened, but the conversation would prove easier the more distance Justine had from Jack.

Wrapped in her dressing gown, she emerged from the washroom.

She froze. Mamie and Florence were both sitting on her bed, frowning in her direction. Florence must have summoned Mamie while Justine was in the bath. This meant Justine's night was about to get even worse.

She sat at her dressing table and began brushing her wet hair. It was easy to ignore her sisters because Mamie and Florence hated silence of any kind. As predicted, they started talking to each other when Justine didn't speak.

"I told you she looked terrible," Florence murmured.

"I thought you were exaggerating," Mamie said. "But I can see you were not."

"Weren't you concerned when she didn't show up to the legal aid society?"

"No. She's been coming and going at strange hours of late. I assumed she was working on another one of her projects."

"Well, you should have been paying better attention. She's been knitting for God only knows how long."

"What about you?" Mamie's voice hardened. "You are the one living in the same house with her. Or, are you too busy with Clay and the casino to keep watch over our little sister?"

"Yes, I am very busy, Mamie. The casino is taking up all my time. I cannot do everything here while Daddy and Mama are away, too."

"Stop it." Justine slapped the brush on the table.

"I am not a child. You needn't keep watch over me. Furthermore, do not discuss me as if I am not in the room."

Her sisters closed their mouths, properly chastised, for about ten seconds. Mamie recovered first. "Justine, your well-being is our responsibility while our parents are gone. We know you are not a child, but you are an unmarried girl visiting dangerous neighborhoods and dangerous men. We have a right to be concerned."

"As you can see, I am perfectly well. I would like to get some sleep, so if you'd get off my bed now . . ." She shooed them with her hands, but her sisters didn't move.

Mamie lifted her chin. "I am not budging from this spot until you tell me what has upset you. Were you hurt?"

Not physically. "No. I'd rather not talk about it."

"Too bad," Florence said. "I am quite content to sit here all night, if necessary. What about you, Mamie?"

"Frank sometimes snores, so I am perfectly happy right here in Justine's bed. I could stay the week, actually."

After living with them for twenty years, Justine knew her sisters were not bluffing. "You two are absolutely awful."

Mamie patted the mattress. "Come lie down and tell us all about it. God knows we've talked to you enough about our troubles over the years."

Florence reclined on a stack of pillows. "Definitely. You've always been our sounding board, Tina. So, let us return the favor and help you—even if it's just listening."

Exhaustion swept over Justine and she crawled

onto the bed. All she wanted at the moment was to sleep. "That's the problem. You don't merely listen. You both run roughshod over my life. You always have. Remember when you convinced me I could get to Paris if I kept running toward the horizon? Or when you made me sled down the dangerous hills first? How about when you told me to touch the electric socket because it wouldn't hurt?"

Florence cleared her throat and exchanged a glance with Mamie. "You make us out to sound like some kind of bullies. But we'd never do anything to seriously injure you."

"That's true. We love you. Good God, you're the best of all of us. How could you ever doubt that?"

"Because you discuss me like I'm a child. Both of you have called me naive more than once. You think just because you've visited dance halls and casinos that you are worldly and experienced. Impervious to danger. Well, I've been to dance halls and casinos and saloons and tenements and brothels and every other place you could imagine in this city. Yet, because I am not sassy like Florence or willfully disrespectful like Mamie, then I must not be capable of looking after myself."

Florence moved closer and clasped Justine's arm. Mamie stretched out on the other side, sandwiching Justine between them. "You're right," Mamie said. "I have often thought you're too nice, too decent for this city. But you're tough, Justine. So much tougher than people give you credit for."

"I couldn't agree more," Florence said. "In fact, I'm envious of all you have accomplished in such a short time. Clay said they call you an angel downtown—"

Mon ange. She could almost hear him whisper it. Tears flooded her eyes.

"Oh, no. What have I said?" Florence sounded horrified. "I meant it as a compliment, I swear."

Justine brushed the moisture from her cheeks. "That's not why I am crying." Neither of her sisters asked, but she could feel how much they longed to. They were both biting their lips, hard, and showing admirable restraint. She sighed. "I broke things off with Jack Mulligan."

"Wait, I thought . . ." Florence flicked her eyes toward Mamie. "I thought that ended some time ago."

"No. I just started coming home at a reasonable hour so you wouldn't suspect I was still seeing him."

Florence's mouth fell open. "That's dashed clever of you. I'm impressed. Mamie, why don't you seem surprised by any of this?"

"Because she knew," Justine said. "Or rather assumed, based on certain cases at the legal aid society."

"You knew?" Florence rose up on an elbow and glared at Mamie. "Why didn't you tell me?"

"Frank was supposed to handle it. He promised to see Mulligan and demand he stop seeing Justine."

"Damn. So that's where Clay went with Frank that afternoon. He was deliberately cagey about the nature of that errand."

"Wait, Frank and Clay went to see Jack? When?"

"Right after you met with Mrs. Gorcey. I assumed he would have told you."

No, he hadn't. But then, why would he? It had

only involved her and her family. How utterly annoying.

"What happened between the two of you?" Florence asked. "Because if he mistreated you in any way then—"

"No, no. Nothing like that. The complete opposite, actually."

"What does that mean?"

"He . . . he gave me anything I wanted. Anything at all. I merely had to mention it and he'd snap his fingers and make it happen. He's like some sort of sorcerer. And admittedly, it was seductive at first. He saved me time and effort. Problems disappeared when Jack was around."

"That doesn't sound so bad," Mamie hedged. "But I sense something happened."

"I wanted to become a police detective—"

"What?" Florence said. "There are no female detectives."

"Not yet. But there are plenty of cases the men won't bother with, issues that involve women and children, mostly. I wanted to take those on."

Florence's expression suddenly brightened. "Actually, I love it. It's the perfect job for you. Obviously Mulligan opposed the idea considering he's on the other side of the law."

"As are others who shall remain nameless," Mamie said under her breath, referring to Florence's illegal casino endeavor.

"Wrong. Mulligan was in favor of it. He met with the Tammany Hall representative and convinced him to offer me an appointment. I was all set to become the first female detective."

"And?" Florence prompted.

"And it wasn't right. They were going to start me out as a detective, not a roundsman."

"What's wrong with that?"

"Everything. Could you imagine the resentment of the other officers when I strolled in, no experience whatsoever, as a detective?"

"I don't see why that's a problem," Florence said. "A lot of men do it all the time, relying on nepotism and favors to get ahead. Why shouldn't you?"

"Because it's not fair. And, it was more than just that."

"It was the spider's web," Mamie said, her knowing gaze trained on Justine's face.

"Spider's web?" Florence asked.

Mamie ignored the question. "I'm right, aren't I?"

"Yes." Justine picked at a thread on her coverlet. "I cannot involve myself with a man who bribes and intimidates and threatens to get what he wants, even if it's for a good cause. Eventually I'd resent it."

"Did you tell him as much?"

"I did. He tried to talk me out of it."

"He can be very persuasive, from what I understand," Mamie said.

"Obviously he's unaware that no one is able to change Justine's mind once it's decided," Florence said.

Mamie's voice softened. "You love him, don't you?"

Justine couldn't answer past the lump in her throat. She concentrated on breathing and the tiny spider crawling on her ceiling. *How appropriate.*

"Oh, Tina." Florence hugged Justine's arm even tighter. "This is exactly what I was afraid of."

"You did the right thing," Mamie said on her other side. "Though I realize it's little consolation at the moment."

"Eventually you'll move on from this," Florence said. "You shall meet someone else and Mulligan will be a distant memory."

The problem was Justine didn't want anyone else. How could any man ever compare? Furthermore, why would she ever risk her heart again? This was unbearable. "I never really understood when you two were going through your man troubles. I thought you were exaggerating. I was so cavalier with my advice when I had absolutely no idea what you felt like."

"One doesn't need to experience tragedy to offer help or sympathy. And you were never cavalier," Mamie said.

"Agreed." Florence rolled off the mattress and came to her feet. "And I think we should stop talking and start wallowing in our misery as men do."

"By doing what?" Justine asked.

"By getting drunk."

JACK THRUST BOTH arms in the air as sweat ran in rivers down his body. His opponent lay at his feet. "There's another one down. Who else thinks they are able to best me?"

The men in the room exchanged wary glances. Over the last two days, sixteen men had climbed into the ring with Jack. None had emerged victorious. Onlookers from the neighborhood had gathered outside the club's windows, watching as Jack pummeled opponent after opponent.

It had started as a way to burn off his rage, exhaust

himself into a dreamless sleep each night. A bonus was that it likely would draw out the man who'd shot at Jack. O'Shaughnessy could not let the failure stand. Sooner or later, Jack would come looking for answers . . . and he wouldn't come alone. The only play was to make another attempt on Jack's life—a successful one this time.

So Jack made himself as visible as possible. He let Cooper and Rye worry about scouting the crowds and watching for pistols. Part of him hoped the assassin prevailed. At least then Jack would cease to pine for a woman who thought of him as poison.

This is not my world—it's yours. And I do not like who I am becoming by remaining in it.

"Come on, fellows," he shouted. "Won't one of you cowards crawl in here to fight me?"

A throat cleared to his right. Rye, and he wanted Jack's attention. Jack went over and collected the towel he'd hung on the ropes and began wiping down his face and neck. "What is it?"

"The boys ain't too keen on fighting you in your current mood. How about you climb out of there and we'll—"

"One more, Rye. Just one more match."

"No, not today. You're near exhausted as it is, not to mention that fresh scar still healing on your side. And when was the last time you tended to the books?"

Five days. He hadn't stepped foot in his office since she left, the sight of the room like a swift kick in the stones. Returning to Bond Street was also out of the question. Probably time to find a real estate agent and sell it because he'd never sleep there again.

"Don't worry about the books," he said. "And I can't stop. We haven't seen the shooter yet."

"It won't matter when you drop dead here on the floor."

"That's ridiculous. I am in excellent health."

"You wouldn't say that if you could see yourself."

"Stop nagging me. If I'd wanted a wife, I would have married a long time ago."

"No, you wouldn't have because nobody'd put up with you—nobody except *her*. And you've kicked her out."

I didn't kick her out. She left me.

"Mind your own goddamn business and find me another fighter."

"I'm busy watching for O'Shaughnessy. If you're so eager to kill yourself then you'll have to do it without my help."

Rye walked away, leaving Jack alone in the ring with his thoughts. That didn't improve his mood. Quite the opposite, actually. He'd rather face down ten O'Shaughnessys than ruminate on *her*. There was no changing the past.

Qui n'avance pas, recule. He would advance or die trying.

Spinning toward the crowd in the main room, he yelled, "One hundred dollars to whoever gets in the ring with me!"

Eyes widened all around him. A few men shook their heads, but a dozen or so appeared as if they might be contemplating the offer. "Two hundred if you last more than ten minutes."

Four men started forward, tall men with thick necks and broad shoulders. *Finally.* He rubbed his hands together. Maybe he'd fight all of them. Whatever he paid them would be worth it, especially if they landed a few punches. At least then he could tend to physical injuries, whereas there was no relief from heartache. The only way to survive it was to ignore it.

"Who's first?" He pointed at the biggest of the lot. "Southern Mike?"

Mike shrugged his assent then climbed through the ropes and into the ring. Jack waved one of the boys forward, who began wrapping Mike's knuckles in cloth. Jack stretched out his arms as anticipation swirled inside him. The darkness receded for a moment, blessed relief from the madness hovering on the edges of his mind. He could focus on the fight, the punches to throw, and lose himself in the pure physicality of it.

Rolling his head on his neck, he stared out the window, beyond the crowd. For a split second he caught the glint of metal. Blinking, he saw it. On the other side of the street, a man stood facing the club, a gun in his hand.

And he was aiming it at the window.

Chapter Twenty-Four

Jack recognized the man and it was not who he'd expected. What the hell?

Instead of hiding, Jack shouted the one word guaranteed to send a room full of crew members scurrying like cockroaches. "Coppers!"

The place erupted into chaos. Tables and chairs were knocked over, glass broken, as men darted for the back exit and secret rooms. Jack didn't move. He stared, almost daring the man across the street to shoot him.

But the man must have realized the opportunity at a clean shot had passed, because he tucked the pistol into his pocket and started down the street. Donning his shirt, Jack slid through the crowd as quickly as possible. Then he was out the doors and on the walk. He spotted the shooter and followed. It was then he noticed that Cooper was also in pursuit. *Good man*.

No way would the shooter get away this time.

The man turned along Bowery, heading south. Jack decided to cut him off, so he crossed the street and darted ahead. When the man noticed Jack directly in front of him, his eyes went huge. He spun on his heel and took off in the opposite direction—right into Cooper.

Cooper grabbed hold of the shooter and yanked his arms behind his back. The man struggled, unable to break free, as Jack slowly approached.

"You fucking idiot," Jack growled and drove his fist into Robert Gorcey's stomach.

Gorcey wheezed and crumpled in Cooper's hold. Pedestrians gave them a wide berth on the sidewalk. Still, this was far too public for what Jack had planned. "Bring him to the club," Jack ordered.

With a nod, Cooper began dragging Gorcey to Great Jones Street. Cooper might appear wiry, but he was strong. Gorcey had no chance of escaping.

At the club's front, Jack jerked his head toward the metal doors that led belowground. "Down there."

They were in the cellar when Rye found them. The older man spat on the ground at Gorcey's feet. "Jesus. One of our own?"

Gorcey's expression was mutinous, his disgust and hatred directed solely at Jack. "You deserve it," he snarled. "Beat me all you want but you deserve killing for interfering."

"By forcing you to act like a decent human being, you piece of filth. Those children depend on you to provide for them—money you earn by working for me, I might add."

"Not anymore. I left—or are you too busy with your whore to notice?"

Jack didn't even think, just reacted. His fist cracked into Gorcey's jaw. "Speak about her like that again and I'll break both your legs."

"Who cares?" Gorcey slurred. "After what I've

done my legs are the least of my problems. Do your worst, Mulligan."

"Are you so cheap you can't spare the money for your family? I know how much you make, Robert. You could well afford it."

"That is not the point," Gorcey said. "I don't want to be married to her anymore. I don't love her or those kids."

"Then why'd you marry her? Why'd you come inside her and make those kids?"

"Because she let me. And she wasn't so plain and boring back then. That's what happens when women have babies. They become plain and boring. She never let me fuck her again after that fifth brat was born."

"Jesus, Mary and Joseph," Rye muttered. "No wonder she didn't want him back."

Jack's eye twitched, his fists clenching. He'd met Mrs. Gorcey and she deserved better than this unappreciative bastard. "A decent woman, sharing your life and giving you babies? That's a goddamn gift. That is a woman you work hard to keep, not one you leave. But I can see she's well rid of you. They all are."

Gorcey said nothing, his expression unchanged. While Jack didn't know the other man well, Gorcey didn't strike him as a genius mastermind. Had he worked alone? "How much did O'Shaughnessy pay you?"

"I don't know what you're talking about."

"Don't you?" He strode closer and leaned down into Gorcey's face. "If you weren't working for me, you were working for someone else. Tell me who, Robert."

"Whether you believe me or not isn't my problem. I'm not working for anyone else."

"Actually it's very much your problem. If you tell me the truth, I might just put you on a train to Kansas. If you lie, however, I'm thinking a ship bound for Brisbane. That's on the other side of the world, Robert. Either way, you'll never return to New York."

"I'm not working for anyone else," he repeated, though Jack didn't believe him.

"Well, it looks as if I've gotten my wish. I was looking for one more man to fight today and it seems I've found him." He rolled his shoulders and advanced on Gorcey.

"You haven't asked the most important question."

"Such as, why don't I just throw you in the East River and be done with it?"

"No. Like how I knew about you and that fancy lady."

A cold sense of foreboding slithered down Jack's spine. "How did you know about her?"

"Everyone knows. Including O'Shaughnessy."

"And?"

"I'll tell you, if you let me go."

Jack's fists clenched as his pulse pounded in his ears. No way would he let Gorcey go, but he had to know what O'Shaughnessy planned, especially if it involved Justine. "I won't let you go, but I may let you live if you tell me."

"Not good enough. Let me go and I'll tell you everything you want to know."

"Robert, you seem to think this is a negotiation. I do not negotiate with men who've tried to kill me."

"Then I guess she dies."

That was all Jack needed to know. O'Shaughnessy had targeted Justine as a way to get to Jack . . . and Jack must move heaven and earth to prevent that.

"Let's go," Rye said. "Right now."

Jack was already moving toward the door.

"Wait," Cooper called. "It could be a trap. If Gorcey's working with him, this is exactly what O'Shaughnessy wants you to do."

Jack paused, fear sinking its claws deep into his chest. This might be a trap . . . but what if it wasn't? What if O'Shaughnessy had kidnapped Justine? The thought turned his blood cold. "I don't care. If she's not there already, then she's in danger. I have to put the fear of God in him; otherwise, she'll always be at risk."

"Agreed," Rye said. "We should take a hundred men."

"No, that's what he wants. A big confrontation in the streets where we all get arrested and chaos descends upon the city. I lived through that once and I don't relish doing it again. This has to be civilized."

Rye shook his head. "O'Shaughnessy ain't civilized."

"He'll come around. Cooper, stay with Gorcey. Tie him up. Rye, let's go."

JUSTINE HURRIED UP the steps of police headquarters, the note tucked in her handbag. She could almost feel the paper in there, burning with importance, as she hurried to Ellison's office. She hadn't spoken to the detective since the shirtwaist factory.

In reality, the visit wasn't that far in the past, but she felt like a different person now, someone a bit sadder and harder.

Thirty minutes ago, she had been leaving the legal aid society when a boy handed her a note.

$10,000 FOR MULLIGAN'S LIFE. YOU HAVE UNTIL SUNDOWN.

Trevor O'Shaughnessy had signed it, along with directions to Broome Street Hall.

Justine had no idea who he was or if he'd really kidnapped Jack but she meant to get to the bottom of it. Ellison's desk was empty, so she searched the building until she found the detective in a meeting with some other men. She didn't care if interrupting was rude; Jack's life might be at stake.

Knocking on the doorjamb, she waved Ellison over. He didn't appear happy at the intrusion, his frown deepening. "I need to speak with you. Urgently," she whispered.

"Miss Greene," a man behind a large desk called. "Come in, please."

The well-dressed man was about her father's age, his hair slightly silver at the temples. "How . . . how do you know who I am?"

"Your father and I are acquainted. You and I have actually met a time or two, not that I expect you to remember. I am Captain Harrison."

Ah, yes. "Your niece is Miss Ida Harrison."

"Indeed, she is. Was there something you needed from Detective Ellison today?"

She didn't hesitate. If Ellison's help was good,

Captain Harrison's was even better. "I received this note not even an hour ago." Pulling out the paper, she handed it to Harrison.

Harrison whistled and passed the note to the other men. "Looks like Mulligan's got himself in a spot of trouble."

That was what scared her. "Who is this O'Shaughnessy person?"

"The man who's trying to take over Mulligan's territory," Ellison explained. "I'm surprised you didn't know, seeing as how friendly the two of you are."

Justine ignored the dig. "Should I be worried? Will he hurt Mr. Mulligan?"

"One of them'll likely end up dead." Harrison shrugged. "Better for us if those types take care of themselves, anyway."

"What does that mean?"

"It means we don't have time to get involved in those downtown gang wars. They sort it out amongst each other. Saves us the trouble."

"But, this is clearly blackmail. Can you not do something? At the very least come down to Broome Street Hall and speak with this O'Shaughnessy person. It might be nothing to worry about, but it also could mean a man's life is in the balance."

Another officer in the room chuckled. "O'Shaughnessy isn't the type to bluff. If he says Mulligan's in danger, then believe it."

That was worse news. "But I cannot get ten thousand dollars by sundown."

Ellison lifted his hands and let them fall. "Then I suppose Mulligan's reign is over. Bound to happen sooner or later."

"Detective! I cannot believe officers of the law would behave so callously over a man's life."

"Now, don't grow hysterical," Harrison said. "I understand this is upsetting to you but it's not something the department can get involved in. I'm afraid Mulligan will need to figure this out on his own."

"What if my father asked the department to become involved? Would you do it then?"

"No, I wouldn't. Besides, your father would understand that these are two violent criminals and the city would be glad to get rid of one of them. He'd let it play out."

With a snarl, Justine snatched the note, spun and marched to the door. And to think, she used to admire these officers. It turned out many of them weren't admirable; they were corrupt and unreliable.

Haven't you learned by now who really has all the power in this city?

She'd have to handle this herself.

Great Jones Street was only a few blocks away. Still, it seemed like an eternity before she stood outside Jack's club. A fight was underway in the boxing ring, everything going on as usual. Perhaps the note had been a bluff.

The boys at the door wouldn't meet her eye as she climbed the steps. "I need to see Mr. Mulligan."

"Beg your pardon, miss," one said as they both moved to block the entrance. "But we have orders not to let you inside."

She rocked back on her heels. "Orders from whom?"

"Mulligan." He pulled at his shirt collar. "I'm awful sorry, miss."

Jack had barred her from the club? Her chest squeezed like it was caught in a vise. "Is he here? Please tell him I need to see him right away. I'll wait."

"He and Mr. Rye left—"

"Shut it, you idiot," the other boy hissed. "He doesn't want her knowing his business."

She ignored the unhelpful one and focused on the boy who spoke first. "Left to go where?"

"I couldn't say, miss."

"He might be in danger. Please, tell me."

The unhelpful boy sighed. "They don't tell us where they're going. We're just supposed to guard the door."

"Is Mr. Cooper here or did he go, as well?"

"He's down in the cellar." This was from the helpful boy, earning him a smack on the back of the head from the other guard.

"Thank you," she told him and hurried to the metal doors that she assumed led to the cellar. "Mr. Cooper! I need to see you immediately. Please, Mr. Cooper." She gave the metal a solid bang for good measure.

The metal door swung open seconds later. "Miss Greene?" Cooper appeared, glancing up and down the street. "What are you doing here?"

"I think Jack's been kidnapped by Mr. O'Shaughnessy."

Frowning, Cooper stepped out of the cellar and drew her away from the boys at the door. "Why do you say that?"

She took the note out of her handbag. "I went to the police first. They wouldn't help me."

"Worthless bastards." He read the note. "Damn it! I knew they shouldn't have gone alone."

"Wait, so Jack willingly went to go see this O'Shaughnessy person? Will he get hurt?"

Cooper made a noise. "O'Shaughnessy would kill his own mother if he thought he could profit from it. Jack thought you were in danger, so he went to talk to O'Shaughnessy."

Justine could only imagine that conversation. Jack would threaten and intimidate the other man to get what he wanted. The encounter would have gone to rot after that. "We have to help him."

"He won't like it. He said that's what O'Shaughnessy wants, a big street fight to upset the balance of power downtown. It used to happen all the time in the old days."

Before Jack. And wasn't that exactly what Chief Harrison told her?

"I don't care what Jack wants. I cannot get my hands on ten thousand dollars, so unless he has that kind of money lying around in the club, we have to think of something else."

"I could maybe get together a thousand or so. Ten thousand? I wouldn't know where Jack keeps that much cash."

She could go to Mamie and Frank. Perhaps Florence and Clay, as well. Between them all, they could likely come up with the money. But there was no time. Light was fading quickly, the sun already low in the sky. If only her father were in town. Daddy would have the money—but whether he'd actually hand it over for Jack was another story.

Furthermore, she wasn't certain any of her family would help. Florence and Mamie were not keen on Jack, especially after Justine had filled them in on her conversation with him the other night. They both thought she was better off without him.

Whether that was true or not, she couldn't allow him to be killed. She could barely stand their separation now . . . and he was in perfect health. If he died, she'd never be able to live with herself—especially if she could've done something to prevent it.

Tilting her head at Cooper, she said, "We have to save him."

"Miss, I'm thinking you should return home and let us handle it. Whatever happens might be dangerous."

"Mr. Cooper, we don't know each other well, but I won't be returning home until Jack is safe and sound. Are we clear?"

Cooper grimaced. "He'll kill me if you're harmed."

"Then blame me, because I'm not leaving. We need to go down there and get Jack out."

"Short of taking every man in the club down there with brickbats, I don't know what we could possibly do."

Her gaze cut to the windows of the club, through which she could see the men shouting and clapping for the fighters. "Would that work?"

"It might. O'Shaughnessy doesn't have as many men under him as we do, but Jack wouldn't want us to do that."

"Then it's too bad Jack isn't here. Come on."

She returned to the front entrance and planted her feet. "Mulligan has been kidnapped. I must speak with everyone inside."

The guards blinked, their jaws falling open. Instead of arguing, they stepped aside and let her through. Cooper was right behind her as she walked into the main room. Putting two fingers in her mouth, she whistled loudly, a piercing screech that cut through the noise. Everything stopped as heads swung her way.

In any other circumstance, the attention would have rattled her. Not today. Jack's life was in danger. She had no time for nerves or second guesses. Every minute counted.

So she hurried to the ring, which stood on a small platform, and stepped up onto the edge. There were at least seventy-five men here, with a lot more in the saloon if the noise coming from the back was anything to judge by.

"Hey now," one man called. "I've got ten dollars riding on this fight. Get down, miss!"

"Mulligan has been kidnapped by Trevor O'Shaughnessy."

The words dropped like a stone thrown into a calm lake, causing disbelief and anger to ripple across the room. "How do you know?" someone shouted.

"I received a note demanding payment in return for Mulligan's safety. It's more money than I can produce in the time allotted, which I suspect Mr. O'Shaughnessy realized when he set such parameters. Regardless, we cannot leave Mulligan to O'Shaughnessy's whims. We have to go get him."

Cooper came up alongside her, steadying himself on the ropes. "She's right. There's no other way. We need to show O'Shaughnessy that we stand behind Mulligan, no matter what."

The men shifted on their feet, exchanging glances, their faces showing their reluctance. She understood the hesitation; they were being asked to go into battle, where they might face injury—or worse. She couldn't tell them of her plan just yet, but she hoped to avoid *worse*.

First, she had to get them to agree.

"I ask you," she shouted. "How many of you has Mulligan personally helped? How many of you would receive the shirt off his back if he thought you needed it? He cares about each and every one of you. Every man here has made him proud. You joined together to create an organization the likes of which this city has never seen—a powerful organization even the police cannot touch. You did that—you and Jack Mulligan. So, are we going to let Trevor O'Shaughnessy take all that away? Or are we going to go over there and get our man back?"

They started nodding before she stopped speaking. By the time she finished, men were filing out of the saloon and pushing closer to the boxing ring. No one moved, all eyes remaining on her.

Cooper leaned in. "Well?"

"What do you mean?"

"They're all waiting for you to lead them over there."

Chapter Twenty-Five

Seething, Jack glared at O'Shaughnessy's profile. How had he been so stupid? The mere thought of Justine in danger had him running here without any consideration for his or Rye's safety. The move had been astoundingly unwise. O'Shaughnessy had been ready for them and Jack hadn't seen Rye in hours. As soon as Jack was subdued, they had separated him from his second-in-command.

O'Shaughnessy had taken Jack to a small room with no windows, tied Jack to a chair. They sat here, just the two of them, while O'Shaughnessy whittled a piece of wood with a long knife. Slivers of wood rained down on the floor at O'Shaughnessy's feet. The other man said nothing, just whittled.

O'Shaughnessy was obviously employing Jack's favorite method of intimidation: silence. And, while Jack hated to cede the upper hand, it was in his best interest to try and convince O'Shaughnessy to let him go.

"This is reckless and irresponsible, Trevor." No response. "I don't know what you hope to gain.

The police won't tolerate any struggles between us. We'll both be taken out and everyone loses."

Nothing.

"If you kill me, you'll have every man under my command coming for you."

More whittling.

Jack sighed. "Listen, Trevor. I understand. I was once reckless and irresponsible, too. Hungry for more power. This, however, is not the way to get what you want."

"Oh, should we talk it out, Mulligan?" the other man sneered. "Would you be reasonable then? Or would you just try to keep me and my men in our small little box on the other side of town?"

"Do you honestly think you deserve more than that?"

"I don't think you have a fuckin' clue what I deserve."

"Then enlighten me."

O'Shaughnessy threw the knife toward the door, and it spun, end over end, until the blade sank into the wood with a thump. Putting his hands on his knees, he faced Jack. "You think the fancy suits and big words make you a gentleman, that you're better than the rest of us. But, you ain't better. Your hands are just as dirty, just as bloodstained as everyone else's in this city. We've tried to respect you and your men, but the island isn't big enough for two leaders. It only needs one—and I'm the one with the balls to do something about it."

"By killing me? Don't be stupid."

"I'll try for ransom first."

"Ransom? From whom?"

O'Shaughnessy's mouth curved into a sinister

smile and Jack's muscles tightened in dread. "Let's see. Who do you know from a well-to-do family? I figure she can afford it—even if it won't save you."

"Tell me you fucking didn't."

"I did. She probably has ten thousand stashed under her mattress. She'll never even miss it."

Christ. Jack closed his eyes briefly, absorbing the news that O'Shaughnessy had dragged Justine into this mess. For that, Jack would strangle the man with his bare hands. Though they were no longer together, Justine was the type to rescue anyone she perceived as in danger. If she showed up here alone, putting herself at risk, O'Shaughnessy wouldn't hesitate to take advantage.

And Jack could do nothing to help her.

Rage streaked through him, a red blur of emotion, and he struggled against the ropes holding him to the chair. O'Shaughnessy just chuckled. "You'll not free yourself of those knots, boyo, no matter how hard you try."

"I'll kill you," Jack snarled. "I'll kill you and enjoy every second of it."

"Lots of luck, then."

They stared at each other for a long moment, and the smug arrogance in O'Shaughnessy's gaze only enraged Jack further. But he had to remain calm. Losing his temper wouldn't solve this.

"If harm befalls her, I won't show you mercy," he promised flatly.

"Save your mercy, Mulligan. You think we should all fear and respect you, but what have you done to earn that respect? Convince a bunch of gutter rats and street fighters to follow your lead? They're on the streets, doin' the hard work, while you sit in your ivory tower counting fucking money. That doesn't earn my respect."

"I don't need your respect, Trevor. But you would be wise to fear me."

"I grew up in Dublin, Mulligan. This is like paradise compared to what I saw there. I don't fear anyone or anything these days."

Jack shook his head. "We could have worked together, you know. It didn't have to end up this way."

O'Shaughnessy's expression hardened. "I did try to work for you. Of course, you wouldn't remember. It was years ago, when I first came here."

Jack had no memory of that. It must have shown on his face because the other man explained. "Was told I couldn't be a part of your crew unless I dressed up, acted like a gentleman. I didn't own a suit, couldn't afford one. So I asked for a loan to buy one—and your man laughed at me. Told me there were no loans, to go out and steal one if I had to."

"I wouldn't have reacted like that."

"You know how it works. The men under you speak for you."

"Just like your men were following my dancers and robbing my policy shops?"

"And I put a stop to both. Those responsible were dealt with."

"You are running a gang of renegade thugs, Trevor. You will drag the city back decades unless you gain control over them."

"Not all of us want to work for a corporation. This ain't a bank, Mulligan. This is every man for himself."

Idiot. "Then you'll never be powerful enough to rid yourself of the coppers and Tammany."

"Your concern is touching. However, thanks to the brothels, I have more men in my pocket almost than you. You'd be surprised the mistakes a man makes when he thinks with his cock."

Was that a pointed dig at Jack and his recent pre-occupation with Justine?

He had to ask. "How did you learn about her?"

"The entire lower half of Manhattan knows. Gorcey was the first one to tell me, though. She's not what I pictured for you. Kind of plain." He lifted a shoulder and scratched his jaw. "Sometimes the plain ones are better to fuck, though. They try harder in bed."

Jack's blood roared in his veins and he struggled against the ropes once more. "You son of a bitch."

O'Shaughnessy threw his head back and laughed. "Like I said, thinking with his cock."

"You had better fucking kill me," Jack snarled. "Because if I get the chance I will end you, O'Shaughnessy."

"Don't worry. You will not get the chance—"

A knock sounded at the door and one of O'Shaughnessy's men appeared. "You'd better come out and see this. We could have a problem."

Without looking at Jack, O'Shaughnessy got up and walked out. Jack was left alone to stew with the dark thoughts inspired by O'Shaughnessy's words. First, he would tie the Irishman up, preferably to a chair. Then, he'd take a knife and ever so slowly drag it—

O'Shaughnessy walked back in and yanked the knife out of the door. Instead of sheathing the knife, he approached Jack with it. Jack braced. He wouldn't beg. Other than never telling Justine how he felt about her, he had no regrets about his life. He'd done the best he could with what he had—and considering Justine had left him, he knew she'd be just fine. She was better off without him in her life.

Jack lifted his chin as O'Shaughnessy walked behind him. He expected to feel the blade against his skin, but instead he felt the tug of the ropes. The bindings around his arms fell to the floor, though his hands were still secured behind his back. O'Shaughnessy jerked him to his feet. "Let's go. I want her to watch while I kill you."

JUSTINE HAD PARTICIPATED in countless marches over the years. Protests for fair wages, suffrage, better working conditions . . . She was no stranger to joining a mass of people in the streets of New York City.

This, however, was totally different.

Hundreds of men had followed her south to Broome Street, with more joining on the way. They streamed behind her and Cooper—well-groomed men with brickbats, brass knuckles, clubs and chains. By the time they closed in on Broome Street Hall, some women had taken up with them, as well.

It would have been a fearsome sight if she weren't already so terrified.

Sunset was upon them, the lamplighters scurrying up their posts to do their duty, and Justine came to a stop outside O'Shaughnessy's saloon. She prayed Jack hadn't been hurt. *I cannot lose him.*

Not now, not when she'd just realized how much he meant to her.

He wasn't perfect, but neither was she. There had to be common ground for them, some way to straddle both of their worlds and create something new and different. Something *together*. After all, her sisters had both settled for unconventional men and made it work. Why couldn't Justine do the same?

Whatever happened, she was not ready to give him up. She'd tried as much and it had only served to make her miserable.

She didn't know whether he would forgive her or not but she had to try—if they could get him out of O'Shaughnessy's saloon alive.

Men began trickling out of the saloon, lining up in front of the building like a brick wall. They also held weapons, and didn't appear all that surprised to find a mob on their doorstep. The air was thick with tension. Despite the show of hostility, she didn't wish for anyone to get hurt. "Let me try and reason with O'Shaughnessy first," she murmured to Cooper.

"Absolutely not. There's no reasoning with him."

"We have to try. If Jack is still alive, then we may be able to avoid bloodshed today."

"If they've killed Jack, the men and I will burn this place to the ground."

Justine almost wouldn't blame them. She would want to hurt Trevor O'Shaughnessy in such a case. "Cool heads must prevail, Cooper, until we know what has happened."

A man emerged from the saloon and walked directly toward Justine. "Miss Greene," he said. "O'Shaughnessy would like a word inside."

"Absolutely not," Cooper snapped. "She does her talking right here."

"O'Shaughnessy says he'll only talk inside. And he said to say that Jack is still alive. But that won't remain the case if she doesn't come in."

Justine's mouth dried out. *O'Shaughnessy isn't the type to bluff.* The policeman's words had her turning to Cooper. "I'll be fine. Stay here with the men. If something happens . . ."

Cooper took her elbow. "This is a mistake. Jack wouldn't want you putting yourself at risk like this."

"O'Shaughnessy won't hurt me. My family is very powerful in this city. Trust me, I will return."

Before Cooper could wage any further arguments, Justine followed the man into the saloon. Lights blazed inside and she needed a few seconds for her eyes to adjust to the bright interior. When she could focus, what she discovered nearly brought her to her knees.

A stocky man with black hair and dead eyes stood across from her, his hand holding a knife to Jack's throat. Jack's gaze burned with recriminations and anger, but he said nothing. Merely stared at her intently, as if terrified to take his eyes off her. His arms were tied behind his back, his clothes rumpled and torn. Blood oozed from a cut on the side of his lip.

He'd fought, obviously. That didn't surprise her. Jack was a survivor, no matter the fancy suits and smooth charm.

Whatever it takes I will get him out of here.

She transferred her attention to the man with the knife. "Mr. O'Shaughnessy."

"Miss Greene. I see you've been busy."

"There are hundreds of men outside. More are on the way. We are prepared to do whatever is necessary to free Mr. Mulligan."

"And are you?"

"Am I, what?"

"Prepared to do whatever is necessary. What are you willing to do for Mulligan's release?"

"Don't promise him a goddamn thing," Jack snarled.

O'Shaughnessy pressed the knife deeper into Jack's throat, and a trickle of blood ran down into Jack's collar. Gritting her teeth, she watched that trickle and ached for Jack. He must be absolutely furious with himself for falling into O'Shaughnessy's hands.

"She'll give me an answer or I'll spill your guts here on the floor. So, what is it, Miss Greene. How would you save your lover?"

There was no debating that word. O'Shaughnessy clearly knew of the relationship before sending her the ransom note. Nor would it help to admit that they were no longer lovers. That she'd walked away and Jack had let her. "I do not have ten thousand dollars. Not on such short notice."

"Pity. But then, I'd never really expected you to pay up."

"Then why send the ransom note at all?"

"Because killing him quickly would have been too easy. And you wouldn't have been here to witness it."

Oh, Lord. He'd wanted her here the whole time? Perhaps Cooper had been right. Perhaps she should have gone home instead.

"He won't kill me, Justine. He won't risk it, not with all those men outside."

O'Shaughnessy's smile turned cold. "You're not the only one with secret tunnels. I'll be long gone before your men make it inside the front door."

"Then what do you possibly want?" Jack asked.

"Maybe I want *her*," O'Shaughnessy said.

"Over my dead body."

"That's exactly what I'm plannin', Mulligan. Too bad you won't still be around to see it."

Justine's heart pounded in her chest as she slipped her hand into her pocket. O'Shaughnessy was planning on raping her? With an army at her back? "You won't get away with it. Not with all of Mulligan's men outside."

"My men will hold them off just long enough until I get you into one of the tunnels."

Lifting her arm, she aimed a loaded pistol at O'Shaughnessy. "Let him go."

The weapon didn't appear to faze O'Shaughnessy at all. "Have you ever fired a pistol? I'm betting you haven't and that your aim is shit."

"Are you willing to risk it?"

"I'm fairly certain I can slit his throat, dodge your bullet and get to you before you can fire again."

"Fairly certain is not certain."

His lips twisted. "I didn't get to where I am today by not taking risks, Miss Greene."

"Living in Jack Mulligan's shadow, you mean?"

Jack's eyes closed briefly, his expression pained, and she wondered if O'Shaughnessy had hurt him again. "Justine," he growled.

She soon understood why. The taunt seemed to

enrage O'Shaughnessy, his eyes bulging and his skin turning red. "Let's see if your aim is any good." He moved his hand as if to slice Jack's throat—

"Wait," Jack blurted. "I'll give you everything."

JACK EXPECTED THE words to hurt or perhaps cause the building to collapse. They were monumental, something he'd sworn never to bargain with: his *empire*. The one he'd built with his own two hands through sweat and blood and cunning. But, he'd offered it up willingly. Gladly.

If it would save her, he'd give up ten empires.

She'd arrived here like an avenging angel with an army behind her to free him from his enemy. Somehow, she'd organized that mob outside, one he could see through the saloon's front window. Then she'd come inside to barter and trade insults with a thug like O'Shaughnessy. Brandished a pistol like Annie Oakley, for fuck's sake.

Look at what you've turned her into. Look at what you've made her do.

This woman who hated violence, who tried to stay on the right side of good, and he'd caused her to become a hooligan, just like him. Christ, he hated himself in that moment. Hated everything he'd ever done in the name of building that empire. Because it had somehow rubbed off on her, tainted her pristine soul.

She did not deserve this. To watch Jack's blood spill at her feet before shooting a bullet at another human being, even if O'Shaughnessy deserved it. Jack couldn't bear the thought of it. And what happened if the bullet missed? It turned his blood to ice.

So, he'd bargain with whatever he had left, pride be damned.

"No, Jack," she started. "Do not—"

"All of it," he told O'Shaughnessy. "You can have it all."

"Now, this I did not expect," O'Shaughnessy said. "I thought you'd go down stoically, not bargaining for your life."

He was bargaining for Justine's life, actually. "Let Miss Greene, Rye and I leave here tonight and I'll give you everything."

"Jack, you cannot do that," Justine said, her pistol still trained on O'Shaughnessy. "I'll shoot him."

And earn a stain on her soul? He couldn't allow that. "Trevor, I swear it."

"How can I believe you?"

"Bring Rye out here."

"Why?"

"Because my word is law. And he won't believe it unless he hears it directly from me."

O'Shaughnessy must have motioned to his men because a few of them disappeared at a side door. Jack tried to even out his breathing, remain calm. The knife remained at his neck, the point digging into the skin at his jugular. He knew that one flick of O'Shaughnessy's wrist would sever that artery and Jack would bleed out on the floor. In front of Justine.

Rye appeared seconds later, the older man's face worried but unscathed. He exhaled when his gaze lit on Jack. "Oh, thank God." Then he saw Justine and the pistol. "Miss Greene, what are you doing with that gun?" He tried to take a step forward but O'Shaughnessy's men grabbed his shoulders, preventing him from moving.

"Rye, I have agreed to turn over everything to O'Shaughnessy."

Rye's eyes grew round but he didn't argue. "What do you need from me?"

"You'll aid in transferring everything over after I tell the men." Rye nodded once. "Trevor, do you promise to let the three of us leave once I speak to them?"

"Yes."

"Then let's get it done. Rye, take Miss Greene and join the others outside."

"Jack, I don't like this." Justine's hand trembled, the pistol still trained on O'Shaughnessy. "Let us stay with you."

Though touching, the offer was unacceptable. He needed her as far away from this place and these men as possible. Somehow, he had to make amends for dragging her into the filth and violence downtown. "It's better if you go."

Hurt flashed over her expression, the same look she'd worn when he told her he'd do his best to forget her. The cruelty pained him but it was necessary. Only when she was safe would he be able to think clearly.

She lowered the pistol and O'Shaughnessy's men quickly ushered her and Rye outside. Through the glass, he could see his men, itching to fight. O'Shaughnessy's crew blocked the saloon, not backing down in the face of Jack's army. If Justine weren't out there, vulnerable, perhaps Jack would let the two sides battle it out. He had the numbers over O'Shaughnessy.

But she was there, worried over his safety, still wanting to save him. The perpetual rescuer. He could not allow any harm to befall her today, not because of him.

O'Shaughnessy and another man dragged Jack out front. The knife remained firmly between Jack's shoulder blades. "Let's see if you're as good as your word," O'Shaughnessy said in Jack's ear.

The crowd quieted when the trio emerged. Jack could see O'Shaughnessy's men all down Broome Street, while his men curled in the opposite direction, toward Bowery. Justine, Rye and Cooper stood in the middle. The sight of her there filled him with both fear and shame.

There was only one thing Jack could do: live to fight another day.

"Men," he called to the faces he'd known for years. "I will be turning everything over to O'Shaughnessy. I ask that you show him the same respect and loyalty you have shown me. This city cannot deteriorate into the blood and carnage of days past. To prevent that, I am stepping aside. I thank you for—"

O'Shaughnessy didn't let him finish. He yanked Jack backward into the saloon. "No need to get maudlin, Mulligan. Not where you're going." The knife returned to Jack's throat.

"Even though you promised to let me go?"

"I'm not known for keeping my promises."

Jack had expected this, actually. It was exactly what Jack would have done in similar circumstances. So, he didn't hesitate. He jerked away from the knife, getting a hand up to block it, then threw an elbow into O'Shaughnessy's face. Bone crunched and blood spurted. He shoved O'Shaughnessy out of the way and dodged the two other men in the saloon with his fists.

They clearly didn't see the need to worry about Jack escaping when the only exit was blocked by hundreds of men. Jack didn't head toward the street, however. He had another destination in mind, one O'Shaughnessy was unaware Jack knew about.

The secret tunnel under the saloon.

No one had more information on the tunnels in this part of town than Jack. When O'Shaughnessy grew more powerful, Jack had made it his business to learn about this building and what lay underneath it. The door to the tunnel was in the storage room below. He flew down the stairs into the cellar and dodged the crates of liquor until he found the false wall on the west side. Slipping inside it, he made certain to close the wall carefully, so they'd never know he'd found it.

Then he disappeared into the tunnels below the city.

Chapter Twenty-Six

It took her a few days to work up the nerve to visit Bond Street.

Justine knew Jack hadn't died at Broome Street Hall, not after O'Shaughnessy came running out looking like a deranged lunatic, blood all over his face, screaming, asking where Mulligan had gone. That Jack somehow escaped filled her with hope, the relief so palpable she nearly collapsed. Then Rye had thrown a man's coat over her head and began smuggling her through the crowd, away from the danger.

"Don't you worry, miss," Rye had told her as she boarded an uptown hansom. "Old Jack always finds a way."

She didn't doubt it. He was the most resourceful and intelligent man she'd ever known. And, now that he'd turned his empire over to O'Shaughnessy, Jack was free to pursue something else. Like a national brewery, or another business opportunity. Anything other than danger and vice.

Which meant they could be together.

She loved him, and the past few days had taught

her that life was short. Anything could happen at any moment. Therefore, shouldn't she grab any happiness she could find while still alive? Jack had said he would try to forget her, but she didn't believe he actually meant it. Not when he'd given it all away to save her and Rye from O'Shaughnessy.

He still cared about her.

All she needed to do was to convince him to give them a chance.

She waited until dark had long settled on the city. Wearing a long cloak, she approached his front door and rang the bell. She hadn't told anyone she was coming, but she knew Jack would be here, plotting the next stage of his life. She desperately longed to be part of that plot.

The door swung open to reveal Rye. His expression softened when he saw her under the hood. "Hello, miss. I was wonderin' when you'd stop by."

She crossed into the entryway and unbuttoned her cloak. "How is he doing?"

"Not sleepin'. Not eating." He shook his head. "I'm starting to worry."

She threw her cloak over the bannister and started up the stairs. Rye called out, "Wait, miss. He's not up there."

Oh. Pausing, she turned on the step. "Where is he?"

"Downstairs. At the bowling lane."

By the time she reached the basement, the sound was nearly deafening. Jack was in shirtsleeves, no necktie or collar, hair askew, at the mouth of the lane. Sweat dampened his clothes, making them stick to his body. At the other end of the lane, Cooper was scurrying to reset the pins.

Jack picked up another ball, his foot tapping with impatience. "Hurry up, damn it."

Justine felt a pang of sympathy for Cooper. "Hello, Jack."

He spun toward her, his expression flat and unwelcoming. "What are you doing here?" He looked terrible. Gaunt and exhausted. Dark circles under eyes rimmed with red.

"I wanted to see you."

"Why?" He weaved, unsteady on his feet, and she feared he might topple over.

"May we sit somewhere and talk?"

"I don't want to talk." Turning, he hurled the ball down the lane, all ten pins exploding at the impact. Cooper jumped out of the way, covering his head for protection.

"Jack, please," she said quietly.

Cooper started walking away, ignoring the mess. Jack put his hands on his hips. "Where are you going? Reset those goddamn pins!"

Cooper kept moving. "I'm starving. I'm going to the kitchen and getting something to eat."

Jack said nothing, merely cursed under his breath. When they were alone, he cocked his head at her. "What do you want, Justine?"

"When was the last time you slept?"

"Hoping to get me into bed? I thought you put an end to all that."

"I am not trying to get you into bed. I am *worried* about you."

"Of course you are. But it turned out you were right. I am poison, after all. At least where you are concerned."

"What are you talking about?"

He returned his ball to the rack then thrust his hands in his pockets. "You said I would corrupt you—and I did."

"Are you referring to what happened with O'Shaughnessy? Because I don't regret any of it."

"You never should have been involved."

"I had no choice. He sent me the ransom note and I went to the police. They wouldn't help me, so I went to Cooper and organized the men."

"Yes, I heard all about your Joan of Arc speech, mobilizing the masses." He shook his head. "Leading a mob down Bowery. Brandishing a pistol. Trading insults with O'Shaughnessy. I wouldn't believe it if I hadn't been there to witness it."

Her back straightened, the words hinting at wounds she'd prefer stay closed. "Why? Because I'm naive and sheltered?"

"Because you are good and decent and the purest person I have ever met in my life!" he shouted, his blue eyes wild. "You almost killed a man because of me. It's not an easy thing, Justine. Do you know what that does to you, the weight on your soul when you take another person's life? You'd see it in your nightmares for the rest of your life."

"I wouldn't think twice if it meant saving you."

"Then you're a fool!"

Her skin burned, the words like a match to her insides. "No, I am in love with you!" she shouted.

Horrified, she covered her mouth with her hand, almost as if she was afraid of what else might escape. She hadn't wanted to tell him this way. Not until she knew if the feelings were reciprocated.

He traded his empire for my safety. The feelings had to be reciprocated. There was no other explanation for what he'd done.

He staggered backward, his skin losing whatever color it had. "Impossible. You cannot . . . love me."

No reason to deny it now. "Too late, because I already do."

"You shouldn't."

She tried to mask the hurt at his reaction. If she'd expected a grand declaration of his feelings, well, the more stupid her. "I do not expect you to return my sentiment now, but it is my hope it'll grow to happen over time."

"There's no chance of that. You said it yourself, this is my world, not yours. You don't belong in it, do-gooder."

Frustration and anger boiled over. "I don't know where I belong anymore! I feel like I am between two worlds. I went to the police with the ransom note and they wouldn't help me. They said it was better for the gangs to fight it out amongst themselves. So I went to Cooper and instantly had an army of men ready to save you. I'm confused, but the one thing that makes sense is you. Whatever you do next, whether it is a brewery or a business, I want to be there with you."

"Whatever I do next?" He lifted his arms and let them fall. "Justine, I am plotting to kill O'Shaughnessy. That is what I am doing next. I am reclaiming my empire."

"But . . ." Her stomach sank. "I heard you give your word."

"Just like O'Shaughnessy gave his word that

he'd allow me to walk out of there? We're liars and thieves. We cannot be trusted."

"Please, Jack. Do not kill him. Do not be that man. You are better than that."

He gave a gruff, bitter-sounding laugh. "No, I really am not."

"You are. Promise me you will not kill him." He said nothing, so she pressed her case. "Don't you see? This is your chance. You could walk away. Disappear. We could go somewhere together. Be happy, just living away from the city."

"I can't do that. This will always be hanging over my head. Waiting to come back and destroy whatever life I've managed to build for myself. O'Shaughnessy cannot let me keep breathing. He knows my men would follow me again in an instant. He will track me down if I don't get to him first."

"So you are choosing this"—she swept her arm to indicate the hidden house—"over a future with me?"

"You were right to walk away. There's no happy ending for a man like me, one with enemies everywhere. And I cannot allow that to ruin your life. You deserve better."

"You are making decisions that affect me without my input. What about what I choose?"

"I won't do it, cara," he said softly. "I watched you put yourself in danger, hold a man at gunpoint, and I was terrified that you'd be hurt and I wouldn't be able to prevent it. Whatever this is between us ends today."

Her throat closed, as if to prevent the hurtful words from reaching her heart. Yet, they did. They sank into every part of her to weigh her down and slice her open. She struggled to speak. "You cannot mean that."

His bright eyes were dull, lifeless as he approached. "I do." He shoved his hands in his pockets and loomed over her. "Go out and save the world, mon ange. I am beyond saving."

He strode past her and she heard him race up the stairs, his feet thumping on every tread. As if he couldn't get away from her fast enough.

Tears gathered in her eyes and she blinked at the pins scattered at the end of the alley. Evidence of Jack's destruction, she supposed. Much like the pieces of her heart.

"You are a goddamn fool."

Jack looked up from his whiskey and glared at Rye, who'd just stormed into the room. "Don't say it."

A quarter of an hour ago Jack had walked out on Justine after telling her to move on with her life. There had been no other choice, even if he wished it otherwise. Wishing was a pointless endeavor for an underworld kingpin. He dealt in realities. Cold, hard truths. The prospect of danger around every corner.

"I will say it once more and you will listen. You're a goddamn fool. Whatever you said had her running out of here in tears."

Jack's stomach rolled over, nausea and whiskey nearly making him gag. He took another sip, even though he hated it, hoping to numb the pain quicker. Beer took too long to get him drunk.

He hadn't wanted to make her cry. She'd been

the first one to realize how incompatible their lives were, not him. He'd merely agreed with her. Even if he'd been willing to try, seeing her point a gun at O'Shaughnessy had certainly changed his mind.

I want her to watch while I kill you.

Jesus, Jack couldn't get the scene out of his head. They'd barely made it out alive. He couldn't risk it ever again. Not with Justine, no matter how many tears she shed.

"You know it's for the best," he told Rye.

"What I know is that you have the chance for real happiness and you're throwing it away."

"Right," he sneered. "A chance for O'Shaughnessy to find me when I least expect it. At least this way, I can kill him and get my business back."

"You don't need to do that. You don't need to be Jack Mulligan anymore. Take her and go start over somewhere."

The idea was ridiculous. "Hide under another name? Work as a plumber or a bank teller out in Omaha? I spent my life creating this for myself. Richer than my wildest dreams, respect and fear from the Bronx to the Battery. You think I'm going to let Trevor O'Shaughnessy take all that away?"

"So you'd rather be gutted or shot in the street like a dog? Because that's what will eventually happen if you don't get out."

"You don't know that."

Rye sent up a bitter chuckle to the ceiling. "Of course I do. You cannot stay on top forever."

"Yes, I can."

"You idiot. You should get out, move in with your lady and start having little Mulligans."

Jack's hand curled into a fist. He liked the sound

of that, so much that it made him angry because he knew he'd never have that kind of future. "No one from our world is allowed to do that, Rye. You should know that by now."

"Clayton Madden did it."

"In a manner of speaking. He's living above what will soon be her casino like a hermit, but they aren't married. And he didn't have near the number of enemies that I do."

"Close—and he also didn't have near the number of loyal men, either."

"I won't corrupt her. You're wasting your breath."

"You think if you leave and go straight that you're corrupting her?"

Why was Rye pushing this? "Someday this life will come back to seek vengeance on me. If not O'Shaughnessy then someone else. I will not watch her suffer for my choices."

"Not if you walk away clean. Tell everyone what you're doing, let it be known that you're going straight."

Frustration boiled in Jack's veins, everything he hated and loved splitting apart his mind. He stood and threw his tumbler against the wall. "I almost got her killed!" he shouted. "Or raped. You should have heard what O'Shaughnessy said. Fuck, Rye. Don't you get it?"

Several seconds passed. "Ah." Rye nodded as if all the problems of the world suddenly made sense. "You love her."

"You're not listening to me, old man," Jack growled.

"I hear every word, even the ones you aren't

speaking. You're scared. You love her and you're scared."

Jack dropped back into the chair, put his elbows on his knees and rested his head in his hands. "How I feel doesn't matter. Not anymore."

"Wrong. You don't believe me, fine. Why not go see the one person who can really help you?"

There was no doubt as to whom Rye referred. "And why would I bother?"

"Because you can't hide out in this big house, alone, for the rest of your life, drinking and bowling yourself to death."

"I won't be alone."

"Yes, you will," Rye said. "Because Cooper and I won't sit around and watch you destroy yourself. Go and talk to him, Jack."

Jack blew out a long breath, bracing himself as he raised his hand to knock. Before his knuckles even met wood, however, the door swung open.

Clayton Madden stood there, a cup and saucer in his hand, his dark eyes suspicious . . . until he got a good look at Jack. Then he relaxed.

And started laughing.

"Well, well," Clayton said, one eyebrow arching. "Look at what the cat has dragged in."

"Fuck off and let me in."

Clayton pulled the door open. "In a charming mood today, I see. I cannot wait to hear what this is all about."

Jack stepped inside the plush top-floor apartments. Clayton was not officially living with Florence Greene yet, but there were feminine touches everywhere, from the bonnet casually tossed on a chair to delicate slippers by the door. Jealousy streaked through Jack, but not because he longed for Florence. It was the domesticity, the intimacy that he envied.

Two days he'd stewed over Rye's words. In that time he'd been drinking more than sleeping, not eating. He knew he looked a mess. He lacked the energy to care, however.

"I'd offer you a drink but it's not yet noon so—"

"Whiskey, if you have it."

Clayton's brows rose but he didn't say anything before going to the sideboard. Jack rested his head in his hands, questioning the intelligence of this visit. He didn't even know what kind of insight he hoped to gain from Clayton.

Yet, something had to give. He felt like he was losing his goddamn mind.

Rye wouldn't speak to him, and Cooper remained at the club. Thoughts of Justine haunted Jack's waking hours, and the dreams of her at night were so vivid, so real that he couldn't bear to fall asleep.

He should be plotting O'Shaughnessy's demise, yet he couldn't focus on anything.

Whatever you said had her running out of here in tears.

"Here. You look like you could use it." Clayton thrust a tumbler in Jack's face.

"Thank you." Jack accepted the glass and downed a quarter of it in one gulp. The whiskey burned all the way down his throat, chasing away the chill in his bones. "Is Florence here?"

Settling in the chair across from Jack, Clayton crossed his legs and took a sip from his china cup.

"Not at the moment. She's not due back for some time. You aren't here to see her, are you?"

"No, I'm here to see you."

"Let me guess. O'Shaughnessy."

Before he retired, Clayton's network of informants had always been impressive. "How did you know?"

"I stay abreast of things downtown. Glad to see you made it out alive."

"Are you?"

Clayton shook his head. "Mulligan, we've established somewhat of an adversarial relationship but that was business. I've always admired and respected you."

"And I you. Which is really why I'm here. I need advice."

"Does this have to do with my sister-in-law?"

"I thought you and Florence weren't married."

"Semantics. We're as committed as any two people in possession of a piece of paper. Which means I think of her sisters as my family." He smoothed the fabric of his perfectly creased trousers. "I heard Justine rallied the boys to get you freed from O'Shaughnessy. I wish I could have seen it."

A smile tugged at Jack's mouth for the first time in days. "It was an amazing sight. Led them all the way down Bowery like the Pied Piper."

"Or perhaps Boudica. She's quite fearsome, from what I understand."

"From Florence?"

"No, surprisingly. Florence and Mrs. Tripp worry incessantly over their youngest sister. I sense they still think of her as sheltered. Childish, almost."

Justine was none of those things. She was stubborn and resourceful, brave and intelligent. "She's a force to be reckoned with when she sets her mind on something."

"A Greene family trait, I'm afraid."

Jack downed another mouthful of whiskey. "I'm in love with her."

"I figured as much. So, what is the problem?"

"Must you ask?"

"I suppose I must. The way I understand it, you've given everything away. There's nothing preventing you from taking up with a woman like Justine Greene."

"You can't be serious. You really think it's just that simple?"

"Yes, I do."

Jack's aching head pulsed with frustration. He threw back the rest of the drink and set the glass on the table as he rose. "I can see I'm wasting my time."

"Wait. Hear me out." Clayton pointed at the seat until Jack lowered himself down once more. "You are attempting to make this complicated, but it's truly not. I assume you are plotting against O'Shaughnessy?"

"Yes." Sort of. If he could stop thinking about Justine.

"It's what I would have done in your shoes, were I unattached. Which you are not."

"I am not what?"

"Unattached. You just said you love her and the feeling must be reciprocated if she launched a rescue mission on your behalf."

Jack studied his shoes. *I am in love with you.* Words he did not deserve from a woman he deserved even less.

He cleared his throat. "You know as well as I do how dangerous an attachment is in our world."

"Yet, you are able to leave that world behind. I did and I've never regretted it."

"Not once?"

"Not. Once." A small smile twisted Clayton's lips. "You know the woman with whom I now share my life. I'd lay aside a hundred kingdoms for that privilege."

"Does anyone really just walk away, without recourse?"

"They do. You remember Mallet Malone?" Jack nodded. Malone had been the leader of the Waterfront Rats, disappeared in '78. "Moved to Vermont," Clayton continued. "Ran a maple syrup farm until he died a year ago."

Jesus. How hadn't Jack known this? "I had assumed he ended up in the East River."

"No, old Mallet lived a happy and healthy life. There are others, too. Including me."

"You've never worried about someone coming after you, a former patron with a grudge?"

"I would be lying if I said it didn't occasionally cross my mind, but I take precautions. It also helps that Florence is capable of handling herself."

"But there's a difference. O'Shaughnessy can't allow me to keep breathing. It's too dangerous."

"He'll let it go if you leave town."

Leave the only city he'd ever known? The streets and buildings were in his blood.

And what of Justine? If he convinced her to forgive him, then he couldn't ask her to leave her family, her work here in New York. No, moving was out of the question.

"I don't want to leave and run a maple syrup farm." He wanted to run a national brewery, but not anonymously and not under an assumed name. That dream, however, felt further away than ever.

"Then what are you going to do?"

"Get rid of O'Shaughnessy, I suppose."

More blood on his hands. More violence in his head. He definitely couldn't go back to her after that. He'd tainted her enough.

Please, Jack. Do not kill him. Do not be that man. You are better than that.

He had no choice. Couldn't she understand? It was why he'd cut her loose. She was better off without him.

"Can't imagine Justine would approve of that," Clayton said.

"She asked me to promise I wouldn't."

"And did you?"

Jack's brows pinched. "Why would I do that? There's no other way to deal with O'Shaughnessy, Clayton."

"Isn't there? Stop thinking about this like Jack Mulligan. Think about it as an outsider would, someone who doesn't know our rules and practices. That's what I had to do when I lost everything."

"How does that help me?"

"It might just solve your problem. It also might help you win the girl. Shall we switch you to coffee?"

Chapter Twenty-Seven

Justine trudged up the third flight of stairs, each step more exhausting than the last. *This is what happens when one stays abed, nursing a broken heart*, she supposed. Muscles weakened and every day became a struggle. "Will you *now* please tell me why we had to come all the way to an apartment house on Broome Street?"

Florence glanced over her shoulder. Secret mirth danced in her eyes, which meant her sister was up to no good. "Not yet."

"For the love of Pete," Justine grumbled. "I am not in the mood for this."

"I realized as much when you started complaining around Eighty-Eighth Street. Just trust me, please."

Justine huffed and followed her sister to the landing. Once there, Florence threw open a side door like she owned the place. An empty room was revealed, two chairs the only occupants. "Who lives here?" Justine asked.

"No one. Come along." Florence shut the door behind them and gestured to the chairs in front of the windows. "Let's sit."

"Why?"

"God, Justine. Stop asking questions and do what I say. We must hurry."

Hurry? For what? She kept the questions to herself, however. Florence could be sharp when pressed and Justine felt raw enough these days.

A week ago she'd visited Jack in his bowling alley. Longer still since she'd faced down O'Shaughnessy on his behalf. In some ways it seemed like a lifetime ago. Yet to her heart, which somehow ached more each day, it felt like yesterday.

On each chair sat a white confectioner's bag. "Oooh, a snack." Florence snatched a bag and sat down. "Popcorn. Yum."

Justine took the other bag and lowered herself down into the chair. Outside the windows she could see Broome Street Hall. A very unpleasant reminder. Jack's men hadn't believed him when he asked them to transfer their loyalty to Trevor O'Shaughnessy. Their disbelief and unhappiness had rumbled through the crowd long after Jack had disappeared. Seeing O'Shaughnessy bloody and angry had only fueled the resentment between the two groups. She had no idea how the issue would be resolved. Perhaps it never would be.

Go out and save the world, mon ange. I am beyond saving.

She didn't believe that. No one was beyond saving. And everyone—even Jack Mulligan—was worthy of redemption. He just hadn't wanted it.

Whatever happened, she hoped he remained safe.

Florence tossed a handful of popcorn in her mouth while staring through the window. Justine frowned. "I cannot believe you are eating that. You have no idea where it came from."

"Of course I do. Try it." She nudged Justine with her elbow. "It's safe, I promise."

Justine tentatively tasted a piece. It was fresh. "None of this makes any sense."

"It will soon enough. Just relax and enjoy being out of the house for once."

Sakes alive, her sister was annoying. Justine ate the popcorn and watched the traffic along the street. "I've only been inside the house for a few days."

"Try a week, Tina."

"Some days I wish I'd been an only child." What must it be like to live without meddling sisters?

"Liar." Florence dropped her head on Justine's shoulder affectionately. "You love us."

She sighed and rested her head atop Florence's. "Yes, I do. Mostly."

Two men walking down the street caught Justine's eye. One of them was . . . Detective Ellison. That was certainly a coincidence. The man next to Ellison looked authoritative, with the bearing of a policeman or perhaps a government official. "What is Detective Ellison doing here, I wonder."

"Hmm." Florence angled closer to the window and tossed another piece of popcorn in her mouth. "I wonder."

"You are annoying," she said. "You know what is happening and you refuse to tell me."

"Because I won't ruin the surprise. Just watch."

Ellison and the other man disappeared inside Broome Street Hall. O'Shaughnessy's headquarters. Strange. Ellison hadn't been in any hurry to come down here the other day, when O'Shaughnessy had kidnapped Jack. She'd practically begged the officers to intervene. Now they were here of their own free will?

Were they in league with O'Shaughnessy?

The possibility sickened her, even as it made sense. Ellison hadn't been all that shocked at the ransom note. Most policemen, she'd learned, were on someone's payroll. O'Shaughnessy was no fool, likely amassing power as they sat here. Poor Jack.

Out of the side of her eye, Justine caught movement on the neighboring street. A large police wagon was coming ever so slowly down Bowery, toward Broome. Tens of men in dark suits hovered near the wagon, uniformed officers there, as well. She sat up, leaning in. "Do you see that? Over there on Bowery?"

"Here we go!" Florence sounded positively giddy.

The group on Bowery halted, waiting. For what? She turned her attention back to O'Shaughnessy's saloon. Minutes later, Ellison and the other man burst through the saloon doors. They each held one of Trevor O'Shaughnessy's arms, the leader's wrists shackled with handcuffs.

She shot to her feet, popcorn forgotten. "Oh, my heavens."

They were arresting O'Shaughnessy.

Ellison put two fingers in his mouth and whistled loudly. The legion of men around the corner started racing for Broome Street, then converged on the saloon like a swarm of locusts. The wagon followed quickly behind. Justine couldn't hear what was being said but O'Shaughnessy looked to be complaining—loudly. He struggled against the men, his face red and angry.

It didn't do any good, however. They loaded him—and several of his men—into the police wagon.

"I cannot believe it," she whispered. Days late, but the police had finally managed to apprehend O'Shaughnessy. Her resentment toward Ellison and the police department eased ever so slightly.

"Believe it," Florence said. "That was Trevor O'Shaughnessy being arrested by the US Secret Service. Along with help from our own police, of course."

"The Secret Service? But, why? They handle counterfeiting cases."

A knock sounded on the door. Justine froze, on guard. Who knew they were here? Florence didn't bat an eye, as if she'd expected the interruption.

"Don't answer that," Justine hissed. "You have no idea who it is."

Ignoring her, Florence called, "Come in!"

The knob turned and the door slid open. Jack Mulligan stood in the doorway.

Justine's jaw fell. How . . . ? Why . . . ? Then she remembered the bags of popcorn. *Of course.* Jack had known this was going to happen, had asked Florence to bring Justine down.

For what? To taunt her with all she'd never have because he would soon return as king of New York's underworld?

That was even more depressing.

She said nothing, merely folded her hands. She

could survive this. Whatever he wanted to say, she would listen and then she would leave. Just a few more minutes and she could escape.

Clayton Madden strolled in behind Jack, his focus solely on Florence. "What did you think, love?"

Her sister ran to her partner and threw her arms around his neck. "It was fantastic. Beyond exciting." She whispered in his ear and Clay's expression turned positively predatory.

Clay shot Jack a glance and hooked a thumb over his shoulder. "We're going to make ourselves scarce in the adjoining room."

Jack nodded once, not paying them any attention. He thrust his hands in his pockets and continued staring at Justine. If she didn't know better, she would say he looked nervous.

The door closed and silence settled in the small room. She didn't know what to say and he seemed in no hurry to speak, either. Her heart gave a twinge of longing and regret at the sight of him. He looked tired but slightly more put together than the last time she'd seen him. That was good. At least one of them was on the mend. Soon he'd return to his charming ways, overseeing the criminal empire he refused to give up.

Good, good.

Finally, she couldn't stand it any longer. "Why am I here, Jack?"

He nodded toward the window. "Did you like the show?"

"You must be very happy that your archenemy is now out of the way. Congratulations."

"I am thrilled beyond measure, but that isn't why you are here."

"No? I assumed you wanted to gloat."

"Gloat?" He approached where she stood at the windows. "What on earth for?"

"That it has all worked out for you, exactly as you wanted."

"Except that it hasn't."

"Well, I haven't a clue as to what else you need. O'Shaughnessy is gone, and you're able to return to your throne. You may continue overseeing your kingdom."

"I still don't have the one thing I need, though. Have you not guessed what that is by now?"

The intensity of his stare was beginning to rattle her. She had never seen him so serious, so focused. "No."

"You, mon ange. I need *you*."

Disappointment crashed through her at the same time that her heart leapt in delight. "You said I was better off without you."

"That's still undoubtedly true, but I can't give you up."

"Too late. You already gave me up."

"That was a mistake."

"I cannot do this again." She rubbed her brow tiredly. "We are still circling round and round when we've both made our feelings clear. It's exhausting."

"No more circles, no more confusion. It's very simple. I've given away my kingdom with no intention of reclaiming it. Furthermore, I have just removed the only obstacle to a future with the woman I love."

"*Love?*" She blinked at him, struggling to comprehend. Had he really said *love*?

"Is that so hard to believe?"

"Yes, frankly. You walked away from me so easily that night at your house. You told me whatever was between us needed to end."

"You did the same to me once, if you'll recall."

True. "And that was the hardest thing I've ever done."

"Justine, nothing about that night was easy for me. I miss you with a ferocity that frightens me. I've been worthless for days. Only until I decided on this plan for O'Shaughnessy have I been able to function."

"Plan? You mean . . ."

The side of his mouth hitched in the most adorable way. "You don't believe the Secret Service just stumbled upon counterfeit bills in O'Shaughnessy's possession, do you?"

She glanced down to the street, where policemen and agents were gathered in front of the saloon. They were carrying out safes and lockboxes, ledgers and papers, loading all of it into a wagon. Ellison and the Secret Service agent were there, directing the operation. "You planted the bills?"

"Well now, that would be wrong." He moved next to her and crossed his arms over his chest, his attention on Ellison and the others. "However, it turns out the Secret Service takes counterfeiting quite seriously."

That was a nonanswer and they both knew it.

"Jack . . ." His name came out on a long, frustrated sigh. "Tell me what is going on."

Taking her shoulders, he gently brought her around to face him. His hands were warm and strong, and the simple touch sent tiny shock waves all through her. "I wanted a future with you, but I had to deal with O'Shaughnessy first. Unless I moved to another city and changed my name, I would always be at risk."

"Except you pushed me away."

"Because I couldn't see a way out. I assumed I would need to wage a war against O'Shaughnessy to get rid of him. At the very least, I thought I'd have to kill him. Instead, I found a way to have him put away for a long, long time."

She tried to feel outrage over Jack's machinations . . . but O'Shaughnessy deserved it. He had tried to kill Jack and threatened to assault her. If given the chance, he likely would have followed through on both. "And you didn't kill him."

His expression softened, tenderness blazing in his bright blue eyes. "You asked me not to."

"So, all of this"—she gestured to the scene below—"was about proving something to me?"

"I want you in my life, by my side. You are more important to me than anything else in the world and I'll do whatever it takes to keep you."

The pressure around her heart eased as happiness took root there. She'd never expected him to say such things or for this incredible man to put her first. It almost seemed too good to be true. "What of your empire of vice and sin?"

"I traded it for a different kind of empire, one of love and laughter. Know any angels who might be interested?"

"I might. Let's hear more about how you love me."

Grinning, he bent until his mouth hovered over hers. Everything in her strained to get closer, to meld to his body like a wet piece of cloth. His hands slid to cup her face in his palms. "I love you, Justine. I am sorry it took me so long to tell you. Please, say you forgive me and that you'll stay—"

She pushed up on her toes and covered his mouth with hers. The kiss was sweet and familiar, their mouths hot and eager. For so long she feared she'd never experience this ever again . . . so she held on tight and let their problems fall away for this one moment. Lips, teeth and tongues collided, their hands grasping and clawing as the kiss wore on.

A knock on the door interrupted them. They broke apart, though Jack didn't release her as they stood trying to collect their breath. The knock came again, so Justine called, "Yes?"

Florence poked her head into the room. Justine couldn't help but notice that her sister looked adorably disheveled. Florence smirked as she looked them over. "I assume from the silence and swollen lips that you two have made up, so Clay and I are going home. But"—she pointed at Jack—"if you ever hurt my sister, I will bury you where they'll never find the pieces."

"Florence!" Justine gaped at her older sister. "Stop threatening him."

Florence lifted a shoulder. "Daddy said it to Clay a few years ago and properly scared him. Figured it was worth a try here. Seriously, Mulligan. Do not cross the Greene sisters or we will end you."

He gave her a nod. "Noted."

"Good night, you two."

After the door shut, Jack asked softly, "Have we made up, cara?"

Justine bit her lip and stared at his chin. She'd always believed in redemption. That everyone deserved a second chance. How could she deny him forgiveness when he'd done all this for her? When he'd confessed his true feelings?

She looked up. "It seems we have. You love me, after all."

"And you still love me?"

"I still love you." That earned her a quick kiss on the mouth. She leaned back to meet his eyes. "Are you certain you won't miss being the most fearsome man in New York City?"

He gathered her close and held her tight to his chest. "Absolutely not. And while I cannot promise I won't attempt any favors or bribes, I do promise to limit them strictly to our bedroom."

"Such a devious mind you have," she said, unable to hold back a broad smile.

"Yes, but only for you from now on."

Chapter Twenty-Eight

The Broome Street Settlement
March 1894

The corner of Bowery and Broome was packed with dignitaries, politicians, society's elite and residents of the neighborhood. All had braved the cold air this morning to hear Miss Justine Greene, founder of the Broome Street Settlement, speak at the settlement's dedication ceremony.

Grinning, Jack watched from his place in the crowd. He was so damn proud of her.

Somehow, she'd convinced her father to turn over her trust fund early and used the money to open this settlement house, which would provide education, resources and assistance for the neighborhood residents. They had a staff of six and many more volunteers, mostly young women who had just graduated from college. Jack loved that O'Shaughnessy's former saloon had been converted for such a noble purpose. O'Shaughnessy would fucking hate it.

"Our goal," she said to the crowd, "is to improve

the community from within. We will work for the neighborhood by working with the neighborhood. No one will be turned away based on ethnicity, education level or religion. Our model will remain similar to that of Jane Addams's Hull House in Chicago."

Many in the crowd nodded, familiar with the name. Jack knew of Hull House and Jane Addams only because Justine had introduced him during a trip there this past October, when he'd researched potential brewery sites in Chicago. They hadn't settled on a location yet, but having Justine to himself for three weeks had been glorious.

The speech soon concluded and applause broke out. The mayor went to shake Justine's hand, the flash of photography nearby sending smoke into the air. It would be several minutes before she could break away so he watched the crowd.

"Don't look now," Clayton muttered at Jack's side. "Here comes your soon-to-be father-in-law."

Sure enough, Duncan Greene was glad-handing his way through the crowd, straight toward Jack and Clayton. Jack straightened off the lamppost he'd been propped against. "Shit."

"Smile. You'll want to make a good first impression."

"Fuck off."

To date, every member of the Greene family had welcomed Jack . . . except Duncan. Even Justine's grandmother had invited him for tea, where they conversed the whole time in French. He'd won her over with humorous stories from his days in Lower Manhattan. By the end of the visit, she'd hugged him and invited him to Newport for Christmas with the family.

Duncan, on the other hand, pretended as if Jack didn't exist. He told Justine he wasn't ready to welcome another former criminal into the fold. Jack didn't care whether Duncan approved of him or not. The only person who mattered to Jack was Justine, and she assured him her father would come around. Eventually.

Clayton chuckled. "The good news is that you make me look like a *saint*."

"Stop grinning," Jack said. "You'll scare the small children."

An out-of-breath Florence slid in next to Clayton. "I'm here. Sorry. I saw him working his way over and so I ran."

"That was unnecessary," Clayton said, kissing her hand. "He's not coming to harass *me*."

"Still, I must protect Mulligan, seeing as how Justine is preoccupied." She turned just as Duncan stepped up. "Oh, hello, Daddy."

"Florence." Her father leaned in and kissed her cheek. "You are looking well. Good morning, Clayton." The two men shook hands.

Jack said nothing, merely waited for the cut direct. *Oh, the horror.*

"Daddy, have you met Mr. Mulligan?" Florence gestured toward Jack.

Duncan grimaced but turned. "Mulligan," he said and stretched out a hand.

Hiding his surprise, Jack shook the other man's hand. "Mr. Greene. A pleasure."

"My wife and my mother have both informed me that I may not hold on to this grudge any longer. I suppose that means we must meet to discuss the terms of your marriage."

Jack hadn't yet proposed, but no use splitting hairs with her father. He would marry Justine when she was ready, not when others pressured them. "No need. I want nothing but your daughter."

"Call me skeptical, but I do not believe that."

"I always say what I mean. And, I have plenty of money."

"Yes, ill-gotten gains, no doubt," the other man muttered. "What about property?"

"I have a home on Bond Street." Justine would soon be moving in, a day he looked forward to with unholy anticipation. He planned to fuck her in every room of that house.

"Oh, so you are not interested in an old factory in Chicago that could easily be converted into a brewery?"

Jack's brows shot up. The crafty old devil. "I might be, if it's the right size. We've been looking for a space there."

"I heard as much from Julius Hatcher. He seems quite relieved that you've given up your former pursuits."

Hatcher had eagerly come on board to the national brewery corporation once Jack had relinquished his criminal empire to Rye and Cooper. The refrigerated train cars were now in production and they were in negotiations to purchase a railroad.

Duncan waved his hand. "Perhaps this property could be traded for stock in the company."

"Perhaps."

"I'd receive double the property value in stock, of course."

"Would you, now?" Was Duncan honestly trying to swindle him?

"Yes, I would." The older man stepped in and lowered his voice. "I figure it's only fair seeing as you seduced and ruined my youngest daughter while I was traveling in Europe."

"What is going on over here?"

Justine barreled into their little group and moved to Jack's side, his do-gooder come to save him. Warmth filled his entire body, pure contentment and happiness the likes of which he'd never known. Ignoring everyone else, he bent to kiss her cheek. "Congratulations, cara. You were magnificent."

"Thank you." She looked at her father. "What were you discussing when I arrived?"

"I have a piece of property I'd like to give your fiancé."

"He's not my . . ." She shook her head, likely realizing the futility in arguing with her father. "That's very generous, Daddy. I'm sure Jack appreciates it." Her eyes widened meaningfully at Jack.

Swallowing his exasperated sigh, he nodded. "Yes, of course. How could I possibly refuse?"

"Excellent. Come see me tomorrow and I'll give you all the information."

They settled on a time and Justine grinned broadly. "I am so happy to see the two of you getting along."

Yes, if one called nearly being blackmailed *getting along* . . . Duncan was more bruiser than gentleman, it seemed. But Jack couldn't bear to disappoint her, so he merely smiled. "You know, I think I will fit right in with your family."

Everyone said their goodbyes and drifted away, leaving Jack and Justine to walk together toward the settlement house. "Your family seems to think we are already betrothed," he said. "Does the misunderstanding bother you?"

"No, not really. I sense it helps them accept our relationship. Also, my mother is anxious to plan another wedding, seeing as how Florence refuses to walk down the aisle with Clay."

"Shall we make it official, then?"

"Was that your idea of a proposal, Jack Mulligan?"

Heat crawled up his neck. He knew women placed importance on these things and he'd now dug himself a hole from which he'd probably never emerge. "I . . ."

A delicate hand landed on his arm and pulled him inside the building, to the room she used as an office. She closed the door and latched it. Seconds later, she threw her arms over his shoulders. "I was teasing you." She nipped his earlobe with her teeth, and a shiver worked its way through his entire body.

"If you recall, you were the one who wanted to wait. I was ready to marry you in August."

She toyed with the ends of his hair. "I remember, but I like this part, where it's new and exciting. Sneaking around and finding ways to not get caught."

"A thrill seeker. How did I not realize this?" He placed his hands on her hips, dragging her flush to his frame so she could feel all of him.

"Hmm." She skimmed her lips over his jaw. "Perhaps marriage wouldn't be all that different, though."

Blood thickened and heated in his veins, and all he could think about was bending her over the desk . . .

"Will you let me make an honest man out of you, Jack Mulligan? Will you marry me?"

"Yes, but not completely honest." He reached down and lifted her right off the floor, then carried her to the desk. "I wouldn't want you to get bored."

She scraped her teeth over the sensitive skin of his throat, causing him to groan. "I think there's very little chance of that."

Acknowledgments

Thank you so much for reading and supporting the Uptown Girls series. It has been a blast to write. Because I love historical research, here are some notes for you.

Jack is loosely inspired by a real-life Gilded Age figure in New York City, Paul Kelly. A legendary criminal, Kelly really did consolidate many of the gangs, dressed like a dandy and spoke multiple languages. Trevor O'Shaughnessy is loosely based on Kelly's rival, Monk Eastman.

The brewery information was largely based on Anheuser-Busch. A-B was the first to produce refrigerated train cars (1876), and the revolutionary beer that Patrick Murphy created was modeled after Michelob (created in 1896).

Marie Connelly (or Connolly) Owens is believed to have been the first policewoman in the US, joining the Chicago Police Department in 1891 as a detective sergeant with full arrest capabilities. It was her success in chasing down wife deserters that got her noticed by the Chicago PD and given a spot in the department.

I could never do this job alone. Much love and thanks to my traveling partner, Diana Quincy, who kept telling me to put more "devil" in *The Devil of Downtown*. I am so very grateful to Sarah MacLean, Sophie Jordan, Sonali Dev, Lenora Bell, Eva Leigh, Michele Mannon and Megan Frampton for their brilliance and friendship in all the things. And thank you to Jenny Nordbak, Jennifer Prokop, Joel Kincaid, Frauke Spanuth, and Adriana Anders for answering my very last-minute questions!

Thank you to the fabulous Tessa Woodward for her support and enthusiasm for my stories, as well as the entire team at Avon/HarperCollins who work on my books, especially Elle Keck, Pamela Jaffee, Imani Gary, Kayleigh Webb and Angela Craft. And thanks to Laura Bradford, who always looks out for me.

As always, much love and gratitude to Rich for his never-ending supply of patience and support.

Don't miss out on the rest of
Joanna Shupe's Uptown Girls series,
available now from Avon Books

The Rogue of Fifth Avenue

**Silver-tongued lawyer.
Keeper of secrets.
Breaker of hearts.**

He can solve any problem . . .
In serving the wealthy power brokers of New York
society, Frank Tripp has finally gained the respect-
ability and security his own upbringing lacked.
There's no issue he cannot fix . . . except for one:
the beautiful and reckless daughter of an important client who doesn't seem to understand the
word danger.

She's not looking for a hero . . .
Excitement lies just below Forty-Second Street and
Mamie Greene is determined to explore all of it—
while playing a modern-day Robin Hood along the
way. What she doesn't need is her father's lawyer
dogging her every step and threatening her efforts
to help struggling families in the tenements.
However, she doesn't count on Frank's persis-
tence . . . or the sparks that fly between them. When
fate upends all her plans, Mamie must decide if
she's willing to risk it all on a rogue . . .

The Prince of Broadway

Powerful casino owner.
Ruthless mastermind.
Destroyer of men.

He lives in the shadows . . .
As the owner of the city's most exclusive casino,
Clayton Madden holds the fortunes of prominent
families in the palms of his hands every night. There
is one particular family he burns to ruin, however,
one that has escaped his grasp . . . until now.

She is society's darling . . .
Florence Greene is no one's fool. She knows Clayton Madden is using her to ruin her prestigious
family . . . and she's using him right back. She
plans to learn all she can from the mysterious casino owner—then open a casino of her own just for
women.
With revenge on his mind, Clay agrees to mentor
Florence. However, she soon proves more adept—
and more alluring—than Clay bargained for. When
his plans are threatened, Clay must decide if he is
willing to gamble his empire on love.